TOM BURKHALTER

Everything We Had

A novel of the Pacific Air War
November-December 1941

Acknowledgements

I would like to thank the members of my writers group, the CVKAWG, for their assistance and moral support through the gestation of this work. This means YOU: Rama Donepudi, J. Paige Straley, Bill Shamblin, Nick Bucher, Nikolai Vitsyn, and last but not least, honorary member Brad Kurlancheek. Members of the Hickory Writers Group who helped with reviews and suggestions include Gwen Veazey, Burke Hicks, Skip Marsden, Karla Bartlett, Roxy Bruntmeyer and Barbara Charles. In the camp of friends who read the story and offered good advice I'm proud to count Marianne Dyson and Karen Moore.

For Sherman Best and Larry Huggins, US Air Force veterans of World War II and Vietnam, respectively, who were good enough to read the work and offer technical advice: you guys have given me the best compliments I can hope for. I don't know how pride can make one humble, but that's how your comments make me feel, proud and humble at the same time.

For John Parker, navigator, 8th Air Force: John, your continued willingness to listen and patience with my endless questions about your service in World War II gave me a priceless window into history and at least one man's heart. Thank you for sharing. In turn, I hope I can share some of what you've given me, to the benefit of others.

For invaluable technical advice on the use of the Norden bombsight in combat I salute Dan Healey, bombardier, 15th Air Force.

For Diana Mowery: babe, you keep me going. I love you.

Foreword

This is a work of fiction based on actual events. As much as I can, consistent with writing a work of fiction, I have used places, names, units and battles as they occurred.

To get a sense of what actually took place in the Philippines, Java, Australia and New Guinea between December 1941 and June 1942 means reading USAAF numbered histories, aircraft manuals, small-press unit histories, personal accounts of the war, perusal of charts and use of that wholly invaluable aid for the historical novelist, Google Earth. It means familiarity with the way things were done back in those days: navigation with plotter, sextant and compass instead of GPS; ring-and-bead gunsights instead of targeting computers and HUDs; bombing with the Norden bombsight instead of laser-guided missiles.

One reason events in the early Pacific war are not well known is a simple matter of logistics. All supplies, from aviation fuel to typewriters, had to come via slow supply ships over a ten-thousand-mile sea route. The humid, rainy, hot climate of that part of the world is unkind to paper and ink. Written records were subject to loss during retreats and air-raids. The participants were more concerned with survival and fighting the Japanese than with keeping and preserving accurate, copious records for the convenience of future historians. The actions of the first six months of the Pacific war have for those and other reasons faded into obscurity, which is one reason I decided to write about it.

Another reason might be that the record of the Allied forces fighting the Japanese in the first six months of the war was a record of retreat and defeat. People tend to remember winners. I disagree with that attitude. Our soldiers, sailors and airmen in the early Pacific war were outnumbered, outgunned and outflanked. They were poorly prepared and supplied for the war they fought. They kept fighting. What it took to do that under the circumstances is a lesson we should all ponder.

My intent in using actual historical figures, and most especially Boyd D. "Buzz" Wagner, is to honor and keep alive their memory. Once they were household words; today they are all too often nothing but footnotes.

But not in these pages.

CHAPTER ONE
Manila

The Verde Passage - Manila Bay

Before dawn on the morning of November 20, 1941, three ships cleared the Verde Island Passage between Luzon to the east and Golo Island to the west. The ships turned north in line ahead, steaming at twenty knots, blacked out, with extra lookouts at the masthead and the bridge wings to watch for fishing boats and inter-island vessels. The heavy cruiser USS *Louisville* led the column. In the cruiser's wake the chartered ocean liner SS *President Coolidge* and the transport USAT *Winfield Scott* steamed. The *Coolidge* and the *Scott* carried troops and equipment to reinforce the Philippines garrison. Aboard the *Coolidge* was a contingent of the 35th Pursuit Group: the 21st Pursuit Squadron with half the group's pilots and the group's mechanics, cooks, supply and headquarters echelon.

A group of young officers from the 21st and another outfit, the 24th Attack Group, crowded into a cabin on the promenade deck of the *Coolidge*. All of them were second lieutenants and wore the silver wings of pilots in the Army Air Corps. The room was fogged with cigar and cigarette smoke. Beer and liquor bottles littered the floor. In one corner a quartet attempted to sing a song that would have made their mothers blush with shame and fury. The quartet went unheard; almost everyone else concentrated on the scene around a table in the center of the room.

In the center of the table was a large pile of cash. Four second lieutenants sat at the table. Beer bottles and ashtrays were at their elbows. In the center of the table was a large pile of greenbacks. Each man looked intently at the five cards in their hands. The lieutenants gathered around the table howled encouragement at the players, stamping their feet and waving beer bottles. The poker game had started just before midnight. The four pilots at the table were the survivors.

One of the lieutenants laid a $10 bill on the pile of cash. As he did he folded his cards and laid them on the table in front of him. Then he leaned back with a toothy smile.

The lieutenant to his right tossed his cards down in disgust. He muttered, "I'm out." No one heard him over the noise. He looked at the lieutenant on his right, who shrugged and laid a $10 on the pile before looking at the man on his right.

The last player leaned back in his chair, yawning. He took a swig from his beer bottle, never taking his eyes from his cards. He looked at them from a couple of different angles. The men behind him whistled and hooted, held up their thumbs, or shook their heads in disgust.

The first player shook his head. He leaned forward and growled, "C'mon, Jack. Ante up or fold."

The pilot thus addressed picked up a bill from the stack next to his ashtray without looking at it. He threw it down on the pot.

It was a $50. Howls of approval greeted the bill. The third lieutenant muttered something and threw his cards down, pushing back from the table.

"See ya and raise ya, Timmy," said Jack. He leaned back and took a swig from his bottle.

Timmy frowned across the table at Jack. His eyes narrowed as he picked up a cigar smoldering in the ashtray beside him, tapped the ash off, and took a slow puff as he regarded his only remaining opponent.

"You're bluffing, Jack," Timmy said. "You didn't even look at that bill."

Timmy smiled and laid a pair of $20s on the pile. The cabin shook as the other lieutenants yelled and stamped and applauded, slapping each other in the back in excitement.

"Think so?" Without looking Jack peeled a card from his hand and laid it face down on the table. He took a card from the deck in front of him. Timmy peeled off two cards from his own hand and took two from the deck.

Jack smiled and took another $50 from the stack in front of him, waving it slowly in front of his face. Timmy shook his head and tossed a $50 on the pile.

In a moment the room quieted down. The drunken quartet in the corner was elbowed into silence.

Jack tossed the $50 on the pile. His voice was low and cool.

"Call," he said.

Timmy laid his cards down one by one: three aces and a pair of jacks.

The crowd murmured loudly and quieted again.

Jack didn't move, looking across the table at the first player. He didn't change his expression.

Then he shook his head, once.

The first player grinned and reached for the pot.

"Kinda hasty there, Timothy," said Jack, and laid his hand face up on the table.

A multi-throated cheer erupted from the crowd. The hand revealed was four kings and a seven of diamonds.

Timmy bit through his cigar.

Jack watched him for a moment as he was pummeled and back-slapped in approval. Someone shoved a fresh beer in his hand. He took it, upended it, and drank it down in a series of swallows as the others chanted *Go! Go! Go! Go! Go!*

When he drained the last of the beer he slammed the bottle down on the table and gathered the pot into the already-large stack of bills in front of him. He pointed at the deck and raised his eyebrows at Timothy, who shook his head in disgust and held up his hands in surrender before putting his right hand out. Jack shook hands with him and started stuffing bills into his pockets.

It took awhile. Finally Jack had bills stuffed in every pocket of his uniform blouse and pants.

"A fond farewell, my friends!" he said. The other pilots jeered and catcalled after him as he left the cabin.

Jack walked down the passage and took a turn through a set of blackout curtains. The roar of young men was replaced by the wash of the sea, spraying back from the bows of the liner, and the wind of the ship's passage sighing along the deck and the rigging. He took a deep breath of the fresh sea air, and then another, blinking his eyes.

A beer or twelve was one thing, but Jack really didn't like tobacco smoke.

He walked forward with one hand on the salt-slicked deck rail of the liner. To the right, across the passage, a faint gray radiance outlined the low hills of Luzon. Above the hills a few clouds turned pink in the rays of the rising sun. On the water Jack saw the truck lights of a steamer heading south. Jack had good eyes, better than the Air Corps requirement of 20/20. He saw a deckhouse under the lights. Here and there smaller, fainter lights, probably fishing boats, dotted the passage.

The light on the clouds grew. The pink became deeper, redder, adding golden yellow highlights. The stars faded. Great red rays of light appeared over the hills. Then the sun climbed above the hills, illuminating the ships and boats in the Passage, and it was day.

Jack watched the sunrise, hands on the rail, the wind of the liner's passage ruffling his hair. Underneath his feet he could feel the thrum of the ship's turbines and propellers. With each revolution, they drove him closer to the convoy's destination: Manila.

Something kicked gently behind his knee, which buckled. Jack caught himself on the railing and turned to see Roy Chant holding out a cup of coffee. Jack took it, smiling, and nodded his thanks.

Chant mumbled something that sounded like "good morning." He sipped his own coffee, leaning against the railing and balancing against the gentle corkscrew motion of the liner.

Jack pointed ahead of them, past the now-visible cruiser. "Look north there, Roy. I think that mountain is Mariveles."

11

"What's so marvelous about a mountain?"

"Mariveles," Jack repeated, sounding the syllables. "It's at the mouth of Manila Bay, north of Corregidor."

"A marvelous mountain north of a corridor?"

Jack laughed. "Cut the act, Roy. Even you aren't that dumb."

Chant grinned at him. The two young men leaned against the railing, looking beyond the cruiser to the land ahead of them.

"Six weeks cooped up on this bucket," Chant said. He sipped his coffee. "I hope we get to fly soon."

"Yeah, me too. This trip was too much like being in the Navy."

"How much further across the bay to Manila?" Chant asked.

"Maybe thirty miles."

"Shoot," said Chant. "We've got hours yet. Let's get some breakfast. Hey, how much did you win, anyway? I never saw a run of luck like you had last night."

"I haven't counted it yet," Jack replied.

Chant shook his head, looking at Jack's bulging pockets. "Pal, you better put that money in the ship's safe, or you might provide too much temptation to some poor, weak sinner."

"What, Roy, like you?"

Chant managed an injured, astonished look. "Me? Jack, I may be poor, but I am *not* weak."

When they came back on deck after breakfast the liner was in the mouth of Manila Bay, heading east. To the left was the island of Corregidor. Beyond Corregidor to the north lay the seaport of Mariveles. A mile south of them was an odd-looking island.

"What the hell is that?" asked Chant, standing next to Jack at the railing. He pointed to the island. Man-made concrete cliffs rose sheer out of the water. On top of the concrete were two huge gun turrets, like something off a battleship, along with an armored observation tower and a wooden barracks. A tiny splotch of red, white and blue showed the American flag flying over the island.

Jack dredged up memories. "Fort Drum," he replied after a moment. "Coast Artillery. 14-inch guns."

Chant looked at the heavily-armed concrete island. "Jesus," he finally said. "14-inch guns over there, and more big guns on Corregidor, right? I think I remember something from ROTC about catching the enemy in a crossfire. Guess they weren't kidding."

"Big guns on disappearing carriages on Corregidor," Jack commented.

Chant frowned at him. "How come you know so much about it, Jack?" he asked.

Jack shrugged. He looked from Fort Drum to the green hills rising from the sea beyond the fort.

"My brother Charlie went to West Point. He thought he'd like to be an artilleryman once and got interested in forts and artillery and stuff like that."

"Did your brother stay in the artillery?"

"No, Charlie's in the Air Corps like us. He flies B-17s."

"Must be in the blood."

"What, because my Dad was a pilot, too? It's not like we're fifth-generation New Bedford whalers or something. Airplanes haven't been around that long."

Chant shook his head. "B-17s. I hear those guys really have it made. I kind of wish I'd been assigned to bombardment."

"Six weeks on this boat, Roy, and I'm just now finding out about this little fetish?"

"Jack, I was never out of North Carolina until I went to Texas for flight school. Kind of got the idea it might be fun to fly for the airlines."

"Airlines?"

"Sure, why not? They've got stewardesses. Besides, I don't think I want to stay in the Army when my hitch is up."

"No? Why not?"

Chant frowned, looking across the water at Fort Drum and its gun turrets.

"You ever see a fort like that?" Chant asked. "Makes you think."

"I guess. What's your point?"

"How much damage could a shell from big guns like those do?"

"I don't know, Roy. Level half a city block, maybe." He frowned. "One shell from a gun like that could sink a battleship, if it hit in the right place. Remember the *Hood* and the *Bismarck*, last year?"

"Yeah. Sort of. A big sea fight? *Bismarck* blew the *Hood* all to hell, but the Brits sank the *Bismarck*, finally." Chant frowned at Fort Drum. "So that's a lot of firepower over there. Enough to sink a battleship."

"Sure. I'm still waiting for you to get to the point, Chant."

"I studied mathematics in college, Jack. If I don't wind up with an airline job, maybe I'll go back to school and teach geometry or something."

"OK. So you're a smart guy. I knew you weren't stupid."

Chant shook his head. "Thanks for the praise there, Jack."

Jack smiled. "OK, so I'm still waiting."

Chant frowned. "It doesn't add up."

"What?"

"None of this. Look at that fort over there, what is it but half a battleship that can't move? How many battleships do the Japs have?"

"I don't know. Not as many as we do."

"Maybe, but how many do you think it will take to blow the turrets off that concrete island?"

Jack leaned against the rail, looking at Fort Drum.

"I don't know," he said.

"Yeah," said Chant. "Me, either. That's what I meant when I said it doesn't add up. Does anyone even know what the Japs have to throw at us?"

They were quiet for a moment. Manila Bay unfolded around them. The green hills to the south slid slowly by.

"You figure there'll be a war?" Chant asked. "With the Japs and maybe the Nazis?"

Jack sighed. "Yeah. Hitler was crazy enough to attack the Russians and the Japs are just plain crazy."

"What d'you mean?"

"You want to talk about stuff that doesn't add up? Look at the war in China. Japan's not that big and it doesn't have that many people. The Chinese could lose ten to one and the Japs would still run out of men first."

"Doesn't look like they see it that way."

"Which proves they really are crazy."

"Crazy enough to attack the Philippines?"

Jack nodded. "Don't you reckon we're here because someone in the War Department is afraid the Japs will give it a try?"

"I guess they didn't send us out here to enjoy the weather and see the sights," Chant answered.

Another group of young lieutenants lined the railing back towards the bridge superstructure, pointing at the different sights around the harbor. Suddenly they laughed and slapped each other on the back.

"What's that all about?" Jack asked.

Chant scoffed. "Aw, that's Brad Williams and his bunch. Bunch of cock-hounds. Reckon they're figuring out which whorehouse they'll visit first."

"Oh yeah? What about you, Roy?"

Chant shuddered. "That VD film they showed us in Basic did it for me. I think I'll just try for pure and sinless thoughts for another year or two."

"That goo might back up and flow out through your ears, you know."

"That's kid stuff, Jack." Chant grinned. "Might make it hard to get to sleep nights, though. What about you? You going to make the rounds?"

Jack scoffed. "Not me."

"You got a girl back home?"

"Yes." Jack hesitated. "We're engaged. She lives in Los Angeles and when I got to Hamilton Field I thought I'd get to see her every now and again, but hell, you remember, I barely got there before we got orders to come out here to the Philippines."

Chant shook his head. "So how long have you known this girl? What's her name, anyway?"

"Irina. I met her here in Manila, actually, three years ago."

Chant looked at Jack, raising his eyebrows. "What were you doing in Manila three years ago?"

"Came out on the Pan-Am China Clipper with my Dad and my brother Charlie. Dad figured maybe it would be a good thing if the Davis boys had one last fling together."

Chant chuckled, shaking his head. "So you flew out here on the Clipper? Where'd you stay?"

"The Manila Hotel."

"Pretty ritzy! So you have dough. More than your pay and your luck at poker, I mean."

"We're comfortable," Jack admitted. "The family, I mean."

"Comfortable. Great day. So that two thousand bucks you won last night is just chicken feed?"

Jack looked at Chant, but the other lieutenant's eyes were twinkling. So he grinned. "Thought I might go into business for myself, some day."

"Two thousand bucks would make a pretty good nest egg. You reckon to get married when we get back?"

"You bet."

"Oh? Well, you got a picture of the lucky lady?"

Jack took out his wallet. He kept a head-and-shoulders portrait shot of Irina, a little the worse for wear now, but whenever he looked at it Jack felt Irina's eyes looking out of it and into his own.

"Gee," Chant said, looking at the picture. "Davis, I might should change my mind about you."

Jack put the wallet away. "What do you mean?"

"Rich, not too ugly, halfway decent pilot and a good-looking girl like that into the bargain? That's too much luck for any one man to have."

"Don't forget modest and soft-spoken."

Chant shook his head. "She's sure a looker. If she's a sweet kid you'd better hold onto her."

"I intend to. Besides..." Jack hesitated.

"What?"

"Something Dad told me once that stuck with me."

"What was that?"

"You'd better not laugh."

"I won't, promise."

"Dad told me I'd be a lot happier in life if I didn't do anything I couldn't look my Mom in the eye and tell her the truth about it."

Chant nodded. "Well, what's so funny about that? Reckon my Dad would tell me the same thing."

"Some of these guys would think it's a little strange. You know."

"Sure. But well, I have a girl back home, too. Kind of."

"Kind of?"

16

Chant blushed. "Don't like to talk about her. I don't really like the way most of the guys talk about women, anyway. It's not respectful."

Jack nodded. "Got a picture?"

Chant reached into his pocket for his wallet. Inside there was a faded black and white snapshot of a smiling young woman in a cheerleader's outfit.

"You've kept this for a while," Jack observed. "Maybe she'd send you a new one. You ever write to her?"

"Aw, well, she was a cheerleader and I was second string on the football team. Her pop owns the local car dealership, an' he's the mayor." Chant grimaced. "My folks weren't that well off."

"So? You're an officer and an Army pilot. That makes you first string now. Is she married? Or engaged?"

"No. Not that I know of. Mom never said in her letters, anyway."

"You ever ask? Never mind." Jack manfully mastered the smile that threatened to erupt on his lips. "Write to her. Keep it light, you know, none of that Romeo and Juliet stuff. Tell her about flying for Uncle Sam in the beautiful tropical paradise of the Philippines and all that and you maybe want some news from home from someone besides your mother. Then just see what happens."

"You think?"

"Well, you can't do much more than write. But we won't be out here forever."

They stood in silence for a moment as Fort Drum drifted astern.

Jack nodded back at the fort. "It's a sitting target, isn't it? Wonder if they've got any antiaircraft guns over there."

"Why would they need 'em?" Chant asked. "The Air Corps will keep the Jap bombers away."

"Let's hope so." Jack looked ahead. The eastern shore of Manila Bay was visible. To the north of the bay cumulus clouds began to build over the land.

Manila Bay - Pier 7 - Nichols Field

Tugboats nudged the *Coolidge* into her berth at Pier 7. An hour after docking Jack and Chant filed slowly down the stairs to the pier with the rest of the pilots. That took a long time, and then the pilots and men of the 21st were held on Pier 7. Fuming, their squadron commander, 1st Lt. Ed Dyess, went off to find someone in charge.

Jack saw the penthouse of the Manila Hotel from where they stood on the pier, trying to find a scrap of shade as the hot morning got hotter by the moment. They were there long enough that the squadron's own mess cooks prepared a scratch meal of hot dogs and sauerkraut. From somewhere iced tubs of Coca Cola appeared.

Chant looked at the last bite of the hot dog in his fingers. He grimaced

"What's wrong, Roy?" Jack asked.

Chant popped the morsel in his mouth, chewed, and swallowed. "I was thinking these hot dogs are OK, but I'm sure going to miss the chow on the Coolidge. I don't think I've had steak for dinner often, and the steaks the other night were absolutely wonderful."

Chant grabbed another hot dog, looked at it, and bit the end off. "Hot dogs are fine but you really don't want to know what's in 'em."

A sergeant in a broad-brimmed hat carrying a clipboard stopped and looked at the pilots standing around the tub of soft drinks.

"Excuse me, gentlemen," the sergeant said. "I'm looking for the 21st Squadron, 35th Pursuit Group."

"That's us," Jack replied.

"Is a Lt. Dyess here?"

Dyess shouldered his way forward. "I'm Ed Dyess," he said.

The sergeant saluted. "Sir, I have trucks here to take your pilots to Nichols Field."

"What about the enlisted men?"

"The ground echelon will come next."

"OK," said Dyess.

18

Jack and Chant stood with their bags in hand. The others crammed down the last bite of hot dog or swilled down Cokes before picking up their own bags.

"Let's go, hotshots," Dyess said. "Next stop, Nichols Field."

The trucks drove for a mile down Dewey Boulevard, then turned left onto a side road. They drove a few more blocks and crossed a little bridge over a smelly creek. The bridge was only wide enough to accommodate one truck at a time. On the other side lay Nichols Field.

Nichols was built east of the creek on top of a bunch of filled-in rice paddies. There was a concrete runway, the only one in the Philippines, and a collection of old 1920s-style institutional-Army looking buildings along a single street by four wooden hangars. A small sea of OD tents sprouted in every available area.

Jack could smell that rice paddy stink, although maybe it came from the creek.

Regardless, looking at the men marching and going about their errands, it was plain that Nichols Field, like every other part of the US Army Air Forces, was bursting at the seams.

None of that interested Jack as much as the antique Boeing P-26 pursuit plane sitting at the end of the runway. The early afternoon sun glinted off the shiny yellow wings and the bright steel bracing wires. The leather-helmeted pilot was clearly visible in the open cockpit.

Jack grinned. It might be old and antiquated, with its wires and open cockpit and twin machine-guns synchronized to fire through the propeller, but the P-26 was the first airplane he'd fallen in love with, and you never quite forget your first, for good or ill. Besides, it had been too damned long since he'd been in the cockpit. Jack was ready to fly a box kite to get in the air again. He looked at the P-26 with longing.

The truck braked to a stop. Jack stood by the edge of the truck's rear gate, watching as the pilot of the little pursuit wiggled his rudder. The blattering roar of its engine swelled. Jack could see the pilot had the elevators in full up position to keep the tail down against the air blasting back from the propeller. In the next instant, the pilot released the brakes and the P-26 rolled forward. The tail came off the ground. In another few hundred feet the airplane lifted from the runway, climbing straight out to the south on the runway heading, the roar of its engine diminishing with distance.

Someone behind Jack said, "Jesus, I hope we don't have to fly those old crates. Stick another wing across the top and we could go hunting the Red Baron."

Jack jumped out of the truck, pretending not to hear the slur on what had been, in its day, a pretty good airplane. Privately, though, he agreed with the sentiment, because in front of a nearby hangar he could see what he'd come all the way across the Pacific to fly: the sleek, long-snouted shape of a P-40E, painted olive drab on top and light gray on the bottom, with white numbers on the fuselage and fin and the red-white-and-blue national insignia bright and proud aft of the cockpit. A couple of mechanics had the cowling open, fussing with something in the Allison engine's guts.

The canopy, though, was open, open as if in invitation.

Jack felt the tingle in his hands and his feet and the seat of his pants. He wanted to start that 1100-hp engine and feel the rumble and rattle of the airframe as the prop wound up to 2000 rpm. Then he wanted to see the ground fall away around him as he climbed into the sky.

He blinked and shook himself. Another airplane had started up.

At first Jack couldn't believe it. He recognized the airplane, a Seversky P-35, but instead of the US national insignia the pursuit was marked with three gold crowns on a blue roundel. Then another P-35 started up. This one had a blotchy camouflage paint scheme, olive drab over bare aluminum, standing out in streaks.

At least this airplane had US markings.

"Those are P-35s, right?" asked Chant. "Whose air force does the one with the three crowns belong to?"

"Sweden," said their squadron commander. He stood beside Jack, looking at the two P-35s. "That's Royal Swedish Air Force insignia, three gold crowns on a blue field."

"What are we doing with Swedish P-35s?" Jack asked.

Dyess shook his head. "The Air Corps requisitioned them," he replied. "Seversky Aircraft had a contract with the Swedes, but I guess we needed them worse."

Someone called Dyess away. He left the lieutenants standing there as the P-35s taxied out.

"At least we're supposed to get P-40s," Chant muttered. "Aren't those P-35s kind of old?"

"Four years ago that was a hot airplane," Jack told him. "The first few models were racing airplanes. Flew in the Bendix cross-country."

"Oh yeah? Four years ago?"

"That's right."

"Swell. Isn't that what they call obsolete?"

"Look. It was the first all-metal, retractable-gear, enclosed-cockpit pursuit adopted by any air force anywhere. It's still better than the fixed-gear stuff the Japs are flying."

Chant scowled. "I sure hope so. Taking airplanes from the Swedes sounds kind of desperate to me."

"Yeah. Well, you see all those crates inside that hangar? Those are P-40s. Hopefully that's what we'll get instead of P-35s."

A corporal ran up to them. "Lieutenants, if y'all will follow me, I'll show you to your billets."

Jack picked up his bags. "OK, corporal, lead on."

The lieutenants of the 21st Squadron came to what the corporal proudly informed them was "their squadron street." The corporal pointed to a guidon at the corner of two paths between a row of tents.

"21st Squadron, 35th Pursuit," the corporal said, pointing to the numerals on the guidon. "Your home away from home. If you gentlemen will get settled in, someone will be by shortly to show you to the chow hall. By your leave, sirs."

The corporal ran off.

Jack and the other pilots stood staring at the six-man pyramidal canvas tents on their "squadron street."

"I remember company streets," someone said. "But that was before I transferred from the infantry to the Air Corps. What the hell is a squadron street, anyway?"

Jack walked to the nearest tent. Chant came with him. The other lieutenants broke up and filtered down the lane between the tents, which was still muddy from recent rains.

On the voyage across the Pacific Jack had come to see Chant as an even-tempered, cheerful guy. Now, though, looking at the canvas tent, Chant's normally cheerful face wore a narrow-eyed, thin-mouthed look of irritation.

"What's wrong, Roy?" Jack asked. "It's just a damned smelly tent like all the others."

"That's just it," Chant drawled. "If I wanted to play Boy Scout, I'd have joined up for the doughboy infantry. I figured the Air Corps would be a little more modern."

Chant waved his hand at the olive-drab tent.

The tent had a pyramidal roof and sides that rolled up to catch the breeze. Mosquito netting was rolled down and tied in place. Inside six cots were already set up.

The tent did indeed stink. Canvas stored away in a warehouse in the tropics developed all sorts of fungus and mildew. Jack saw a faded stencil at one corner of the doorway flap but he couldn't make out the letters and numbers.

He pushed aside the flap and went inside. The six cots were arranged in two neat rows of three. No one had claimed the cots yet. Jack put down his duffle bag and said, "Roy, any of these cots strike your fancy?"

"No, I reckon not, Jack."

Jack put his duffle bag down on the cot nearest the door and sat on the cot. It had a rough, scratchy wool blanket and a thin, limp pillow without a cover. The tent pole in the center of the floor had a kerosene lamp suspended from it. He looked up at the canvas roof. The sun shone in through myriads of tiny pinholes.

"Crap," he muttered.

"What?" asked Chant, who had chosen the cot opposite Jack's. Chant followed Jack's pointing finger and sighed, examining the roof.

"Well, at least we already know it's gonna leak when it rains," Chant said. "So, a leaky roof, no mattress, no fans, no electric lights and the latrine is fifty yards thataway down the street. And obsolete pursuits to fly."

"Could be worse," Jack said. "Tomorrow maybe we can go look for a place off base."

Nichols Field O-Club

It cooled off after sundown. Jack ate with the guys he came over with in the *Coolidge*, mostly because, like him, they were relative newcomers to the 21st Squadron. Besides Roy Chant, there was Bruce Kearns, from Oklahoma City; Evan Toland from Atlanta, Georgia; Rich Carlson from Kansas City, Missouri; and Matt Cooper from some little town he'd never heard of in Montana, Choto or Choteau or something like that. "Does sound French, doesn't it?" Cooper said cheerfully the first time they talked about where they were from. "Used to be a lot of trapping in that part of Montana, I guess. Probably a bunch of French-Canadians named Choteau."

They left the mess hall and headed toward the Officers' Club. From the noise outside it was easy to tell it was crowded and rowdy inside. Over two thirds of the officers in the Air Corps were young second lieutenants, and that was evident in the group standing at the bar or sitting at the tables. The highest ranking officer Jack saw was a captain, sitting with a couple of first lieutenants, and it looked like the rest of the officers were all second lieutenants like himself and his friends.

In one corner someone was trying to play a battered upright piano. Jack couldn't recognize anything like a tune. Cigarette smoke drifted up towards the ceiling, stirred by slow-moving fans. There was a smell of spilled beer, like a college frat house on Saturday night. Jack thought that wasn't too far off the mark. Almost everyone in the room was in their early twenties and almost all of them had at least two years of college, the minimum required by the Air Corps to enter pilot training.

So it was what a sergeant with stripes and hash-marks up and down his sleeves might describe as a roomful of dumb college boys, far from home and momma's apron strings. Jack grinned and walked to the bar. The rest of the guys pushed their way through behind him.

He ordered a beer. When the bartender set it down before him the lieutenant standing next to Jack at the bar took it before Jack could.

"You're too slow for a pursuit pilot," the guy said.

Jack shrugged and motioned for the bartender to bring him another beer.

"First one's on this joker," he told the bartender, jerking a thumb at the other man.

The other lieutenant tried to grab the second beer from the bartender. Jack pushed the man's hand aside with his right hand and took the beer with his left.

"Thanks," he told the bartender.

Jack looked at the lieutenant standing next to him. The guy was a little taller and had a few pounds on Jack.

"I may be slow but I'm not stupid enough to try the same trick twice and think it'll work," Jack told him.

"Well, just who the hell do you think you are, God's gift to the Air Corps?" the lieutenant sneered. "Maybe I should take you outside and show you a new trick or two."

"I thought we were here in case the Japs start something," Jack replied. "If you think you're as tough as one of those little yellow bastards I might step outside with you. Otherwise drink your beer."

Without warning, the lieutenant reached out to shove Jack. Jack avoided the blow by stepping back a half-pace. The other lieutenant stumbled against the bar, saved from falling only by an outstretched hand at the last minute.

"Hawkins, go to your quarters," said a new, dead-level voice. It cut straight through the rest of the noise in the Officers' Club and made itself instantly heard.

The lieutenant looked up at the newcomer, as did Jack.

A first lieutenant in khakis stood there. The silver wings over his left breast pocket had the slightest amount of tarnish to them. The man's hair was black and wavy. He wore an old-style aviator's wisp of a moustache.

"Yes, sir," Hawkins said at once. His tone was subdued. He turned and left the club.

Jack looked at the first lieutenant. "Thanks," he said. "I didn't want to start anything my first night on base."

The first lieutenant smiled briefly. "Good policy," he said, and turned to go.

"Excuse me, sir," Jack said. "But would you mind if I bought you a beer and asked a few questions?"

"Well, I wouldn't mind a beer," the first lieutenant said.

"You buying, Jack?"

Jack turned to see his own squadron commander, Ed Dyess. "Sure thing, boss," he said.

"Me, too?" Chant asked hopefully at Jack's elbow.

"Damn, Ed, is this half your squadron?" the other first lieutenant asked. He indicated the young men standing behind Jack and Chant.

"No, Boyd," Dyess replied. "I guess the others are around somewhere and if they haven't made it here yet they will soon."

Jack looked at the other first lieutenant, the one Dyess addressed as "Boyd."

The man held out his hand to Jack. "Wagner, Boyd Wagner."

Jack shook hands with the senior lieutenant. "Davis, Jack Davis."

"Hey, Jack, I think we'll catch up with you later," said Carlson. "I think I see a poker game in progress."

"Suit yourself," Jack said. Chant stuck with him; the others left to find the poker game.

Wagner led them out to a screened-in porch off the main bar and signaled a Filipino barman, who came over.

Jack had a beer already and said, "Beer's on me, or whatever else these gentlemen want."

"Beer's fine," said Wagner.

"Me too," said Chant.

"I'll have one," Dyess said, sitting down.

The bartender brought the beer in foaming mugs with cold moisture beaded on the outside. Jack tasted his. It was a little different from Stateside beer. He asked Wagner about it.

"They brew it locally," the older man said. "But I have a feeling you aren't actually interested in beer, Davis."

"No, sir." Jack glanced at Dyess. "I want to know about the situation here."

Wagner sipped his beer, looking over the rim of the glass at Jack. "You take it straight or sugar-coated?"

"Straight," said Jack.

"Me, too," Dyess chimed in. "If Jack here hadn't asked I would have."

25

Wagner nodded. "OK. Well, in short, we're on the ass end of a ten thousand mile supply line, as you guys know because you just traveled along it. The Japs can cut that line anytime they want. We're short of everything, and I mean everything from bunks to .50-caliber ammo." Wagner hesitated. "And, I'm afraid, a certain amount of brains."

"What d'you mean, Boyd?" Dyess asked quietly, sipping his beer.

"You'll see for yourself after you've been here a few weeks, Ed, and really, maybe I'm being unfair. A lot of it is too few people trying to do too many things without enough to work with. You know how the Air Corps is expanding from what, just a dozen or so groups two years ago to maybe two hundred in another two years? That's a lot of men and equipment to conjure out of thin air, don't you think?"

Dyess nodded.

"When you expand that fast there are bound to be problems, and buddy, let me tell you, most of them have come right out here to the Far Eastern Air Force." Wagner sipped his beer and brooded for a moment. "I got myself in a bit of trouble a month ago. We went to Iba Field out on the west coast for gunnery practice. We didn't have P-40s yet, so we were flying P-35s. There's not enough .50-cal. ammo to expend any for practice and the .30-cal. guns in those airplanes have had the rifling pretty much worn out of the gun barrels. It was not a rewarding experience."

"What did you do?" asked Dyess.

Wagner shrugged and drank from his beer. "None of my boys had any gunnery training back in the States. Like I said, the guns in the P-35s had the rifling shot out of them, so we may as well have been shooting smoothbore muskets for accuracy. It was a little frustrating. So I wrote a report about it and kicked it upstairs, hoping if people got mad enough at me they'd at least take a look at the problem and maybe make some changes."

Wagner scoffed.

"I'd guess you weren't court-martialed," Dyess said. "What did the brass do?"

"Not much," Wagner said shortly. "I got called on the carpet and told not to stick my nose into policy matters. Then we got P-

40s and that was a whole new set of problems, starting with the fact that most of my boys had never even seen a P-40."

"Mine either," said Dyess. "We were just starting to convert into P-40s when we got shipped out here."

"What were you flying before that?"

"P-35s and P-36s."

Wagner nodded. "Well, you know the P-40 is pretty much just a P-36 with an inline engine instead of a radial. When we got P-40s I thought things would start to look up, but it didn't work out that way."

"No? Why not?"

"The kids we're getting out here are good stuff, by and large, but since they expanded the training program I think the brass is more concerned with numbers of pilots graduated than producing pilots who know what the hell they're doing with an airplane," Wagner replied. "We've had way too many accidents, stupid stuff, stuff I would've thought any cadet would know not to do, much less a lieutenant with his wings even if he is just a few months out of flight school. We're lucky we've only had one guy killed, but we've torn up a lot of airplanes."

Dyess frowned, nodding. "Experience counts for something, too," he pointed out. "Most of my boys are class of '41C or later. I doubt they average more than 250 hours total flying time in their logbooks. And these goddamned pursuit airplanes the Army has now are more like racers that only hot pilots would've flown a few years ago."

Chant exchanged a glance with Jack. "Even the P-35, sir?" he asked.

"The P-35 was developed from a racing airplane," Wagner replied.

Jack drank his beer. "What, Roy, you doubted me?"

"Just keeping you honest."

"But that brings us right back to the original point," Wagner said. "Your kids are pretty green. We don't have enough P-40s to equip your squadron yet. You'll be stuck flying P-35s for awhile."

"Oh, gosh, Boyd, I'm pretty sure they told me we'd have P-40s ready and waiting."

"I note you don't seem too surprised, Ed," Wagner replied drily. "You may have noticed the Air Corps is scraping the bottom of the barrel for airplanes. Some of those P-35s were intended for the Royal Swedish Air Force. The instruments read in metric and they've even got Swedish insignia."

"Metric?" Dyess frowned. "That could cause real problems. I doubt most of my guys know metric. I'm not sure I do, myself."

"Well, join the club, pal. Fortunately we have an engineering officer who knows the conversion factors from metric to English. He marked off stall speeds and never-exceed speeds and temperature red zones and stuff like that."

"I guess that's better than nothing."

"Yup. We also have some airplanes that were supposed to go to Thailand. They're basically just AT-6 trainers with bomb racks and four .30-cal. machine guns. The Army calls 'em the A-27. You can guess what we've been calling them."

"Jesus."

"You said it. But airplanes aren't the worst of it. Those silly bastards back in the States didn't think to ship us an oxygen plant so half the time we can't go above ten thousand feet."

"So much for high-altitude interceptions."

Wagner nodded. "Pretty much. Then there's the little matter of Prestone, as in we didn't have any."

"Hold on," said Dyess. "What d'you mean, no Prestone? You can't fly a P-40 without coolant."

"Don't preach to the choir, bishop. We had twenty-odd P-40s assembled and ready to go, but we couldn't even start slow-timing the engines on 'em because there wasn't any Prestone. I hear FEAF went to Supply about it, and some chair-warming colonel old enough to remember when the Army moved on horse-drawn wagons wanted to know why the hell we needed anti-freeze, anyway, and didn't we know we were in the tropics?"

"Boyd, no offense, but…"

"But you find that hard to believe? So did I. The fact is we didn't have any Prestone, and no one could explain why. We just got enough to start flying two weeks ago, and even then there's precious little of it."

Dyess shook his head. "Is it true they've got an actual cavalry regiment out here?"

28

Wagner laughed. It didn't sound amused. "Hell, there's a troop of cavalry right here on Nichols Field, the 124th US Cavalry Regiment is up at Fort Stotsenburg, right next door to Clark Field." He frowned. "They even conduct saber drill at Saturday parade."

Dyess blinked. "Guess they didn't hear what the Wehrmacht did to the Polish cavalry two years ago."

"Well, who the hell knows. It happened to the other guy, not to us." Wagner chewed on the stem of his pipe, puffed, looked in the bowl, and tapped out the ashes. Then he took a pouch from his pocket, refilled the bowl of the pipe, and relit it. When he had the tobacco burning he looked from Dyess to Jack.

Jack returned the scrutiny. Wagner was only a few years older than he was, and only a first lieutenant. But Wagner's eyes looked right into Jack's with just a hint of amused challenge. Dyess looked back and forth between them and chuckled.

"Go ahead and try, Boyd, but I don't think that will work," he told the other squadron commander.

Wagner puffed his pipe and casually looked away from Jack. "Oh? What won't work, exactly?"

"I don't think you'll unnerve Davis here just by staring at him."

Wagner shrugged. "He wouldn't be worth a crap if I could."

He looked back at Jack. "What class did you graduate in?"

"Kelly Field, Class of '41D."

"Well, at least you learned at Kelly. That's something. Total time?"

"Civilian or military?" Jack asked.

Dyess turned to Jack and raised an eyebrow. "Civilian time, Jack? Why am I just now finding out about this?"

"I didn't tell anyone at Kelly because I didn't want to be an instructor. I did that for awhile. Didn't like it much."

Dyess shook his head. "I thought you were a little too good. But here I thought you were a hot pilot."

"I am a hot pilot," Jack said.

Wagner's mouth hid the ghost of a smile. "So break your total time down for me."

"Civilian, about four hundred hours. Military about three hundred."

"How long you been flying, then?" Wagner asked.

"Got my license in 1938."

"You say you gave flying lessons?"

"That's right. Mostly for the Civilian Air Training program."

Wagner grinned suddenly. "Well, I bet you collected your share of thrills. What was your first assignment after flight school?"

"31st Pursuit Group, flying P-39s."

Wagner looked at Dyess. "I hear that little bitch is a real handful, speaking of hot airplanes. What did you think, Davis?"

"I liked it. Kind of sensitive on the elevators. Fair roll rate. Not much go above 17,000 feet, though, just like the P-40. A little faster than the P-40, maybe, on the straight and level." Jack frowned.

Wagner nodded. "Same engine, same single-stage supercharger. You get any time in the P-40?"

"About five or six hours when I got to Hamilton Field before we shipped out."

Wagner snorted. "Hell, that makes you an expert P-40 pilot in the Far Eastern Air Force." Wagner looked speculatively at Davis.

"Don't even think about it, Boyd," Dyess warned. "I need my experienced guys just the same as you do."

"Can't blame a man for thinking," Wagner replied. "No hard feelings, I hope?"

"Not if you buy the next round," answered Dyess.

CHAPTER TWO
Hamilton Field

Hamilton Field, California

Captain Charles Davis stood with his flight engineer and the line chief looking sourly up at the No. 1 engine of his B-17D heavy bomber.

"That's a brand-new engine. Why won't it start, Chief?" Charlie asked.

"I hate to tell ya I don't know, Captain, but I don't know," the mechanic answered. "Every check I can make without takin' the damn thing off the mounts I've done. Nothing has done a damn bit of good. We changed out the plugs and the ignition harness even though they were working fine. I even called a guy I know at the Wright engine factory. It stumped him too."

Charlie scowled up at the engine. There was a team of mechanics on a platform around the engine, coaxing a sling into place.

"So you're going to take the engine off and put it on a test stand?"

"Yes, sir. That's all I can figure to do."

"In the meantime I've got a four-engined airplane with three engines. Hell, Chief, we were supposed to be on..." Charlie stopped. The movement of his bomber was at least technically a military secret, even though he was sure it was about as open as a secret got.

The line chief nodded. "I know, sir."

"Yeah. Well, I'm open to suggestions."

The line chief hesitated. "Captain, there's nothing wrong with the turbocharger on this engine mount, an' I think I've got a line on an engine we can hang on this ship. But that engine is on a C-model B-17 down at March Field. That airplane's been used pretty hard and the engines have at least a hundred hours on them. The idea was to send you guys to, ah, Plum, I guess it is, with new ones."

Charlie stifled a grin at the chief's use of the code word "Plum." He nodded slowly. "I'd need to clear that for you, wouldn't I?"

"Yes, sir. You know how it is."

Charlie did know. The Army Air Forces were undergoing a traumatic growth spurt, and that meant engines – along with spare parts, tools, hangar space, barrack space and most important of all, trained personnel – were in ridiculously short supply for a country like the United States.

After a moment he nodded once, decisively. "OK, Chief," he said. "I'll go talk to Colonel Miller. How long will that old 'C' be down even if we don't swipe one of her engines?"

"My buddy down at March tells me a couple of days at least. She's overdue for her 100-hour inspection and some modifications they've been putting off to bring her up to 'D' standard."

"Right then. I'll be back."

"Yes, sir."

Charlie turned and walked around the side of the hangar to the main avenue leading to the headquarters building. The street was filled with trucks and jeeps going back and forth from the hangars and the flight line. To his right were H-shaped white stucco barracks and ahead of him was HQ, another single-story, white stucco building with a red-tiled roof. It was a short walk on a pleasantly cool California day with the salt and mud smell of

San Francisco Bay mingled with aviation fuel, exhaust, and hot metal. A formation of P-40s screamed overhead, the lead pursuit peeling off to enter the landing pattern, followed by the others. Charlie grinned a little, shaking his head, thinking about his brother Jack. Until a month ago Jack was at Hamilton Field with the 35th Pursuit Group. Charlie found out that the lead echelon of the 35th Pursuit was at Plum, though, along with Jack's squadron, the 21st.

As he walked Charlie returned salutes from privates, sergeants, and the occasional lieutenant. He entered the HQ Building, nodded at the corporal at the entrance desk, and strode down the corridor lined with offices. There were rooms filled with filing cabinets and cubbyhole offices with junior officers jammed into them, most of them shouting on telephones or frantically taking notes while listening to someone on the phone. At the far end were the senior officers. Charlie went to the door labeled "Special Operations" and entered.

There was a bored-looking, tough-looking staff sergeant seated at a desk before the closed door leading to the colonel's inner sanctum. The sergeant looked up when Charlie entered and frowned.

"Captain, the colonel's kind of busy right now," he said.

"You bet, sergeant, and so am I," Charlie replied. "I've got a busted engine and a Fort I need to get to the Philippines."

Charlie deliberately pitched his voice to carry and penetrate. He knew the walls of all the offices in this building were little better than paper-thin.

The sergeant rolled his eyes at this obvious chicanery. Just as he opened his mouth to ask Charlie to have a seat Colonel Miller himself threw open the door to the inner office.

"What the hell, Davis?" he roared. "Why aren't you already halfway to you-know-where instead of mooning around in my office like this?"

Charlie came to attention and matched the Colonel's volume. "Sir, I regret to inform the Colonel that my ship isn't going anywhere until I get a new engine. But I have a potential solution, sir, although one you may not like."

The colonel, a short, stocky man with a red face and thick white hair, glowered at Charlie from under bushy white eyebrows. "Well?" he growled.

"Chief Wilson can get an engine from a Fort down at March Field that's undergoing 100-hour inspection. He can put that on my ship, sir, and I can go after the rest of my squadron."

"They should be landing on Midway sometime today, isn't that right?"

"Yes, sir."

"Crap. I'll have Lew Brereton on the blower to me five minutes after they land at Clark Field if they're one short. And two minutes after he hangs up it'll be Hap Arnold himself on the phone."

"Yes, sir."

The colonel turned to his sergeant. "Voorhis, get on the phone to the 122nd Group down at March. They own that B-17C. Tell them I authorized the engine switch and that it is to proceed very quickly indeed."

"Yes, sir," said Sergeant Voorhis, as he reached for the phone.

"If Col. Goins gives you any guff put him on the phone with me." Miller turned to Charlie. "Anything else?"

"Any word about a new navigator, Colonel? Mine is still in the hospital recovering from appendicitis."

"Navigators? Jesus Jumping Jehosophat, son, you think I keep navigators in my hip pocket? Tell me, you can find your way around a sextant, can't you?"

"Yes, sir, if necessary."

"Right. Tell you what." Miller went to his desk. He pulled a file from a stack of them. "Here's something. There's a half-dozen second lieutenants sitting down in Operations. They just got out of Navigator's School. They were on their way to March Field and got diverted by weather. I doubt they could find a full moon on a clear night with a pair of binoculars but I'll give you one if you're willing to take a chance."

Charlie grimaced. "I'll take what I can get, sir."

"Good! Head on down to Operations. By the time you get there Voorhis will have one ready for you." The colonel glared at Charlie. "Anything else?" he growled.

Charlie came to attention. "No, sir!" he barked.

The Colonel chuckled. "Get the hell out of here, Charlie. When you talk to your mother give her my regards. And you, be careful out there. There's going to be a war soon, like it or not, ready or not."

The Colonel held out his hand. Charlie shook it. "Thank you, sir, I will."

Charlie left the Admin Building and stood on the sidewalk for a moment. Then he started walking back to the flight line. Base Operations was in an office below the control tower that overlooked the flight line.

Welcome to the 19th Bomb Group

Alvin Isaiah Stern, 2nd Lieutenant, US Army Air Forces, wriggled into the hard wooden seat in the corner of the reception area of Base Operations. He pulled his trench coat over his skinny body, trying, for the hundredth time, to shut out the clacking tongues of the other lieutenants gossiping in the room. Al wasn't particularly tired, but he closed his eyes as if he was, because he didn't want to be drawn into the endless, fruitless speculation on the endless rumors floating around about the possibilities of war.

What pissed Al off about all the speculation was how obvious it had been for the last six months that the US was about to get involved in another world war for which it was completely unprepared. For second lieutenants to speculate about when that war would start, when Major General Hap Arnold, commander of the Army Air Forces, and his bosses, including the President, Franklin Delano Roosevelt, didn't know, was a complete waste of time as far as Al Stern was concerned.

The phone rang. Al opened his left eye enough to see the sergeant at the desk answer it, nod as he jotted something down, and hang up again. The sergeant reached for a file and opened it, writing on papers in the file. The sergeant looked up and took in the occupants of the room.

"Lieutenants, if I could have your attention," he called out in what Al thought of as the "sergeant's voice." The Sergeant's Voice wasn't particularly loud but it tended to be dry, penetrating, and often wearily cynical, especially when the sergeant in question was addressing young men years his junior who nominally outranked him.

The seven lieutenants in the room looked at the sergeant. Al opened both eyes and sat up.

"Gentlemen, a Captain Charles Davis will be here momentarily, looking for a navigator volunteer," the sergeant said. "Captain Davis is with the 19th Bomb Group and I am informed that he will be heading to Hawaii within the next twelve to twenty-four hours. I am also informed that if he doesn't get a volunteer he has authorization to select one of you at his pleasure."

That made Al sit up a little straighter. Who the hell was this Captain Davis that he had that kind of clout?

The other guys immediately went into kaffee-klatsch mode, jabbering like a bunch of jackdaws. Al thought about what the sergeant had said. The key phrases were "19th Bomb Group" and "Hawaii." Al figured that for window dressing. There were plenty of rumors about where the 19th was headed and "Hawaii" wasn't included among the possible destinations. The only other US possession of any size out in the western Pacific was the Philippines. The Philippines meant fighting the Japs, and that was just a sideshow. The real war was going to be in Europe, fighting Hitler.

Al Stern's family was Jewish but they weren't Zionist. Not exactly. But a lot of synagogues in the USA contributed to Zionist causes such as helping the colonists in Palestine, and no Jew was blind to what was going on in Germany and Europe. Most of the reason Al dropped out of medical school and went into flight training – OK, so he wasn't cut out to be a pilot, he was good with numbers so he became a navigator – was because he figured the USA was, sooner or later, going to fight the Nazis.

Al thought it likely that, within the next six months, he and his classmates would be in England, bombing Germany. The US Navy was fighting U-boats in the Atlantic, even though neither the US nor Germany had declared war on each other. Yet. But most of the jabbering done by the jackdaws concerned the likelihood of further Stateside training while Hap Arnold or FDR, or whomever, got around to deciding what they wanted to do with this enormous Air Force they were building.

A captain walked in. Al subsided back into his chair, still pretending to sleep while keeping one eye open enough to watch.

The captain wore an A2 leather jacket with some sort of insignia on the left breast that Al couldn't quite make out. It looked like a blue shield and a gold sword. The jacket looked worn-in, not old and beaten-up, just lived-in and comfortable. The captain's hat had the stiffener taken out, and the officer's insignia on the front was just slightly dull. The man himself was maybe a little over average height, 5'9" or so, and maybe 150 or 160. More to the point the guy didn't look like a kid playing dress up, like most of Al's classmates, or an actor playing a role. This guy looked comfortable with who and what he was.

The room went quiet as the captain walked over to the sergeant's desk and spoke with him. The sergeant had risen, nodding as the captain spoke, and then indicated the lieutenants in the room.

"Take your pick, sir," Al heard the sergeant say. There was nothing of the Sergeant's Voice in the non-com's tone when speaking to the captain, who must be Captain Davis. Then Al noticed the ring on the captain's finger. He hadn't been around the Army too long, but he'd seen one or two of those rings, and others like it, enough to know it was a West Point class ring.

The captain turned to face the room.

Charlie looked around the reception area of Operations, taking in the lieutenants standing there. There was one in the back, kind of a sleepy-looking little guy, just coming to his feet. None of them looked any older than fifteen or sixteen, even though he knew they had to be in their early twenties. That, along with the new uniforms and insignia, and most of all the bright, shiny new navigator wings, proclaimed what they were to anyone who knew how to look.

Total new guys, inexperienced and maybe even dangerously ignorant. Charlie had been around long enough to know how new the art of long-distance aerial navigation was. When he reported to the 2nd Bomb Group at Langley in 1940 he was taught to act as a bombardier and navigator as well as a pilot. Charlie was sure that was the point of Colonel Miller asking if he could still find his way around a sextant. Looking at these kids he wondered if he'd be better off doing it all himself.

Charlie suppressed a sigh. A little voice whispered in his ear about what it might be like around midnight tomorrow night. They would be close to the halfway point between Hawaii and California over the dark ocean, with a copilot who could barely fly and a navigator who might not be able to take a proper star sight. That put everything on Charlie's shoulders: responsibility not merely for a half-million dollar airplane and its crew, but the portion of war-fighting capability it represented. One man, one rifle, one bomber, might make all the difference between defeat and victory. West Point drilled that principle in him until it was second nature.

Charlie turned the sigh into a deep breath. He'd bet on himself and hope for the best.

"I'm going to the Philippines and I need a navigator," he said abruptly. "Anyone want to go?"

One of the navigators said, "Respectfully, captain, I'd need a day to plan a trip like that. Unless you've already got the route laid out."

Charlie's former navigator had done that, in fact, but Charlie wasn't going to say so. Just because the route was laid out didn't mean the navigator could sit back and make tick marks on the chart. Not when the worst legs on the route involved two thousand miles of over-water flying trying to find relatively small islands in the middle of nowhere. Not when the weather over the route had changed over the last four days. Not when a pencil line on a chart was the merest beginning.

One down, Charlie thought to himself. He knew he wasn't going to find experience in this bunch. He decided he'd have to settle for nerve, if he could find it.

So he shrugged and said, "What you're saying, lieutenant, is you don't know how to do your job? That Uncle Sam just spent I don't know how many thousands of dollars teaching you to be a navigator? Hell, all we're doing is going from point A to point B, even if it is 2400 miles from here to Hickam Field."

The lieutenant reddened but said nothing. Charlie looked from one to the other of the lieutenants.

He was struck by the little guy on the other side of the room, who stood apart from the other lieutenants. The little guy shrugged into a greatcoat a size too big for him. He seemed a little older than the others. He had olive skin, finely chiseled features, brown eyes and black curly hair. He was slender and maybe five-foot-four. When Charlie looked at him the lieutenant met Charlie's eyes directly but without challenge.

"What about you, lieutenant?" Charlie asked him.

"The Philippines is likely to be a war zone pretty soon, isn't it?" the navigator asked.

"So I hear. Does that scare you?"

"Yes, sir."

"Good. It ought to. It sure as hell scares me."

"Why us, Captain?"

"What do you mean?"

"We're all of us fresh out of Navigator's school. We were told we'd be assigned to a new bomb group and train to go to Europe."

"I'm sure they told you exactly that. You haven't been in the Army long, have you, lieutenant?"

"About seven months, sir."

"Alerting you to go to the Panama Canal Zone and then ordering you to Alaska is pretty much the Army, lieutenant, all the way. As for why you, specifically, it's because you just happen to be here when I need a navigator. So by any chance do you have a hankering to see the exotic Orient?"

"Not really, Captain, meaning no disrespect. But aren't the Japs kind of a side show?"

"What's your point?"

"We keep hearing Hitler's the one to beat."

"May be. I'm going to the Philippines. You want to go or not? I'm in kind of a hurry."

The lieutenant nodded. "All right. I'll go if you'll take me."

Charlie thought about it for a moment. Then he nodded. "OK. Get your gear and come with me."

"Don't I have to report to somebody or something?"

"You do. You report to your immediate superior. That's me. As for the rest of it…"

Charlie turned to the sergeant behind the desk. "I'll take this one, sergeant. Will you handle the paperwork?"

"Yes, sir." The sergeant handed Charlie a manila folder. "Here's the lieutenant's travel orders. I'll have the rest of the paperwork routed to the 19th Bomb Group."

"In triplicate?"

"Of course, Captain." The sergeant smiled.

"Good. Thanks, sergeant. Lieutenant, you got all your bags with you?"

"Yes, sir."

Charlie turned to the other lieutenants, who were still standing in a little group, looking at him uncertainly.

"Good luck in Europe, gentlemen," he told them.

The lieutenant he'd chosen got his duffle bag over this shoulder and picked up his barracks bag. Charlie walked forward to help but the little guy looked at him and shifted the bag.

"I've got it, Captain," the lieutenant said.

"OK, then, let's go," Charlie said. He went and held the door open, then led the lieutenant out to the flight line.

"Welcome to the 19th Bomb Group," Charlie said. "What's your name, anyway?"

"Stern, Captain, Al Stern."

Charlie nodded. "Davis, Charlie Davis. You call me Charlie and I'll call you Al until you screw up, and then I'll call you some other names. OK?"

Stern grinned at Charlie. "Sure thing, boss. So, where are we going?"

"Transient flight line," Charlie replied. "That's my airplane, down there."

Al looked around. There was a single B-17 among the P-40s. "This kind of looks like a pursuit field, Charlie."

"It is. It also happens to be a lot closer to Hawaii than March Field. The 19th staged out of here to get to the Philippines."

"I think I remember something about that. Back in September, wasn't it?"

"That's right."

"But that was a whole squadron going at once."

"That's true. We were part of a squadron movement, too, but now we're trying to catch up."

"We're going alone? I mean, just the one B-17?"

"That's right."

"What happened to the rest of the squadron?"

"Nothing. I think. Probably halfway to Clark Field."

"What happened to you, then?"

Charlie grimaced. "We were about an hour out when the No. 1 engine decided it was time to quit, which it did."

Stern looked at him and looked away. "Must have been fun," he said.

Charlie barked a short laugh. "Loads," he said.

The scene played itself over again in Charlie's mind. The No. 1 engine gave no warning of failure besides a cough, a rumbling vibration across the port wing, then a *CRACK* from inside the engine accompanied by a shower of sparks and an abrupt streamer of fire from under the engine cowling. It had been a busy couple of minutes in the cockpit until they got the fire out and the engine shut down completely, with the prop feathered and the airplane trimmed to fly on three engines.

At night, two hundred miles off the California coast with nothing but the dark ocean underneath them. At that it could've been worse. The engine could have failed further out to sea, or maybe the fire extinguishers wouldn't have put the fire out. None of which was worth worrying about any further, and Charlie put it out of his mind.

"So what happened to your navigator?" Stern asked.

Charlie shrugged. "Appendicitis. He came down with bad stomach pains after we landed. The docs took his appendix out. That'll put him in hospital for a couple of weeks. I can't wait that long."

Stern nodded. "I haven't been in the Air Corps long, Captain, but I guess if an engine catches fire it should be replaced."

"I've known mechanics who aren't as smart as you, Al."

"Why, thank you, Captain, sir. You get a replacement?"

"Yep. It won't start. No one knows why. Now we have to wait for another one, and that's three days down the drain."

"Engines must be in really short supply."

"So is everything, Al, in case you haven't noticed."

Stern snorted. "Did your guy leave his charts?"

"Yeah. We didn't think we'd be stuck here this long, so he left all that in the airplane. Charts, navigator's kit, even some spare pencils."

"Spare pencils? That should cover it, then. Did your guy have the trip planned?"

"What, you don't think you can find Hawaii on your own?"

Stern looked at Charlie. "I hear Hickam Field is on Oahu, sir."

Charlie chuckled. "So it is, Al, so it is. Do you know where Midway Island is?"

"Sure. More or less west northwest of Hickam about a thousand miles."

"Close enough without a chart. How about Wake Island?"

"That's the stop for the Pan Am flying boats after Midway. I know Wake is southwest of Midway, again a thousand miles or so, probably more."

"How about Port Moresby?"

"What's at Port Moresby?"

"I don't know. A harbor, I guess, and some sort of airfield. The 19th went through there in October. It's on the south coast of New Guinea."

"New Guinea?" Stern thought it over. "Wouldn't it be easier to go through Guam if we're headed to the Philippines? I mean, that's what Pan Am does on the way to Manila."

"That's right," Charlie agreed. "How do you know so much about Pan Am?"

"The instructors at navigator's school worked for Pan Am. We went over the Clipper's route to Manila from San Francisco as an example of over-water navigation."

"Good. I hope you remember most of that. It'll come in handy. We won't go via Guam because it's only about a hundred miles from Saipan and Tinian, which belong to the Japs."

"Ah," said Stern. "The Japs. I keep reading nasty things about them in the papers."

"You actually read?"

"It's a defect," Stern admitted graciously. "And a bad habit, too, but I can't seem to control myself."

"Well, I'm a comic book man myself, so I don't have much room to talk."

"That's OK, sir. They taught us in navigator's school that pilots aren't too bright, or they wouldn't need a navigator to tell them where to go."

Charlie laughed. "Brains and a screwy sense of humor. You'll go far in the Air Corps, Al."

"Sir, with respect, I just want to get this war over with and go back to school."

"School?"

"Yes, sir. I'm premed."

"Premed? Is that actually a degree?"

"No. I was studying biochemistry."

"What else do you do?"

"A friend of my father's is a doctor. He also has a little hospital, and I had a job there doing different things."

"Yeah? You learn first aid, stuff like that?"

Stern nodded. "I'm not a corpsman, Captain, but I can bandage a wound and give morphine."

"It's not really my business, but why did you enlist?" Charlie asked.

Stern looked at Charlie. He shifted the barracks bag on his shoulder. "You mean, I could've gotten a deferment and gone on to medical school, doctors being important to the war effort."

"Something like that. There will be plenty of hospital jobs, too, especially once we get into a shooting war. Hand a Tennessee farm boy a rifle and he makes a pretty good infantryman. I'm not so sure about teaching him to read an X-ray."

"I'm Jewish, Captain. And I'm American. This country for all its faults has been good to my family and to me. I don't want to sit in school for another year and then another two years as an intern or a resident in a hospital in Boston or Baltimore or whatever while everyone else, including most of the guys I grew up with, fights Hitler or Tojo."

Charlie thought about it. "Look, Al, as long as you do your job, which is to get my airplane where I need to go, I don't really care why you do it. But I know most of the bomb groups we're training will go to Europe to fight Germany once the war starts. I know what the Germans say about the Jews, so why don't you want to go over there?"

Stern shrugged. "Maybe we'll go to war against Germany, and maybe not. The Navy is out in the Atlantic shooting at U-boats right now, and Herr Hitler hasn't done a thing about it. But the Japs? That could start any time."

"Oh? Why?"

"Because the President cut off exports to Japan last spring. No oil, no scrap metal. The English and the Dutch did the same thing. How long can the Japs keep their navy going, much less their war in China, without oil or gasoline?"

Charlie nodded. When FDR embargoed trade with Japan earlier in the year he figured that was a declaration of war in itself. The Japs might be little yellow bastards but they were tough little yellow bastards, and nothing in their history showed they were shy about going to war. One of Charlie's instructors at West Point had studied the Japanese siege of the Russians at Port Arthur in 1905, and Charlie had made a point of studying the Japanese military since.

There wasn't a lot to study. No one collected military intelligence on the Japs because no one took the Japs seriously. Charlie figured that was a mistake a lot of American kids would pay for.

"The truth is, sir, it's going to be six months to a year before we can do much in Europe," Stern continued. "I mean, the scuttlebutt I hear is that we have one, just one combat-ready group of B-17s, and that's the 19th, and it's gone to the Philippines. So I figure if I go out to the Pacific and learn my trade I'll have something to contribute by the time we're ready for Hitler."

Charlie smiled. "Maybe so, Al. Tell me something. Have you ever been in a B-17?"

"I've been through one. An old "B" model."

"You mean you've never flown in a Fort?"

"No. They were going to take us up in that old B but the Air Corps sent it off to the Royal Air Force or something."

Charlie sighed. "The flight to Hickam Field takes about twelve hours. By the time we get there you'll know the airplane pretty well."

"Yes, sir."

During the walk Charlie noticed his copilot, Lt. Mike Payne, pacing back and forth in front of their airplane. The No. 1 engine had been removed but no one else was around.

Payne saluted Charlie as he got out of the jeep. Charlie returned the salute and took in Payne's frown and the way his shoulders bunched up.

"What's the matter, Mike?"

"It's our waist gunners, sir. Corporal Caniff and Private Milton have been transferred off our crew."

Charlie took a deep breath. "Jesus Jumping Jehosophat. OK. Mike, this is Al Stern, he's our new navigator. He's never been up in a B-17 before. Take him through the airplane and answer any questions he's got, OK? I've got to go back and see Colonel Miller."

"Yes, sir."

"And if anyone, and I mean anyone, tries to take any more of our crew, you hold 'em off at gunpoint if you have to."

"OK, skipper, but my .45 is back at the BOQ."

"Mike, I don't care how you do it. We keep the rest of our crew together. I'll be back as fast as I can. Where did Chief Wilson go?"

"Down to March Field to get the engine off that other B-17."

"Good. Al, you stay here with Mike. You heard what I told him about keeping the crew together. Help him if it comes to it."

Stern blinked. "Yes, sir," he said.

Al Stern looked up and down the flight line as Captain Davis hurried away. Other than the B-17D in front of him the only other multi-engine airplane on the ramp was the Lockheed Lodestar he and the other navigators flew in on earlier this morning. A pair of P-40s taxied past, engines making a muttering rumble unlike the radial engines Al was used to hearing whenever he flew. The pilot in the first airplane gave them the finger as he taxied by. The pilot in the second airplane waved and grinned. Payne thumbed his nose at the pilot of the first P-40. Al shook his head and waved back at the pilot of the second.

Al took a deep breath. There was that tang in the air he was getting used to, the tang of engine exhaust and raw aviation fuel and lubricating oil.

When the P-40s taxied far enough away to talk without shouting Al turned to Lt. Payne and held out his hand.

"Al Stern," he said.

"Payne, Mike Payne," the copilot replied. He shook hands with Al, then grinned abruptly. "Just graduate?"

Stern nodded warily.

"Me too," Payne informed the navigator cheerfully. "Class of '41-J. I wanted to be a pursuit pilot but that's the Army for you."

"You fly the B-17 much?"

"Me? Nope. Maybe eight or nine hours with Captain Davis, is all."

Al started to ask Payne if he thought he could land the B-17 if Captain Davis were injured and unable to fly. Then he decided he didn't want to know.

"You think my bags will be OK here by this big tire?" Al asked. He looked around for a spot on the concrete unstained by oil or gasoline.

"That's the left main gear," Payne informed him. "I doubt anyone will bother your bags. If it were a tool kit it might be different. Put 'em down and I'll show you the airplane."

Payne led him around the vertical fin of the airplane, which Al thought looked something like a shark's fin, and through an access door on the right side of the bomber.

It was, Al thought, something like climbing into a sewer pipe. At 5'4" he didn't have any trouble standing upright, but Payne was closer to six feet tall and had to stoop as he made his way forward over a narrow wooden floor. The floor was the only covering over the skin of the aircraft. There were exposed wires, tubes, boxes and ribs all down the fuselage. A couple of big machine guns were stowed next to Plexiglas ports molded into the side of the bomber.

"Careful stepping around the lower gun tub," Payne said, pointing to a hole in the bottom of the fuselage.

Al stepped gingerly around the hole. It went down into a kind of platform below the fuselage where a gunner would crouch, firing twin .50-cal. machine guns below and behind the bomber.

"I hear the new B-17E has power turrets instead of all these gun tubs," Payne said over his shoulder. "But this is what we have for now."

Payne led Al forward past what seemed to be the radio operator's compartment, judging from the dials and the telegrapher's key and black boxes in racks. The muzzles of another pair of machine guns eyed him from a storage space under the upper fuselage. To Al it looked as if you could stick your thumb and maybe your little finger in the muzzles of those guns.

"Watch your step over the catwalk," Payne said.

The bigger man passed through the door at the forward end of the radio compartment and maneuvered himself with difficulty over a very narrow metal walkway over an empty space. Al guessed it was the bomb bay. The navigator looked at the racks and pins but had no idea how bombs were supposed to be placed in them to drop smoothly from the aircraft. There wasn't much light in the bomb bay, but he could see the same wires and tubes that led up and down the fuselage running through guides in the ribs.

The airplane sat at an angle to the ground and from the waist they had been climbing uphill. They passed through another bulkhead.

"Here's the cockpit," Payne said with a grand gesture. "I'm the copilot, I sit on the right. Captain Davis sits on the left. And look here."

Payne turned slightly to the right and pointed up. Underneath a chair on the right-hand side of the flight deck a tear-drop shaped Plexiglas bubble showed the sky above them. The bubble was big enough for a man's head.

"You'll take star sights through that bubble," Payne said. "So I'm told, anyway. That chair is where the formation commander sits if we're carrying one."

"Why there?" Al asked.

"Because the chair can be raised and swiveled so you can look around through that bubble," Payne replied.

"So where's my station?" Al asked.

Payne grinned. "Good thing you're a little guy. Follow me."

Al saw a rectangular opening under the deck where the pilots' seats were mounted. He blinked in surprise when Payne got down on hands and knees and crawled into the opening and forward. Al squatted down and looked. Beyond Payne he could see a sort of tunnel, with light from windows in the nose of the airplane.

Another narrow little board led along the bottom of the bomber, with more wires and little boxes and oxygen bottles and tubes attached to the ribs of the airplane. There was an open hatch on the left hand side. As they passed Al could see the left main gear with his bags leaning against it. Then Payne passed through another doorway set in a bulkhead and crawled forward to a sort of pedestal with a tiny stool in front of it.

"And here you are, Lt. Stern, your happy aerial home away from home," Payne said, sitting on the little stool facing Al.

Al sat back on his heels and looked around.

The nose compartment of the B-17 was maybe eight feet long and six feet in diameter, as near as he could measure by eye. Al figured that Payne sat at the bombardier's station; the top-secret Norden bombsight was kept in a secure storage facility when not in use, so no surprise that there was only a mounting pedestal in the nose.

He looked to the left. There was a little wooden table there and another tiny stool in front of it, almost under his left hand. Al crawled forward and sat in the stool.

Two little windows less than a foot square were in front of him. Through them he saw the two engines on the left wing. Fastened to ribs on either side of the window, or bolted to the floor, were the instruments he'd been introduced to in navigator's school: flux gate compass, altimeter, airspeed indicator, thermometer, drift meter, intercom, oxygen connection and blinker, stopwatch and clock. There was a cased sextant under the table and maps in a folder on the table, along with an aerial computer, a plotter and dividers.

A half-dozen yellow pencils stuck out of a pocket on the map folder. Al took one out; it was a standard No. 2 pencil with a good point.

"That was Bobby's stuff," Payne said. "I guess it's yours now."

"Bobby was your navigator? Captain Davis told me he came down with appendicitis."

Payne grimaced. "When we landed after the engine fire he started having stomach pains. Doc said it was appendicitis and the next thing we know he's in the hospital for an operation. Charlie wants to get the hell on out of here, and I guess that's where you come in."

"I guess," Al said wryly. He started looking through the charts. Then he turned to Payne. "Tell you what. Maybe I should start looking over this stuff. If you need me to stand off thieving sergeants, yell."

"I'll do that," Payne said with a grin.

Payne started to squeeze by Al, who pushed as far against the table as he could.

"Hey, Mike," Al said.

Payne was turning around in the passage to let himself down through the open hatch. He looked up at Al.

"Yeah?"

"What was it like the other night when you guys lost the engine?"

Payne thought about that for a moment and shrugged. "I don't mind saying I was scared," he replied. "There was a pretty good fire, but it was on the skipper's side. I couldn't see much except the glow of the fire. Charlie's hands were all over the cockpit for about five seconds, and the next thing I know he's got the fire out, the prop feathered, the engine shut down, and the plane trimmed to fly with one dead engine. It all happened too fast to get really scared and then we turned for home."

Al nodded. "Thanks."

"Sure thing." Payne swung himself down through the open hatchway and vanished.

Al looked out the window in front of him at the two engines. He wondered what he would have felt, looking out the window, watching a fire in the engine attached to a wing full of aviation fuel.

Payne's description of the incident confirmed Al's first impression, that Captain Davis was the kind of pilot who knew what he was doing.

Al took a deep slow breath, let it out, and opened the map folder.

The first chart showed the eastern Pacific. A bold pencil line stretched from San Francisco to the island of Oahu. Al took out the plotter and laid it across the line, reading the initial heading from the protractor on the plotter. He looked through the other charts. He was relieved to find some of them familiar from school navigation problems, the same islands Pan Am used as their way stations across the Pacific: Oahu, Midway and Wake.

Instead of going to Guam, though, the charts showed the Central Pacific and the island of New Guinea. Another chart showed the northern coast of Australia. The last one showed the Philippine archipelago.

There wasn't a lot of internal detail in the charts of New Guinea or Australia.

Al started to wonder if he'd made a mistake, volunteering to navigate this airplane across the whole damned Pacific Ocean, with a crew he'd never met and had only hours to get to know. He looked at the incomplete charts. The incompleteness was like something out of the 17th Century, except there wasn't any notation about "Here be dragons."

Then he turned back to the first chart, showing the Pacific between California and Hawaii, and began planning the flight.

A Gunner for Charlie

For the second time that afternoon Charlie found himself Colonel Miller's office, but this time Sgt. Voorhis stopped him with an upraised palm.

"Sir, you really can't go in there," the sergeant said earnestly. "The colonel's got General Smith on the phone."

Charlie nodded and sat down. "By the way, sergeant, be sure and thank Colonel Miller for me," he said quietly. "That engine change is going through and I have a new navigator. He's green but I think he'll do."

Sgt. Voorhis nodded. "Always happy to help, sir."

"What's the general want?"

"Meaning no disrespect, sir, but what do generals always want? More of this, more of that, and why wasn't it done yesterday?"

Charlie suppressed a smile, but he knew his eyes were twinkling. "Better not let the colonel hear you talk like that."

"Like what, sir?"

"Exactly."

In a moment there was the sound of a telephone slamming back into its cradle and a barely-suppressed stream of profanity from inside the colonel's office.

"You might want to let him simmer down for a minute before you poke your head in, sir," the sergeant told Charlie.

Charlie nodded in agreement.

"Who the hell are you talking to, Voorhis?" Colonel Miller's voice boomed from behind his door. "Send them in or send them away"

Charlie grimaced. Voorhis got up to open the door for him and crossed his fingers at Charlie.

Colonel Miller was writing furiously on a notepad when Charlie entered. He thought it best to come to attention in front of the Colonel's desk.

"Yes?" Miller growled.

"Sir, thanks for the engine and the navigator," Charlie said.

Miller stopped writing and looked up at him.

"I know you didn't come here just to thank me, Charlie," Miller said. "What do you want now?"

"Waist gunners, sir."

"Waist gunners?"

"Yes, sir. My waist gunners have been shanghaied."

"And I suppose you want me to replace them."

"Yes, sir."

"Captain, let me call to your attention what should already be obvious to an officer even of your relative lack of experience. The Air Corps is expanding. Cancel that, it's just plain exploding, bursting at the seams, and all I hear is I need men for this and men for that. You've got a navigator and except for your two gunners you have a full crew, is that right?"

"Yes, sir."

Miller sighed. He rubbed the bridge of his nose and Charlie noticed for the first time that the older man looked tired, even fatigued.

"I never liked the Philippines all that much, but I wish to hell I was going out there instead of being stuck at this damned desk," Miller said. "Look, Charlie, I haven't the faintest idea where you're going to find gunners. I don't have any up my sleeve. You saw I scraped the bottom of the barrel to find you a navigator. My best advice is, once you get to Clark Field, look for someone who wants a change of duty. More likely than not you won't need gunners until then. They're sending you around via Port Moresby and Darwin, right?"

"Yes, sir."

"Then you'll only have to worry about flying over the Jap mandated islands north of New Guinea. You're supposed to overfly them at night, anyway."

"Yes, sir. I understand."

"Good luck again, Charlie. Be careful."

"I will, sir."

Charlie did an about face and left the Colonel's office. On his way out Voorhis motioned to him.

"I can get you at least one gunner if you aren't too particular, sir," he whispered, handing Charlie a note. "Take that to the Provost Marshal and ask for Sergeant Jim Matthias. He might be able to persuade the provost to let a certain Private Lefkowicz go on condition that when he goes, it's far, far away. If it works out, give me a call and I'll square the paperwork."

Charlie took the note and smiled crookedly at Voorhis. "You, sergeant, are why they teach officers who really runs this man's Army."

Voorhis winked solemnly.

Once, very shortly after graduating from West Point and upon reporting for duty involving flight training at Kelly Field in Texas but before his flight training began, Charlie found himself stuck with the post of assistant duty officer to the Provost Marshal at Kelly Field on a busy Saturday night that devolved into a busier Sunday morning. There had been brawls and fights in the nearby town of San Antonio. Buses with drunken enlisted men and cars with drunken officers were waved through the gate until nearly dawn.

It was the smell of the brig Charlie remembered afterward. The smell was sweat, vomit laced with beer and cheap whisky or rum, blood, urine and feces, all mixed together, sometimes all on one person.

There was only a whiff of that as Charlie entered the cell block of the Provost Marshal's office with an MP sergeant as escort, but it was enough to bring that night back in vivid detail.

"Here he is, sir," the MP sergeant said. "Hey, Lefkowicz, atten-hut!"

The sergeant stopped in front of a jail cell occupied by one man, lying on a bunk in the cell with his back turned.

Lefkowicz appeared to be of medium height. Charlie judged from the shoulders on the man that he was of stocky, even muscular build. That suited Charlie. There wasn't a hell of a lot of head room in the waist gun position. A gunner of medium height was best, with plenty of muscle to wrestle a .50-caliber machine gun against a 200-mph slipstream.

There did seem to be a problem with the man's attitude, however, since he didn't move or otherwise indicate that he had heard the MP sergeant.

"Leave him to me, sergeant," Charlie told the MP.

The MP nodded. "Sing out if he gives you any trouble, sir," the MP said, and walked out of the cell block.

Charlie looked at Lefkowicz's back for a moment. "Private Lefkowicz, my name is Davis. Captain Charles Davis. I'm flying a B-17 to the Philippines tomorrow. I need a gunner. Do you want the job? It comes with complete forgiveness for what seems to be your multitudinous sins."

"Screw you and screw the Air Corps," the man lying on the bunk muttered. "I've had it."

Charlie frowned. "With what, exactly?" he asked.

"Huh?"

Charlie bit off the nearly reflexive demand that the man in the jail cell address him as "sir."

"Look, soldier, you're lying there feeling sorry for yourself, and I don't know or care why. I want a gunner for my airplane. I'm told you have some skill with a machine gun. That makes it a match made in heaven, except there's this little problem with your disciplinary record, like maybe you'll be breaking rocks in Leavenworth for the duration of the war. If that's what you want, lie here and feel sorry for yourself. I'm leaving tomorrow evening. Be on the flight line ready to go by 1500."

"Screw you."

"Fine. If you change your mind let Sergeant Matthias know. But if you decide to come, Lefkowicz, leave the attitude in this jail cell. There's no room for it on my crew or in my airplane."

Charlie turned and walked out of the cell block. Sergeant Matthias looked up as he came out.

"Didn't think he'd go for it," Matthias commented.

Charlie nodded. "Kind of a long shot," he agreed. "But I'm pretty desperate for a gunner. I told him if he decides to come along in time to get to the flight line by 1500 to let you know. That OK?"

Matthias nodded. "Sure. The Provost Marshal had a talk with the aggrieved party, who agreed it might perhaps be in the best interests of the Air Corps if the matter just dropped and the paperwork disappeared. Be a lot easier if Lefkowicz got the hell out of the States for awhile, though."

"Filing errors are a terrible thing," Charlie agreed. "Fight over a girl?"

"Yes, sir."

Charlie shook his head. "Be interesting to find a woman it was worth getting in this much trouble for, wouldn't it?"

Matthias grinned. "I reckon so, sir. But my old Pop used to say there was something in favor of the quiet life."

CHAPTER THREE
Settling In

The Establishment of Senor Guttierez

Jack slapped a mosquito as he dug through his barracks bag. The bag was dappled with the sunlight shining through the pinholes in the tent roof. It had rained during the night. The inside of the tent was damp and stank of mildew.

"What are you looking for, Jack?" Chant asked.

"You remember Colonel Miller, back at Hamilton Field?"

"Yeah. Good old duck, but kind of starchy."

"He's a family friend. He told me about a place...ah, here it is." Jack took a letter out of his bag and opened it. "Right, that's what I thought. Colonel Miller knows a guy we should look up. Has a kind of a boarding house. What do you think?"

"A kind of a boarding house? That could be really good or really bad."

"Bad as last night in this tent?"

Chant looked around. During the rain last night the occupants of the six-man tent frantically dug ponchos or other rainproof garments from their duffel bags to drape over their cots, whose bedding was already wet. The wooden floor was still wet. The other guys had already left to look for a shower and grab some breakfast.

"Good point. Dyess did say we could live off base as long as we were within a few miles. Where is this place?"

"Does 22 Las Estrellas Avenue mean anything to you, Roy?"

"Nope."

"Me, either. Get dressed. We'll hire a cab and check this place out. You suppose these other guys will care if we speak for them?"

"After last night? No, I don't think so, not if it's dry and halfway decent."

Ten minutes later they were walking down the street. Chant looked in at the squadron office tent and left word with the duty officer where they were going.

Trucks rumbled back and forth across the wobbly bridge over the smelly creek flowing sluggishly towards Manila Bay. At Chant's wave one of the outbound trucks slowed long enough for them to swing aboard. It let them off at the intersection with Roxas Drive, where they waited in the hot sun for another five minutes before a rickety-looking cab slowed.

The driver leaned over. "Give you ride, soldiers?"

"Sure thing," Jack said. They climbed into the back.

"Where to?"

"You know 22 Las Estrellas?"

"Ah, the establishment of Senor Guttierez? Close by, a few moments only."

Chant looked at Jack as the cab lurched into the traffic. "Seems your friend is well-known."

"Hell, that probably means he's full-up. Bet we don't get rooms there."

"Senor Guttierez does not let his rooms to just anyone," the cabbie informed them. "He prefers older gentlemen of means, who appreciate peace and quiet."

"Peace and quiet," said Chant. "You like that idea, Jack?"

"We'll get plenty of excitement once we start flying again. Might be nice to have a quiet place off base."

57

The cabbie waited for a break in the line of trucks headed from the docks to Nichols Field. Then he turned into a side street lined with small neat houses. He made one more turn, taking them closer to Manila Bay.

"Here we are, gentlemen," the cab driver said. "22 Las Estrellas Avenue."

Jack handed the driver a 50-peso note. "Wait for us."

"Hokay, Joe."

Jack and Chant got out of the taxi and stood for a moment on the sidewalk, looking up and down the street curiously.

"Looks like the old part of San Antonio back in Texas, near Randolph Field," Chant remarked. "All red tiles and white stucco and cobblestones."

Jack nodded, listening. There was a background murmur of traffic on Roxas Drive a few blocks away. They were close to the shore of Manila Bay, and from out on the Bay a ship's horn moaned. Overhead a pair of P-35s muttered and rumbled as they entered the landing pattern for Nichols Field.

"Not as quiet as all that, Jack," Chant observed.

Jack grinned up at the pursuits as they flew past. "Aw, that sounds like home to me, Roy. Might seem too quiet if someone didn't fly over us now and then."

Chant grinned and shook his head. "Well, let's see what the man has to say."

Jack went up the steps to the front door of 22 Las Estrellas and knocked. The door was mahogany, stained and carved into intricate scroll-work and fluting. A pair of small glass portholes looked out from the interior upon the porch. Faint steps sounded from behind the door, which opened to reveal a man of medium height in an immaculate white suit. A stiff, slightly old-fashioned celluloid collar topped a white shirt with a black tie. The man's hair glistened with pomade, brushed sharply back from his broad forehead. Dark brown eyes glittered over a hooked nose that had been broken at least once. The eyes flickered rapidly over the two young lieutenants before fastening on Jack.

"How may I be of assistance, lieutenant?" the man asked in courteous tones.

"Are you Senor Ramon Guttierez?" Jack asked.

"I am. And you?"

"I'm Lieutenant Jack Davis, and this is Lieutenant Roy Chant."

"A pleasure, gentlemen." Guttierez cocked a politely inquisitive eyebrow at them.

Jack said, "A mutual friend told me to inquire whether you still provide rooms in your house to young military men."

"Indeed?" Guttierez replied. "Who might that be?"

"Colonel Joseph Miller."

"I see," said Guttierez. "Well, for friends of Colonel Miller, a place might be found here in my establishment, for a price. Is it just for the two of you, or perhaps others as well?"

"There would be six of us, if that would be convenient."

Guttierez nodded. "So it may be. Did the Colonel inform you of the rules of my establishment?"

"No women, no alcohol, up early and eat all that is set before you, but only at breakfast, where you serve the finest coffee in all Manila."

The Filipino smiled. "This does not trouble young men, especially young pilots, loose in a foreign land? Who might reasonably be expected to sow the wild oats?"

Jack grinned. "Colonel Miller said you were the sort of gentleman who respected the privacy of others, so long as matters requiring privacy did not take place under your own roof."

"And how is the Colonel?"

"Well when I last saw him. He wished to be remembered to you."

"He is a true gentleman. Well, come in, and let us see if my humble establishment suits you."

Guttierez turned and walked down the dim flagstone corridor of the house. Jack looked at the rooms opening on either side of the corridor. They were spacious and airy, with shuttered windows and slowly-turning ceiling fans. As they passed through the door they left much of the day's heat behind them. A gentle breeze moved down the hallway, wafting a spicy scent along with a hint of freshly-brewed coffee.

Jack studied the way Guttierez walked. There was a certain grace in the man's stride, with the least hint of swagger. The image that came to Jack's mind was a Spanish cavalier of the

59

sixteenth or seventeenth century, complete with rapier, doublet, hose and ruff, or maybe the armor and helmet of a conquistador. Jack had seen professional boxers move like that, out of the ring: never off balance, sure of themselves, and with that same hint of swagger.

"Here are the rooms," Guttierez said, gesturing down a hallway that opened off the main corridor. "Look them over, and then come to the kitchen. We will have coffee, and if you like the rooms we will set a price."

With that, the Filipino walked on down the hall and turned into a room at the far end.

Jack looked at Chant, who grinned and shrugged.

"I could see that fellow in some sort of Oriental spy novel written by Dashiell Hammett," Chant whispered. "Wonder what his story is?"

"You actually know who Dashiell Hammett is, Roy? I'm impressed. I thought you just read tech manuals."

"What I want to know, Jack, is how *you* know who Hammett is. I thought you just read highbrow stuff."

Jack rolled his eyes and they looked into the first bedroom.

The bedroom was small and reminded Jack of the descriptions he'd heard of a monk's cell, complete to the crucifix hanging on one wall. Even though it was small it was pleasing to the eye. The floor was tile in different colors, laid to form squares and stars. The walls were whitewashed stucco that brightened the room. There were subtle whorls and ridges in the plaster. A little writing desk stood under the double windows which opened on a view of the Bay. The bed was narrow, but the pillow was plump. Neatly folded white sheets covered the mattress. That bed looked inviting indeed after the night they'd just spent on wet cots in a stinking tent, sweating the night away as rain dripped on them through the leaky roof. A pleasant breeze wafted through the windows, stirring the gauze curtains. Overhead a fan turned slowly. It was still warm and humid, but it looked good to Jack.

"Pard, let's pay that old boy whatever he wants," Chant whispered. "I think the other guys will fall right in with us."

"Damn right," Jack replied. "Especially if he brews a good cup of coffee."

<u>Waiting to Fly</u>

Jack walked through the heavy oak door and down the cool hall of 22 Las Estrellas as the sun set that evening, carrying his bags. Chant and the others were still detained on the field.

"Good evening, Lt. Davis," Ramon said.

"Good evening, Senor Guttierez," Jack replied. "I trust your day was satisfactory?"

"Eminently. And yours?"

"No flying until tomorrow. Other than that, not bad, only boring."

Guttierez nodded gravely. "It is a terrible thing for a young man to be bored. It leads to difficulties."

Jack quirked a smile at his host. "Guess so."

"Will the other lieutenants be along?"

"Squadron business delayed them at the field. They should be here shortly. Now, if you will permit me?"

Jack put his bags down on the tiled floor and reached into his pocket. He pulled out American dollars and handed them to Guttierez.

"Will this be sufficient for two months?"

Guttierez took the money, counting it in the swift professional motion of a veteran card player.

"It is more than we agreed," he said.

Jack nodded. "Something on account, for good will."

Guttierez nodded. He folded the bills and placed them in his inside jacket pocket.

"The other gentlemen understand the rules of the house?"

"They have been informed. I'll make myself responsible for them."

Guttierez inclined his head to one side, studying Jack.

"As you wish," he said. "Do you have plans for the evening?"

"For myself, I think I will write some letters. Mr. Chant likes to read. As for the others" Jack shrugged. "I fear they are bored, and may seek amusement in town."

Guttierez' face did not change, but there was a twinkle in his eyes. "Let us hope they do not find insuperable difficulties, then. You have dined?"

"I have, thank you."

"Then I will bid you good evening."

Guttierez glided away with that easy grace, vanishing into the kitchen.

"That guy was a boxer or something," Jack muttered to himself. He picked up his bags and walked down the hall to the room chosen earlier. It took awhile to hang up his clothes in the wardrobe. Finally he took off his tie and shoes. The room had not yet cooled down with the coming of the evening, so Jack took off his blouse as well, and sat at the desk in his undershirt.

He took a notebook and a fountain pen from his B4 bag. The notebook was battered and carried entries starting in 1939. Jack thought he'd write something about Manila today and how he remembered it from 1938, just to put some words on paper.

He opened the notebook and wrote until he heard footsteps from down the hall and a tap on his door. Jack turned to look at Roy Chant leaning against the door frame, grinning.

Jack smiled back. "What are you so happy about?"

"Word is we might get to fly tomorrow."

"About damned time."

"Also, I hear Dyess is looking for someone to be assistant squadron maintenance officer."

"You thinking about volunteering?"

"Maybe. You get to fly a lot. The more flying time I put in, the more likely I am to become a flight leader."

"Roy, you confuse me. I thought you didn't want to go places and do things in this man's Army."

"Not quite what I said, pard. I just said I didn't want to make a career of it. I wouldn't mind at all being a flight leader."

Jack snorted.

Chant craned forward, looking at Jack's desk. "What are you doing? Oh, hey, are you trying to write? Want me to make myself scarce?"

Jack shook his head. "I thought I might jot down a few thoughts, is all. Or maybe write some letters. What are you going to do?"

"I actually thought I might work some geometry problems."

"Geometry? Isn't that high-school stuff?"

"Only if it's Euclidean. I thought I might see how well I do studying Riemannian geometry and Cauchy-Riemann integrals on my own."

"Now what the hell is that?" Jack held up a defensive hand when Chant started to reply. "That's OK. I don't mind math but I'm the practical type."

"It is practical," Chant insisted. "We just aren't sure how yet."

"Pal, if you tell me, I believe you. I think I'll stick to pen and paper for now."

"Suit yourself," Chant said. He winked at Jack and walked off down the hall. Jack caught snatches of talk that sounded something like, "Stuck in the mud, mired in ignorance, never to lift his eyes to the stars, condemning his children to..."

He listened, smiling, as the words faded away. Then he turned back to his pen and notebook. Jack looked at the blank pages, listening to the sounds coming in through the open window. It was Monday, and they'd been in Manila for four days, and no one knew when they were going to get to fly again.

Maybe he should do something about that.

A Dogfight

In the end finding a flying job wasn't hard. Nichols Field was a major repair depot for the Air Corps in the Philippines. Not only was it the assembly point for the P-40s, but the P-26 and P-35 pursuits of the Far Eastern Air Force broke down or needed maintenance. When they did, regulations required the airplane be test-flown to check that it was indeed airworthy.

The line chief was sympathetic and pointed to a couple of P-26 pursuits. "Those aren't exactly a priority for us, lieutenant," he told Jack. "They're supposed to go to the Filipinos, and we've been tied up putting these P-40s together to do much about it. So knock yourself out."

The line chief corralled an enlisted man to help Jack start the airplanes. The P-26 had an inertial flywheel starter that had to be cranked by muscle power, a hard, sweaty job on a hot humid morning.

"You ready, sir?" the enlisted man asked.

Jack tugged his restraints tight, wiggled his ass on the parachute, and nodded at the enlisted man.

"Anytime, Cletus," he said.

Cletus inserted the crank in the side of the fuselage and threw his weight on the bar. The crank turned slowly against the inertia of the flywheel, but it turned faster and faster until Cletus unshipped the crank and nodded at Jack.

Jack cracked the throttle open, mixture to AUTO-RICH, and engaged the flywheel. The high note of the flywheel changed. The propeller kicked over, the cylinders fired and pearl gray smoke gusted out of the exhaust. The engine popped, banged; the propeller whirled, glittering in the sunlight. The rough banging of the engine smoothed to an even rumble. He relaxed, leaning back against the high head-rest, toes on the brakes. The propeller blasted wind around the open cockpit. The air blasting over the rudder and elevator surface made the controls tremble under his hands and feet. The engine gauges came up to operating range. Jack gave Cletus a thumbs-up. The enlisted man nodded and threw Jack a salute.

"Nichols Tower, Army Five Two at the ramp, request permission to taxi to the active," Jack radioed.

His headphones crackled. "Army Five Two, this is Nichols Tower. Taxi to Runway 18 and hold."

"Army Five Two, taxi to Runway 18 and hold."

Jack set his altimeter to the field elevation, released the brakes, and began to taxi in S-curves toward the departure threshold of Runway 18. At the threshold he turned at an angle to the runway that let him look up at the final approach to Runway 18.

"Army Five Two, Nichols Tower, you are clear for takeoff."

Jack taxied onto the runway and pushed forward on the throttle, easing back on the stick as the speed came up. The wheels of the little P-26 pursuit rumbled down the runway, bumped gently, and then the airplane climbed away from the sod runway of Nichols Field. Jack had never flown a P-26 before, but the feel of it matched what he'd heard, that it was a good airplane with solid control response.

He pulled up on the flap handle as the P-26 climbed above 100 feet. He checked the impulse to retract the landing gear – the P-26 might have been the Army's first monoplane fighter, but it was also the last with fixed gear. His left hand was on the throttle and mixture control as he listened to the roar of the engine over the rush of the slipstream. The P-26 also had an open cockpit, and lessons learned from his first days of flying came back, separating the sound of the engine from the quivering thrum of the wing bracing wires and the propeller wash blasting around him.

There was something about the engine's note he didn't like, a roughness just perceptible, a vibration felt mostly in the seat of his pants. Jack scanned the sky around him before looking at the engine instruments, which seemed to be in their proper positions for oil pressure and temperature, fuel flow, electrical system and cylinder head temperature. Jack moved the throttle back a notch, leaning the mixture a little as well. The roughness faded but didn't quite go away. Jack grimaced. This airplane had been built in 1932. He doubted the engine had been changed in at least a year. As far as the remaining vibration went, that could be the result of who knew how many hard landings and high-g turns over the years, bending the wing spars and the fuselage in ways not quite predictable to Boeing's engineers.

When he pulled back on the throttle he pushed forward a little on the stick. The rate of climb indicator changed from around 900 feet per minute to 700. He looked over his shoulder at Nichols Field, which was well within gliding range if his engine quit right now.

Jack continued scanning the sky around him for clouds and other aircraft. Then he pulled back on the stick, listening to the sound of the wind over the wing, around the open cockpit, the changing pitch of the vibrating bracing wires, darted glances at the wingtips as his angle to the horizon changed, looked at the needle-and-ball, the airspeed and rate of climb indicators. The altimeter showed he was still climbing. Everything else told him he was fast running out of airspeed and approaching a stall.

Ailerons, elevator, rudder – controls in an airplane approaching a stall lost effectiveness in that order. Just as the ailerons and elevator lost their bite on the air Jack pulled back on the throttle and gave the pursuit left rudder. Nose and tail switched places, and as the nose fell through the horizon he saw the city of Manila and then below him the waters of Manila Bay. The plane picked up speed rapidly as gravity exerted its hold, more rapidly still as Jack pushed forward on the throttle, feeding power to the engine. Jack pulled back on the stick and leveled out, looked around to be sure he was clear of traffic, and started in with some aileron rolls.

The aileron rolls let him feel out the roll rate and the aileron sensitivity. He pulled out of the last roll, climbed to nine thousand feet, and started a turn, tightening it gradually, the g-force piling on, feeling for the first flutter of an accelerated stall, easing off the elevator, easing back again, repeating until he could tell the first nibble of a stall in a turn.

Jack grinned. It might be old and antiquated, with its wires and open cockpit and twin machine-guns synchronized to fire through the propeller, but the P-26 was the first airplane he'd fallen in love with, back in 1938, and for good or ill you never quite forget your first love.

Docks and ships crowded the shoreline of the Bay. He picked out Dock 7 where the *President Coolidge* was tied up, still discharging cargo for the Philippines garrison. Just east of Dock 7 was the Manila Hotel and Rizal Park.

The P-26 picked up speed as Jack took in the view. He pulled gently back on the stick as a glance at the airspeed indicator showed the P-26 flashing through 250 mph. Once again gravity piled on his shoulders, squeezed his lungs, plucked with steel fingers at his feet on the rudder pedals and his hands on stick and throttle. He pulled vertical. The nose of the P-26 passed above the horizon, and the line between land and sky vanished. Over the nose of his pursuit was only blue sky and white cloud as he climbed, altimeter rising rapidly, airspeed falling off until he was stationary in the sky, the noise of the wind and the slipstream fading, leaving only the roar of the engine and the propeller straining against gravity.

In the moment before falling airspeed made his rudder ineffective he stepped firmly on the right rudder pedal. The propeller hissed and swashed as it arced sidewise through the air. Nose and tail, earth and sky switched places. For the briefest instant, as the last of Jack's upward momentum fell to zero, the P-26 hung still in the sky. Then gravity and propeller thrust snatched the pursuit earthward. Jack let the speed build up to two hundred miles an hour, then pulled out into first a sharp left and then a hard right turn.

He rolled the P-26 level with the horizon, held it there for a moment, then snap-rolled to the right, grinning as the blue of Manila Bay swapped places with the blue sky and its white puffy clouds. The snap-roll became a diving turn to the left as Jack looked around, checking again to be sure he was clear of other aircraft, before pulling out into a slight climb to regain altitude.

That was when he saw the P-40, hovering above him, the light gray paint of its underside making it almost invisible against a cloud above it. The P-40 perched a good five thousand feet higher than Jack, who swept the area for traffic again before turning back to look at the P-40.

The other pursuit made a leisurely turn, staying above and just behind Jack, who grimaced up at the P-40 through narrowed eyes behind his goggles. Jack knew his own airspeed was just above 200 mph. That meant the P-40 was deliberately staying above and behind him, since the P-40 cruised around 250 mph.

That guy wants to play, Jack thought. *At the very least he's thinking it over*.

Jack, studying the other airplane, realized the P-40 was climbing as he climbed, keeping the same altitude difference between them. Jack leveled off at ten thousand feet, as high as he could safely go without oxygen, and saw that his airspeed was 220 mph, compass heading 355, almost parallel with the shore of Manila Bay at this point. The city of Manila was below him to the right and the north; Nichols Field, the main pursuit base in Luzon, was behind him, about ten miles away. Just over the edge of his right wingtip he caught a glimpse of the Manila Hotel and adjoining Rizal Park. Then he looked above and behind him.

As he looked back the P-40 dove. The pursuit's pilot didn't peel off, split-S, or anything else, he just shoved his stick forward and dove at Jack like a hawk stooping on a rabbit. Jack knew most pilots hated what they called "eyeballs-out g", the uncomfortable feeling of having your stomach trying to climb up through your esophagus and your eyeballs pop out of your skull with negative g. Jack nodded to himself. Whoever this guy was he wasn't afraid to mix it up and that meant Jack was in for a real fight, even if it wasn't for real.

That was fine with Jack, even if he was in an airplane that could hardly stay in the same sky with a P-40, whose top speed was at least one hundred mph faster than the P-26. There was one thing the P-26 could do in a fight with a P-40, and Jack watched the diving pursuit astern of him, waiting for his moment.

He inched forward on the throttle as the P-40 dove and when Jack figured the P-40 to be entering firing range he banked hard to the left, climbing slightly in the turn. Jack's seven hours flying time in a P-40 taught him that the thing dove like crazy but you had to hold hard left rudder in the dive. A turn to the left in a diving P-40 could be done, but it wasn't easy.

The P-40 made a quarter-turn to the left with ailerons, trying to turn inside Jack for a deflection shot, then gave it up, straightened, and pulled out into a climb. Jack looked over his shoulder in time to see the sun flash off the other pilot's goggles; the pilot's face was hidden by an oxygen mask. Jack continued his turn until he was headed back towards shore, darting glances behind him at the P-40.

The other airplane nosed down, the wings rolled, and the pilot came out of the first half of a barrel roll with a lot of rudder, leaving the P-40's nose pointed at Jack again. This time the other pilot was attacking with a shallower dive angle, meaning he wouldn't have to hold left rudder quite so much.

That's okay, pal, I know some tricks too, Jack thought. He remembered his father telling him about timing, about timing being everything. He waited on the other pilot's approach to gun range. This time he didn't try to turn away. Instead he pushed forward on the stick in the first half of an outside loop, coming upright at the bottom and looking over his shoulder as he pulled into a hard left bank.

The P-40 was already pulling out of its dive, banking gently to keep Jack in view. Jack continued his turn until he was headed back towards the shoreline, figuring his best bet on shaking this guy would be to get him closer to the traffic pattern of Nichols Field or that other airfield, north of Nichols, Nielsen Field or something like that.

The P-40 climbed about a thousand feet above Jack, then made another hammerhead turn, paralleling Jack's heading for a moment. Jack could almost feel the other guy's thoughts, like some kind of calculating machine, figuring the angles and the distances, and when the other guy made his move once again there was no hesitation, no preliminaries. One second the P-40 was straight and level, then he rolled left and pulled into a diving pursuit curve, tracking that future point in space and time where his bullets would strike Jack's airplane.

Jack banked hard to the right into the attack, looking back at the P-40, which once again pulled up and away. Jack rolled wings level and started to climb, still looking over his shoulder at the P-40, who pulled up into an Immelmann turn and dove down on Jack.

Jack pulled hard on the stick, the seat of his pants and a glance at the airspeed indicator telling him he could manage it, barely, to climb into the first half of a loop and convert this diving attack into a head-on pass. The glance, the decision, the pull, those were the work of split seconds. Jack craned his head back, watching the P-40. Relative speeds and angles changed. Jack didn't bother rolling upright, climbing inverted into the P-40 with his airspeed falling away. The P-40 came down like a crack freight on a steep grade, already big, filling the ring of the P-26's crude gunsight. Jack held the P-40 in his sights until it thundered just over him, the turbulence of its passage making his airplane rock and skid. Jack popped some rudder to right the airplane, put it into a dive to recover airspeed, and looked frantically for the P-40.

The P-40 climbed slowly to Jack's altitude. Jack watched warily but he had the feeling the fun was over. In moments the other pursuit pulled alongside Jack. His eyes widened as he saw the snow-owl symbol of the 17th Pursuit Squadron painted on the rear fuselage, right behind the white band denoting the squadron commander's aircraft. The pilot pulled off his oxygen mask, revealing a pencil-thin line of moustache over a grin. He saluted Jack casually and peeled off towards Nichols Field.

Wagner! Anyone might be flying a P-40 with squadron commander's markings, but Jack remembered Wagner from the other night at the club.

Jack took a deep breath and got permission to land from Nichols Tower.

That left Jack with his next problem, namely, he had never landed a P-26 before. He glanced swiftly over the instrument panel and noted the position of the flap indicator. The P-26 had fixed gear, so he only had to worry about slowing down enough to use the flaps without tearing them off the wings.

He entered final and pulled the flaps down. The nose tried to come up as the flaps changed the center of lift of the wings; Jack countered with a smooth application of elevator. The P-26 felt solid and controllable at 90 mph and full flaps. Jack kept that combination going to just above the runway, then pulled back all the way on the throttle and came back on the stick, gingerly, feeling the airplane out, not wanting to balloon into a steep climb ending in a stall and a sudden return to earth.

The main wheels in their streamlined spats kissed the runway with the lightest of bumps, then rumbled over the concrete until the tail came down. Jack applied the brakes, feeling the wind diminish, keeping the pursuit headed straight down the runway until it came down to walking speed.

That was better. He figured there couldn't be anything wrong with the P-26 after that workout. He'd sign it off and take the next one up.

Maybe he could get into a P-35 later on. Jack loosened his jacket against the heat, watching for the airman to wave him into place on the ramp. If he worked at it he might get enough flying time in to qualify for flight pay this month.

Over to one side was a line of P-40s. One of them bore the markings of a squadron commander and the white-owl insignia of the 17th. Beside it stood a slim figure in a flying jacket with a parachute over his shoulder and a leather helmet in his hand, talking to a couple of airmen in coveralls who looked like mechanics.

Wagner, Jack thought.

Welcome to the Philippines

The next morning Jack Davis didn't remember where he was when he first opened his eyes. The room was dimly lit by orange

70

light, slanting in through the open window. Overhead a ceiling fan turned slowly, making a faint *click-clack-click-clack* sound as the blades turned, stirring the warm, humid air. A glint of reflected silver light caught his eye, and drew his memories complete from sleep. The silver light was the morning sun reflecting from the pilot's wings on his uniform blouse, hung neatly from the rack in the corner with his other clean uniforms.

He sat up, yawning and blinking. He could see his notebook and fountain pen on the desk under the window. He got out of bed and went to the chair, staring out the open window whose gauzy curtains stirred lightly in the morning breeze. The breeze brought the smells of the city of Manila with it, mixed in with the smells of nearby Manila Bay: mud, rotten fish, humid salt air, sweat, human waste, exotic spices, brick cooling in the early morning breeze before the heat of the day. He looked down at the notebook, where he had written a single sentence: *Manila is not the way I remembered it, and the situation here is not what we were told.*

He sat at that desk for hours last night, looking at that single line, remembering that trip to Manila in 1938. Mostly he was remembering how Irina looked the first time he saw her. That led to an inspection of the picture she gave him, the last time they met. That was in Bern in 1939, just before the Germans invaded Poland.

Jack leaned back in the chair, looking out the window. Across the street there was a white stucco two-story building, as Spanish in appearance as anything in southern California. Shadows played over it in the light of the rising sun. A man in a white suit came out onto the verandah of the house and sat at a little table there. In a moment, a woman came out with a silver tray and coffee service. She poured for both of them, then sat with the man drinking coffee while the sun rose.

Over the faint sigh of the wind and the *click-clack* of the ceiling fan another noise grew. It was a cough, a collection of coughs, then a muted rumble in the distance, a little ragged at first, and then growing to a sustained bass hum, muted by distance; engines, Jack knew, aircraft engines belonging to the airplanes based at Nichols Field about a mile to the south. The sound made his heart beat a little faster. He closed the notebook, put it in a drawer of the desk, and picked up his shaving kit.

He went across the hall to the bathroom. He put a little shaving soap in a mug, mixing it with his brush, and lathered his face. He shaved quickly and carefully with a straight razor that had belonged to his father, wiped the soap from his cheeks and chin, felt for stray whiskers, splashed on some aftershave, and went back across the hall to his bedroom.

In the little house around him he heard the waking noises of other young men, and then down the hallway came the welcome waft of coffee.

An oddly-accented voice belonging to Jose, the Filipino house-boy, bellowed down the hall: "Wake up, American bums! You hurry to eat breakfast, I have hungry pigs to feed! Chop-chop!"

Jack dressed, quickly and carefully: khaki trousers with the regulation brass buckle, uniform blouse with the collar and shoulder insignia of a second lieutenant, properly placed and shined, field scarf knotted and tucked in between the first and second buttons of his blouse. His shoes looked properly shiny; he put them on and grabbed his garrison cap and B4 bag, heading out the door of his room and down the hall towards the smell of coffee.

At the breakfast table Ramon sat, immaculate in his white suit, sipping coffee and reading a newspaper. On the table was a coffee service, a plate of sweet buns and another of bacon and eggs.

It smelled like the ambrosia of paradise.

Jose poured coffee into a white china cup as Jack walked in.

"Good morning, Mr. Davis," said Jose.

"Good morning, Jose," Jack replied. He took up the coffee cup and sipped, smiling. "What's new in the world, Senor Guttierez?"

"Wars and rumors of wars, Mr. Davis."

"Ah. The usual." Jack sipped the coffee again.

"I've had worse coffee in New York hotels, Jose," he said. "What's your secret?"

"New York," Jose said dismissively. "My family grows coffee in Mindanao, many years. Family blend, many, many years old. Glad you like it."

72

"It's great coffee," Jack said, sipping again before taking a sweet bun from the plate in the center of the table.

Senor Guttierez looked up for a moment from his paper. He met Jack's eyes.

"You sure you never boxed before, Ramon?" Jack asked as he bit into the bun.

"I am, Mr. Davis," Ramon replied gravely. He poured himself another cup of coffee as the other lieutenants stumbled in. They were all more or less Jack's age and general build, young men of medium height and weight, the easier to fit into the relatively small cockpits of pursuit airplanes. The young men were all dressed the same, too, in khaki uniforms with pilot's wings and the brass bars denoting their rank as second lieutenants.

They mumbled good mornings to each other as they walked into the dining room and sat down to coffee and sweet buns, helping themselves to bacon and eggs. The last in was Roy Chant, smiling and looking chipper.

"Morning, fellas," Chant said. "Fine day, ain't it?"

"The hell you so happy for, Chant?" grumbled one of the other lieutenants.

Chant sat down next to Jack, picked up a bun, and ate it in two bites. Then he took a long sip of his coffee, setting the cup down with a satisfied sigh before reaching for another bun.

"Sure is good coffee, Jose," Chant said. "Makes a man appreciate the start of a new day."

"Thank you, Mr. Chant," Jose replied.

Jack regarded his fellow officer with some degree of exasperated amusement.

Jack shook his head. "Anyone would think you had good news from home or got promoted to Admiral," he said.

"Admiral?" Chant asked. "I thought we were in the Air Corps. Do we have admirals in the Air Corps? Wasn't it always General this and General that back at Kelly Field? I don't remember any admiral so-and-sos."

One of the other lieutenants drew back his arm, intent on throwing it at Chant. Jose picked the bun deftly from the man's hand.

"You hungry, you eat," Jose said. There was reproof in his voice. "Don't waste food, American bum."

73

"This is great bacon, Jose," said Chant, taking a slice and chewing it. When he swallowed, he asked, "Where do you get your bacon and eggs?"

"The farm of Senor Guttierez. My father runs it."

"I grew up on a farm. How many pigs you got?" Chant asked. "My folks keep pigs at our farm in Carolina."

"Plenty pigs on our farm, Mr. Chant, and pigs always hungry. They don't waste food. Eat every bite, every time. Not like American bums."

The men around the table laughed. Jack finished the last of his coffee and stood up.

"Thanks for breakfast, Jose," he said.

"You welcome, Mr. Davis. God go with you."

"And with you."

The other lieutenants looked at the clock on the wall. It was almost 0645. From the street outside a horn blared. As Jack walked out, they hurriedly drained their cups and finished their buns. Chant snagged another bun off the diminished plate as he walked out.

"God bless, Jose, and don't worry about it going to waste," he called over his shoulder.

"Bless you too, Mr. Chant, and about you I don't worry," Jose replied.

Outside on the street an aging Army truck waited, idling as if it had asthma. The truck was an old Ford with a round radiator whose markings proudly proclaimed it as belonging to the Nichols Field support squadron. A sleepy-looking private was at the wheel, nodding his good mornings as the lieutenants climbed into the back of his truck.

"Hey, Jelabin, don't we get a salute this morning?" Chant called to the driver.

"Naw, suh," replied the private. "Beggin' the lieutenant's pardon, but if I salute I gotta take my hand off the shifter, an' then the engine might fall out. An' regulations require I gotta keep one hand on the wheel at all times, so there you are, suh."

"He's got you there, Chant," Jack said. "Hey, Jelabin!"

"Yes, Mr. Davis?"

"You just get us to the field in one piece and I'm a happy man."

74

"Me, too, lieutenant. Now all you gents hang on."

Private Jelabin drove carefully until he was on Roxas Drive. The early morning stream of traffic consisted of small trucks, automobiles, horse-drawn wagons, trollies and even an ox-cart drawn by a ponderous water buffalo. With a clash of gears Jelabin drove out into the stream of traffic, ignoring squawking horns, braying horses and shrieking profanity alike. The lieutenants waved at the people behind them as the truck accelerated down the road through the suburb of Baclaran.

The truck crossed the now-familiar rickety bridge over the smelly creek that meandered slowly to Manila Bay a half-mile or so to the west. Jack, leaning over the side of the truck, saw two P-40s lined up ready to take off. He punched Chant in the shoulder and pointed.

The two P-40s had the snow-owl markings of the 17th Pursuit Squadron on their fuselages. As they watched the pursuit planes accelerated down the runway and took off, staying low as they sucked up the gear and flaps, then turning into a graceful chandelle to the right over the bay, still climbing and heading north.

"Maybe we'll at least get to fly today," Chant said. "Sure would be nice."

Jack nodded. He felt a little guilty, not letting Chant in on the test-flight gig. It was only in the P-26s going to the PCAF, but it got him off the ground. Besides, there had only been a half-dozen of the antiquated pursuits.

Private Jelabin braked the truck to a stop in front of the operations shack. The operations office for Nichols Field was partly underground; the second floor was a barracks, empty already, with the men either eating breakfast at the mess hall or marching to work on the airplanes crowding the field.

Jack and the other lieutenants climbed down from the truck. The driver waved, clashed the truck into gear, and drove off in the direction of the motor pool.

The 21st's operations shack was a tent adjacent to the taxiway. Nine other lieutenants stood around outside the tent, and as Jack came up their squadron commander, 1st Lt. Ed Dyess, came out of the tent and looked around.

Dyess grinned. "Glad to see you guys all bright and chipper this early in the morning, because I have some news. Some you will like, some you won't, so here's the good part first. Today we start flying again. In the next day or so everyone will get a chance to go up."

That raised a ragged cheer, but before it could spread Dyess held up a hand for silence. "Well, like I said, there's the good and the bad, and the bad is that we won't get our P-40s for at least another week. In the meantime we're getting P-35s. Before we get those, you guys are going to have to take a check flight."

Dyess gestured towards the flight line.

Jack didn't bother to look at the Seversky P-35A pursuits parked there. Beyond them were the modified AT-6 attack planes, the A-27s taken from the Royal Thai Air Force.

"We'll go up in alphabetical order," Dyess continued. "You guys go get your coveralls and parachutes, then report to the Operations Shack. We'll start in twenty minutes."

"Who's giving us the check ride, sir?" Jack asked.

"Boyd Wagner from the 17th and his flight commanders. I'd do it but I haven't flown any more in the last two months than any of you guys. I've got some time in P-35s. I'll go up this morning by myself and peel the rust off. In the meantime, let's see. Abernathy, Bertram, Davis, you guys are up first. Davis, hold up a minute. The rest of you take off."

Davis stood until the rest of the squadron filed off. Then Dyess looked at him and shook his head.

"Jack, I just happened to find out you volunteered to help Chief Jones with a little problem he had."

"Yes, sir."

"So you like the P-26?"

"It's a nice airplane, Ed, but mainly it's better than nothing."

Dyess snorted. "There's that. Tell me, how much time did you get?"

"Oh, about eight hours."

"All in the P-26?"

"Yes, sir. They were supposed to go the Philippine Air Force but they needed to be test-flown first after overhaul."

"Overhaul? They actually have that?"

"Sort of."

76

"You're still alive. That says something. I heard some other rumors, too."

"Rumors, sir?"

"Something about a P-26 dogfighting a P-40. Odd, though, although everyone says it looked like a hell of a fight no one could say who won."

Jack grimaced. "Probably that bastard in the P-40. The best you can do in a P-26 is go head on. That gives you two .30-cal. machine guns against six .50s. Those aren't great odds."

"Nope. Know anything else about it?"

"Skipper, you already know I was in that P-26."

"Yeah, and I know Boyd Wagner was in the P-40. He's a hot pilot, Jack. Should I be impressed with you?"

"Maybe next time."

"Next time?"

"Next time I might have the advantage. Better airplane, better position, surprise, something, anything. I did the best I could, Skipper. In a real war I would've gone down in flames."

Dyess nodded, scowling. He looked over at the flight line and the hangars where mechanics swarmed over P-40s and P-35s.

"OK, Jack, we'll have to work on that. A P-35 is a step up from the P-26, at least. Go make me proud."

Jack wore an aviator's chronograph his mother gave him when he graduated from flight training. It showed he still had five minutes to go when he trotted up to the 21st Squadron's operations shack, wearing his flight suit and carrying his own leather helmet and goggles and Switlick parachute, also a gift from his mother. Wagner sat in a chair with his feet propped up on a crate. Like Jack, he was in a flight suit, but his had a certain air about it, just the right amount of fading, one or two patches, some stains from oil or hydraulic fluid that hadn't quite come out despite the best efforts of the post laundry. In short, the man had the look of a veteran pilot.

Wagner knocked the ashes out of his pipe and swung his feet to the floor.

"Morning, Lt. Davis," Wagner said. He put his hand out. "You ready to fly?"

"Yes, sir," Jack replied. He shook Wagner's hand.

"Tell you what. For right now, you call me Boyd, at least until you screw up. Which might be in just a few minutes from now." Wagner grinned. There was something challenging, even a bit daunting about that grin.

"OK, Boyd," Jack replied.

"You did pretty good the other day in that P-26," Wagner continued. "Let's see what you do in something a little more complex."

Wagner rose, picking up his own parachute where it lay beside his seat. "Come along, then, and tell me about the AT-6." Wagner started walking towards the nearest A-27. He waved at an enlisted man standing next to the airplane.

Jack blinked. "The AT-6 is an all-metal, single-engine, two-place monoplane. The power plant is a 600-hp Wright Wasp Jr. radial engine. The airplane has a top speed of 180 mph and a best cruise speed of 150 mph. Normal takeoff speed, fully loaded, is 75 mph. Gear down, flaps down stall speed is 90 mph. Stall speed in clean configuration is 80 mph. The airplane carries 70 gallons of 101-octane aviation fuel, enough for about four hours of flight at best cruise. The propeller is..."

"OK, OK," said Wagner. "You obviously got through advanced flight school. You like the AT-6?"

"Yes, sir. Much better airplane than the BT-13."

"We call this one the A-27. Basically it's an AT-6 with a couple of machine guns, so the empty weight is greater, which does what for the stall speed?"

"Raises it. 5 mph or thereabouts."

Wagner nodded. "Close enough."

By now they were at the wingtip of the A-27. The enlisted man, a chunky youngster with a shock of blond hair under his sun hat, had opened the canopy for them.

"How's it looking today, Jones?" Wagner asked the enlisted man.

"Ah reckon she'll fly, sir," Jones replied. "She's topped off with gas 'n' oil, an' the guns are loaded in case you-all want to shoot at somethin'."

"OK. Thanks."

Wagner reached into the rear cockpit and pulled out a set of earphones that he attached to his flying helmet. Jack hesitated a moment and climbed up the wing to the front seat.

He shrugged into his parachute, making sure the harness was snug, and then got in the airplane. A set of earphones hung from the instrument panel and he put them in his helmet, then settled the helmet on his head, fussing with the fit a little before he tightened the chin strap. At once he could feel the sweat start out from under the leather. He wiggled a little bit in the seat to make sure the parachute was solidly against the seat pan, then fastened the safety harness and pulled it tight.

Jack looked at the instrument panel. All the instruments appeared to be in the right places, but they were marked in strange loopy, swirly letters that must be, he thought, what they used for an alphabet in the Kingdom of Siam. Some of the instruments had tape labels beside them, and there was a printed warning label at the top of the panel that read: INSTRUMENTS INDICATE IN METRIC UNITS. He looked up at the crew chief, Jones, who had climbed up on the wing beside him.

"Metric units?" he asked.

Jones shrugged and grinned. "Sir, that's the way they came to us. An' dang if Ah know what one means in the other. But look here."

Jones reached in and pointed. "This here's the oil pressure gauge. See that mark? If the needle falls below that, y'all are in trouble. Here's the temp gauges. The red means bad an' the green means good."

Jack looked again at the instrument panel. After a moment he could see where someone had painted marks on the airspeed indicator gauge at 50, 100 and 150 mph. Similar marks were on the other instruments.

"OK," he said. "Has anyone pulled the prop through to clear the cylinders?"

Jones grinned again, looked back at Wagner and gave him a thumbs-up. "No, sir," Jones replied. "I'll do that right now if y'all will keep your hands off the engine switches."

Jones got down off the wing and walked around to the front of the aircraft, where he pulled the propeller through five blades of revolution. After that he walked to the front left of the airplane, looked at Jack, and made a "wind 'em up" motion with his right hand.

Jack looked over his shoulder at Wagner, who said, "It's your airplane, Jack. After takeoff climb to seven thousand feet out over the bay and we'll do a little air work."

"Yes, sir," Jack said. He reached for the start checklist, but it was written in Siamese. He looked at the incomprehensible letters for a moment, put it on his knee for luck, and called the checklist up from memory.

Two minutes later he sat behind a rumbling engine. The propeller was a silver blur in the sunlight and the engine gauges looked more or less the way his memory told him they ought to look. There was a crackle in his headphones.

"Tell the tower this is a local familiarization flight," Wagner said over the intercom. Our number is Army 334."

Jack switched the radio from intercom to transmit and picked up his own microphone. "Nichols Field, this is Army 334 at the ramp, request permission to takeoff for local familiarization."

"Roger, Army 334, permission granted. Altimeter is two niner niner one, wind from the southeast at 6. Take off to the west."

"Roger, Nichols Field, ah, request permission to take off to the east."

"Permission granted, 334."

Jack looked up at the control tower, which was little more than a roofed enclosure about twenty feet off the ground. There was a wind sock on top of it that agreed with the southeast wind. It wasn't standing out very much. Jack looked at the trees around the airstrip. Mostly they were palm trees of some kind and he had no idea how much wind it took to move a palm frond, but these hardly stirred. OK, six mph for the wind.

"You don't like downwind takeoffs?" Wagner inquired.

"No, sir."

"OK. Taxi down to the other end of the field, then, and we'll do it your way."

Jack taxied in careful S-turns down the taxi area adjacent to the runway. Here and there the taxiway was rutted and there were half-dried mud puddles. When Jack got to the west end of the runway he stopped short and ran up the engine, standing on the brakes, and checked the magnetos. Then he worked the controls to be sure they were free, lowered the flaps to takeoff position, and called the tower for clearance.

"Roger, 334, pattern is clear, takeoff at will."

Jack looked up and checked the approach to the runway, took off the brakes, and fed power to the engine. The runway was bumpy and rough. Jack eased forward on the stick a little as their speed increased, feeling for the increased pressure against the elevator, and when it felt about right he gave the stick another forward push until the tail came off the ground. The bumping decreased. Jack eased the elevator back to the neutral position, then pulled it back a little more.

The rumbling of the landing gear over the runway's uneven surface ceased and the ground fell away underneath them. Jack raised the gear and the flaps. Then he trimmed the airplane for best angle of climb. The airspeed indicator needle was just below the painted mark for "100".

Jack turned north and then west. He relaxed into the seat, looking all around the airplane as he straightened out on 270 and crossed the shore of the bay, passing through 2000 feet and still climbing.

"What are you looking for, Jack?" Wagner asked.

"Other airplanes," Jack replied. "Also still getting used to how things look."

To the north Manila Bay curved around to the west with the entrance to the bay in plain sight thirty miles away. The hills and central plain of Luzon, where Clark Field was located, lay somewhere beyond and below the thunderheads forming over the plains.

Because the altimeter was marked in meters Jack couldn't be completely sure when he was at 8000 feet. He leveled out and cranked in neutral elevator trim when the short fat hand pointed at the painted "8" outside the altimeter and the long skinny hand pointed at "0".

That was when Jack saw the two P-35s another three thousand feet higher at seven o'clock, maybe two miles away.

"Traffic at seven o'clock," he said over the intercom.

"Welcome to the Philippines, Lieutenant Davis," Wagner said. "Those are Japanese fighters and you're going to be under attack as soon as they see you. What are you going to do about it?"

Jack bit back an angry retort and a feeling of injustice. Two against one wasn't even a good estimate of the odds. Even the obsolete P-35 was one hundred mph faster than the A-27. These were worse odds than flying against Wagner the other day.

"Guess we'll find out, sir," he said.

The P-35s were now about two and a half miles away and appeared to be heading to the north. Jack pulled back on the stick, advanced the throttle, and turned due south.

He kept looking around the sky because there was a little voice in his mind that sounded like his father's. It said, "Son, the Hun we worried about wasn't the one in the sun, it was the one we just didn't see period. Even if you aren't in a shooting war you shouldn't assume you're alone in the sky. And just because you have your eye on one airplane doesn't mean there's not another."

So Jack kept looking and found a second pair of P-35s below and behind him, catching up quickly.

"Sure be nice if I had a wingman, sir," he told Wagner sourly.

"Sure would," the squadron commander replied cheerfully.

"I guess those P-35s down there are Japs, too."

"Sure are," Wagner agreed. "Catching up fast."

Jack looked over his shoulder at the two P-35s.

"Are you strapped in tight?" he asked Wagner.

"Always. It's your airplane, Davis, I'm just a passenger."

Jack looked up at the high P-35s, who were still proceeding to the north. Then he looked at the low P-35s.

He rolled hard to the right, pushed forward on the stick, kicked right rudder as the A-27's wings rolled vertical, and chopped the throttle. Sky and sea switched places, for a moment they headed straight down at the Bay and gravity took them, accelerating the airplane as the nose continued to pull through the vertical, then plastering them hard into their seats as Jack centered the rudder and ailerons and pulled back on the stick, feeding full power to the engine as he did. The engine roared. As their nose pulled up to the horizontal there were the low P-35s, still climbing to meet them but closer and closing fast.

There was an old-fashioned fixed gunsight in front of Jack, just a ring with a cross inside it. Jack centered the sight on the lead P-35 and kept it on the center of the Seversky's radial engine.

The P-35s split to left and right around Jack, who chopped the throttle again, pulled back on the stick and reefed into a hard left turn after the lead P-35, who crossed in front of Jack in a vertical right turn. Jack kept his heading straight into the other airplane, who leveled out and broke underneath him.

Jack looked astern. The trailing P-35 was on his tail and closing fast. The two P-35s heading north reversed heading and dove on him. Jack turned hard to the left. The bigger, faster P-35 with its higher wing loading tried to stay with Jack in the turn and overshot, leveling out and climbing away.

Two P-35s were diving on him from the north, easing away from each other to catch him whichever way he turned. One P-35 was below him but turning and climbing back into the fight, another P-35 rolling over to dive on him from above. Jack rolled right and pulled hard into the turn, rolling wings level and pushing the throttle to the stops with his nose down slightly. He glanced at the airspeed indicator. He knew the A-27 was already pushing safe maneuvering speed for the lighter AT-6 it was adapted from, but no one had thought to put a mark at the do-not-exceed airspeed.

Jack pulled into an Immelmann turn, up and into the loop, rolling out on top just as two P-35s crossed on him, one from either side. Another came up from below and the fourth came at him from a dive. Jack put his old-fashioned World War One style gunsight on the diving P-35 and held it there until the P-35 broke away rather than collide.

"Pepsodent Whites, Pepsodent Whites, this is Pepsodent Leader," he heard Wagner say over the radio. "Knock it off and return to base. Out."

The stick banged against Jack's knees, the old familiar "I've got it" signal from flight school days. Jack raised his hands above his shoulders and put his feet on the floor.

The A-27s throttle came back and the nose went down, then up, as Wagner pulled them into a loop. At the bottom of the loop he rolled left, then right, then did an eight-point roll. For about ten minutes Wagner flew the airplane with as delicate and precise a demonstration of aerobatic skill as Jack had ever seen. During that time Wagner didn't say a word, and Jack felt himself getting angry.

He'd taken on four opponents in better airplanes and maybe he hadn't won and in a real war he'd be dead, but God damn it, he hadn't lain down and died! Jack was sure he'd gotten at least one of those guys, maybe two. He did everything he could, and then this sonofabitch in the back seat decides he wants to fly an aerobatic series without saying a word! Twice Jack stopped himself from saying something bitterly insubordinate, and the second time he decided he'd just keep quiet rather than give Wagner the satisfaction.

Finally Wagner rolled out on an easterly heading. Manila was directly in front of them, and Jack could make out the ships in the bay below and a slight haze over the city. There was a thunderstorm rolling down on them from the north. He looked southeast of the city for the field and found it, could even make out, just barely, the last of the Pepsodent White flight of P-35s landing.

"Take us home, Jack," Wagner said over the intercom. "And by the way, that was pretty good flying. Let's get you checked out in the P-35 tomorrow."

"Er...yes, sir."

Jack looked around them and called Nichols to report their position. The thunderstorm was almost to the outskirts of Manila, and Jack put the nose down to beat the storm to the field.

CHAPTER FOUR
Goodbye California

A New Engine

Charlie spent most of the day on the flight line, watching as Chief Wilson's crew mated the "new" engine to his airplane. Since Chief Wilson was short-handed Charlie had his crew helping. Wilson had taught snot-nosed kids about engines for twenty years, and Charlie figured anything these guys learned would be to the good and besides, this kept them all in one place and away from scheming personnel sergeants.

He pitched in to help with the engine change, partly to set a good example, but more because he wanted to know himself. He'd heard rumors that the airfields the Air Corps was building out in the Philippines were kind of rough and that the supply situation might be just as rough. Anyway, if they had an engine go bad in Darwin or New Guinea, where he was sure parts and mechanics would be unavailable, a little extra knowledge might be the difference between continuing the flight or sitting on the ground in some Godforsaken place.

So Charlie got his hands greasy, pinched his right index finger in the engine sling, got cussed out in a polite way by Chief Wilson, and learned a hell of a lot in the six hours he spent with his crew changing the Number 1 engine.

Chief Wilson stepped back once they had all the fuel, oil and electrical lines reconnected to the engine. His men had the propeller on a sling and were coaxing it in to place.

"Captain, why don't we see if that engine starts up before we put the cowling back on?" the boss mechanic suggested.

Charlie nodded. He looked up at the sun, which was well on the way to the western horizon.

"Kind of late in the day for a test flight," he said. "What time do you usually get started of a morning, Chief?"

"Normally about 0700," said the mechanic. "You'll want to do a test flight before you start for Hickam, so why don't I meet you here about then?"

Charlie nodded. "Right. I'll get clearances for a local flight. We'll go wheels-up around 0800, if everything goes well."

About that time Al Stern levered himself out of the hatch in the nose and dropped to the ground. "What time should I report?" he asked.

"We're just going to stooge around for a bit, Al," Charlie said. "Me, Mike, Chief Wilson and Lloyd." Charlie pointed to Sgt. Lloyd Turner, the flight engineer.

"Well, how long were you planning to stay up? More than an hour?"

"Probably right at an hour, yeah."

"I'd still like to come along."

Charlie shrugged. "OK. It'll give you a chance to get used to the ship. Make sure you bring a parachute, oxygen mask and your cold-weather flying gear. We'll climb to 25,000 feet and give the turbos a good workout."

"I don't have any of that stuff," Stern said. "Where can I get it issued?"

Chief Wilson spoke up. "I'll take you over to Supply, Lieutenant," he said. "They'll fix you right up."

"Thanks, Chief," said Charlie. He looked up to where the mechanics were tightening the last bolts on the propeller. "Let's see if that engine will start."

Three Minutes

Charlie was reading in the BOQ lobby that evening when the PA system announced, "Captain Charles Davis, your call is ready in Booth 3."

Charlie put a bookmark in his place and went to the phone booth.

"Captain Davis," he said to the receiver.

"One moment, sir," said a crackly female voice. Then, "Hello? Mrs. Davis, are you there?"

"Right here," said his mother's voice from across the continent.

"Go ahead, sir," said the operator. "You have three minutes."

"Charlie, are you all right?" his mother asked. She had spent most of her adult life in Connecticut or New York, but Charlie thought he could still hear a hint of Dixie in her voice.

"I'm fine, Mom. Just wanted to say hello, is all."

"Oh, is that all?" Even over the crackly line he could hear the amusement in her voice. His mother was one of the sharpest people he knew. She'd figure out everything he needed to tell her from the hints his sense of military security would allow.

"Sure, Mom."

"Well, then, are you behaving yourself and being safe?"

"Aw, Mom, the guys already call me Grandma. I don't like to take chances, you know that."

"Good. I'd like to see you live long enough to give me grandchildren. Have you heard from your scamp brother?"

"Jack? You know the Army, Mom. Even if he told me I couldn't say. But we did have a little visit about a month ago. Didn't you get my letter?"

"That half-page or so?"

Charlie grinned at the wall of the phone booth. "Come on, it was at least three-quarters of a page."

"Hm! Maybe someday you'll venture to a whole page and a half."

"I might remember too many things if I did that," Charlie said.

"Oh?"

"Sure. Just the other day I was thinking about that last trip Dad and Jack and I took."

There was a heartbeat's worth of silence on the other end. "That was a nice cruise. Jack and your father always talked about it."

"I bet they did." Charlie thought his mother's use of the word "cruise" was a nice touch. The trip in question wasn't a cruise, since it involved flying on the Pan American Clipper to Manila. "All we did was play shuffleboard and drink rum drinks."

"Do you think you might run into Jack anytime soon?"

"You never can tell."

"A very nice young lady came to see me the other day while I was in New York."

"Oh?" Now Charlie was puzzled. He had no idea what his mother was talking about; this wasn't their little personal innuendo code. "Who?"

"She said she met Jack on that little cruise and asked to be remembered to him."

"No kidding. Ash blonde hair, medium height?"

"Legs like a showgirl and a shape that would make a young man howl at the moon."

"Jeez, Mom!"

Laura Lea laughed. "You know it's the truth."

"How is she? Was her uncle with her?"

"That darling Mischa? Of course. He and Irina are both fine. Mischa had some business in Boston. They were on their way back to Los Angeles." Laura Lea hesitated. "I told her where Jack was."

Charlie blinked at the dark wood wall of the phone booth, trying to imagine his mother in their apartment near Central Park. She'd be sitting in her damask-covered settee by the window so she could look out at the park and the city skyline.

"I thought she knew," Charlie said.

"I barely knew," his mother replied. "Your brother wants to be a writer, and he's worse than you about writing."

"That's the way things are right now, Mom."

Laura Lea sniffed. "She knows that. Tough, that one. I doubt she'll let Jack get away as easily as all that. So Jack's fate is settled. What about you, eldest son?"

"Aw, Mom, I'm a career army officer. Don't have time for a family just now."

"Perhaps not, but you won't have the excuse of a war forever."

"I sure hope not."

"Me, too."

There was a click and a hum on the line. "This is the long-distance operator. Your three minutes are up."

"I love you, Mom," Charlie said.

"I love you, Charlie. Be careful and if you see your brother, give him my love."

"I will. G'bye." Charlie hung up the phone and sat for a moment, looking at the black Bakelite receiver.

Point Reyes

Charlie gathered Stern and Payne together first thing for breakfast, where they planned their flight in accordance with the clearances Charlie obtained the night before: take off from Hamilton, circle the field a few times to check the engines, climb to 25,000 feet, fly west to Point Reyes on the coast, then return to Hamilton, where Chief Wilson would do a final servicing of the engines and prep the airplane for the first and longest leg of its trip to the Philippines.

"So if we make it 2400 miles to Hickam Field we ought to be able to make it the rest of the way," said Charlie. "Although you can never tell."

At 0700 the Hamilton Field flight line was already a busy place. There was the whine, cough and roar of radial engines being coaxed into life which blotted out almost all other noises, so that if two men wanted to talk they had to lean close together and speak loudly.

Al Stern looked nervously at the airman standing close by with a bright red fire extinguisher mounted on wheels.

"What's that for?" he asked, pointing.

"That's in case an engine catches fire," Charlie said.

"Does that happen often?"

"Once is too much." Charlie looked at Chief Wilson and winked. The Chief raised his eyes to heaven. Charlie knew what he was thinking: *Pilots*.

"OK, here's the deal. We're cleared to fly out to Point Reyes on the coast and back. Interceptor Command might send up some P-40s to play with us, so keep your eyes open. Al, Point Reyes is on our heading to Hickam Field, so this will give you a chance to practice a little. Chief, you're acting as flight engineer. It's 60 miles, more or less, from here to Point Reyes, so in all we should be gone less than two hours, more like an hour and a half. Any questions?"

Stern hitched at the parachute harness he was wearing. "Have I got this damned thing on right?"

Charlie looked at it. He reached out and took hold of one of the straps. "It's kind of loose. Tighten it up some or the crotch straps will do a number on your testicles if we have to jump."

"Does that happen often?" Stern asked. He tightened the straps on the parachute harness. Payne snickered.

Charlie looked at him. "Some people jump and some get pushed, Al," he said drily, looking at Payne. "And I'll point out that the day is young. Let's preflight. D'you have the checklist, co-pilot?"

Payne hesitated. "It's in the cockpit," he admitted.

"Well, go get it. I'd like to be you-know-where before Christmas if that's OK with you."

Payne nodded, levered himself up the open hatch in the nose compartment, and disappeared inside the airplane. In a moment he returned with the preflight checklist and offered it to Charlie.

"Ump-umm," Charlie said. "You do it. Chief Wilson and I will look over your shoulder and be sure you've got it right."

Payne nodded.

Thirty minutes later Charlie, with a wink at Chief Wilson, was convinced that the airplane would fly, and that, perhaps, Mike Payne might someday know what his duties were as copilot.

"Let's go," Charlie said.

Thirty minutes later San Francisco and the Bay area was spread out below and to the southwest of them when they leveled out at 25,000 feet. At 15,000 feet Charlie switched engine controls to the turbochargers as required by the manual as Chief

Wilson looked on over Payne's shoulders. But the switchover went smoothly and quietly, and even the "new" Number 1 engine turned out its required RPMs in synch with the other engines.

"Pilot to navigator," Charlie called over the intercom. "How you doing, Al?"

"Uh, navigator to pilot. It's kind of chilly, but other than that, OK."

"Keep an eye on your oxygen indicator. At this altitude the oxygen supply line could freeze up. How are we doing on heading and speed?"

"You are on heading for Point Reyes, heading 252. Groundspeed 260 mph. We should be over Point Reyes in about ten minutes."

Charlie looked at the temperature gauge mounted on the cockpit bow and did a little mental arithmetic. Given the outside temperature and the altitude, his indicated airspeed of 175 mph probably did translate to about 260 mph true airspeed, or speed over the ground. A quick glance at the compass showed that Payne, who was flying the airplane, maintained a fairly constant heading that averaged 252 degrees, or a little bit south of west. Charlie looked over his shoulder at Chief Wilson, who had been studying the engine instruments for the last twenty minutes as they climbed to altitude.

Chief Wilson looked at Charlie and shrugged. "Looks good to me," he said. "So far."

"So far? That's comforting."

Wilson's eyes crinkled. His grin was hidden under his oxygen mask. "So whaddya want, Captain, a money-back guarantee?"

"Absolutely."

"You want a guarantee like that, Captain, you gotta talk to the people out at the Wright engine plant in Dayton. I just work on the damned things."

"Sissy."

"Not once in my life, I promise. Well, not since I was two, anyway."

Charlie grinned behind his oxygen mask.

Ahead of them, pointing like a finger out to sea, was Point Reyes with Drake's Bay to the south. Charlie knew there was a lighthouse on the end of the peninsula – he'd taken a girl out there during the summer, last time he had leave – and below the lighthouse the surf crashed and surged against the rocks at the very tip of land, and beyond that nothing but the broad Pacific for 2400 miles, until you got to Hickam Field.

Charlie studied that dark blue horizon where the lighter blue of the sky made a line that was, he knew, about two hundred miles away. *Go to that horizon twelve times*, he thought, *and we're in the landing pattern at Hickam.*

"Navigator to pilot."

"Go ahead, Al."

"We're above Point Reyes, Charlie."

"How'd you do on your time estimate?"

"Nine minutes 53 seconds. Seven seconds off."

"Not bad. Chief Wilson, what do you think?"

"I already signed off on this airplane, Captain. She's good to go."

Charlie refrained from pointing out that Wilson had signed off on this airplane five days ago and Charlie had brought it back with a dead engine. Wilson was a good chief; the engineering of aircraft engines was still a new science.

"OK. Co-pilot, your airplane. Put us over Hamilton Field with 5000 feet of altitude remaining. Talk to the navigator for heading and speed as necessary."

"Uh, roger, pilot."

Charlie ostentatiously took his hands off the controls and folded them over his belly. Then he smiled under his oxygen mask as Payne put the airplane into a left turn.

Hell, the kid barely had three hundred hours total time, and maybe six of that was in the B-17. Payne needed to fly the airplane every chance he got, for all their sakes.

A Woman that Beautiful

The rest of Charlie's morning and early afternoon passed in a blur, with last-minute servicing for the B-17, fueling, weather checks and other preparations for the long flight over the Pacific to Hickam Field. Charlie spent much of the day with Bob Payne and Al Stern. Payne attempted to supervise the mechanics

93

making last minute adjustments to the airplane; he finally learned he wasn't supposed to do that much, since the mechanics knew a lot more about their job than he did. Stern was inclined to hang up on the arcane symbols used by the meteorologists, but Charlie helped him through that. In the end the B-17 was ready by 1300. Charlie sent everyone off for lunch at the mess hall, thinking he'd follow in a few minutes after he took one last look around the airplane with Chief Wilson. As he finished a private drove up, braking to a screeching halt just in front of Charlie.

"Captain Davis?" the private called.

Charlie exchanged salutes with the private, who had jumped from the jeep and braced to attention.

"That's me," Charlie said. "What can I do for you, private?"

"Sir, Colonel Miller requests you come down to HQ at once," the private replied.

That made Charlie blink. He turned to the Chief, who waved impatiently.

"I'll finish up, sir," the Chief said. "You'd better not keep the Colonel waiting."

"Thanks," said Charlie. He got into the jeep. The private slammed the vehicle into gear and wheeled it around in a tight circle that had Charlie clinging to his hat and the side of the jeep.

"Who d'you know in Hollywood, Captain, if you don't mind me asking?"

"Nobody personally," Charlie replied. "Why?"

The jeep flashed past the transient ramp and roared between two hangars. Beyond the hangars were the four-story enlisted barracks on either side of the road, white stucco with the red tiles that gave the whole base a California-college-campus sort of feel.

"Well, sir, there's a big black car with a chauffeur out in front of HQ, and the prettiest sweetheart I've ever seen in my life, on or off the silver screen, got out of it. The Colonel himself came out to talk to her, and they carried on like old friends. I reckon she's a movie star, sir, but I sure can't place her."

"She must be a real looker," Charlie said. The driver accelerated and Charlie held onto his hat.

"Oh, you bet, Captain, just wait 'til you see her! An' look up there, sir, by the flagpole in front of HQ."

The private pointed without slackening speed. Charlie resisted the impulse to snatch the wheel from the youngster and looked ahead.

There was indeed a long black limo, a Deusenberg or a Daimler or something equally elegant and ostentatious, parked in front of HQ. A uniformed chauffeur polished an imaginary spot on the gleaming chrome of the rear fender as the private screeched to a stop only inches behind the man's rump. The chauffeur stood up indignantly. Charlie jumped out of the jeep to the curb. He preferred to do the driving himself if he had to fly that low, especially without wings.

A familiar voice called, "Charlie!"

He turned to see Colonel Miller on the porch of the HQ building, waving at him.

Next to Colonel Miller stood a young woman. She was perhaps two inches taller than the colonel, who was a short stocky man, and perhaps her slender body next to his broad one emphasized the difference in height. Maybe, too, the high heels she wore had something to do with it, along with the well-tailored pale green satin dress. The dress itself came to just below her knees and covered her shoulders and upper arms. She wore a wide-brimmed hat, which she lifted to look at Charlie. Her light blonde hair stirred a little in the breeze, framing her face as she smiled at him.

Then he knew her, even though he had only met her once, years ago in Manila of all places.

"Holy jumpin' Jesus," Charlie breathed.

"Told ya, Captain," said the private smugly. "She's a real peach."

The chauffeur sniffed and went back to polishing his fender.

Charlie walked forward, saluted Colonel Miller, and then took off his hat.

"Let me see if I remember," he said to the young woman. "It's Miss Irina Alexandrovna Aradhana, is it not?"

The lady thus addressed smiled and offered her hand, not to be shaken, but for Charlie to kiss. It was the simple unaffected gesture of training and upbringing. Charlie was an American and didn't really believe in the old world aristocracy, but in this case he was willing to make an exception. Irina Alexandrovna was

White Russian aristocracy; would, in fact, have been known as Countess of Tolzenoy, the fiefdom of the Aradhanas, if the Soviets had not intervened.

He found himself bowing over her hand and kissing it in as respectful a fashion as his West Point instructors in deportment could have wished – or, perhaps more to the point, his own mother, Laura Lea Davis.

"A pleasure to see you again, Captain Davis," said Irina Alexandrovna. She squeezed his hand gently. He straightened up, abruptly conscious of his greasy flying suit and somewhat battered leather jacket. He noted there was nothing but amused approval in Irina's eyes and remembered this was no ordinary woman. His brother Jack fell for her at first sight; Charlie looked in those blue eyes and saw something of ice and steel in them, along with the warmth.

"Down, Charlie," said Colonel Miller affably. "Miss Aradhana has been most cruelly deceived, and it's partly my fault. We're both hoping you can help rectify the situation."

Charlie looked away from Irina with an effort. Colonel Miller smiled at him.

"Beg pardon, sir?" he managed.

Irina laid a hand with the gentlest of pressures on Charlie's shoulder. "I was given to understand that Jack was here," she said.

Charlie loved the sound of Irina's voice. It was the accent; she spoke perfect, flawless English, and yet there was a soft lilting inflection in the accent. It was not French. It certainly did not have the guttural quality one might expect from a Russian. He wondered if it was something uniquely her, or perhaps in part the White Russian aristocracy from which she sprang, where French was spoken as a matter of course and Russian was the patois of the people, a mere lingua franca spoken by all in a hegemony including dozens of ethnicities each with their own tongue.

"That was true until quite recently," said Colonel Miller.

"So I heard as well," Charlie added.

Irina nodded gravely. "I am now given to understand it may be possible that you will see Jack soon," she said.

Charlie looked at the Colonel, eyebrows lifting in surprise. Charlie knew that all movements of men and materiel to the

Philippines was a closely guarded military secret. Irina Alexandrovna was a most unlikely spy but she was still a civilian, and this was very close to a breach in security.

"Even if that were so, you will understand I may not speak of it," Charlie said guardedly, looking back to Irina.

Irina smiled. It was a brief, gently condescending smile revealing a flash of even pearly teeth.

"Even a mere woman understands the needs of military security," she said softly. "I am Russian, and I am told we Russians understand these things in our genes. Whatever, I had hoped to see Jack before..."

It was the slightest of pauses but Charlie felt it squeeze his own heart. The realization came to Charlie that the beautiful, slender, fragile-looking woman in front of him was the product of generations of what was, in truth, a warrior aristocracy; that blood told her Jack was being sent in harm's way.

"I understand," Charlie said. He paused. "How may I help?"

Irina looked into his eyes. "I know you may not speak of where you will go and what you will do there, but perhaps it may be you will find a way to put this in Jack's hands?"

She handed Charlie a stiff manila envelope, big enough to hold a sheet of regular typing paper without being folded, or an 8x10 picture.

"Naturally I can make no promises," Charlie said, but he took the envelope. "If it is in my power, though, I'll see that Jack gets this."

"You understand, it is only for Jack," said Irina. "I should blush for anyone else to see it."

She touched the envelope gently with her hand. Charlie noticed the address then, written in an old-fashioned script with a broad-nibbed pen:

Lt. John T. Davis, USAAF
21st Pursuit Squadron
35th Pursuit Group
APO San Francisco

"Forgive my ignorance, but a pursuit group, that is something like a regiment of cavalry, is it not?" Irina asked.

"In spirit if nothing else," Colonel Miller supplied. "Bomber types like Charlie and myself, well, we're more like the infantry."

"There are many sorts of bravery, each one meritorious," Irina replied. A bleak look came and went in those blue eyes. "I remember my father saying that once."

"He was right," said Charlie. He hefted the envelope. "I'll keep this safe until the next time I see Jack."

Irina smiled, stood on tiptoe, and kissed Charlie on the cheek. "Thank you," she said, and turned to Colonel Miller.

"I must go, but thank you for your kind assistance," she told the Colonel, holding out her hand. The Colonel bowed in a courtly, old-world fashion Charlie knew belonged to another age. Then Irina turned back to Charlie.

"I will not say goodbye, Captain Davis, for I'm sure we will meet again. Thank you, and God keep you safe."

She smiled and walked away. The limo driver jumped to open her door. Charlie saw the private leaning against his jeep, watching her. The private's closed mouth did little to hide his unhinged jaw.

The driver closed the door behind her and got in. Irina faced them through the window, smiled, and waved her hand. Charlie felt his hand go up to wave in response, but it was as if the hand belonged to someone else. He was quite unaware of any decision to wave back.

"Wow," he said, as the limo drove away. "I remembered she was gorgeous, but..."

His voice trailed away.

Colonel Miller sighed. Charlie looked at him. The colonel's face was sad, watching the limousine drive off toward the front gate.

"What is it with you Davis boys?" he asked softly.

"Beats me, Colonel," Charlie said. "Jack's the one with all the luck."

"No kidding." Colonel Miller blinked. "Sweet Jesus. I remember the first time I met your mother, in Paris in 1917. She might have given Miss Aradhana a run for her money on looks."

Charlie looked at Colonel Miller in surprise.

"You be sure that envelope gets to your brother, Charlie," Colonel Miller told him. "I don't think it would do to disappoint the lady."

Departure

Charlie stood on the ramp in front of the Hamilton Field Operations building. The fuel trucks had just pulled away. Kim Smith and Al Stern levered themselves into the airplane through the nose hatch. Bob Payne was already on the flight deck. It was time to go.

He stood for a moment looking around the flight line at all the sights and sounds familiar to an air field in the States. He'd been to Clark Field once, years ago, while he was still a cadet at West Point. That was only three years ago, and Clark Field hadn't been much more than a couple of hangars and a long sod field. He wondered if it had changed much. For just a moment he felt cold and alone, looking to the west, knowing it was very likely that he'd be at war soon.

Charlie was confident of his airplane and himself. That confidence didn't extend to his crew, not yet. He'd have to take every opportunity he could to train them as they crossed the Pacific to the Philippines. He sighed and looked at his watch.

It was time to start engines.

Charlie shook off the reverie, knowing he was just postponing the moment when he'd have to board the airplane and make that long flight over the Pacific. He started toward the open hatch and put his hand on the sill.

A horn honked insistently as a truck drove up to the bomber. It came to a stop a few feet away. Charlie recognized Sergeant Voorhis sitting next to the driver, an enlisted man Charlie didn't know.

An MP stepped down from the back of the truck. Another man followed him out. Charlie recognized Private Lefkowicz, and was surprised to see that the young man was in handcuffs. Sergeant Voorhis climbed down from the truck and reached back in for a duffle bag and a manila envelope.

Voorhis marched up to Charlie and saluted smartly. "Reporting for movement with a party of one, Captain," he barked.

Charlie returned the salute. "Rest, sergeant." Then, quietly, "Lefkowicz doesn't look like he changed his mind to me."

Voorhis matched Charlie's tone. "He didn't, sir, but the paperwork says he did."

Charlie looked Voorhis in the eye. "Why are you doing this, Sergeant? And what makes you think I'll take Lefkowicz under these circumstances?"

Voorhis hesitated. "Sir..."

"Go on. You're trying to help me out, too, and I appreciate that. I'm just not sure I think it's the best idea. I've got an airplane and a crew to think of. I'd rather go short-handed than take some gold-bricking goofball with me. So sell me on the idea."

"Yes, sir. Look, I know this kid. We come from the same neighborhood back in Chicago. I know his family, too. They're good folks and Lefty is a good kid."

"Lefty?"

"He's a southpaw, sir. Throws a mean fast ball. Played minor league before he enlisted. Ahead of the draft, I might add."

"OK. Go on."

"The only thing wrong with him is that girl I told you about. Probably the first piece of ass he ever had. You know what that's like. She jilted him, told him she wanted this other guy. Probably said some other things. You can imagine what. Lefty's young. He's only twenty. Honest, Captain, that's why he's behaving this way."

"OK, so he's unlucky in love. Can he do anything useful?"

Voorhis nodded. "His first sergeant says the kid's a natural-born gunner. Picked up the whole manual on both the .50-caliber and .30 caliber machine guns, even that damned old Lewis gun from the last war. The kid's as good as anyone who's been through armorer's school."

Charlie thought that over. Gunnery training was one of those subjects passed over in the drive to build airplanes and train pilots, navigators and bombardiers. Very little time or money was allocated to it. The B-17D, however, carried five .50-caliber guns and one .30-caliber machine gun. The .30-caliber was in the nose and in Charlie's opinion was only just better than no gun at all. Regardless, it was what they had to fight with if it came to that. Having someone aboard who knew how to care for the guns would be helpful.

He looked at Lefkowicz, standing next to the MP, who was undoing the handcuffs. Lefkowicz didn't seem to be paying any attention. He just stared down at the concrete of the ramp.

Charlie felt a wry grimace twist his face. He looked at Voorhis.

"Well, Sergeant, like I said yesterday, we've all been there."

"Yes, sir."

"I gather that's his gear?"

"Yes, sir."

Charlie dearly wanted to ask Sergeant Voorhis how he had gotten orders detaching Lefkowicz from whatever outfit he belonged to and transferring him to the 19th Bomb Group, but as he opened his mouth Voorhis cleared his throat slightly. His eyes pleaded with Charlie.

Charlie decided he didn't need to ask any further questions.

He shook his head. "Major Pattison didn't tell us the half of it."

"Beg pardon, sir?"

"He was one of my instructors back at the Point. He was fond of telling us cadets that it was sergeants who ran the Army."

"I don't know what you mean, sir," the sergeant said piously.

Charlie sternly suppressed a smile. "I'm sure you don't, Sergeant. Well, let's get Romeo aboard. I was supposed to be in Hawaii six days ago."

"Yes, sir," Voorhis said. Then, quietly, "Thank you, sir."

"For what, Sergeant? If you're right on this you've done me a favor."

Lefkowicz, freed from his handcuffs, walked slowly to the waist section of the airplane with Voorhis and the MP behind him. Charlie looked in the door; Lefkowicz made his way forward to the bench where the crew sat before takeoff and was buckling himself in.

Charlie quirked an inquiring eyebrow at Voorhis, who shrugged. "You work with machine guns, you fly on Forts sometimes," he said. "I guess, anyway."

"I guess," Charlie replied. He put a foot on the waist hatch and started to climb aboard. There was a hand on his shoulder. Charlie turned.

Voorhis stepped back. He and the MP came to absolutely rigid, parade-ground attention, and saluted.

"Good luck, sir," said Voorhis.

Charlie returned the salute. "Thanks," he said, and climbed aboard.

CHAPTER FIVE
Life In the PI

No Hollywood Stuff

Jack Davis turned on final for Nichols Field, double-checking to be sure his landing gear was down and locked and flaps fully extended. He scanned the runway below and ahead of him, noting the ruts and the mud puddles and the ugly smear in the grass where Lt. Williams ground-looped his P-35 and tore it all to hell.

Stupid bastard, Jack thought. *Don't be like him, Jack Davis, keep it loose, keep it steady, keep your eyes open and fly smart.*

Just above the runway Jack eased all the way back on the throttle. The Seversky P-35 pursuit lost airspeed as Jack pulled smoothly back on the control stick. The wings stalled just as the mains kissed the ground; Jack fed in just a hair of forward stick to keep the tail up as airspeed bled off. The tail came down of its own accord as the airspeed indicator showed the airplane dropping towards zero, which was no forward motion regardless of whether the gauge was calibrated for miles or kilometers per hour.

The pursuit slowed to a walking pace and Jack fed in a little throttle, fishtailing gently to keep a lookout ahead as he approached the apron. He'd gotten the pursuit down in one piece; he didn't want to ruin things by taxiing into a parked airplane, like Lt. Dunne had done this morning. He could see the P-35's crew chief waiting with the cut-down old Ford truck that served as an airplane tug, so as he approached the edge of the concrete he stood on the left brake, turned the airplane in a half-circle, put on both brakes, and ran the engine up to clear the plugs before shutting it down.

Jack sat in the cockpit for a moment, feeling the heat of the sun, the muggy humidity of the tropical air, listening to the quiet, broken by the sound of the Ford tug's engine and the *tic-ting* noises made by the radial engine of the P-35 as it cooled. He didn't sit there for more than a few seconds, because he was very aware of the slender figure of Ed Dyess sitting comfortably in front of the Operations tent, feet propped up, puffing on a cigarette.

The other thing Jack was very, very aware of was the P-40E Kittyhawk at the far edge of the apron in front of the hangars. It was shiny; it was new; it looked sleek and fast and full of promise. Jack looked at the pursuit, looked away and did not look back. Instead he undid his straps and stood up in the cockpit, then climbed down onto the wing.

"How'd she do, Mr. Davis?" the mechanic asked.

"Pretty good, Melville. I had her up to 300."

The mechanic chuckled. "English or metric?"

Jack smiled. "Well, somewhere in between, then. You want a hand with the tow bar?"

"Naw, that's OK, sir. Besides, I think the boss is giving you the high sign." Melville jerked his chin towards the Operations office. When Jack turned to look he saw Lt. Dyess motioning to him.

"OK. Thanks, Melville. You got the Form One?"

"Yes, sir. Right here." Melville produced the form. Jack scanned it quickly, scribbled "All OK" and signed it.

He shrugged out of his parachute harness and slung it over his shoulder. Dyess had gone back to reading something – a file, Jack thought – as he puffed on a cigarette. Inside the hangars someone started a radial engine, and the familiar, homey *put-a-put, put-a-put, put, put* sound as the engine coughed, sputtered and finally began to idle smoothly was a comfort.

Jack, walking across the grass from the apron to the Ops shack, carrying his parachute under a tropical sun and sweating freely inside his flight suit, took a deep breath and felt a smile at the corners of his mouth. For a few moments he wasn't conscious of much else, just the swing of his legs, the heat of the sun on his back, the sweat trickling down between his shoulders, the weight of the parachute over his shoulder, the feel of the ground under his feet, the memory of the blue sky and cool air at 10,000 feet as he checked out the P-35 he'd just landed. That P-35 was one of those that had suffered minor damage as a result of a landing mishap two days ago. Regulations required that the airplane go through a test regimen after repairs, and Jack, as the newly assigned squadron assistant maintenance officer, drew the task of the test flight.

Dyess kept reading for a second, puffing on his pipe, as Jack mounted the two steps up to the veranda and stood before him. Then Dyess looked up.

"Know what I've got here, Jack?" Dyess asked.

"No, sir."

"It's your personnel file. I've been reviewing it. I got curious about your time with the 31st Pursuit last summer."

Jack shrugged the parachute harness off his shoulder and hooked it on the back of a nearby chair. Then he took off his leather helmet.

"So how did you like the 31st?"

"It's a good outfit."

"But you requested a transfer. I can't think it was because you'd heard something about the 35th being sent to the Philippines and you wanting to be in the middle of the action. That move was top secret at the time."

"Yes, sir." Jack hesitated. "Truth is, sir, my fiancée lives in Los Angeles. I figured if I were at Hamilton Field I might have a better chance of seeing her."

Dyess lit another cigarette. "Looks like that transfer went through pretty quick. You know someone in Personnel?"

"Well, sir..."

"Never mind. That question was pretty much rhetorical. Of course you do. But I guess it backfired on you."

Jack shrugged. "Only half the group was sent out this time. I could've been with the other half."

"But you didn't try. Not that I remember. Hell, you were in my flight at Hamilton before they made me half a squadron commander."

"Ed, asking a favor is one thing. Asking two is another. I won't say I was happy, but it didn't look like there was much even Colonel Miller could do about it."

Dyess grinned. "You know Joe Miller?"

"He and my father served together in France."

"OK. Well, that makes some sense. I know the Colonel, as it happens, and you're right. You could've pushed for two favors, but I doubt you'd have gotten a third."

"Yes, sir."

"Boyd Wagner tells me you did pretty well yesterday. I had to remind him I needed you again. I think he'd like to shanghai you. So how d'you like the P-35?"

"I hope we get P-40s soon, but the P-35 isn't a bad airplane. Handles really well. Not so sure about those engines, though."

"What do you mean?"

"They need to be replaced. At the least they need to be overhauled. The one I was just in was thirty hours overdue. Stateside, the line chief would've pushed it back behind the hangar if he couldn't change the engine."

"So he would have. But we're not Stateside. I keep hearing we could be in a war zone any minute. Would you rather have a P-35 with a tired engine, or no airplane at all?"

Jack scoffed. "Ten minutes into my first dogfight it might not matter."

"That bother you?"

"Hell, yes."

"Good. So you know, I don't like it either, and I hope we get P-40s soon, too. Speaking of which, how well do you remember the Allison engine in the P-39?"

"Fairly well."

Dyess regarded him in silence for a moment. The squadron commander took another drag on his cigarette, then put it out in the ashtray on the table next to his chair.

"Sit down, Jack," Dyess said.

Jack dragged up the chair his parachute hung on and sat.

"Remind me, how much civilian time do you have?" Dyess asked.

Jack blinked. He'd started flying in 1938, just before his father was killed at the Cleveland Air Races. But since he'd been accepted for the Air Corps he hadn't thought much about his civilian hours. It was mostly cross-country and stunt flying or cloud-chasing in a Waco biplane. He told Wagner that he'd been a flight instructor, and that was true, but he'd only taught for a couple of months before he went into the Air Corps.

"I don't remember exactly," Jack replied. "Four hundred hours or so, I think."

"You didn't log it down?"

"Yes, sir. But that logbook is back home and it was made pretty clear to me at Kelly Field that whatever I'd learned as a civilian I'd better unlearn or better yet, just forget."

Dyess' grin came and went. "I see. Well, that means, given the time I see here in your file and what I estimate you've flown here with me, that you have something like 700 hours total flying time."

"Is that a lot?"

"Yes and no." Dyess gestured at the pilots and mechanics gathered around the P-40E across the apron. "Things were different in 1938 when I got my wings. The syllabus was a lot more detailed and training was a year instead of nine months. Nowadays, you kids come out of flight school with a set of shiny silver wings and about 200 hours flying time. Then the Air Corps puts you into something like a P-39 or a P-40 and invites you to do your best to bust your ass. Darwin might like that approach but I've got a squadron to run. How much time did you get in P-39s with the 31st?"

"About 50 hours, I think."

"That's close. 52 and some change, according to your file. How did you like the P-39?"

Jack smiled. "Like I said the other night, she's fun to fly but you've got to watch your elevators. With the engine behind the cockpit like that she's real sensitive to pitch changes. Some of the guys claimed she'd tumble end over end in an accelerated stall."

Dyess nodded. "37mm cannon in front of the cockpit, Allison engine behind it, center of gravity not as far forward as on most airplanes, yeah, I could maybe see that."

Jack waited. He could see Dyess was thinking something over.

"OK," Dyess said finally. "You're a pretty good pilot. I knew that after flying with you back in the States. Wagner thinks you're pretty good, too, and he isn't the type for unnecessary praise. Your record bears that out. I've heard enough about the P-39 to think that it got out of the Bell Aircraft factory with maybe one or two interesting flight characteristics most pilots find out about the hard way. Again, it adds up to Jack Davis being a pretty good pilot. Now I'm going to tell you something you won't like, Jack, but I want you to bear with me. You're going to be one of the last pilots I put in the P-40."

Jack blinked and sat back a little. He thought of that beautiful airplane sitting on the apron about two hundred yards away from him.

Dyess grimaced. "I figured you'd take it like that. I have a good reason for it, though. Jack, I think you can go up in the P-40 anytime you want and learn the airplane quick. You've got experience in the P-39, which is a trickier airplane and has the same engine, so that should make it easier for you." Dyess paused to light another cigarette. He took a draw on it and pointed it at Jack while he exhaled a cloud of smoke.

"But out of the thirty pilots in this squadron you're one of maybe a half-dozen, myself included, with the combination of skill and experience to make that happen. I can't run a squadron with six pilots in it. I need the other fourteen guys, if not to the same level, at least trained up enough that when I put them in the P-40 we don't lose half of them in silly accidents in the first week." The squadron commander paused.

"So here's the deal. I'm making you an unofficial instructor pilot. You're going to take these guys up in an A-27 and evaluate them. You see any really bad habits or deficiencies, you let me know. Then we'll work with them in the P-35. After that, as we figure the guys are ready and as P-40s come available, they go into the P-40. It's going to mean a lot of flying and a lot of work on the ground and in the air. Are you up for it?"

Jack started to grimace and quit; started to sigh and stifled it. "Yes, sir," he said.

Dyess leaned back in his chair and grinned. "You know, Jack, what we're doing here, it's not about flying and having a good time. This is a pursuit squadron. Our job is to kill people in other airplanes. We can't do that nearly so well if we lose half our guys to accidents because they don't know what they're doing."

"I understand, Ed."

"It's just you had your itty bitty heart set on flying that P-40, didn't you?"

"Yes, sir."

"So tell me, have you re-read the manual for the airplane?"

"Yes, sir."

Dyess nodded. "What's your flaps down, gear down stall speed?"

"What airplane weight?" Jack asked.

"7500 pounds."

"Manual says 75 mph."

"What do you say?"

"It varies a few knots from airplane to airplane. With flaps and gear up she's supposed to stall at 85 mph, and at 7500 pounds my landing speed is 90 mph. Get much below 100 mph and things will start to get squirrelly pretty quick, is my feeling."

"Define squirrelly."

"Well, the manual also says the airplane has no tendency to enter a spin from a stall. But it also says when she does spin she drops her nose, whips hard to the left and spins violently. You get below 100 mph and you're close to stalling anyway."

"And you can't enter a spin until you stall," Dyess agreed. "OK. Think you can start an Allison engine?"

Jack shrugged. "It's been a couple of months. I'd have my crew chief look over my shoulder as a backup and take my time going down the checklist."

"Most of these guys would think that kind of sissy, having your crew chief look over your shoulder."

"They can think what they like. Any Air Corps crew chief worth a damn knows the airplane better than I do, or at least as well. The crew chief's job is to make sure the airplane is airworthy. He's on my side and I don't mind having him right there, looking over my shoulder."

Dyess thought for a moment. "Your dad was a racing pilot, wasn't he?"

"Yes, sir. Every race I ever watched, when he started up, he had his mechanic looking over his shoulder."

"You learned some good habits. OK. This is what I want you to do. If I'm going to make you an instructor it's going to be easier for these guys to listen to you if they know you know what you're talking about. I want you to go fly that P-40 on the apron. Take her up, wring her out, get reacquainted. If you feel comfortable with the airplane make a low-level high-speed pass over the runway, but Jack, make no mistake. This is not an invitation to do any Hollywood stuff. No aerobatics on the deck for awhile, OK? In particular I want you to remember that the manual specifically prohibits intentional spins, so don't get into any unintentional spins, either."

Jack grinned. "I think I can manage that for you, Skipper."

"See that you do. Come on. Let's go make you the envy of all eyes."

The crowd around the airplane fell silent as Dyess walked up to it with Jack in tow. The pilots grinned in anticipation when they noticed Jack was in his flying gear and carrying his parachute. One or two of them exchanged glances. Roy Chant caught Jack's eye and winked.

Dyess went to stand beside the left wing root and put a hand possessively on the fuselage. He ran his hand over the smooth aluminum skin of the airplane, smiling for a moment, and then turned to face the other pilots.

"Beautiful airplane, isn't it?" he asked, the smile still on his face. "I hear they're being set up pretty quickly now, even if it might be another week before we get ours."

The pilots, without being told, edged closer to Dyess. Jack stood back a little, watching the rest of them, and watching the squadron commander.

He couldn't decide what it was about Dyess. The pilots crowding around him were young, but only a few years younger. He was a first lieutenant, and the rest of the pilots were second lieutenants, most of them not long out of flight school. Dyess wasn't particularly handsome or strong or otherwise distinguished.

But it was a fact that Dyess was, as Jack was unashamed to admit (at least to himself), the best pilot in the squadron, maybe the best pursuit pilot in the FEAF, with the possible exception of Buzz Wagner. Jack had no intention of letting things stay that way, but Dyess set a high standard as a pilot. Now, watching him with his pilots, Jack realized the man set a high standard as a leader.

So maybe it was the man's easy confidence in his own ability, the absolute assurance that he could take an airplane, make it do exactly what he wanted it to do, and remain master of any situation that might arise. That, Jack realized, looking at the faces of the other pilots as well as into his own heart, was a real achievement.

It was something to remember, something to study. While Dyess spoke to his pilots Jack studied the P-40E.

From the prop spinner and the hefty oil cooler under the Allison engine back to her well-formed tail the P-40 was every inch a pursuit airplane. It *looked* tough and self-reliant, like the kind of airplane that should have a bunch of Jap flags – well, Japs, Krauts or whomever, he corrected himself – painted under the cockpit. He looked along the leading edge of the wing and saw the muzzles of three .50-caliber machine guns. He could see the armament panels in the wing just behind the guns, where the ground crew would feed in the ammunition belts. Before he actually knew what he was doing he began to identify features on the airplane he'd read about in the manual, looking down the line of the air scoop above the nose to the mechanical ring gun sight in line with the optical sight just above the instrument panel inside the cockpit, down to the six exhaust stacks that poked out of the engine nacelle, still gleaming and looking factory-new. That thought made him frown to himself; it meant they'd have to slow-time these damned engines. That thought brought up another: had the machine-guns been sighted in? What the hell good was a machine-gun if it didn't shoot where the pilot's gun-sight pointed?

"Lt. Davis," he heard Dyess say.

"Yes, sir."

Dyess beckoned and Jack pushed through the crowd to Dyess' side.

"I'm sure you all know Jack by now," Dyess said. "And in what I'm sure will be a popular decision, Jack here is going to be an instructor pilot. Which means he's going to be stuck in P-35s awhile longer, so as a consolation prize he's taking the first flight in our first P-40."

Dyess turned to the line chief. "Chief, is she ready to go?"

"Sure 'nuff, Lt. Dyess. Just baby the engine a little."

"You hear that, Jack?"

"Yes, sir," Jack replied. "Perhaps the Chief would look over my shoulder while I start the engine?"

Jack lined up on the runway, waggled the rudder, and looked at the tower. The airman standing there with the light gun gave him a green. Jack looked over his shoulders, tried the stick and rudder one last time to be sure the controls moved freely, and stood on the brakes. Throttle all the way forward. He watched the RPM indicator climb, set the manifold pressure for 45 inches, glanced at the oil and cylinder head temperatures – everything looked OK. He let the engine run for a few seconds at takeoff power and then let loose the brakes, feeding in right rudder to counteract the propeller torque.

The P-40E accelerated, bumping over the rutted sod runway, the power of the engine through the whirling propeller pushing him back against his seat. Jack watched the runway, his wingtips, the engine instruments; the airspeed came up and he eased forward the least bit on the stick to get the tail off, centering the stick as the tail came off the runway. Some of the bumping smoothed out and he felt the extra acceleration as the drag of the tail wheel came off. He was at 80 mph, and he could feel the air slamming over the ailerons and the elevators, dancing now on the rudder pedals instead of the brake to guide the airplane down the runway. He held the pursuit down until the airspeed indicator edged up over 95 mph and then gently, gently eased back on the stick. The main gear gave a rumble and a bump and there it was, that moment when the horizon started to fall away and grow all around you.

Jack hit the lever to retract the main gear and milked up the wing flaps a little, then eased back on the throttle. As the speed came up he closed the flaps on the oil cooler to lessen the drag. With a spaced pair of thumps the gear came up into their wells and locked in place. Jack's airspeed climbed towards 140 mph.

He pulled back on the stick and held his airspeed at best rate of climb, about 145 mph. The vertical speed indicator was next to the turn and bank indicator, and showed he was climbing at 2100 feet per minute. That was pretty close to the manual, and the engine temp and coolant gauges were within normal ranges for this RPM setting.

Jack nodded to himself. Then he looked all around, checking the sky and his tail. Just in case. It seemed that he was all alone for once.

Five minutes later he leveled off at 10,000 feet. He'd been cautioned by Dyess against going higher, since the P-40's oxygen tank was empty. More problems with the sole oxygen production plant, which was always lagging behind demand.

Jack scanned the sky all around him again as the airplane accelerated. He made a sharp turn to get the field in sight below and ahead of him, then put the ship into a slight dive. He passed through 8000 feet, pushing 400 mph, and found the rudder and elevators hard to work. The ship had a tendency to yaw to the right and drop the right wing, too, which he found a little disconcerting. He knew he could put in some aileron and rudder trim to counteract it and make maneuvering easier, but decided he'd keep it the way it was for now, just to see what difference it made performing aerobatics. He pulled up into a loop, compensating on the controls as the tendency to yaw right faded along with his airspeed at the top of the loop.

After twenty minutes of aerobatics Jack dropped the right wing and pulled elevator in the turn, huffing as the g-load came on, pulling it tighter and tighter until his vision narrowed and began to gray. He held it there through a complete 360-degree turn and then pulled out, taking a deep breath and then another as the g's came off. He gave it a minute, breathing slowly and deeply, until his vision came back.

"Nichols Field, Nichols Field, this is Army Two-Zero-Two," he radioed.

"Go ahead, Two-Zero-Two, this is Nichols."

"Who's in the pattern?"

"Pattern clear, Two-Zero-Two."

"Roger, Nichols, keep it that way. I'm coming down."

"Roger, Two-Zero-Two."

Jack grinned. Then he pulled back hard on the stick until the P-40E was climbing straight up, hanging on the prop as the airspeed bled away under the pull of gravity. The airspeed fell below 100 and Jack kicked hard right rudder as the airplane started to stall. Instead nose and tail switched places, pointing down at the green rice paddies below with the brown scar of Nichols Field in the middle of them. He throttled back to ease the load on the engine but the airspeed built up as rapidly as it had fallen away during the climb. He had the ship headed straight down with nothing but earth in his windscreen.

Jesus jumping Jehosophat, Jack thought, *this thing dives like crazy!*

At 3000 feet he began his pullout, firm and gentle against the control forces as the g's built up, but he'd timed it right and the P-40 leveled out just above the treetops at over 400 mph showing on the airspeed indicator, the air screaming past his cockpit and the rudder and elevator feeling like a half-dozen big men sat on them. The tower rushed towards him and he flashed over the approach end of the runway, still indicating over 400 mph, easing it down until he clipped along the runway at lawnmower height, paying no attention to the group of men standing on the apron watching him fly by, instead watching the trees at the far end of the runway, judging his moment, waiting, then the gentle pull back on the elevators and the P-40 shot up into the air like a rocket, and he let her roll to the right, laughing out loud as he climbed into the sky. He kicked rudder again at the top of his climb and went into a dive to make one more pass down the runway, maybe even a little lower this time, and climbed away more sedately to pattern altitude, throttling back.

"Army Two-Zero-Two to Nichols Field, request permission to land," he radioed.

"Permission granted, Two-Zero-Two. Winds negligible, altimeter two-niner-niner-five."

"Two-niner-niner-five, thank you, Nichols," Jack replied.

He was at pattern altitude on the downwind leg showing 275 mph. He brought the propeller back to 2300 RPM and closed the throttle to 18 inches, feeling the tremble of the slowing airframe through the controls and the seat of his pants on the hard parachute pack, and turned hard onto the crosswind leg, bleeding even more speed in the turn. As he turned on approach he dropped the gear, waited until the airspeed dropped below 140 mph, and gave it full flaps. He opened the canopy and air rushed in, plucking at his clothes and his scarf as he continued his approach.

There it was, that one spot on the runway he liked, the exact spot where he was going to place his main gear. He darted a glance at the wind sock, hanging lifeless on its staff, and kept the P-40 the way it was, the way he liked it, minor corrections to stick and rudder, until that point in space and time where it all came together in his mind and he pulled back on the stick and the throttle. The mains kissed the sod, rumbling and bouncing, and he pulled the throttle all the way back to IDLE. He held off the tail for a bit but it too came down, bouncing a little, and he was on the ground again, feeling that moment of brief regret that came and went whenever a flight was over. Then he taxied in slow S-turns to the apron and shut the engine down, exactly according to checklist. The propeller spun to a halt.

As he started to undo his safety straps he felt the airplane sway as someone climbed on the wing. He looked to the left as Ed Dyess crouched on the wing and looked at him. There was something a little sardonic in Dyess' eye, something of a challenge in the set of his mouth, which crinkled at the corners in a wry smile.

"So, hotshot," Dyess said. "How does she handle at low level and high airspeeds?"

Mail

Chant stopped at Jack's door. Jack was putting a final polish on his shoes. He sat in his trousers and undershirt, trying to sweat as little as possible before putting on his uniform tunic. The tunic was laid out carefully on Jack's bed, buttons gleaming, metal devices such as his silver wings polished to a satiny gloss, second lieutenant's bars shining like gold instead of brass, the brown bill of his officer's hat new and crisp.

"Where you going, Jack? Having dinner with MacArthur?"

"Something like that."

"No, seriously."

Jack looked at his reflection in his shoe, turned the shoe this way and that, then nodded slightly before looking up at Chant.

"The Skipper gave me 24 hours before I have to start this instructor thing," he said. "I figured I'd see if they had a room at the Manila Hotel."

"You get tired of the coffee here already?"

"No. It might be the last chance I get to be a pretend civilian for awhile, though."

"You reckon on spending some of that gambling pot?"

Jack put his right foot in its shoe and started lacing it up. "I reckon," he said, smiling.

That was when he noticed the sheaf of letters in Chant's hand. "Mail?" he asked.

"Oh! Yeah, since Dyess made you assistant maintenance officer, I got the booby prize. Mail and morale officer." Chant riffled quickly through the letters and handed three to Jack. "Here you go."

"Thanks, Roy."

Chant smiled. "Have fun."

"You bet." Jack laid the letters down on the bunk next to him and tied his other shoe before picking them up again. The first one, as he'd more or less expected, was from his mother. The second was from his brother Charlie.

He held the third letter in his hand and felt dizzy. Then he realized he wasn't breathing. Deliberately he drew in a breath, surprised at the effort it took. It made him angry.

116

She's just a girl, he told himself. And immediately replied, *yeah, right.*

He pulled his B4 bag from underneath his bunk. He'd already packed it with enough for an overnight stay, some toiletries, a change of socks and underwear, light slacks and a shirt for tropical wear. Jack had figured he'd sit on the terrace at the Manila Hotel and watch the sun go down over the bay and sort through some memories while sipping something cool, fruity and alcoholic. That was still his plan, but the letters added something to it.

Jack tossed the letters in his B4 bag and zipped it closed. Then he finished dressing and walked across the hall to Chant's room.

"You get any mail?" Jack asked.

"You remember that girl I told you about, from back home?"

"The cheerleader?"

"Right, that one. Look here." Chant took a picture from the envelope in his hand and held it up for Jack.

The picture was of a smiling, dark-haired girl in a nurse's outfit, waving at the camera. Jack could see the cheerleader's face from Chant's faded picture, a little older.

"I'll be damned," Jack said. "So how did she come to write to you?"

"She was home from nursing school in Chapel Hill. The local paper published a list of local boys in uniform. She saw my name on it and decided to write me."

"Second string or not, pal, you must've made an impression."

Chang grinned. "Well, maybe, but it says here she's writing a couple of other guys too."

"So what? Just remember what I told you, keep it light and cheerful when you write back. Flirt a little. Say how great she looks in that nurse's uniform, and ask where she's planning on going."

"Jack, you said something. I reckon I'll do just that. You off to the Manila Hotel?"

"In about two shakes. Just wanted to see how you were doing first."

Chant placed the picture back in the envelope. "Buddy, I'm doing fine. Enjoy yourself."

A Drink on the Terrace

Jack got out of the taxi in the entrance drive to the Manila Hotel. He paid the driver and stepped onto the sidewalk, looking up at the canopied entrance. The major difference three years made to the hotel were the two armed guards at the entrance. Jack figured that was because General MacArthur and his family still lived here, as well as most of the rest of the brass in the islands.

He gave a tug to his tunic, glanced down at the gleaming shine of his shoes, and flicked his eyes left and right to reassure himself that that brass second lieutenant bars did indeed shine as if they were gold. When he looked to the left he caught the silver gleam of his wings just above his breast pocket. He nodded ever so slightly and mostly to himself, and walked past the guards into the hotel's foyer.

It was the same as he remembered: polished mahogany, bright mirrors, crystal chandeliers and tables with sprays of red, orange, yellow and purple tropical flowers, whose scent wafted over you as you passed them, sometimes new and fresh enough that the scent could make you a little giddy. Then, just as he remembered it, there was the bar on the left, already noisy and convivial with men in dress uniforms or Class A's, with their women in evening gowns and cocktail dresses; and directly ahead the desk with its shelves of pigeonholes and gleaming brass room numbers.

The man behind the counter looked vaguely familiar, part Filipino, part Chinese, with a gleaming bald head, a black moustache, and eyes that missed nothing. The desk clerk's eyes passed over Jack, registered him, and kept moving. Jack walked up to the desk.

"My name is Davis," he said. "I'd like a room for the night."

The desk clerk looked at him. He had what Jack thought of as a professional face, bland, a polite if non-committal smile, but otherwise without expression.

"You have reservation, Lieutenant?" the man asked.

"No. But I'm expecting a telegram and a letter of credit addressed to me, Second Lieutenant John T. Davis, US Army Air Forces."

The Manila Hotel was one of the grandest of grand hotels, on a harbor that was one of the crossroads of the world. Jack's request was neither new nor even unusual.

"Card?" the clerk asked.

Jack produced his wallet and flipped it to his Army ID card. The clerk looked at the picture of Jack on the card, looked back at him for a moment, and nodded.

"Good picture," the clerk said. "One small minute, sir, I check."

The clerk went to a door beside the pigeonholes with keys and room numbers. He opened it and spoke for a moment. Another man, dressed in a tuxedo, came out of the room. He held a small envelope in his hand.

"Lt. Davis?" the man asked. "I'm the concierge. We've been holding this for you."

Jack took the envelope, opened it, and looked inside. It was a draft on the Bank of Manila.

"Thank you," he said.

"Balthasar tells me you would like a room for the night. I believe that may be arranged, Lt. Davis. Would you like to draw on your letter of credit?"

"No, but if I may, I'd like to leave some cash with you."

"Of course, sir."

Jack took the two thousand dollars he'd won at poker from his pocket. The concierge raised an eyebrow, the corners of his mouth turning up slightly.

"Cards?" he asked.

"Poker," Jack replied. He handed $1500 to the concierge, who got a receipt book from behind the counter and gave Jack a receipt for the money.

"Enjoy your stay, sir," the concierge said, handing Jack the receipt and a business card.

"Thanks."

The concierge made a courteous bow to Jack and gestured to the desk clerk as he turned to leave.

Balthasar scanned the pigeonholes behind the desk.

"Mm. Might have small room, fourth floor. No balcony, but windows open on the Bay. Good bed. Ten dollars for the night. That hokey-dokey?"

"Suits me."

The desk clerk handed Jack the guest register and indicated where he should sign. Jack took the fountain pen the man offered and signed, then handed him ten dollars.

"Have luggage?" the desk clerk asked.

Jack hefted his B4 bag.

Jack followed the bellhop up to Room 417. He changed into the light slacks and civilian shirt he had brought with him, then went out on the terrace by the hotel's swimming pool. The sun was setting in fiery, gaudy tropical reds and yellows, with purple-gray clouds changing colors as the sun continued its travel below the horizon, and the yellows losing ground to the red, which deepened in color as the stars came out and the lights on the ships in Manila Bay came on. Jack signaled a waiter, ordered Scotch, and sat under a striped umbrella to drink it when it came.

"Hey, Jack! What the hell ya doin' out here all by yourself?" a voice asked.

Jack turned and saw one of his squadron mates, Lt. Evan Toland, with a couple of other guys from the 21st. They were in uniform and obviously looking for a "good time," and elected to start with a few drinks at the Manila Hotel.

"Pull up a chair, gentlemen," said Jack. "Hell, I thought I'd have the place to myself, that's what I'm doing here. Couldn't stand the thought of olive drab or khaki another second and here you are anyway, all decked out in your Class A's."

Toland sat down, pushing his uniform hat back on his head. The other two lieutenants with him sat down as well. Jack tried to remember their names, but besides remembering that the tall blonde one was Smitty something or other and the stocky guy with dark hair was called Duane he was damned if he could remember anything else about them.

A waiter darted unobtrusively to their table, took orders, and was back momentarily with tall frosted glasses full of some sort of rum concoction.

Toland held up his glass. "Here's to the Japs!" he said. "Let 'em stay in Tokyo."

Smitty laughed and drank. Duane scowled.

"Bullcrap," Duane said. "Let the little yellow bastards come on down. We'll show them a thing or two about fighting, and then we'll send those B-17s to Tokyo and bomb it to wooden splinters."

Jack eyed Duane, sipped his drink, and said nothing. Duane was still flying the A-27; Lt. Dyess hadn't yet seen fit to trust him with a P-35. From what Jack observed of Duane's flying that was a reasonable decision. It wasn't that Duane was a bad pilot. His flying lacked a certain decisiveness, in Jack's opinion. He was one of those pilots who got through flight training by screwing up as little as possible, sticking as close to the rule book as he could, and taking no chances. That was all well and good, but a pilot who wouldn't push his own limits from time to time wasn't very interesting to Jack.

Smitty said, "Maybe you should see if that attack outfit that came over with us on the *Coolidge*, the 24th I think it is, needs pilots. I don't think Lt. Dyess likes you, Duane."

Toland snorted. "The 24th has plenty of pilots. They just don't have any damned airplanes. Supposed to have A-24 dive bombers but they haven't gotten here yet and who knows when they will."

"That's pretty screwed up," Smitty observed.

"But pretty normal for this place," Duane growled. "Jesus. Talk about scraping the bottom of the barrel. The A-27s were supposed to go to the Siamese and the P-35s were supposed to go the Swedes. I guess we'll get whatever the goddamned English didn't want next, while we send all our best airplanes to the RAF."

"You don't think we should help the English?" Jack asked.

"I think we ought to equip ourselves first before we send everything over there," Duane retorted. "We don't even have anti-aircraft guns, not proper ones, just some old 75-mm stuff that might not even work, the fuzes are so old."

"Are you spreading rumors or do you know this for a fact?" asked Jack. He took a sip of Scotch.

"I'll tell you how I know, Davis. I'm from New Mexico and my brother is over here up at Fort Stotsenburg with the 200th Coast Artillery, which despite its name is actually an anti-aircraft outfit. And not only is the damn ammunition ten or fifteen years old but the powder train fuzes they used back then are only good up to 20,000 feet. It's a good thing the Japs don't have any airplanes worth a shit, or we'd be in real trouble."

Jack blinked at him. "Don't you read the intelligence reports, Duane?"

"The hell you talkin' about?"

Jack signaled the waiter for another Scotch. When it came he sipped before looking at the glowering Duane. "I'm talking about the Mitsubishi bombers that have been bombing Chinese cities. You know, all those atrocity stories the newspapers keep writing."

Duane scoffed. "Newspapers. Those reporters don't know nothin'. Probably got all their guff from some doped-up Chinaman who wouldn't know a Jap bomber from a pair of chopsticks."

"Well, maybe so, but Intelligence seems to think those Jap bombers might be able to reach as high as 23,000 feet."

"Maybe they got one or two squadrons of modern bombers," Duane allowed. "But most of their stuff is ten years behind us. They don't have anything to match the P-38."

Jack bit off the retort that formed almost instantly, which was, neither do we, since all the P-38s are sitting back at the Lockheed factory in Burbank while the engineers figure out why you can't pull one out of a high-speed dive without the tail coming off.

Toland looked from Jack to Duane and then said brightly, "Who d'you guys like for the Rose Bowl this year?"

Smitty glanced at Duane and said, "Stanford. Don't know who they'll play, but Stanford's going. With Albert at quarterback and that Kmetovic guy running the ball they'll walk all over whoever they play."

"Aw, baloney," said Duane. "Those guys ain't so hot. The Cornhuskers have a pretty good team, too, and you can't ever count out Notre Dame."

Smitty snorted. "Irishmen and Catholics, what the hell do they know about football?"

With that Smitty and Duane were at each other over football. Jack sat back a little and looked at Toland, who winked solemnly at him.

Irina's Letter

Jack went to the elevator with two more Scotches in him than he really wanted. Toland tried to get him to come along with them, but Jack declined. He felt a little wobbly but not too bad. The elevator dropped him off on the fourth floor.

So once the door was locked behind him he sat on the bed, propped himself up with the pillows, and opened his B4 bag. The letters were on top, and he opened the one from his mother first.

His mother's letters always made him smile. Over the last year, since he joined the Air Corps, she gradually stopped reminding him to change his socks every day, or brush his teeth, or wash his hands before dinner, or any of those things that a mother of willful young boys has to pound into her sons on a regular basis. Instead she added political commentary: acerbic notes about President Roosevelt, whom she always referred to as "Mr. Roosevelt" or "that man in the White House;" grumbles about the state governor and the mayor of the nearest town, both of whom, Jack knew from personal observation, were terrified of Laura Lea. Both men had made the mistake of telling his mother that a woman had no place in politics. Jack was sure she had smiled sweetly and subsequently demonstrated to them the power of a Southern woman to work behind the scenes her mission to accomplish.

Saying that his mother was strong-willed was a little like saying that the sun is hot in August in Manila. He chuckled, reading her description of the misadventures of their new maid, a young woman of Italian descent, who evidently had droves of admirers among the young men at the nearby Army camp, where she also volunteered to work in the canteen. "I shall have to volunteer to work there myself, I fear," wrote Laura Lea, "if only to keep an eye on the girl." Besides, with both her boys in the service, she felt a little useless rattling around that big old house with nothing to do but supervise the staff and work in the rose garden.

Jack read the letter twice before putting it back in the envelope and opening the one from his brother Charlie.

The letter made him frown in thought. He decoded the family references and understood that the letter was written after the

35th sailed for "Plum" aboard the *Coolidge*. The letter referred to Charlie's first ride in a bomber and how he was looking forward to seeing the target of his first bomb run.

Jack knew perfectly well what Charlie was telling him. In 1938, he, Charlie and their father visited Manila, where then Lt. Col. Joseph Miller got Charlie a ride in an old Martin B-10. Charlie conducted a simulated bomb run on Clark Field.

Jack thought about hiring a car first thing in the morning and driving up to Clark Field. That was the only airfield in the Philippines that could handle the B-17s, even though he'd heard the engineers were scraping out new fields all over the islands. Besides, he'd seen a formation of B-17s the day before yesterday, sailing serenely along at 20,000 feet and still climbing as he sat in his P-35 at 10,000 feet with no oxygen, again.

Jack picked up the room phone and hung it up before the operator could answer. There wasn't any use driving up to Clark Field, not even knowing if Charlie was there. He couldn't call from a civilian line, either, for security reasons. He'd call when he got back to Nichols tomorrow afternoon.

When he hung up the phone he looked at the unopened letter still in his B4 bag and realized he'd been putting off reading it. He drew the envelope from the bag and turned it over in his hands, resisting the temptation to smell it. Finally he opened the envelope and drew out the letter.

It wasn't very long, only two pages, written in black ink on that cream-colored stationery Irina liked. When he opened the envelope a picture fell out. It was about wallet size, and it was another, more recent head-and-shoulders portrait shot of Irina, wearing her hair up in a way that emphasized her slender neck, looking slightly to her left into the camera, smiling in a way that made Jack catch his breath. He looked at the picture for a long time before he picked up the letter.

Her handwriting was looping and old-fashioned, mostly because she was taught to write by White Russian governesses whose penmanship was a product of the 19th Century. The words and letters were evenly spaced. He thought of her as he had first seen her, in the lobby of this very hotel, in June of 1938.

She was in an overstuffed chair in the lobby, reading a magazine, wearing a black sheath dress. Over her platinum-blonde hair she wore a pillbox hat with a gauzy veil. The dress came down to mid-calf. She wore long heels and the legs hidden by the dress were hinted at by curves beneath the fabric of the hem of her dress and the curves of her shapely calf. She looked up from her magazine as Jack passed by, and at first he thought she was much older than himself. He was 18 at the time, and thought she was in her twenties at least. It was an air of sophistication, experience, worldliness, even confidence, that she had. When she looked up at him Jack saw that her eyes were deep blue, a blue with hints and tones of violet, and her skin was creamy and fine-grained, only a few tones darker than alabaster. Her face had high cheekbones, her lips were relatively thin, but between her lips and her eyes there was a mobility, almost a dance between the two, that he thought hinted at some secret amusement, and then, as her eyes looked into his own, he seemed to be dropping into some vast depth, if only for a moment.

It was quite a strange sensation, he thought, remembering it: that feeling of falling when you know your feet are firmly on the floor, looking at her before he knew her name or anything else about her, as she broke contact with him and blinked, looking up and to her right as another man, a man in an Army uniform, stood in front of her as the elevator doors closed.

Jack blinked and consciously took his mind away from that memory. He looked at the letter.

Dear Jack, he read.

The last time I wrote I mentioned that Uncle Mischa was determined to move his interests to the States. So, by the time you get this letter we will be in Lisbon, where we will take the Pan Am flying boat to New York, some time before Christmas. You may remember I do not like to fly, but sailing across an Atlantic full of Nazi U-boats seems a temptation to Fate.

The last I heard from you, you were flying someplace you could not tell me about, in an airplane you liked but which most of your fellows did not. A handful, I believe you called it? I hope this makes you happy, but you know how I feel about pilots. I do not call love a misfortune, and in the horrible madness the world seems determined to fall into I see there is no safety for anyone.

It is simply my fate to care for a man who is determined to face needless peril even in time of war. Please, Jack, please, remember when you fly, and when you fight if it should come to that, that my heart rides with you. I have lost too many of those I love to lose you too.

Uncle Mischa and I will take an apartment in Los Angeles, but he speaks of finding something more permanent in Beverly Hills. He enjoys being a "money man" to the Hollywood film industry. He never speaks of it to me – I am, after all, a young woman of gentle upbringing – but I am not so inexperienced as to be unaware of his interest in young actresses, of which there seem to be an endless supply, working all sorts of different jobs and hoping to be noticed for a part in the movies. I rather thought we'd end up in New York. After all, Uncle Mischa is a banker, and for that the best place to live after Bern or London is your New York City. Maybe nowadays New York City is even better. Hitler doesn't have a navy that can take his tanks across the Atlantic, and the Japanese already have their hands full in China, after all. But Uncle Mischa says your President Roosevelt may have underestimated the Japanese when he cut off oil and steel exports to Japan. If people cannot trade for what they want, he said, then they will take what they want.

I do not want to leave my home, but I think Uncle Mischa is right. But then, if we live in Los Angeles, perhaps we may see each other again. I often think of our little time here in Bern together. It seems so long ago, and I would like for that time to come again.

I would like that very much, Jack.

With all my love,

Irina

Jack sighed, looking at her signature, and looked at the picture again. It was the first one she had ever sent him. She looked the same as he remembered; maybe a little older, more like the woman he thought he had seen the first time he saw her.

She loved him. It made his heart squeeze in his chest, it made the blood rush to...well, an inconvenient place under the circumstances. He wondered what it would be like, seeing her again. He looked at the picture for a long time before he finally put it away.

He stripped and climbed into bed before turning out the room light. It took a lot of staring at the shadowed ceiling with its slowly turning fan before sleep came.

CHAPTER SIX
To Hickam Field

Simple Confusion

Al Stern yawned and shook his head, staring down at the logbook on the tiny desk.

There wasn't much light in the nose of the B-17. Ultraviolet lights caused the luminescent dials of his instruments to glow. It was cool and noisy with the rush of the air around the fuselage and the roaring engines on the wing. The nearest one was only twelve feet away.

Captain Davis, Al reflected, was right about this trip. He was learning a lot about the B-17. He was learning how to crawl up that little tunnel between the nose and the flight deck with his octant and notebook and pencils, then climb up into the astrodome and take star sights, then crawl back down to this little desk with its dim light and repeater instruments and work out his position fix. He'd done it seven times already, taking them halfway to Hickam Field from Hamilton Field. Captain Davis felt so comfortable before the last fix he announced he was taking a nap, and promptly corked off.

Al looked at the clock, yawning again. Speaking of that crawl up the tunnel, it was about time for another star sight. He'd taken sights, checked them against his dead reckoning, allowed for observed wind, checked again against the radio bearings from radio stations in California. For the last three hours, though, those bearings had grown more uncertain as the radio stations wavered in and out of audibility. He hadn't been able to take reliable bearings with the radio compass for two hours now, and probably wouldn't until they got closer to Honolulu.

He gathered up his octant and notebook, glancing at the gyrocompass. The heading would change about two degrees to the south this time, he thought, and...

Al stopped dead, looking at the compass. It was steady on heading 234.

The only problem was it was supposed to be 243.

Al reached out and tapped the face of the instrument. It wobbled a tiny bit and steadied back on 234.

For a moment Al thought the gyro must have gone bad, but when he looked at the magnetic compass, it read 237. That allowed two degrees for magnetic variation and another degree for the wind slightly out of the west.

Except the magnetic compass should have read 246.

They were off heading by 9 degrees.

Al took a deep breath. "Navigator to copilot."

"Yeah, go ahead, Al," Payne replied.

"Mike, what heading do you have on the autopilot?"

"Two-three-four," said Payne.

His voice was so normal and matter-of-fact that it made Al stop and wonder if that was the right heading after all. He looked down at his logbook. His notes showed a progression of small heading changes over the last seven hours, a degree or two at a time to keep the bomber on the great circle route between Hamilton and Hickam.

The heading should be 243.

Al got his kit together and crawled up the tunnel to the flight deck. Payne grinned over his shoulder at him. The grin faded when he saw the look on Al's face.

The flight deck was a noisy place. Al leaned close to Payne's ear to make himself heard without shouting.

"Mike, we're supposed to be on heading 243."

"No, you said..." Payne stopped in mid-sentence, looking at the gyrocompass and the autopilot.

Then he looked at Al.

Out of the corner of his eye Al saw Captain Davis stir and sit up, stretching in his seat.

Davis looked at the instruments and stiffened when he came to the gyrocompass. Al met his eyes when he turned to look at them.

It wasn't easy, but he did it.

"We're off heading," said Davis.

"Yes, sir," said Al.

"How long have you known about it?"

"I just figured it out, sir."

"You just figured it out? Navigator, how long have we been off heading?"

"Since my last sight, sir. About an hour."

Charlie held Al's eyes for a moment. Then he looked at Payne.

"Mr. Payne? You have something to add?"

"It's my fault, sir. I put the wrong heading on the autopilot."

Charlie looked from Payne to Stern and back. "You're only partly right, Mr. Payne. It's not just you. We're all in this together. *We* screwed up. I screwed up by taking a nap. You, Payne, screwed up because you put in the wrong heading when you should've been paying more attention. Stern, you screwed up because you didn't double-check the heading Payne put in. So here we are, off heading and our fuel running low. What do you intend to do about it, Mr. Navigator?"

Al blinked.

"Don't give me that look, Stern. I already know what we should do. I want you two to figure this out, and I'm going to give you about two minutes to do it."

Al said, "Recommend we come to heading 243 right now, sir."

"Oh? Without taking a star sight first and establishing our position?"

"We've set south of our heading, sir, but not all that far. On 243 we'll still hit the Hawaiian Islands. That will give me time to work out our position and a new heading."

130

To Al's surprise, Captain Davis nodded at once. "All right. Payne, take the auto-pilot off. Hand-fly on heading 243. Do it now."

"Yes, sir!" Payne flipped off the autopilot and gently banked the B-17 to the right until the gyrocompass read 243.

At a look from Davis, Al took the two steps to the flight commander's chair and lifted it into the astrodome.

Al found there was adrenaline in his blood. It made his hands shake a little. He took a deep breath, and then another. He thought, *If I'm this scared now, what will happen when someone shoots at me?*

He brought up the octant, steadying it on the lip of the astrodome. He peered through the octant's eyepiece and clicked the trigger.

Building a Crew

Charlie didn't look around when Stern came up the tunnel from the nose. He kept a slight frown on his face, because Payne was stealing looks at him from time to time as if to see how angry he was. So Charlie kept frowning, and looked out the flight deck window into the night sky to port, where he could see the silver wings of the bomber gleaming faintly in the starlight, which also reflected from the waves of the ocean six thousand feet below them.

The truth was that Charlie was pleased with events. Payne's relatively minor error – minor, of course, only because it had been caught before it became a major problem – presented Charlie with what his instructors back at the Point had called an opportunity to demonstrate leadership.

Upon awakening from his nap, Charlie's first act had been to scan the instruments, especially the engine gauges. The even rumble and vibration told him a lot, but the gauges confirmed that the four Wright Cyclones were running just the way they should. Then Charlie looked at the flight instruments; his eye slid past the gyrocompass and then jerked back at once as he realized the airplane was ten degrees off heading. His first impulse was to yank off the autopilot and turn the airplane to a westerly heading.

Then training asserted itself. Bob Payne seemed like a fair pilot, but inexperienced; Stern impressed him as having a certain degree of nerve and presence of mind, but with even less experience than Payne. They desperately needed to learn to work together as a team, because a bomber crew that didn't work together as a team was going to end up in a smoking hole together some day.

Charlie knew exactly what had happened. Stern had called up the heading correction to Payne, who had entered the wrong heading by transposing the last two digits. Then neither copilot nor navigator had caught the error by double-checking each other. In short, they had not communicated.

It surprised and gratified Charlie that Al Stern, instead of going mute like Bob Payne, came up at once with a workable plan to get them back on heading. Charlie might have gone a few degrees north of 243 to start making up the distance they'd gone to the south, but the geometry of the problem was pretty obvious. So, maybe not the absolute best plan, but workable, and more to the point, it was offered at once.

Charlie didn't miss the slight surprise in Al Stern's voice when he agreed to Al's suggestion. Agreeing that way was also part of the opportunity; teamwork meant trusting each other, and rebuilding that trust was part of it. If it didn't mean compromising the safety of his crew and his airplane, that is.

After Stern came down from the astrodome and went to compute his fix Charlie leaned over and spoke to Payne.

"Why didn't you ask Mr. Stern about the heading? Weren't you paying attention?"

"Sir, we were on autopilot, and..."

"The god-damned autopilot is just a machine, Bob. It does exactly what you tell it to do, and if you tell it to do the wrong thing, it's going to do just that."

Payne had no reply to that.

Twenty minutes went by and Stern didn't call for a heading correction. Charlie left his seat and went down the tunnel to the nose compartment. He could see Stern's back as the navigator hunched over in the dim light, just enough to see his work. Charlie hung back in the shadow, crouched down on his knees.

Stern was looking back and forth between a sheet of paper on the desk and a table of numbers. After a moment, he started to crumple the piece of paper.

Charlie noticed there were two other crumpled sheets at the foot of the desk.

"What's wrong, Al?" he asked, pitching his voice to carry over the engines and the wind.

Stern looked at him. "I keep coming up with a number that's way too small," he said.

"Too small? You mean, all this time you've been trying to convince yourself we really are only about thirty miles south of where we should be?"

The little navigator blinked at Charlie in surprise. "Well...yes, sir."

Then Stern blurted, "How did you know?"

"It's just a little simple trigonometry," Charlie told him. "So what's the problem?"

"It's...Captain, we were off heading."

"That's right."

"But..."

"But you think you ought to be shot for dereliction of duty?" Charlie grinned. "I'm happy you take your responsibilities as a navigator seriously, Al, but the truth is, as foul-ups go, this one isn't bad. Now what heading should we be on?"

"Two four three," Al said. His voice was just audible.

"Hm. You're sure about it?"

"Yes, sir."

"OK. Go tell Payne. I'll be right behind you."

"Don't you want to check my work?"

"No, Al." Charlie looked Stern in the eye. "You're the navigator. I'm not always going to have time to check your work. You made a mistake, but it wasn't in your navigation. Just thank God this wasn't an expensive mistake."

Lefkowicz Wakes Up

It was another seven hours to Hickam Field, but as they neared their destination it became clear to Charlie that there were two things he could count on. First, that Payne would absolutely, positively not make that mistake again. Payne's embarrassment, his recognition of the position he'd put the entire crew in, and the look of naked determination on his face made that obvious. Second, the growing realization that, despite his own statements to the contrary and Charlie's feeling that Stern's education as a navigator had been dangerously rushed in order to fill slots on combat crews, Al Stern had all the makings of a competent navigator.

The blinking surprise on Al's face, coupled with first a little worry, and then that indefinable look that comes across a man's face when he realizes you trust him with more than just being right, came and went. It wasn't easy to see in the dim fluorescent light over the navigator's desk in the cramped nose of the Boeing, but Charlie and Stern were crouched on the deck shoulder to shoulder.

But that had been the middle of the night over the empty Pacific with all the uncertainty and worry that implied. Now it was early morning with Oahu dead ahead, confirmed by an RDF bearing. The sun rising behind them brought the crew awake from the semi-doze of the long night flight.

There was one more surprise in store.

Two hours before they landed at Hickam, Pvt. Lefkowicz came up to the flight deck. He had, as far as Charlie knew, gone to sleep not long after the airplane took off and stayed that way. Now behind them there was the first hint of salmon-pink dawn. Ahead of them, below the horizon and still in the dark, lay the island of Oahu. Sparks had been in radio contact with Hickam for the last hour and they were expected.

Charlie felt a tap on his shoulder. When he turned he saw Lefkowicz standing just behind his seat, crouched over in the low ceilinged flight deck.

"What is it, Lefkowicz?" he asked, a little more brusquely than he intended.

"Skipper, I got to looking at the waist guns. I don't think they've been cleaned in awhile and there's nothing to clean them with aboard. Not that I could find."

That made Charlie blink. "Are they operable?"

"Well, yes, sir, but your chances of a stoppage are pretty good. I'd feel better stripping 'em down and giving 'em a good going-over. Any chance we can get a couple cleaning kits and some solvent at Hickam?"

Charlie thought that one over. God knows where the guns on this airplane had come from, and if the waist guns were in bad shape, the others should be checked as well. For that matter there was the little problem that they hadn't taken aboard any .50-caliber ammunition, to save weight for the flight to Hickam.

"We'll stop overnight at Hickam before we go on to Midway Island," Charlie had told Lefkowicz. "I'll see what I can do about some kits and ammo then."

Lefkowicz nodded and then hesitated.

"Go on, Lefkowicz."

"Sir, one of the mechanics left some rags in the waist section. If I could have maybe a little gasoline, I could go ahead and field strip the guns. I can't do anything about the bores without a cleaning kit, but at least I can be sure the action is good."

Charlie nodded. "Flight engineer, pilot," he said over the intercom.

"Pilot, flight engineer, go ahead."

"Kim, Lefkowicz needs about a pint of gas to clean the waist guns. Can you help him out?"

"Sure thing, Skipper."

"Thanks, Kim. Pilot out."

By the time they had touched down at Hickam, Lefkowicz had the waist guns clean and functional. He had even produced a small tool kit and a chamois cloth from his duffle bag. Once Smith saw what he was doing he took his upper guns from stowage and got Lefkowicz to show him the finer points of stripping and cleaning the weapon.

CHAPTER SEVEN
Realities

Follow Me, Two

Jack Davis looked around the sky through the ribbed canopy of the P-35. Off his right wing the P-35 flown by Roy Chant bobbed gently in formation. Ten thousand feet below them, at ten o'clock, were three lumbering B-18A Bolo bombers in an arrowhead formation. Jack scanned across the Seversky's instrument panel and scanned the sky again, looking for the interceptors protecting the city of Manila, in sight ahead of them, fifteen miles away across the bay.

The last two days had meant a lot of flying, sunup to sundown, up and down the pattern at Nichols Field in the back seat of an A-27, but by sundown yesterday he'd flown with all the other guys in the squadron. Dyess gave him a list of things to do, habits to check on, stuff intended to shake the rust of seven weeks at sea off a bunch of young pilots who didn't have that much time to begin with. Jack didn't think he'd enjoy the work when he started. After the third student, though, he began to enjoy himself.

As a reward Dyess told him to take Roy Chant and go up to Clark Field with a couple of P-35s to fly escort for a flight of creaky old B-18 Bolo bombers on a practice mission. That was early this morning.

Somewhere in this vicinity, Jack was sure, there would be an enemy interceptor force, led by Buzz Wagner and flying P-40s. He grimaced under his oxygen mask, looking up into the sun.

The service ceiling of the P-35A was a little over 31,000 feet. That was with a new or at least a well-maintained engine and a relatively new airframe, none of which applied to these P-35s.

Over 17,000 feet the P-40's single-stage supercharger was ineffective and the airplane's performance fell off. Jack hoped he could use that to his advantage, even in a P-35 with a worn-out engine.

That was why Jack and Roy Chant took off from Clark Field twenty minutes before the B-18s did, to climb to their present altitude of 23,000 feet. Even though the service ceiling of the P-35 was alleged by the Seversky engineers to be 31,000 feet, Jack felt he was lucky to get up to 23,000 considering the well-worn engines in the P-35s.

His orders from Dyess had been pretty vague; his squadron commander said only, "There's a flight of Bolos starting from Clark on a practice mission to Manila. You and Chant take a couple of P-35s and act as escort. The 17th will run a practice intercept on you somewhere between Clark and Manila. Any questions?"

Jack had questions but he knew they'd be futile, so he and Chant flew up to Clark Field instead.

"Cherokee Blue Leader from Hightower, come in."

"Hightower" was the call sign of the Bolo flight leader. Jack keyed his radio. "This is Cherokee Blue Leader, go ahead, Hightower."

"Cherokee, we're starting our bomb run now."

"Acknowledged, Hightower."

"Lead from Blue Two."

"Go ahead, Two."

"I got a funny feeling, Lead."

"Feel all you like, Two, do you see anything?"

"Negative, Lead."

Jack took a deep breath and checked his armament panel to be sure his switches were off. He didn't want to get his adrenaline running and start shooting by mistake.

"Two."

"Go ahead, Lead."

"Check your armament panel. Gun switches off."

"Ah, roger, Lead, gun switches are off."

They neared the shore at the eastern end of Manila Bay. The shipping in the harbor was plain to see as well as the city itself. At the mission briefing the bomber pilots condescended to inform the two pursuit pilots that their intended target was the building on Neilsen Field that housed the headquarters of Colonel Hal George's Interceptor Command. The bomber guys seemed to think that was pretty funny.

What was funny, Jack thought, as he scanned the sky around him with increasing perplexity, was that they were damned near the target and there wasn't a sign of interception. Wagner and his boys might be waiting to bounce them during egress from the target.

"Two, keep your eyes peeled. Maybe they'll jump us after the Bolos finish their bomb runs."

"Roger, Lead."

Jack continued his scan, kicking his rudder to look behind him and clear his tail. There wasn't much the bombers could do if they were attacked, anyway, since the Bolo only carried three .30-caliber machine guns for defensive purposes, one in the nose and the other in a retractable dorsal turret amidships. There was one that was supposed to fire from the belly of the airplane somewhere but Jack had never been able to figure out where it was mounted. There wasn't a gun tub like the ones on a B-17.

"Cherokee Blue Leader, this is Hightower. Bombs away."

"Acknowledged, Hightower."

The Bolos began a majestic sweeping turn to the north. The Bolo had the big wing of a Douglas DC-2 and its twin engines were the same as a B-17 carried. It was slow as a pig and about as graceful as your average cow. "Majestic" was the most charitable way to describe the unhurried standard-rate turn performed by the bombers.

Jack looked south of Manila. He could clearly see the runway at Nichols Field, but at 23,000 feet detail was lacking. It was a hell of a view, though. He could make out the volcano north of Clark Field, Manila Bay to the west with the island of Corregidor in plain sight south of the Bataan Peninsula. Everywhere you looked there were green and brown islands and the hundreds of shades of blue and green water common to the tropics.

Jack turned to follow the B-18s, which were now a mile north and still ten thousand feet below.

There was a glint, a hint of motion. Something white moved across the green-brown land six miles below.

"Bandits, four o'clock low," he called. "Hightower, Hightower, this is Cherokee Blue Leader, bandit at your five o'clock, climbing to your altitude. Two, you see him?"

"Roger, Lead, got the bandit."

Jack looked again and saw another P-40 trailing the first one, climbing to the altitude of the B-18s.

"Two, how many bandits d'you count?"

"Lead, Two sees two repeat two bandits. Shall we go after them?"

"Two, hold your position. There's no hurry."

Jack cleared his tail again and froze.

A thousand feet above and maybe two miles back were another pair of P-40s. He could tell them by the dihedral of the wings and the skinny nose in front view.

Jack looked over his shoulder at Chant, pointed emphatically astern, and then held his finger up in front of his oxygen mask in a "Sh" gesture. Chant looked at him for a moment, then nodded and looked astern. When he looked back he held up two fingers. Jack nodded.

That sneaky bastard Wagner! He launched the high fighters early, way early, because it took half of forever to climb to 24,000 feet in a P-40. "Service ceiling" didn't mean you couldn't go higher; just that above the service ceiling you couldn't coax anything more than a hundred feet per minute out of the airplane. Jack looked back at the trailing P-40s.

The pursuers were clean. Either they had already jettisoned their aux tanks or they had taken off without them to reduce weight and drag. Jack didn't think that was right; the P-40 would

139

burn the fuel in the aux tank climbing to this altitude. The P-40s in pursuit couldn't have a lot of fuel left.

So here were the two P-40s tailing them, getting ready to bounce them from the rear when they went after the P-40s climbing to altitude after the Bolos. A nice little hammer and anvil job.

"Two, with me," Jack said. He advanced his throttle to the stop and eased back on the stick. At this altitude you couldn't move too suddenly or you'd stall; the thin air wouldn't support the wings the way it would at lower altitudes with denser air.

He was betting they could out-climb the P-40s behind them, maybe even make them stall out and tumble, then bounce the low flight before the high pair recovered.

Jack swept his engine instruments and looked over at Chant, who gave him the "OK" sign with thumb and forefinger. Then Jack looked astern at the P-40s, who looked a little bigger; they were accelerating, using their superior altitude to trade for airspeed and overtake the P-35s before they could climb above them. Jack nodded, thinking fast.

Was it Wagner back there? If Buzz was in the cockpit of one of those P-40s what Jack had in mind might not work, and there was only one way to find out.

The P-40s were close now, not quite in gun range, and Jack eased his P-35 into a left turn. Chant followed him, Jack looking over his shoulder to check his wingman and the P-40s astern of them.

Both pursuers entered a turn.

The P-40's wing loading was higher than the P-35's. In a turn at this altitude there was a good chance the P-40 would stall first.

"Stay with me, Two," he radioed, and steepened the turn while still climbing. Airspeed dropped as the g-force increased, weighing him down into his seat, until Jack was a few knots away from an accelerated stall.

Chant was with him but seemed to be falling slightly astern, easing out, bank angle not quite as sharp; Jack was tempted to tell him to close it up and realized he could make the situation work to his advantage.

Jack looked below at the P-40s pursuing the bombers; they were still way behind the Bolos. Jack still had a few minutes. He

140

couldn't dive on the low P-40s without having the guys behind him crawl up his backside, and the P-40 would catch a P-35 in a dive.

Suddenly one of the P-40s behind them snapped over in an accelerated stall. The P-40 was in a spin, tumbling for the ground below; not, as Jack recalled, a maneuver recommended in the manual.

"Two, we'll settle the guy behind us first," he radioed. He hoped the guy behind them was listening, because he'd just figured out it wasn't, couldn't be Wagner.

"Two, can you close it up a little?"

"Lead, she feels a little wobbly as it is."

"OK, Two. Hold her at that."

Even if Chant wasn't turning with Jack both of them were still turning inside the P-40, which was slipping farther and farther behind. By now they were on opposite sides of a circle. The P-40 pilot looked up through his canopy at Jack. Gingerly, delicately, Jack took his left hand off the throttle, being very careful not to disturb the balance he was keeping on his controls, and waved at the other pilot.

The other guy waved back – and promptly stalled and began to spin out.

Nope. Definitely not Wagner.

"Follow me, Two," Jack radioed.

He leveled his wings and pushed over into a dive. Chant closed in. Jack looked to the right and saw the first P-40, still tumbling in a wicked spin below them.

Below them the two P-40s pursuing the bombers were still climbing, overhauling the bombers, which had gone to full throttle to extend the pursuit. "Full throttle" for a Bolo was only about 200 mph, but every little bit helped.

Jack looked over his shoulder. The first P-40 came out of its spin, righted a little too hard and spun out again. The second P-40 recovered and dove in pursuit.

It was going to be close. Jack pushed the throttle forward a little more and the engine howled out a few more RPMs.

"C'mon, baby," he whispered.

The P-40s below them began to turn away from the bombers, attempting to convert Jack's bounce into a mutual head-on pass.

"Two, take the guy on the right," Jack called.

"Lead, he's in my sights."

Jack looked over his shoulder again. The first P-40 was spinning and looked dangerously low, but that meant he was out of the fight. The second P-40 was catching up awfully quick, but the two low P-40s had left their evasive turn a bit late.

The P-40 in Jack's sights grew, grew, expanding until its olive-drab wings were beyond the sight ring, and Jack felt the near-involuntary pressure of his finger on the trigger. He released it convulsively.

"P-40, you're dead," he called over the radio.

"Other P-40, you're a flamer," Chant responded.

Jack leveled his wings and reduced his bank angle. The P-40s kept turning away from him.

"OK, Two, on my call, break right."

"Roger, Lead."

Jack watched the other P-40 a moment longer.

"Two, break break, BREAK NOW."

Chant broke hard right, Jack pulled hard left. The P-40 was by them like a locomotive, turning hard to the left after Jack but overshooting.

"He's yours, Two," Jack called.

Jack watched as Chant pulled onto the tail of the P-40, who promptly put his nose down and dove away from the fight. Jack looked back for the other P-40s but they were all headed for Nichols, low on fuel. To the north the B-18s were still in their "V" formation, headed for Clark Field, and now nearly over the north shore of Manila Bay.

He swept his instrument panel. Good engine, but fuel looking a bit low.

"How's your fuel, Two?" he called.

"Gonna have to head for a gas station soon, Lead," Chant replied.

Jack looked around again. Except for the B-18s head back to Clark to the north and the P-40s entering the landing pattern at Nichols the sky was clear of other aircraft.

"Two, keep your eyes open. I have a feeling this isn't over."

"OK, Lead, just as long as we head to the barn."

"Roger that."

Jack turned south. "Nichols Field, Army Two-Four-Five," he radioed.

"Go ahead, Two-Four-Five, this is Nichols."

"Two-Four-Five with a flight of two, request landing instructions."

"Roger, Two-Four-Five. Is that you north of the field, at ten thousand feet?"

"That's us."

"Field should be clear by the time you get here. Wind two-three-two at seven mph, altimeter two-niner-niner-niner."

"Two-niner-niner-niner," Jack replied, setting his altimeter. "Cherokee Blue flight inbound, Nichols."

"Understood, Two-Four-Five."

Jack looked over his shoulder at Chant, whose head was down, looking at something on his instrument panel.

"Two from Lead."

"Yeah, go ahead, Lead."

"You OK back there?"

"Oil pressure gauge dropped real sudden-like, Jack, and then came back up slow."

"I'll look you over."

Jack throttled back, descending slightly, until he could look up at the gull-gray underside of Chant's P-35. The oil cooler looked fine and there weren't any obvious streaks of oil or anything else that might identify an oil system leak.

He moved from under the other pursuit and came up alongside it. Chant looked at him across the space of their wings.

"Don't see anything but paint, Roy. What are the rest of your gauges doing?"

"Oil pressure is OK but now the cylinder head temps are coming up."

"OK. Let's throttle back. We've got plenty of altitude. I'll radio the field we're coming straight in. No fancy stuff this time, just a straight-in approach and landing."

Chant nodded emphatically inside his cockpit. "You're a mind-reader, Jack."

Jack throttled back and keyed his radio again.

Before he could speak there was a bright streamer of flame from under Chant's engine cowling, like a burning yellow flower

143

engulfing the entire fuselage aft of the cowling. There was a puff of black smoke. Flaming parts flew out of the engine. The propeller jerked to a sudden stop and Chant's airplane slowed radically.

"Roy! Bail out, bail out, get out of there! Roy!"

Jack instinctively moved away from the burning airplane. As he did Chant's P-35 suddenly pulled straight up, trailing flame and smoke behind it, climbing until it stalled and fell over in a spin.

Jack flew in a wide spiral beside the spinning, burning pursuit, yelling and pleading over the radio for Chant to bail out, bail out, get the hell out of there you stupid bastard *Chant, get the hell out of there!*

Chant's P-35 continued its flaming spiral all the way down to the blue waters of Manila Bay. Jack pulled out and away, circling over the spot where Chant went in, marked only by steam, a fading streamer of smoke, and a few bits of floating debris.

Let's Fly

Jack pushed the throttle forward, ran the engine up for a moment, then shut it down. The propeller of Jack's P-35 windmilled to a stop. There was silence for a moment except for the pop-ting sounds of the radial engine cooling. Then the aircraft rocked as someone climbed on the wing, and put a hand on Jack's shoulder.

Jack looked up into the face of Ed Dyess, who was crouched by the cockpit.

"What happened to Chant?" he asked.

Jack looked up at Dyess. It was a moment before he could speak, and he saw Dyess' eyes widen and blink. The squadron commander's lips parted.

"His engine caught fire, Ed," Jack said. "Nothing but flames from the cowling back. The fuel pump must have been spraying gasoline into the fire once it started."

Dyess nodded. "Come on. Let's get you out of there."

Dyess reached in and hit the quick-release lever on Jack's safety harness. Jack stood up and climbed down from the cockpit as Dyess backed down the wing.

144

Jack leaned against the fuselage and undid the straps on his parachute harness. He watched his fingers moving over the straps and buckles with unhurried sure motions, a little surprised at how easily they moved, not altogether sure those were his fingers. He shrugged out of the harness and put the parachute pack on the wing before he pulled off his helmet, running his fingers through his sweat-soaked hair.

He looked over Dyess' shoulder at the Ops Shack. It looked like the whole damned squadron was gathered there, standing on the porch, smoking or staring aimlessly down the runway or up into the sky.

Dyess followed his look. When he turned back he said, "Why don't you wait here, Jack."

Jack nodded and sat down on the trailing edge of the wing at the wing root. He unzipped his jacket and laid it on the wing. It was hot and humid, like it was always hot and humid in the Philippines. Jack felt the sweat running from his armpits and down his back. He sighed and turned his face up to the sky, eyes closed, feeling the sun's heat on his eyelids.

Behind his eyelids he could see the fire of his father's airplane, strewn across the ground and burning next to the south pylon at Cleveland. He could feel the rough hands on his arms, holding him back from running to the wreck. But he could still see his father sitting in the cockpit of that damned racing airplane, and through the flames, just for an instant, he looked into his father's eyes.

Just before the flames obliterated everything Jack saw his father wink at him.

So what was Chant thinking as the fire rushed back over the fuselage? Did it torch into the cockpit? Did it come through the oxygen system, searing his lungs and his throat? Was that why Chant never answered his radio calls, even to scream? When the P-35 pulled up and stalled, was that because the control cables were burned through, or because Chant pulled back on the stick in agony, oblivious to everything but the fire consuming his flesh?

Jack deliberately opened his eyes, letting the sun sear into them, blinking the light away. He took a few deep breaths,

145

looking down at the ground, blinking against the spots left by the sun's glare.

Chant lay at the bottom of Manila Bay in what was left of his airplane. And Jack was here, looking at the scraggly grass beside the runway at Nichols Field, alone with the fact that Chant was dead.

"Jack."

He looked up. Dyess had come back. Lt. Mahony, the base operations officer, was with him.

"Come on," Dyess said. "Let's get the report out of the way. There'll have to be an accident investigation. Mahony here will be the investigating officer."

Jack looked at the man with Dyess. Mahony was about Dyess' age and also a first lieutenant.

"Yes, sir," Jack said.

Mahony sat with Jack and Dyess in a corner of the Ops shack. Mahony had a pad of paper and some sharpened pencils. An enlisted man brought them cold Coca-Colas to drink.

Mahony led Jack through the escort and intercept exercise with questions about height, fuel consumption, time of sighting the P-40 interceptors and maneuvers during the fight.

"And that was all Lt. Chant said? That his oil pressure gauge was fluctuating and the cylinder head temps were climbing?" Mahony concluded.

"Yes, sir. Then I looked over the underside of his P-35. I didn't see any oil coming out of the engine or anything obvious."

Mahony nodded as he wrote. Then he paused, tapping his pencil absently on the pad, before looking at Dyess.

" Break in the fuel line downstream of the pump?" he asked the squadron commander.

Dyess shrugged. "The guys in the tower had binoculars on Chant's ship most of the way down. Their description of the fire matches what Davis described. So yeah, something had to be pouring gas into the fire at a most ungodly rate."

Mahony frowned and nodded. "We'll have to see if the Navy will pull the wreck up. I'll get on the horn to the liaison at Cavite Navy Yard and see what they can do for us. They had a rescue launch out mounting a search for debris anyway, so they should know pretty well where the crash site is."

Dyess said, "See what assistance they need from us, if anything."

Mahony nodded in reply. "OK. That's all I need for right now, Boyd. I'll have my notes typed up and Lt. Davis should review them, make any additions he thinks are necessary, then sign them and get them back to me."

"OK, Grant."

Mahony stood and left. Dyess looked at Jack.

"Let me ask a silly question, Jack. How are you doing?"

Jack shook his head. "I'll be OK."

"I'm glad but it isn't exactly what I asked."

"Yes, sir. I'm just trying to understand."

"Understand?" Dyess frowned. "What do you mean?"

"I'm not even sure myself," Jack said softly. He thought of his Dad winking at him before the flames came up over the cockpit of the racer. He thought about the way the horizon looked as he climbed up above the runway. He thought about the times he'd been scared in an airplane, when he didn't understand what it was doing, and how the fear left him when he did understand and could do something about it.

"Nothing, I guess," he went said after a moment. "Chant's dead. We're not."

"That's right," said Dyess. He looked at Jack a moment longer before nodding incrementally. "You want to take the rest of the night off, go get drunk somewhere?"

"No, Skipper, not really."

"What would you like to do?"

"I'd like to go flying."

"OK. I'll come with you. We'll take one of the A-27s."

Jack looked up at Dyess, who was standing. Dyess' face was expressionless, but the eyes, something about Dyess' eyes; Jack thought of refusing, saying he'd rather be by himself, but the expression in Dyess' eyes stopped him.

"Yes, sir," he said.

Shallow Waters

Dyess climbed into the front cockpit of the A-27. After a moment's hesitation Jack climbed into the back, buckled himself

147

in, and crossed his hands in his lap. Dyess handled it all; signing the Form One, talking to the ground crew, starting the engine, getting clearance from the tower, taxiing into the wind and taking off. As soon as they were in the air Jack looked over the edge of the cockpit at Manila Bay to the west. At about the spot he remembered there was a boat of some kind, too big for a fishing boat, too small for anything commercial, more like a fast yacht of the sort his fraternity brothers from New England liked to play around with in the summertime. The boat wasn't moving but didn't appear to be anchored. Jack wondered how deep the water was at that point.

As soon as Dyess had the flaps and gear up he turned northwest and headed for the boat.

Jack looked over the right side of the airplane as they passed over the shore. He could see the Manila Hotel below them and the walled city of Intramuros across the avenue to the north of the hotel.

"How about it, Jack?" Dyess asked over the intercom. "Are they in the right spot?"

"Pretty close, Skipper," he replied. "Maybe we could do a circle over the boat when we get there? I should be able to tell for sure."

"What altitude were you at when you pulled out?"

Jack looked at the altimeter. They were at one thousand feet above field elevation, which seemed about right. "Hold this altitude."

A moment later Dyess dipped the left wing and did a pylon turn around the boat, or launch, or whatever it was. Looking at it Jack was pretty sure it had been a motor yacht. The decks were polished and gleaming, some sort of brown wood like teak or mahogany, and the hull was still snowy white. The sailors looked up and waved. As Jack watched one of them dove over the side with a line attached.

"Guess the water here is pretty shallow after all," he remarked. "They just sent a guy down with a line."

Dyess circled the launch. Jack alternated between watching the sky around them and the sailors on the launch. In a minute or so the diver surfaced and clung to the ladder over the side of the launch. He rested for a moment. The A-27 was low enough that

Jack could see the diver was breathing deliberately in and out. Then the man dove again. When he came up he motioned to the sailors on deck, who began to pull on the line that went into the water.

At first the sailors pulled without any result. The diver went back down. While he was down the sailors started pulling again, hand over hand this time, and the diver broke the surface and went up the side of the launch. Another sailor dropped a weighted line into the water with a bright yellow float attached.

Then something dark broke the water, attached to the line the sailors were hauling on.

It was what was left of Chant's burned and blackened body.

The sailors pulled Chant's body out of the water and laid it on the forward deck of the launch. One of the sailors covered it with a blanket. The launch started to move away towards the Cavite Navy Yard. Dyess turned the A-27 and made a low pass beside the launch, rocking his wings in salute. The sailors on deck waved in reply.

A Powerful Instinct

Jack sat at a desk looking at the notes Lt. Mahony's clerk had typed up. It was on a form for Preliminary Accident Investigation and the notes, reduced to terse officialese, conveyed nothing to Jack except a sense of numbness. He sighed, reread the same sentence for the third time, and managed to get through the last paragraph. At the bottom there was a line for his signature; the clerk had already typed in his name. Jack signed the report and walked back to Dyess' office.

Dyess looked up from his own report at Jack's knock and beckoned him to come in.

"It looks pretty complete to me, Skipper," Jack said. He put the report he had signed on Dyess' desk.

The squadron commander looked at it briefly and placed it in a manila file folder.

"Sit down, Jack," Dyess said, motioning to a chair in front of his desk.

Jack sat. Dyess pulled a cigarette from the pack lying on his desk. He struck a kitchen match, waited until it had a steady flame, and then lit up. He exhaled a cloud of smoke at the ceiling, where it was promptly dispersed around the room by the ceiling fan.

"We haven't talked about the intercept exercise," Dyess said.

Jack looked at him. "Skipper, I..." he started.

Dyess cut him off. "You're what? You're tired? You're grieving? I'm sure. So am I, for that matter, and more. But none of that matters." He leaned forward, studying Jack for a long moment.

"I've never been in a war, Jack, but Chant's not the first pilot I've seen die since I've been in the Air Corps. If the Japs come south how fast d'you think we're going to lose pilots? Those guys in the RAF in the Battle of Britain, they were losing two or three a day, maybe more. The ones who live through it are going to have to go up again the next day, and if they're smart they'll sit down and try and figure out how to fight better, smarter, safer. That's what we have to do. So tell me about the intercept exercise."

"OK," Jack said. "But I thought Wagner was going to lead the exercise."

Dyess shrugged. "He sent the high element off early and figured they'd give you something to think about. How'd that work out?"

Jack took Dyess back through the exercise. Dyess made notes, nodding and asking questions from time to time. When Jack told him about the second pilot spinning out Dyess looked up sharply.

"He waved at you when you waved at him?"

Jack nodded.

"Well, I guess the dumb bastard won't do that again. Why did you decide to go high yourself, Jack?"

"I knew the interceptors would be P-40s and they'd have a tough time getting that high. That gave me the altitude advantage."

Dyess nodded. "Did you have a tough time getting that high?"

"It took about thirty minutes. We took off ahead of the bombers."

"I see," said Dyess. He wrote a few words. "So you shook off the high element and dove on the low element, who turned into your attack. Head-on pass. How do you think you did?"

Jack shrugged. "We were flying down each others' throats. The P-40 has more and heavier guns than the P-35. Assuming everyone has about the same level of marksmanship, that gives the P-40 the advantage. But..."

Dyess waited. He leaned back in his seat, puffing on his cigarette. "Go on," he said.

"Something my dad told me."

"Your dad?"

"He flew in the last war. SPADs with the 26th Squadron."

"Do any good?"

"Seven kills."

"Wish he were here with us. He could teach us a thing or two. So what did he say?"

"He said someone shooting at you took a little getting used to, because self-preservation was a powerful instinct."

Dyess snorted. "That sounds about right. What do you think the interceptors could be doing better?"

"Well, Skipper, how much raid warning are we likely to get?"

"That's a good question. The answer is, I don't know. I keep hearing we're going to have radar set up to provide early warning but as far as I know the one set up at Iba Field is the only one running. For the rest of it, Interceptor Command has a network of observers who report by telephone."

"The Philippine telephone system?" Jack asked skeptically. "How vulnerable is that to a little judicious sabotage? Chop down some posts or cut some wires just before the war starts, say?"

Dyess nodded. "It took you thirty minutes to get to 23,000 feet. I'm not sure these P-40s can do that reliably, and besides, with the single-stage supercharger on that airplane, performance will go to shit above 17,000."

Jack sat back in his seat. "So what you're saying is that we can't do our job."

Dyess shook his head. "No, not at all. We can at least keep the Jap bombers high and I don't see how those little fixed-gear pursuits of theirs can come this far south from Formosa. So we can do our job, but we may be doing a lot of low-level work like strafing the Japs on the ground if they try to invade. If they can get a beachhead with some kind of landing strip on it, enough that they can fly pursuits out of it, they might give us some trouble."

Jack frowned. "What about those reports of a new Jap fighter?"

"Yeah," said Dyess thoughtfully. "I've heard about that. Chennault in China sent in reports about some new Jap pursuit last year. I think Army Intelligence concluded he was, shall we say, exaggerating."

"What if he wasn't?"

"Then I guess we'd better be ready for anything." Dyess leaned back in his chair. He looked at Jack for a moment. "How you doing?"

"I don't know."

"First time you ever lose someone?"

Jack looked at Dyess for a moment. In that moment Dyess' expression changed.

"No, sir," Jack said quietly.

"Christ, Jack, I didn't mean..."

"It's OK, skipper," Jack replied.

They were quiet for a moment.

Dyess said, "Why don't you go back to your quarters, Jack? Get Chant's stuff together so we can send it home to his folks."

"Yes, sir."

Here's to Us

Whenever Jack closed his eyes all he could see was fire. There was that first bright yellow-red bloom from under the cowling of Chant's P-35. There was the puff of smoke and the sudden flames around the cockpit of his father's racer, lying in pieces at the north pylon at Cleveland.

Fire took a lot of pilots. He remembered his father telling him about Raoul Lufbery, who jumped to his death rather than stay with his burning Nieuport. Lufbery wasn't the only pilot who felt that way in the days before parachutes. Airplanes twenty years ago were built of highly flammable fabric and wood, running on hi-octane aviation fuel. Engines failed frequently and tended to catch fire when they did, so fire was constantly on the mind of the early aviators. Progress hadn't changed that very much.

152

Engines still failed. Fuel tanks still ruptured. Fuel lines broke. Airplanes crashed and burned, too often with their pilots.

He closed his eyes, and saw the flames again.

There was a knock on his door. Jack opened his eyes.

He hadn't bothered to close the door. Ramon stood there.

"Senor Chant will no longer be with us?" the man asked quietly.

"That's right," Jack said.

Ramon nodded. "It is a sad thing. Senor Chant had the manner of a fine gentleman. I shall not ask for particulars, but I hope his passing was not painful or prolonged."

"It was quick, at least."

"Will the other gentlemen be here this evening?"

"Yes, but probably late, and probably drunk."

"A wake for Senor Chant? You do not go?" Ramon gestured. Jack looked down at himself. He had thrown himself down on the bed still clad in his coveralls.

"I don't know, Ramon."

"You will be hungry, later?"

"I thought the deal was just for breakfast."

"Perhaps breakfast may come early, or late, sometimes."

"Thank you, but right now..."

"It is nothing." Ramon left.

Jack sat up and looked out the door. He went to the window. The sky in the west was turning to the red and yellow of flames, backlit by cumulus clouds and the tracery of cirrus.

Footsteps came closer down the hall. When Jack looked up Ed Dyess stood in the door.

"Get dressed, Jack," Dyess said.

"Is that an order, sir?"

"No. Consider it a suggestion from your commanding officer."

Jack rolled his eyes but stood up. "I'll take a shower."

Dyess leaned in and sniffed. "Probably a good idea."

Thirty minutes later Jack and Dyess were in a beat-up Ford coupe headed towards Rizal Boulevard.

"Where we going?" Jack asked.

"Manila Hotel."

"Not the O-Club?"

"No. Most of the 24th Pursuit Group will be at the O-Club. Tonight I'd rather it just be the 21st Pursuit Squadron. What do you think?"

"I'm with you, Skipper," Jack replied.

"Why do you think we're having so many accidents, Jack?" Dyess asked.

"Maintenance, for one thing," said Jack. "We've got a lot of good mechanics at the Depot, but you can only fix an engine for so long before it's better to just replace it."

"Like the engine on Chant's ship?"

"Maybe. Probably."

"Not much we can do about that. It's what we've got, and I don't think FEAF has any spare engines for those ships."

"They're pretty beaten up."

"Well, we'll be getting P-40s pretty soon. In less than a week, anyway. Brand new airplanes."

"With brand-new engines that have to be slow-timed. Machine guns still packed up in cosmoline."

"You're just a regular ray of sunshine there, Jack. How do you know so much?"

"I talk to Chief Jones."

"Yeah? Well, he's worth talking to. You ready to start flight-testing our P-40s?"

"Yes, sir."

"At least those are brand-new airplanes."

"Yes, sir."

"Your repartee is brilliant," Dyess observed. "Don't you like your job?"

"You either don't like me much or you have a hell of a lot of faith in me."

Dyess smiled. "You took a lot of money off me playing poker on the way over, Jack. Do I still owe you money?"

"Nope. You paid it all on the spot."

"Good. Then you know I don't gamble if I figure I can't pay the winner. I figure you can take care of yourself, Jack. I don't plan on losing this bet."

"OK. Start tomorrow?"

"Sure thing."

They arrived at the Manila Hotel. A steady stream of cars and taxis paraded slowly past the front door. Uniformed Army and Navy officers got out, some with women on their arms.

"Pick us up about midnight, Private," Dyess told their driver.

"Yes, sir," the private replied.

When he passed through the entrance past the two armed sentries at the door there was that same feeling of nostalgia some guys claimed to feel on New Year's Eve or their birthdays or something. *She was standing here, and I was standing there*, he thought, looking around the marble lobby. *Yup*, the dry voice went on, *and right there by that marble column is where Captain Calhoun puked all over my shoes, the drunk sonofabitch.*

"Ed, you ever meet a guy named Calhoun, Tommy Calhoun? He was a captain in the Air Corps out here in 1938."

"Jack, I graduated flight school in 1938. How old was this friend of yours?"

"Not exactly a friend. I'd put him at about thirty or so by now."

"Thirty? And he'd already made captain back then? Must've known a couple of generals."

"Well, mostly, he seemed like a decent guy."

"Mostly?"

"Long story."

The lobby was crowded with men in Army and Navy uniforms, mostly older, with their wives. Most of the officers were majors or lieutenant commanders or higher. Jack was glad he'd put extra effort into shining his brass and making sure his uniform was just so. Not a few of the Army officers were frowning their way. Jack could almost hear them thinking along the refrain of *Air Corps showoffs*. That was okay with him; he was thinking *fat-ass Regular Army blowhards*. Then he started studying insignia and medals.

Almost all the field-grade Army officers present had the multi-colored ribbon denoting service in the Great War. A few of them had ribbons for gallantry: Bronze Stars, mostly, with the "V" for valor, a few Silver Stars, and one little wisp of a colonel with hard blue eyes who had a DSC. They were mostly infantry officers, from the crossed muskets on their collars, but the

155

crossed cannons of the artillery and the crossed sabers of the cavalry were well-represented.

"What the hell's all the brass doing here, skipper?" Jack whispered to Dyess.

"Damned if I know. Maybe MacArthur's going to start giving out knighthoods," Dyess whispered back. "Hopefully we've got a nice quiet spot out by the pool."

"Are the rest of the guys there?"

"Yeah."

"Well, look, speaking of all that poker money, I've got a room here. We can get 15 guys in there if they don't mind being chummy, and we can get room service."

Dyess stopped and looked at Jack, raising an eyebrow. "I know you were stuffing bills in your pocket like you'd robbed a bank, Jack, but... "

"It's covered, skipper. Look. I'll see if there's an adjoining room and round up some whisky and ice and stuff."

Dyess grinned. "You stopped just short of giving a superior officer an order there, Jack."

"But I *did* stop."

"OK. See what you can do. I'll round up the thundering herd."

Jack went to the desk. He looked for but didn't see Balthazar; a youngish, bland-faced man stood with some others behind the long polished counter. Jack reached into his pocket for the card the concierge gave him when he first engaged the room and showed it to the nearest clerk, who bowed.

"How may I be of assistance, sir?" the man asked.

"I'm Jack Davis, Room 417. Do you have any adjoining rooms free?"

The clerk glanced over his shoulder. "Yes, sir. Shall I put it on your bill?"

"Please. Also, perhaps, some refreshments?"

"Of course." The clerk snapped his fingers, looking over Jack's shoulder.

A uniformed bellhop hurried to Jack's side. The clerk spoke rapidly to the bellhop in some language Jack didn't understand. Finally the bellhop nodded vigorously and turned to Jack.

"Others joining you, sir?" the bellhop asked.

"Yes."

156

"Here is your key, sir," said the clerk. "One night only for the extra room?"

"That'll be fine," Jack replied. The bellhop took the key from the clerk.

"Follow me, sir," he said.

They went up in the elevator to the fourth floor. "How many in your party, sir?" the bellhop asked.

"Fifteen," Jack said. "Thirsty. Beer on ice and Scotch whisky. Maybe a fruit basket and some rolls."

"You have dinner sent up? Dining room open for two more hours."

Jack thought about it. "Nah. I'll let 'em know and if any of them are hungry they can go downstairs."

"Very good, sir. Fourth floor."

"I know the way. Maybe if you could see to the booze?"

The faintest twinkle of amusement came and went in the bellhop's brown eyes. "Of course, sir."

Jack handed the man a 100-peso note, which he caused to disappear with a gravely courteous motion of his hand.

"Moments only, sir," the bellhop promised, as the doors of the elevator closed.

Jack unlocked 415, the room next to his, and opened the adjoining doors to turn it into two connected rooms. He turned on the lights and went to the window, drew the curtains wide, and opened the windows to let the breeze in.

Trampling footsteps filled the hallway. There was a loud knock on the door.

"Hey, Davis! You in there?"

Jack opened the door and the squadron boys pushed in, herded along by Ed Dyess and his flight commanders. Hot on their heels, as promised, came the bellhop and a small crew of waiters with three trolleys. One trolley held an iced tub full of beer; the second had plenty of ice, soda siphons and six bottles of Haig & Haig Scotch; the third tropical fruit and snacks. Jack tipped the waiters and the bellhop again, then turned to the assembled pilots.

"Gentlemen, we're here for Roy Chant," he said. "So everybody help yourselves."

"What's this, Jack, no rum?" someone asked.

157

"Screw you," Jack said, pouring neat Scotch into a glass. "Officers, gentlemen and pilots drink Scotch. Or maybe bourbon once we're back home. There's soda if you can't take your whisky straight, ice if you need to cool it down, and beer if you just can't take the hard stuff. Whatever, you bums, grab a drink."

Catcalls and raspberries greeted this speech but the pilots gathered around the trolleys. A few took a beer, and Jack noted Ed Dyess was one of them. He caught Jack's eye and winked. Jack nodded.

When there was a glass or a bottle in every hand, Jack whistled for attention.

"I said we're here for Roy Chant and I meant it," he said. "But we're not going to drink to Roy. An old pilot taught me that was bad luck. So raise your glasses, boys, and I'll give you a toast."

Jack raised his glass, there in Room 417 of the Manila Hotel, surrounded by the squadron boys who one by one raised their drinks and faced him. He looked around the room and thought for a moment, back to that night when his father and Colonel Miller got so drunk and told this story from their own youthful glory days. It all came back to him, in a rush, mixed in with the bright flames behind his eyes that was Roy Chant's funeral pyre.

"Here's to us," Jack said softly. Then, louder, "Here's to us! Who's like us? Damned few, and they're all dead."

He drained his glass in a moment filled with silence and the weight of eyes on him.

"All dead," he repeated, when he'd finished the whisky. "But here's to us."

"Here's to us," Dyess said. He put the beer to his lips and began to drink.

"Here's to us!" the others said in a ragged chorus, and drank as Jack refilled his glass.

CHAPTER EIGHT
New Places

Enroute Port Moresby, New Guinea

The eastern horizon lit with dawn. A golden sliver of sun peeked up above the Pacific, gilding the clouds and casting rays of gold and white through the sky, catching the B-17 droning along at 8000 feet above the sea.

Charlie yawned and shifted in the pilot's seat, blinking in the direct sunlight. His ass was dead. Numb. Completely without sensation. He wished to hell he had a hot fresh cup of coffee. If there was anything left in the Thermos jugs they'd taken aboard at Wake Island it was ten hours old and cold by now.

It was a long flight over the ocean, dodging thunderstorms and trying to stay awake. The crew, though, was functioning more and more like a team, and it had been getting better at it every mile since Hickam Field. It started with the navigation error over the eastern Pacific, and continued in Honolulu before they took off for Midway Island.

Once they got to Hickam Field and had some rest Charlie looked for ammunition and cleaning kits. Everywhere, though, the claim was, "We ain't got none to spare, Captain, you know how it is." Charlie did know; he knew that supply sergeants everywhere might be benevolent within their own organization, but to anyone on the outside, forget it. Charlie couldn't even scrounge ammunition, and if he couldn't find cleaning kits or ammo at Hickam Field, he despaired of finding any to spare at Midway or the even more exposed outpost of Wake Island. And God alone knew what would be available at Port Moresby or Darwin, which were run by the Australians, so likely he wouldn't have ammunition or clean weapons until they got to Clark Field in the Philippines and the 19th's own supply organization could help them.

A half hour before departure for the flight to Midway, Sgt. Smith and Pvt. Lefkowicz mysteriously vanished. Charlie fumed through the preflight and the last minute paperwork. He had come to the conclusion he would have to postpone his flight and notify Base Operations that he had missing crewmen when a covered 4X4 truck drove up. It was driven by a sergeant he didn't know, kind of an old guy, old enough, actually, to have served in the last war. This sergeant braked the truck to a stop in front of Charlie's B-17 and got out, saluting.

"Captain Davis, sir?" the sergeant asked.

"That's me, Sergeant. What can I do for you?"

"You can take a couple of misguided kids off my hands, sir," the old sergeant said grimly. He beckoned to Charlie, who followed him around the side of the truck. The sergeant raised the canvas cover.

Two very sheepish crewmen peered back at Charlie from inside the truck.

The sergeant waved a hand at them. "These two characters were about to go AWOL, Captain," the sergeant said. "I caught them trying to sneak into an ammunition locker."

"Can't imagine what they were thinking, sergeant," said Charlie piously, while the miscreants looked down at the oil-stained concrete apron.

"I'm sure, sir," said the sergeant drily. "But I hear these Flying Forts could sometimes use a little ballast. Got something here

160

that might work. Maybe your guys could load it onto the airplane for you."

The sergeant opened the tarpaulin covering over the back of the truck. On the truck bed there were four ammunition boxes whose stenciled legend proclaimed them to hold .50-CAL. BALL 500 ROUNDS AP. There was also another crate, smaller, and Charlie could make out the stencil on it. It was a tool and cleaning kit.

"Thank you, sergeant," said Charlie quietly. "I think that will do just fine."

"Sorry I can't spare more, Captain," the sergeant said. "Things are pretty short around here, but I know where you guys are going, and I've got pals in the Philippines myself."

Charlie held out his hand as Smith and Lefkowicz loaded the ammo boxes and cleaning kit on the airplane.

"Good luck, sir," the sergeant replied. He shook hands with Charlie, saluted, and drove off as Smith and Lefkowicz finished loading the ammunition aboard the B-17. That was three days ago. By now every gun on the ship, including the popgun .30-caliber in the nose in front of the bombardier's station, was clean and functioning.

"Pilot, navigator," Al Stern said over the intercom.

Charlie's mouth quirked. Even over the scratchy, tinny-sounding intercom, he could hear the satisfaction in the navigator's voice.

Charlie rose up in his seat and looked over the bomber's long nose. Dead ahead of them it was still pretty dark.

"Go ahead, navigator," Charlie said.

"There's an island up ahead, there, Skipper, and I'm pretty sure it's New Ireland."

"Only *pretty* sure, navigator?"

"I could be wrong, but it's a long skinny island right where a long skinny island is supposed to be."

Charlie suppressed another yawn. "OK, so we're what, what did you tell me, hopefully about 90 miles north-northwest of Rabaul?"

"Hopefully that's an affirmative."

"OK. Radio operator, pilot."

There was silence on the intercom. Charlie repeated himself.

"Pilot, waist gunner. Sparks is asleep, sir. Want me to wake him up?"

"Yeah, Lefkowicz, go ahead."

Charlie reached across the space between his seat and the co-pilot's seat and punched Payne in the shoulder. It took two punches before the co-pilot snorted, blinked and looked around. Charlie menaced him with a third punch. Payne held up his hands in mock surrender.

A groggy voice came over the intercom. "Umm. Ah, pilot, radio operator. Go ahead."

"Sparks, you think you're awake enough to find the frequency for the RAAF station at Rabaul?"

"Rabaul, Skipper?"

"Rabaul, Sparks. And don't tell me you don't have the frequency, I saw you write it down."

"Roger, Skipper."

Payne leaned over and spoke over the noise of the engines. "Can you get along without me for a couple minutes?"

"Go ahead. You can spell me when you get back."

The copilot nodded, unbuckled his safety belt and unplugged his radio jack. He got up out of his seat in sections, wincing as he did. Charlie kept his face straight. Ten hours in the same chair wasn't any joke, and the people at Boeing hadn't been aiming for comfort when they put those seats in the airplane.

As the sun rose Charlie thought he could see mountains rising up over the horizon across a stretch of water to the south-southeast. The mountains were more or less on the right bearing for Rabaul, which was at the north end of the island of New Britain.

"Pilot, radio operator."

"Go ahead, Sparks."

"I've got Rabaul on the Morse key, Skipper. Bearing on that station is 158."

"Radio operator, navigator. Sparks, did you say 158?"

"Affirmative, Mr. Stern."

"Hey, Charlie, tell that guy to call me Al, will you?"

"Sparks, call Mr. Stern Al," Charlie said, grinning.

"Thanks, Charlie," Al said.

"Al, what do you think, position-wise?"

162

"Given that bearing to Rabaul and what I'm seeing of this island ahead of us, I'd say we're on heading. That makes us about 550 miles from Port Moresby. You're flying 211 degrees. Stay on that heading."

"OK, heading two-one-one." Charlie double-checked the heading set into the Sperry autopilot. It was still set for 211. He nodded to himself. "Sparks, call Rabaul again, ask them to let Port Moresby know they should start looking for us in about how long, Al?"

"Oh, are you talking to me or Sparks? I thought all this intercom chatter was supposed to be just two people at a time."

"Sparks, call him Mr. Stern."

"OK, Skipper."

"All right, all right! Touchy bunch of goyim, aren't you? Sparks, you tell Rabaul we're estimating arrival at Port Moresby in about 3 hours, more or less. I'll refine that figure when I can get a drift sight."

"OK, Al, will do."

"That's more like it. Navigator out."

Payne came back to the cockpit looking a lot more alert.

"Better?" Charlie asked.

"Heck, yeah. Want me to take it for a bit?"

"Sure. Al says if we stay on heading 211 we should make Port Moresby in three hours."

"Jeez. Three more hours?"

"Relax. The worst of it is over. I'm going to make a tour around the ship and make sure everything is shipshape."

Payne rolled his eyes as he fastened his safety belt. He plugged himself back in to the radio/intercom set as he scanned the engine gauges and autopilot settings.

"OK, Skipper, I've got it," he told Charlie.

"Your airplane," Charlie said.

Getting out of the seat for Charlie was about as much fun as it looked to be for Payne. Charlie found his legs were a little asleep, which accounted for the lack of feeling in his toes, and his back was stiff. When he levered himself up and around to get over the engine instruments pedestal between his seat and the co-pilot's seat he stifled a gasp as something twisted in his back, not bad, but enough to make him notice. Once he was out of his seat

163

there wasn't any way to really stretch those cramped and constricted muscles until he made his way to the catwalk over the bomb bay, which was now occupied by extra fuel tanks. He chinned himself on the overhead girders and bent over, carefully, to touch his toes. A few minutes of that was a big help.

When he finished stretching he stood for a moment. The bomb bay was in shadow, with only the faint light of dawn coming from fore and aft, but he could hear the roar of the four Wright engines and underneath that, the whir of electric motors and the pop-click of the hydraulic system. Everything sounded right to him, down to the way the metal catwalk trembled under his booted feet and swayed slightly as the autopilot compensated on the controls.

Charlie went on aft. Dobson, the radio operator, looked up as he entered his compartment.

"Morning, Skipper," he said.

"Morning, Sparks. Rabaul have anything else to say?"

"Wished us a good trip and warned us to be careful going over the mountains."

Charlie frowned. "What mountains?"

"Don't know, sir. That's all they said. You want I should ask 'em?"

"Yeah. Find out where and how high."

"Will do, Skipper."

Charlie continued through the radio operator's compartment into the waist section. The B-17D had two guns in the waist, mounted in teardrop-shaped windows on either side of the fuselage about halfway between the wing trailing edge and the leading edge of the horizontal stabilizer. It was cool in the waist, and with the windows shut not much wind blew through.

Lefkowicz was by the port waist gun position, looking down and ahead. Charlie stood next to him.

"Anything out there to look at, Lefkowicz?"

"Some good-sized mountains southeast of us, Skipper. And we're passing over that long skinny island Mr. Stern was talking about." Lefkowicz pointed down.

Charlie looked at the shoreline a mile and a half below them. Breakers fringed the white sand, green jungle started almost at the water's edge. He looked to the south-southeast at the cone-shaped mountain, outlined against the early morning sky, that the maps and the route briefing told him to expect to see at the north end of Simpson Harbor. The RAAF had some kind of station there near the town of Rabaul.

"Not like those little coral islands we've been looking at for the last two days," Lefkowicz commented.

"Not at all," Charlie agreed. "You doing OK, Lefkowicz? Need anything?"

"No, Skipper, I'm fine."

"Thanks for waking Dobson up. Saved me a trip."

Lefkowicz smiled faintly. "Anytime, Skipper."

Charlie smiled at Lefkowicz and went forward again.

There was a certain feeling of confidence in the way the crew came together. That had been especially pronounced last night when they went on oxygen and climbed to 25,000 feet to overfly the Japanese mandated islands in the central Pacific. He didn't think the Japs had working night fighters but even if they didn't he was happy to be fully armed. They had flown over the Japanese-held island of Ponape, visible as a dark mass with a few electric lights, five miles below them in the moonlight, with all hands scanning the darkness while they breathed rubbery oxygen. Payne did crew checks over the intercom every five minutes. A half-hour after passing over Ponape Charlie began a slow let-down from 25,000 feet to conserve as much fuel as possible. Port Moresby was still 1300 miles south of them, but the danger of detection from the Japanese had passed.

As he walked forward Charlie grinned, thinking that the landfall over Ponape had been a minor triumph for Al Stern, since they overflew the island within five minutes of his prediction.

Dobson pulled an earphone off as Charlie passed back through the radio compartment.

"The Aussies at Rabaul say the mountains are called the Owen Stanley Range, Skipper," he said. "They run kind of east-west down the center of eastern New Guinea, with tops estimated at 10 to 15,000 feet."

"Estimated?"

"That's all they could give me, Skipper."

Charlie grimaced. "OK. Thanks, Sparks."

Dobson nodded and went back to his radio. Charlie passed over the catwalk and back onto the flight deck, where he leaned over to speak to Payne.

"Bob, how's our fuel?"

"We're fat, according to the gauges. Enough for another five hours."

"OK. We may have to climb over some mountains. The Aussies told Sparks they aren't sure but maybe there's some stuff ahead of us that reaches up to 15,000 feet."

Payne frowned and nodded.

"Right. Keep us on this heading and altitude. I'm going forward to check on Al and Bill."

Payne nodded. Charlie squeezed into the narrow tunnel between the flight deck and the nose section.

The cone-shaped nose of the bomber gave an unobstructed view of the sea and islands ahead of them. At the moment those islands were mostly on their left, which, if Charlie remembered his look at the somewhat meager chart they had, was New Britain. The coast of New Guinea was ahead of them but still out of sight.

Al Stern looked up as Charlie came through the tunnel. Bill Smith, the sergeant bombardier, was asleep with his parachute for a pillow, propped against the right side of the nose compartment underneath the right cheek window.

"How's it coming, Al?" Charlie asked.

The navigator shrugged. He'd been up most of the night, taking star sights and calculating their position so they wouldn't stray any deeper into Japanese territory than they had to. Charlie had heard discussion of another route to Australia, going via some little islands whose names he had heard but forgotten, that led southwest and west instead of going west and then south, eventually ending up in Noumea, French Caledonia, only a few hundred miles from the Australian coast.

Technically, Charlie knew that the French colonies were administered from Vichy France, which signed a separate armistice with the Germans and so were considered neutral parties, more or less. Charlie didn't think that would last if the Japs came south, but there was no way to know.

"It's a little easier to navigate at night, some ways," Al said.

Charlie nodded. "Did you hear what Sparks told me about mountains in New Guinea?"

"Yeah."

"Nobody knows much about this part of the world. I think I read somewhere that the Aussies have been flying machinery into the interior of New Guinea and flying gold out, but other than the fact that there are mountains and gold in there, damned if I know anything else."

Stern nodded. He flipped a hand over his chart. "This thing is OK for the coastline but not much else."

"Right. When Sparks asked the Aussies at Rabaul about it, they couldn't tell him if the mountains were 10,000 or 15,000 feet high. I want you to be as careful as you can about our position and make notes about the mountains you see." Charlie tapped the altimeter set in the small panel above Stern's desk. "Especially I want you to note our height. It won't be really accurate without knowing the local sea-level atmospheric pressure but it'll give some indication if we or some other guys have to come this way again."

Stern nodded. "No problem, Charlie."

"You doing OK? You need a nap before you start all the higher mathematics?"

Stern smiled. "I'm OK, boss. Just don't run us into a mountainside or some silly crap like that."

Charlie smiled back. "I'll do my very best, Al."

When he got back up on the flight deck he levered himself into his seat and looked all around. To the east the sun was well above the horizon, and directly off the port wingtip was the volcanic cone marking the town of Rabaul, still below the horizon, with the coast of New Britain just visible. Ahead of them there was some sort of cape or peninsula jutting out from the western coast of New Britain, forming a bay. The western coast of the island crossed their flight path, but was still mostly right on the horizon.

"I'm going to take a nap," he told Payne. "We should cross this island ahead of us, come to another stretch of water, and beyond that is the New Guinea coast. Wake me up when those mountains come in sight. We'll have to climb over them on oxygen."

"You got it, Charlie," Payne said.

Over the Owen Stanley Mountains

"Charlie!"

He blinked and came back to the noisy, sunlit world of the B-17's flight deck. There was a vicious crick in his neck and a foul taste in his mouth. He looked ahead. Visible over the nose of the bomber was a broad stretch of land from horizon to horizon, and dead ahead were mountains, rising up into clouds whose tops were clearly above their present altitude.

"You awake?" Payne asked.

"Yeah," Charlie said. "Gimme a minute."

He stretched as best he could in his seat. Payne handed him a canteen. It was still half-full of water. Charlie drank a little, swished his mouth out, and swallowed it as he studied the mountains ahead.

"Pilot to crew," he said. "We've got some mountains ahead and we're going to have to climb over them. Prepare to go on oxygen. I'll give the word as we approach ten thousand feet."

A chorus of tired *rogers* came over the intercom. Charlie pushed the throttles forward and eased back on the controls.

The Fort began to climb. At this altitude he should get around 700 feet per minute, and the VSI confirmed it. He looked at the engine instruments, which were sitting right where they should be, even with the increase in RPMs and fuel consumption.

"Crew, pilot," he said. "Oxygen, guys."

Tops of mountains estimated at between ten and fifteen thousand feet, he thought to himself sourly.

"What d'you think of those clouds, Bob?" he asked his copilot.

"I think I remember someone telling me clouds might have rocks in them," Payne replied. "The cloud tops don't look that high. Let's climb over them."

The bomber crossed over the coastline as they flew through 11,000 feet, tasting the cool, rubbery oxygen from their masks. At 17,000 feet Charlie leveled out above the cloud tops, which seemed to march away on either side of the airplane.

Ahead and behind them the ocean glittered blue in the morning sun. To either side of them, stretching out of sight to east and west, were high mountains, as high as most of the Rocky Mountains back in the States according to his altimeter. They were just above the cloud tops, but the clouds weren't solid and the mountains weren't that far below.

"Radio operator, pilot," he said.

"Go ahead, Skipper."

"See if you can raise Port Moresby and get a DF steer."

"Roger."

"Pilot, navigator."

"Go ahead, Al."

"I'd say we're looking at mountaintops that are maybe two to three thousand feet below us. Call it 15,000 feet, but I see stuff lower than that."

"So the Aussies were right."

"It's their island, after all. Isn't it?"

"I think so. They're all over it, anyway."

"Pilot, radio operator."

"Go ahead, Sparks."

"Skipper, I've got Port Moresby on voice. It's a little shakey, maybe 3 by 3. They're bearing about five degrees right. Local altimeter is two-niner-niner-one."

"OK, thanks, Sparks." Charlie made a slight adjustment to the autopilot. He looked to left and right again. The mountains were giving way to a broad coastal plain that stretched on south to the Coral Sea.

"Navigator, pilot," Charlie said.

"Go ahead, Charlie."

"Refresh my memory on Port Moresby."

"The airfield is seven miles northeast of the harbor. Don't be misled by the little strip three miles east of the harbor. Look for the one a little further away to the northeast. The town of Port Moresby is on a peninsula pointing to the southwest."

"Thanks, Al." Charlie looked at his copilot. "OK, Bob, let's start the descent."

A Dusty Country Road of an Airstrip

They flew over the harbor and saw a little tropical town of tin roofs and whitewashed buildings on the peninsula. There were some rusty looking freighters in the harbor and a flying boat near the shore. Charlie looked twice before he recognized the seaplane as a PBY Catalina in RAAF markings. They turned southeast along the shoreline until they came to an inlet and turned left, flying up the long narrow bay.

Charlie and his copilot craned in their seats, looking ahead. Sparks had relayed that the airstrip was three miles inland from the northwest end of Bootless Bay, but dead ahead of them all they saw was forest or jungle with low hills all around and mountains to the north.

"Pilot, bombardier."

"Go ahead, bombardier."

"Skipper, I think I see it. Dead ahead of us. Jeez, it looks like a dirt road in that valley."

Charlie motioned Payne to drop flaps and gear as he continued to look for the strip.

He saw it five seconds later, just as his right hand began to tension up on the throttles, getting ready to go around. When he finally saw it he realized Frye's description was accurate and understated. Seven-Mile Drome was nothing more than an aisle in a scrubby-looking forest among some hills.

"Jesus," Payne said over the muted rumble of the engines. "I hope it's wide enough."

"The guys that came through here last week must have made it," Charlie replied. "All right, gentlemen, hang on tight. Here goes nothin'."

Seven-Mile Drome

As soon as the propellers came to a stop Charlie opened his side window. The heat and humidity of Seven Mile Drome hit him like a fist and left him gasping for breath. He could feel the sweat pour from him as the early afternoon sun promptly and enthusiastically heated the interior of the bomber.

"Holy Christ," said Payne. "It's this hot in wintertime, what's it like in summer?"

Al Stern poked his head out of the tunnel to the nose compartment. "You can't be serious, Payne. You think this is wintertime, here in New Guinea?"

"It's December, you kike bastard. What the hell else?"

"It's December below the equator. The seasons are reversed. This is summertime in New Guinea, about as bad as it gets, you goy moron."

Charlie shrugged out of his seat belt and stood awkwardly. Every move made him break out in sweat. He could feel it soaking into his underwear. He took off his leather flight jacket and hung it over his seat.

It wasn't any better outside the airplane. Inside the fuselage they were out of the sun but the heat was stifling because of the enclosed metal space. Once outside the sunlight slammed down on them with force enough to make them gasp for breath.

Charlie took a deep breath that seemed to be mostly water vapor. He took off his hat, wiped the sweat from his forehead, put his hat back on and looked around.

They had followed some sort of beaten-up truck with a FOLLOW ME sign to a sod ramp bordered by tall trees. The airfield itself was surrounded by low hills populated by scrubby trees.

Al Stern and Jack Frye climbed down from the nose of the bomber. Charlie went to stand in the shade cast by the airplane's left wing.

Another, larger truck came towards them. It was followed by another with a collection of 55 gallon drums on the back. Charlie sighed when he saw the drums.

"Aw, crap," said Payne. He pointed at the second truck. "Does that mean what I think?"

"Probably," said Charlie. "But we're goddamned well going to get some chow before we start fueling this airplane out of drums. That'll take hours."

"Not much shade here, either, Skipper," said Lefkowicz. He dug a fatigue cap from a pocket of his coveralls and put it on. The gunner's clothes already showed dark rings of sweat.

The trucks pulled up in front of the B-17. A lanky, sunburned Australian in khaki shorts and a short-sleeved shirt, wearing a Digger hat, which Charlie thought was something like a cowboy hat with one side turned up, got out of the first truck and walked toward them. There were something that looked like miniature crowns on the man's shoulders. Searching his memory from West

Point classes, Charlie remembered that in the Royal Army, as well as the armies of the British Commonwealth nations, that made the man a captain.

At least he doesn't outrank me, Charlie thought.

"G'day," the Australian said. "I'm Captain William Fulbright, Royal Australian Army. Who are you fellows?"

Charlie extended his hand. "I'm Charles Davis, Captain Fulbright. 19th Bomb Group, US Army Air Forces. This is my crew."

As Charlie introduced his men other Australians climbed down from the trucks and gathered behind Captain Fulbright.

"We had a squadron of the 19th come through here last week," Fulbright said when the introductions were over. "They said another bunch might be through in a bit."

"Reckon that's us," Charlie said. "There might be others. Hard to say."

Fulbright grinned and nodded. "Things a bit dicey back in the States at the moment, eh? No worries. Reckon you fellows are tired and hungry. You going to try to press on to Darwin tonight or first thing in the morning?"

Charlie looked up and down the runway. It was paved after a fashion, but there was pierced steel planking at the east end of the runway.

"What's with the steel planks at the east end?" he asked.

Fulbright grimaced. "Aw, that's where the water line for the town runs," he said. "Now and again it breaks and floods that end of the runway, which is why we've got the planks down at that end. Something else you might want to know. In the heat of the day the tarmac gets a bit runny. Too much bloody asphalt in the bloody paving mix. Most of the RAAF types like to fly off at daybreak unless there's a mucking good reason to do it later in the day."

Charlie nodded. "Well, then, Captain, maybe we'll spend the night. It was a long trip."

"See anything interesting?"

"Lots of water. Tried to pass over the Jap islands at night."

"Good-oh, then." Fulbright turned to a man dressed as he was but wearing sergeant's stripes. "Sergeant, get those drums unloaded, an' head back when you're done. We'll get the Yanks a bite to eat and then help them gas up tonight."

"Yes, sir," the sergeant replied.

Fulbright turned back to Charlie. "Come along, then, mates, and we'll see what we can find for tea."

It cooled off a little in the night but Charlie didn't sleep a lot. He, Al Stern and Bob Payne were in one tent. The enlisted men were quartered in a grass hut. The tent stank of mildew, and about sundown it rained like the forty days and forty nights. Almost immediately the tent floor was under water. Their bedding and uniforms were soaked.

When the rain ended the mosquitoes came out. Payne caught one in the beam of his flashlight and expressed the opinion that it was an Australian training aircraft. Stern scoffed and replied that it was obviously a Japanese spy sent to obtain American blood specimens for some darkly inscrutable purpose. They bantered like this for awhile as the mosquitoes zinged and hummed in the tent, finding every hole in the mosquito netting covering their cots, biting through the stifling, soaked woolen blankets.

The fatigue of the long flight, coupled with the hours of fueling their airplane with the help of the hand pump, straining the fuel through a chamois rag, finally took its toll. Charlie slept, but like the others he awoke itching from mosquito bites.

"Christ, what a hole," Payne observed as they left the tent. They were beset by flies that were not to be driven off even by persistent hand-waving in front of their faces. The same flies followed them into the tent that served the Australians as a mess hall. Charlie got a cup of tea and spat out a suspicious lump. Finally he poured the tea out, filled a canteen from a water billy, rounded up his crew and headed for the air strip.

It was relatively cool inside the B-17. They preflighted and ran down the checklist by the dim light of battery-powered torches, taxied down the runway behind the beaten-up FOLLOW ME truck, and turned to face west while Charlie ran up the engines to full power.

It was also still dark. Overhead the stars were only starting to dim and behind them there was a faint pink line on the horizon, visible mostly by the silhouette of the hills flanking Bootless Inlet.

"Let's get the hell out of here, Skipper," Payne said. "I think about half those mosquitoes hitched a ride in my shorts."

Charlie took a deep breath, exhaled, and pushed the throttles forward as he and Payne stood on the brakes. A second or two to build up to full takeoff RPMs and they came off the brakes. At the far end of the runway a faint light came on, the headlights of the Aussie FOLLOW ME truck.

The B-17 accelerated slowly with a full load of fuel. The truck's headlights at the far end of the field got closer with equal slowness, but then seemed to rush at them. Charlie pushed forward gently on the controls, felt the resistance as the air rushed over the elevators, but not enough, not quite enough yet; he held the elevators forward until he felt the rumble of the tail wheel quit as the tail rose and the bomber lumbered forward on its main wheels.

Charlie looked at Payne from the corner of his eye. The copilot had his left hand firmly against the engine throttles, holding them all the way forward. In the dim light of the instruments Charlie could see Payne grimacing. Charlie watched the approaching truck headlights and thought about the trees at the far end of the field. The airplane weighed 57,000 pounds with this fuel load; the runway was a little over 5000 feet long. With all four engines turning at 2500 RPM for takeoff they should come unstuck at around 3000 feet.

At seventy mph indicated airspeed Payne started calling out the airspeed every 5 mph. As he called "85 mph" Charlie felt the controls start to feel about right, and at "90" he eased back gently, very gently, on the controls, enough to break the wheels loose and keep them in ground effect while he accelerated without the drag of the wheels along the ground.

The B-17 lifted, bounced gently, then lifted into the air and stayed up. As the airspeed reached 100 mph Charlie eased back still further on the controls.

"Flaps up," he told Payne.

The bomber picked up speed as the drag of the flaps came off. He motioned for wheels up as they cleared the trees beyond the end of the airstrip. The B-17's rate of climb picked up with the airspeed. Charlie looked left and right, but it was still too dark to see the hills at either side of the runway. They climbed away from Seven-Mile with the lights of Port Moresby and a freighter in Fairfax Harbor winking behind them.

"What's the heading for Darwin, Al?" Charlie asked.

"Steer two-six-one," Al replied at once. "ETA Darwin about 1400 this afternoon."

"Maybe they'll have beer," Payne said. He reached down and scratched himself vigorously where the mercilessly avid mosquitoes had bitten him.

CHAPTER NINE
The Last Leg

Batchelor Field, NW Territory, Australia

Batchelor Field, southwest of Darwin, was another hot place scratched out of the wilderness due to its proximity to some point of perceived strategic significance. Or maybe, Charlie thought sourly, it was picked for heat, dirt and inconvenience.

He swatted at the flies that swarmed around his face. The heat made the sweat run down his back and pool under his buttocks where he leaned against the right main gear. The RAAF obliged them with a tarpaulin stretched from poles to shield Charlie's flight engineer, Kim Smith, who had the cowling of No. 2 engine open so he could tinker with the fuel pump. The pump quit operating on the flight from Port Moresby, leaving Charlie to bring the B-17 in to Batchelor on three engines.

Next to Smith stood an RAAF aircraftsman, handing him tools.a

"Goolsby, you got a wrench in that kit?" Smith asked.

"A wrench? You mean a spanner, mate?"

"What the hell's a spanner?"

"What you Yanks call a wrench. Or so I'm told."

"Does it turn righty-tighty down under?"

"Beg pardon?"

Charlie grinned, listening to the easy back-and-forth between the two mechanics. On the whole, he had to give the RAAF mob high marks. They were stuck out here in this godforsaken outback where the only thing they had to look forward to was the beer ration. The beer had to be flown in. The same bulldozers and earth-movers that hacked out an airstrip among the six-foot-tall termite mounds had hacked out a road from Darwin. The RAAF's mechanics had only the most rudimentary tools and the only spare parts available were from a wrecked Lockheed Hudson, which at least used the same engine as the B-17D.

After looking the fuel pumps over it was clear that the crash did them no good. Charlie told Smith to pick whichever pump seemed least damaged and they'd try it out, since it was that or wait here in Batchelor in the goddamned outback for replacement parts that could be months arriving. The flight engineer looked around at the termite mounds, grimaced, and got to work.

A Ford truck drove up and the RAAF base commander got out of the passenger side. He was a squadron leader, equivalent to a USAAF major, so Charlie came to attention and saluted. Squadron Leader Plum returned the gesture returned with that easy palm-out salute favored by the British and their Commonwealth forces.

"G'day, Captain," said Plum. "Any luck?"

"Sergeant Smith has high hopes, sir," Charlie replied.

"Good-oh," Plum said. "So you'll stay the night, then?"

"Afraid so. Maybe we can do a test flight this afternoon if Smith gets lucky."

Smith mumbled something which made the RAAF aircraftsman grin and which both officers ignored.

"Then we'll see to it you've got a bunk and some tucker," said Plum. "Which is to say, Captain, that I'll tell the mess sergeant to expect a few more for dinner."

"Thank you, sir."

"Quit the 'sir' business if you like. Call me Mike an' I'll call you Charlie."

"Good-oh, Mike," said Charlie, grinning.

"That's the spirit! If you can get the engine running you'll press on for the Philippines early tomorrow morning, then?"

"Just before dawn, Mike. If the blasted engine fires up at all," Charlie answered. He glared at the offending piece of machinery.

"Right. We'll send the petrol bowser round after sundown an' then top you off first thing in the morning. Anything else the RAAF can do for you, Charlie?"

"No, sir, and I want to thank you for your courtesy."

Plum laughed. "Well, Charlie, you're welcome, but ulterior motives, you know. If the bloody little yellow men come south we'd like to see them stopped as far north as possible." Plum's smile evaporated. "What with most of our lads off fighting Jerry in North Africa or reinforcing Singapore we've got bugger-all left to stop them with here in Oz, so the Commonwealth of Australia is quite happy to do what it can for the US Army."

Charlie nodded. "I understand, Mike. I'm not a general but stopping them in the Philippines is the plan as it's been explained to me."

The Australian nodded slowly and looked round the horizon. Then he said, "Bring your officers up to the club for a can when you're done. The NCOs will make sure the rest of your crew is looked after." Plum grinned suddenly. "I think those blokes in the NCO mess managed to get more of the beer ration than is quite fair, but that's a pack of ruddy sergeants for you."

Charlie laughed. "We'll be up in a bit, Mike."

Plum got back in his truck and drove off. Charlie sighed and wiped the sweat from his forehead with a bandana. Then he took off his officer's hat and carefully wiped the sweat out of the headband.

Before Jesus it was hot. It was the sort of heat that made him wish he'd stayed in the States and trained to bomb Germany. The Luftwaffe was probably a tougher outfit than the Japs but at least it was cool in England.

At that, Charlie thought, looking around the sparse trees and scrub surrounding the airfield, Batchelor wasn't as bad as Port Moresby, except maybe for the flies.

Kim Smith straightened up, mopped his face with a bright red kerchief, and called down, "I think we can give her a try now, Skipper."

178

"Well, let's do it," Charlie replied. He looked at the Australian mechanic assisting Smith. "Goolsby, will you stand by the fire bottle? I'm not sure my guys can work it right. Might be backwards from what they're used to."

Leeds chuckled. "No fear, Captain."

"OK, thanks. Smith, wait until Bob and I check the ignition, then pull the propeller through three revolutions and come on up to the flight deck. Leeds, will you watch for fuel spilling out from under the cowling?"

The aircraftsman nodded. "That, or anything else that looks suspicious, and I'll give you the wave-off."

"Ready when you are, then, Skipper," said Smith. He gestured to the gunners, who were squatting next to the right main gear as much out of the sun as possible. They came forward to help Smith pull the propeller through.

It might not have been as bad as Seven-Mile in terms of insect life but the tropical heat focused itself in the aluminum fuselage of the bomber just as fiercely. Charlie felt the sweat pouring down his back and tailbone and wished he had about a gallon of ice cold water, some to drink but most of it to pour over his head.

Once in the cockpit he stuck his head out of the window and looked down at Smith and Goolsby, both of whom gave him a thumbs-up. Charlie nodded.

"Ignition's off," he called. "Pull it through."

The airmen made a relay of pulling the prop blades through. Charlie nodded, satisfied, when Goolsby squatted down to look under the cowling and shot Charlie a nod.

"Fine so far, Captain," Goolsby called.

Charlie nodded and pulled his head back inside the cockpit.

"Let's have the checklist," he said to Payne. They went down the checklist for No. 2 engine. Smith came in when they were a few lines down and stood between them looking at the engine instruments. Charlie started the fuel pump on No. 3, which primed the rest of the fuel pumps in the system. Payne's fingers went to the switch for the No. 2 fuel pump and looked at Charlie, who shrugged. Payne flipped the switch.

Smith studied the instruments. "Primer pressure's not quite 7 psi, Skipper. It's a little low but not too bad."

Charlie nodded and leaned his head out of the window again.

"Clear prop!" he called. He waited to see the airmen move away from the propeller arc before looking back into the cockpit.

"Start No. 2, Bob," he said.

"Starting 2," Payne replied. He moved the starter switch to START, held it down, and unlocked the primer for No. 3, pumping vigorously.

"Fifteen seconds," Smith said, looking at the instrument panel chronometer. The starter whined up to a high pitch and sat there.

"Thirty seconds," said Smith.

"Mesh," Charlie called over the whining starter.

"Mesh," Payne repeated, moving the starter switch to the MESH position.

The propeller on No. 2 cranked slowly. Charlie darted a look at Goolsby, who squatted down to watch the underside of the cowling on No. 2 with one hand on the fire bottle.

The engine coughed out a torrent of pearly gray smoke, then coughed twice more. Charlie moved the mixture control for No. 2 to the AUTO RICH position. The engine coughed again, ran a few RPMs, coughed, sputtered, and caught. It ran rough for a few seconds before smoothing out.

"No. 2 primer to OFF," Charlie called over the rumble of the engine.

"No. 2 primer OFF," Payne replied, flipping the switch.

"Fuel pressure holding on No. 2, Skipper," Smith said.

Charlie looked at the fuel pressure gauge. It climbed into normal operating range. Charlie nodded and looked at the No. 2 oil pressure gauge. It stirred and began to move up, indicating oil pressure was rising to operating range.

No. 2 ran easy at idle RPMs now, making that normal *chugatachugatachugatachug* sound of a radial engine warming up and working into the groove. Charlie watched the engine gauges for a minute before turning to the flight engineer.

Smith shrugged. "Give her the gun, Skipper. She either works or she don't."

Charlie put his hand on the throttle for No. 2. He looked out the window at Goolsby, who flashed another thumbs-up.

"Here goes nothin'," Charlie said, and pushed the throttle slowly forward.

No. 2 responded smoothly as Charlie ran it up to full throttle, without any of the coughing or hesitation of a fuel-starved engine. Charlie and Payne stood on the brakes to keep the B-17 from moving forward. The airframe shimmied and rattled as the wind from the No. 2 propeller blasted over the fuselage and the horizontal stabilizer, kicking out a cloud of dust behind them. Charlie scanned the engine instruments, which showed everything operating normally.

After a minute at full throttle Charlie eased it back to cruise RPMs for another minute. The engine ran as before. He nodded.

"Let's shut her down," he said.

Payne moved the mixture control to ENGINE OFF and killed the fuel pump. The noise and blast from the propeller fell away at once, dropping to nothing as the engine came to a halt.

Charlie mopped his forehead. "Good work, Kim. Maybe that'll get us to Clark Field."

"I sure hope so, sir."

Charlie grinned at the engineer. "What's the matter, Kim? You don't like Australia?"

"Aw, Australia's fine, sir. It just reminds me too much of New Mexico in the summertime, except a lot more humid."

"Get used to it. The Philippines are worse."

Warm Beer on the Veranda

The RAAF officer's mess was in a building with a wide veranda and a corrugated iron roof. The veranda was screened in to keep out the flies. Charlie thought the screening was about half successful and wondered about the dysentery rate, but didn't think he could ask their hosts about it.

"Ah, Charlie," said Squadron Leader Plum, rising from his chair. "Join us and introduce your friends."

"Lieutenants Bob Payne and Al Stern," Charlie replied, indicating his copilot and navigator.

"Welcome, gentlemen," said Plum, shaking hands with Stern and Payne. "What'll it be? Whisky, gin or beer?"

"Beer for me," said Charlie.

"Me too," said Payne.

"I'd love a beer," Stern chimed in.

"Good-oh," said Plum, and waved his hand. White-coated mess men, perspiring in the heat, brought mugs of beer and passed them out.

Charlie took a sip of the warm Australian beer and watched Stern and Payne as they thanked the messmen and sat down with their beer. He was pretty sure neither of his lieutenants knew that the Australians, like the English, drank their beer warm. In Charlie's opinion it lent a whole new meaning to the phrase "pour it back in the horse," but it was still good beer, even warm, and it went down gratefully after the heat of the day.

Stern blinked as he tasted the beer but sipped without comment and smiled. Payne, however, took a manful pull at his beer and choked on it.

The Aussies laughed. "We always get at least one Yank with that one," Plum chortled. "Although why you fellows like your beer served cold is beyond me. It's bloody tasteless when it's cold."

Charlie smiled. Payne recovered and took another, more cautious pull at his beer, and allowed as how it was pretty good after a hot day, which brought another laugh from the Aussies.

"Cobber, you've got that right," said Plum.

The sun went down and the stars came out. The Australians served mutton and potatoes, a little heavy for Charlie's taste, but he was hungry and it wasn't as bad as the unidentifiable contents of what the Aussies at Port Moresby cheerfully referred to as "M&V" rations. Charlie's stomach rumbled all the way across the Coral Sea and the Gulf of Carpentaria yesterday afternoon.

Finally Plum said, "First light is at 0500, Charlie. Did you want to try to get off then?"

"Yes, sir," Charlie replied. "I'll have my guys aboard the airplane about 0400 and Bob and I will start preflighting. Maybe we could get the tanks topped off then?"

Plum nodded. "I've already laid it on. We'll get a couple of trucks out to shine their lights down the runway, and I'll set out the flare pots."

"That sounds great, Mike."

Payne looked at his watch. "How did it get to be 2300?"

"It's the wizard time you're having," Plum assured him.

"OK, then, we'll preflight about 0400, start engines about 0430, and with any luck at all we'll be wheels-up by 0500." Charlie rose. "Mike, thanks for your hospitality, but we'd better get some sleep."

Clark Field Next Stop

Kim Smith and the other enlisted men looked as if they had made a later night of it than Charlie had, but Charlie doubted that he, Stern or Payne had gotten any more sleep. The mosquitoes and flies had buzzed incessantly and it was still hot, hot enough to leave a man gasping for breath, until well after midnight.

They finished preflighting as the RAAF petrol bowser topped off the fuel tanks. Two trucks, driven by yawning aircraftsmen, turned their lights on the bomber. With the headlights and their flashlights it was enough to see by and get their preflight done: checking to be sure the gust locks were removed, that the tires were properly inflated, that the oil and fuel tank filler caps were tight, that the oil and hydraulic tanks as well as the fuel tanks were filled, and the wing and propeller leading edges had no obvious nicks or dings. Finally Charlie signaled his crew to board the airplane.

He stood for a moment, looking out to the east. The truck headlights threw out enough light to illuminate the scrub all around the airfield, and the mowed grass where the RAAF had cut down the bush to make parking areas for transient aircraft. It was also enough light that Charlie couldn't see the eastern horizon effectively; just a hint of gray in the sky to the east.

He sighed and rubbed his eyes.

"Charlie."

Al Stern stood by his elbow.

"Morning, Al."

"You OK?"

"A little tired."

"Hungover?"

"After four beers and six hours of sleep?" Charlie took a deep breath. "How far have we come, Al?"

"Here, to Batchelor Field?" Stern thought for a moment. "At least eight thousand miles. Over halfway around the world. In about a week."

"That's a lot of flying." Charlie took his hat off, ran his fingers through his hair, and jammed the hat back on his head. "OK. Let's get to where the hell we're supposed to be. How do we get to Clark Field from here, Al?"

"Initial heading 340, about 2100 miles."

"About?"

"Maybe a little less. Call it 2100, though. Why? You think your gas gauges are that accurate?"

Charlie grinned a little. "Guess not. What day is today?"

"The 4th," Stern said promptly, and then hesitated. "No, it's December 5. I keep forgetting about the International Date Line."

"Fine navigator you are, not even knowing the date."

"Hey, I've gotten us this far, haven't I?"

"You've done a pretty good job," Charlie said. He punched Stern lightly on the shoulder. "Let's go. Maybe we'll get the weekend off when we get to Clark Field."

The RAAF trucks moved to shine their lights down the dirt runway. Charlie looked at the tiny pair of lights at the far end, nearly a mile away, and hoped they wouldn't need that much runway to get airborne.

He keyed the intercom. "Pilot to crew. Here goes nothin'. Next stop, Clark Field."

Charlie pushed the throttles forward and held them there. He and Payne came off the brakes. The B-17 accelerated down the dark runway, aiming at the intersection of the lights from the truck on either side, then lifted into the air and thundered off to the north. To the east, the first pink light of the sun spread over the horizon.

CHAPTER TEN
Transfer

Nichols Field, PI – Clark Field, PI

"**Mr**. Davis? Mr. Dyess wants to see you up to the Operations Shack."

Jack shrugged out of his parachute harness and nodded at the enlisted man standing by the wingtip of the P-35A.

"OK, thanks, Duncan."

"Yes, sir."

Jack draped the parachute over his shoulder, took off his leather helmet, and ran his fingers through his sweat-soaked hair. He put on a broad-billed baseball cap before walking to the Operations Shack. The "shack" was actually another of the old canvas pyramidal tents with the 21st Pursuit's guidon on a flagstaff outside the tent. Over the doorway a neatly hand-lettered sign proclaimed its function. The sides of the tent were rolled up. Inside Jack could see Lt. Dyess, who, from the way he stood leaning slightly forward with his fists on his hips, seemed to be arguing with another man. Jack could see Major Maverick and Lt. Mahony in the tent as well, all of them making placating gestures at Dyess.

185

"It's just temporary, Ed," Jack heard Maverick say. "It'll work out better in the long run anyway."

"Major, today, just today after being on this station for a week and a half, we're getting the P-40s we were told we'd have when we got here. You can't just take one of my best pilots when I need him to help transition my squadron into P-40s."

As he walked closer Jack saw Boyd Wagner standing in front of Dyess.

"Ed, like it or not I've got to have more experienced pilots," Wagner said. "My squadron has the night intercept mission but I don't have four pilots other than myself who can fly instruments. Five pilots aren't enough for the job and there's no sense in cracking up more airplanes because of inexperience."

"You take Davis and the experience level of *my* squadron drops," Dyess countered. "Then when the goddamned Japs head this way who am I going to use for flight leaders? Some of these kids with two hundred hours, Boyd?"

"Gentlemen, enough," said Maverick. "Is this Davis?"

Everyone in the Ops Shack turned to look at Jack, who judged it wise to come to attention, salute and bark "Lt. Davis reporting as ordered, sir!"

Dyess returned his salute, frowning. "Well, Jack, it appears you're being shanghaied," he said.

"Beg pardon?"

"Lieutenant, you're being temporarily assigned to the 17th Pursuit," Major Maverick said. "You may have heard about the night intruders we're trying to intercept?"

"Yes, sir, I have."

"Good. That's Lt. Wagner's problem, and now it's yours as well." Maverick turned to Dyess. "Ed, I'll either get you a new pilot somewhere or you can have Jack back when the balloon goes up. Fair enough?"

"It's not fair at all, Major," Dyess said stubbornly. "But I can follow orders as well as the next man."

"That'll do."

Dyess turned to Jack. "You heard the man, Jack."

"Yes, sir," Jack said.

"Come with me, Davis," Wagner said. "We're going to fly up to Clark Field in a half-hour, so get whatever you'll need as far as clothes and such for a week."

Jack looked at Dyess, who grimaced, shrugged, and made a shooing motion with his hand. Wagner marched past Jack, who turned to follow the older man.

"I hope you're not pissed off about this," Wagner said over his shoulder.

"Would it matter if I were?"

"Not at all."

"Then I'll just do my job, sir. How are we getting up to Clark Field?"

"I've got my P-40 here. You'll pick up one from the Depot that's been repaired."

"What happened to it?"

"Engine overheating. I'm told it's been fixed."

Jack considered that. Wagner's tone implied a warning, and the warning was consistent with everything that had happened since he got to the Philippines. *I'm told it's been fixed* translated to something on the order of *watch your ass, Mister, or you might bust it.*

"All right," Jack said.

Wagner stopped walking and turned to face Jack. "By the way, you're part of the family now, so you call me Buzz and I'll call you Jack, at least until you screw up. Fair enough?"

"Yes, sir, Buzz."

Wagner grinned, nodded, and headed towards the hangars. A pair of P-40s stood there.

A pair of mechanics buttoned up the inspection panels over the engine on the left pursuit. Jack went up to the left wing root and threw his parachute up into the cockpit.

"Excuse me, sir, but..."

"It's OK, corporal," Wagner said. "Mr. Davis here is with me."

The corporal nodded and went back to the panel. Jack climbed up on the wing root and looked into the cockpit. This airplane was new enough that it smelled mostly of engine oil and leather on the inside. He put his parachute on the seat pan and climbed down off the wing.

187

It took him a few minutes to preflight the pursuit. The airplane was in good shape. There was the barest streak of oil and soot behind the engine exhausts. The olive-drab paint looked fresh, and the squadron markings and national insignia stood out bright and bold. Jack paused, looking at the taped-over muzzles of the machine guns. The machine guns were fresh out of crates and installed in haste with traces of cosmoline preservative still on the barrels. He hoped the barrels were clear, at least.

He opened the inspection panel on the cowling and checked the oil, peering up into the recesses of the engine compartment. An overheating engine could result from many different things. The cooling system in the P-40 wasn't the best and the Allison engine loved to overheat.

Pvt. Jelabin drove up in his old truck as Jack finished the preflight. The private pulled Jack's B4 bag from the seat beside him along with another, smaller bag.

"Thanks, Private," Jack said, taking the bags.

"Yo welcome, Mistuh Davis," said Jelabin. "Suh, they didn't give me too much time, and Mistuh Dyess, he just said y'all was gonna stay a couple nights, so I didn't pack your Class A uniforms."

"That's fine." Jack looked in the B4 bag and the smaller barracks bag. He pulled out a holstered .45 automatic and looked at Jelabin. "You know something I don't, Jelabin?"

The private shrugged. "Y'all never know when a good pistol might come in handy. What if y'all have to hit the silk and find yourself out in the woods? I hear they is some mighty mean hogs runnin' wild out there, and I mean mighty mean."

"Buck teeth and all?"

"And maybe little slanty eyes, too, suh, if you see what I mean."

"I do, Jelabin, and thanks. Hopefully I'll be back in a couple of days, but you look after things around here for me, OK?"

"I'll do that, suh." They exchanged salutes. The private got back in the truck and drove off.

Jack shook his head. It was the first time Jelabin had ever saluted him.

"Guess there's a character like that in every squadron," Wagner said from behind Jack. "You ready, Davis?"

Jack nodded. He stowed the bags in the compartment behind the cockpit, but he kept the holstered .45 out.

Wagner raised a sardonic eyebrow when Jack put the pistol harness on, clipping the loop through the belt of his coveralls.

"You never know," said Jack. He pulled the pistol, took out the clip, and checked to be sure there wasn't a round in the chamber before replacing the clip in the pistol and the pistol in its holster.

"Ready, Tex?" Wagner asked.

"Ki-yippy-ki-yay, Buzz."

The squadron leader shook his head and went to his own plane. Jack climbed into the cockpit of the P-40. One of the mechanics climbed up on the wing root and helped him with his harness.

"Thanks," Jack said. "You the crew chief?"

"No, sir. We just got this thing fixed here at the Depot. I'll help you get the engine started when you're ready."

"Good. I been flying those damned old P-35s for the last week. Might not remember how to handle a real airplane."

"You'll be fine, sir," the mechanic said. "We'll just take it from the top."

Ten minutes later Jack sat at the end of the active runway, behind and to the right of Wagner. Jack's headphones crackled.

"Nichols Tower, this is Army Seven Three Six with a flight of two, ready for takeoff."

"Roger, Seven Three Six. You are cleared for takeoff."

"Thanks, Nichols."

Wagner looked over his shoulder at Jack, who held up his right hand, thumbs-up. Wagner nodded.

Jack's eyes swept once over his engine instruments and fed in throttle and boost as Wagner accelerated down the runway. He came in with right rudder, gently, a little more as the tail came up and the pursuit accelerated even faster. He felt the little pressures in the stick that was the airplane's way of telling him it was ready to fly, and eased back on the stick. Ahead of him Wagner was sucking up gear and flaps. Jack did the same, then pulled into the wingman's slot off Wagner's right wing.

"Lead to Two," came over his headphones.

"Two, go ahead, Lead," Jack replied.

"Jack, we'll climb to nine thousand on heading 327. We'll set up for normal cruise, which should put us at Clark Field in a half-hour or less."

"Roger that."

"Just in case you're wondering, no hijinks on the way. We need to conserve these airplanes, especially the engines."

"Aw, shoot, and I was looking forward to a little rat-racing."

"You'll have plenty of fun tonight, I promise."

"Swell."

The city of Manila spread out below them. Manila Bay was on the left, with ships of all descriptions at anchor in the harbor. Ahead of them cumulus clouds built up over the land, and in the far distance to the west he made out the island forts at the entrance to Manila Bay.

At nine thousand feet they leveled out, over the northeast shore of Manila Bay. Clark Field was forty miles north.

Jack listened to Wagner talking to the Clark Field tower over the radio as they flew over the bay and crossed the shore. In the distance he could see Mt. Penatubo, just to the north of the field.

They entered the downwind leg of the approach. Clark didn't look much different from the last time Jack flew in, the day Roy Chant died. There were B-17s parked uncomfortably close to the edge of the sod runway and the P-40B's of the 20th Squadron in front of the hangars. Two B-18s and three P-35s were parked at the ramp along with some O-46 and O-52 observation aircraft. The roofs of the hangars were painted in a bold red-and-white checkerboard pattern for easy visibility. As he fishtailed his P-40 for spacing behind Wagner, Jack wondered why no one had thought about at least painting the roofs of the hangars brown or green, or anything but that bright white and red, which made a wonderful aim point for any bombardier.

Jack turned crosswind, kept his eyes open for other aircraft in the pattern, sparing a glance to look straight up and behind him, put his gear down and slowed the airplane, turning on final and dropping flaps. There was a puff of dust on the sod runway as Wagner touched down. The dust drifted a little to the left. Jack looked at the wind sock on top of the tower. Hardly enough crosswind to matter. Jack came back on the throttle as the ground came up, and his main gear touched the runway at nearly the same spot as Wagner's, the rough *chirp* of the tires on the sod lost in the rumble of the airframe. The P-40 vibrated with each minute undulation of the runway, bleeding off speed until the tail came down of its own accord. Jack applied brake until the airplane slowed, then started a gentle fishtail to the ramp so he could see what was ahead of the airplane despite the long snout of the P-40. An airman directed him to a spot on the ramp next to Wagner's pursuit. Jack swung his airplane on its brakes, ran the engine up to clear the plugs, and shut it down.

Wagner walked over to Jack as he climbed down out of the cockpit. "Come on, I'll introduce you to the guys."

Jack followed Wagner to another tent. This one had a wooden counter set up in front of it and a neatly-lettered sign that read "17th PURSUIT SQUADRON – OPERATIONS." A canvas awning provided rudimentary shade. A half-dozen pilots sat on a ramshackle collection of chairs surrounding a tin tub full of ice and Coca-Colas. They were dozing but looked up when Wagner came in.

"Sammy, where's John?" Wagner asked one of the pilots.

"Racked out in his tent," the pilot replied. He looked at Jack. "Who's this?"

"Jack Davis from the 21st. He's with us for awhile. Have a seat, Jack, and grab yourself a Coke."

Jack sat down in one of the two available chairs and took a Coke from the tub. The other pilots went to sleep, except for John, who looked at Jack without any particular warmth.

"Jack Davis from the 21st, huh?" Sammy said.

"That's right," said Jack. He opened the Coke with the key hanging from the tub and took a long swig.

"What the hell are you doing here?" Sammy asked. At his tone two of the other pilots opened their eyes.

Jack looked at Sammy. "Well, I'll tell you, Sammy. About two hours ago I was wringing out a P-35 just out of the repair shop. When I came down your boss was arguing with my boss about who had dibs on my services. Major Maverick sided with your boss, and here I am."

"Here you are. Yeah. But I still haven't heard what you're doing here."

Jack took another drink from the bottle. "Then you must be deaf, pal, 'cause I did tell you what I'm doing here. I'm following orders. That good enough for you or is this some frat I need an initiation to join?"

"This here is the 17th Pursuit, Jack," Sammy replied. "We've been out here longer than anyone, and not just anyone flies with us."

"Not exactly what I heard," Jack replied. "I guess you take whomever the Army sends you. Now look, you have some kind of beef with me. Are you just the kind of idiot who wants to cause trouble or do you want to see if I'm going to back down?"

Jack took another swig from the Coke and kept eye contact with Sammy.

Wagner came out of the interior of the tent. Out of the corner of his eye Jack saw Wagner take in the situation with a swift glance.

"Sammy, go check on Two-Four-Three, will you?" Wagner asked conversationally. "Chief Willis says it's ready."

For a moment Sammy kept his eyes on Jack's. Jack stayed perfectly relaxed, looking Sammy in the eye. Then Sammy said, "Yes, sir," without looking away from Jack .

Sammy walked away. Wagner watched him go, sat in the seat he vacated, and took a Coke from the tub.

"Didn't think you knew any of my guys, Jack," Wagner remarked conversationally.

"I'm the sort who makes friends wherever I go, Boyd," Jack replied.

"I see that," said Wagner drily. "Am I going to have to referee, or can you behave yourself?"

"I'm just sitting here minding my own business," Jack said. "What's the drill?"

"Get some rest. We go on 5-minute cockpit alert at sundown."

"Will I fly the same plane I brought in?"

"If you want."

"OK. Is the crew chief with the airplane?"

"He can be."

"I'd appreciate it. I'd like to take the airplane up and wring it out a little bit, especially if you want me to fly instruments tonight."

"Whatever you need, Jack."

"Any idea how high the Japs are when they come over?"

"Don't know for sure it's the Japs," Wagner observed.

"Guess not. So how high are they?"

"Good question. Nobody knows. The radar at Iba indicates direction of a blip, not height."

"That's not much good."

"Better than nothing."

"Can I have some oxygen? I'd like to test the engine at high altitude in daytime before we do a climb in the dark."

"Sure. I'll see to it." Wagner grinned. "Anything else I can do for you?"

"Will we have some .50-cal. ammo for tonight?"

"You bet."

"Great. Thanks, boss."

28,000 Feet

Jack kept the airplane in a standard rate turn as he climbed, scanning the sky around him while keeping a close eye on the engine instruments, especially the cylinder head temperatures. He wanted to be sure the mechanics had fixed whatever caused the engine to overheat. Landing with a dead engine at night was nothing he wanted to have to try, any more than he wanted to make a night parachute jump into the jungle.

The engine purred out an even rumbling song. It got cool in the cockpit and kept getting cooler, even with the heat turned up all the way. Jack took a deep slow breath of oxygen, glancing at the oxygen blinker on the panel. The engine instruments looked good, everything in normal operating range.

The cloud tops were at his level or below. Above him there was only deep blue sky, with the sun falling to the west.

At 28,000 feet he figured he was high enough. It would take fifteen minutes to add another 3,000 feet anyway to reach the service ceiling. His auxiliary fuel tank ran dry. Jack switched to the main fuel tank, listening for the engine to hesitate, but it ran smoothly. He relaxed as he leveled out, running to the north. At this altitude he could see all the way to the ocean beyond the north end of the island of Luzon. Lingayen Gulf spread out

193

before him at 10 o'clock low. He saw a ship cruising near the shore of the Gulf.

Jack looked north again.

More likely than not the Japs would come from that direction. The island of Formosa, rumored to be lousy with Jap Army and Navy airplanes, lay due north of Luzon, 500 miles away, more or less. He doubted the Jap bombers would come with fighter escorts, but it wasn't hard to imagine a flight of Jap bombers coming down the west coast of Luzon. A surprise attack before war was declared could stay over international waters before turning east to attack Manila or the shipping in Manila Bay. Jack wondered what it would be like, to spot a few glints in the sky, and have those glints turn into airplanes full of bombs and machine guns and men ready to kill you on sight.

Jack set his throttle and mixture for cruise conditions and resumed a standard rate turn, maintaining his altitude, watching the engine instruments and the sky around and below him. Clark Field came into sight below, and the silver glitter of an airplane in the pattern. The size made it a B-17, which made him think about Charlie and wonder where he was. The B-17 was nearly six miles below him. He watched it land, wondering if it would be as easy to spot Jap bombers.

He reversed his turn, watching the sky for a few more minutes. Then he eased the throttle to idle and gently pulled the stick back, feeling his way into the stall, put the nose down at the first shuddering warning in the elevator and the stick, then racked the P-40 into a diving turn. Jack kept the dive gentle at first, not wanting to build up his speed too quickly, then tightened his turn until the pursuit nibbled at the edge of an accelerated stall. At this altitude the wings would lose lift and stall in the turn at higher airspeeds than they would at low altitude. In turns you bled energy to maintain speed, losing height in the process. Jack reversed his turn, feeling out the effect of the roll on drag and airspeed over the wing, almost lost it, put the nose down and tried again. He kept it up until his fuel ran low. Then he dove towards Clark Field, keeping his throttle on idle to set up a dead-stick approach to landing.

The New Guy

"That's what we've seen the last two nights," Wagner said, standing in front of the blackboard. " Even with the radar at Iba feeding us vectors we've been playing hide and seek with the intruders. Weather tonight is supposed to be partly cloudy, with no moon until tomorrow morning at 0451 . Any questions?"

Jack looked around the tent.

Replacements and personnel shifts had left five of the original thirty-five pilots in place in the 17th Squadron. The others had gone to provide needed experience to the other pursuit squadrons of the 24th Pursuit Group. Wagner's statement this morning, that he had only five experienced pilots in his group, was correct.

Jack raised his hand.

"Yes, Jack?" Wagner asked.

"Sir, have we considered airborne patrols starting after sundown? Put a couple of ships up and let them orbit at 10,000 feet, conserve fuel and oxygen until the radar picks something up?"

Wagner frowned. "That's been considered. I'm told a standing air patrol would be wasteful of fuel and hard on the engines. For now, we'll do cockpit alert and wait for the radar at Iba or the observer net to give us a warning of unidentified aircraft. John, you and Talbot, you'll take the first watch, 1800 to 2200. It should be dark by about 1830. Davis, you and I will take 2200 to 0200. Simpson, you and Burns, 0200 to 0600. Any other questions?"

Wagner looked around. "OK, then, that's all. Jack, come with me."

Jack followed Wagner to a collection of tents close to the flight line. They were the typical six-man pyramid tents common to the Army and its need for temporary housing in odd places. Wagner indicated the first tent in the row.

"There's a spare bunk in there. Supper's in about twenty minutes. Grab a bunk and we'll go grab a bite."

Jack threw his helmet, parachute and Mae West on the nearest bunk and went with Wagner to the mess hall.

The mess hall was crowded. Jack stood in line with Wagner, who started talking to another first lieutenant Jack didn't know. A captain got in line behind Jack. He wore pilot's wings but Jack didn't know him.

"Excuse me, Captain," Jack said to the man. "Are you with the 19th Bomb Group?"

"That's right," the captain replied.

"My name's Jack Davis, sir," Jack said. "My brother, Charlie Davis, is with the 19th."

"Charlie? You're Charlie's kid brother?"

"That's me. I wondered if you'd heard from him lately. I thought he'd be out here by now."

"Charlie's with the 93rd Bomb Squadron," the captain said. "They got here three days ago. Charlie wasn't with them. I'm pretty sure I heard his airplane had some engine trouble on the way to Hawaii."

"Any way I can find out if he's still back in the States?"

The captain looked around the crowded mess hall. "Over there in the corner, see that colonel? That's Gene Eubanks. He's CO of the 19th."

Jack looked where the captain pointed. In a corner of the mess hall was a table reserved for senior officers. A tired-looking colonel sat with a red-faced major, nodding as the major talked.

"Who's that with him?" Jack asked.

"Rosie O'Donnell. Hell of a good guy. He's my squadron commander."

"Eubanks is nodding a lot."

The captain grimaced. "Hell, I heard they're sending about half the bomb group to some pineapple field down in Mindanao. You may have noticed there's not a hell of a lot of room for heavy bombers here at Clark."

"You guys do seem to have those things parked close to the runway."

"We don't like it any better than you pursuit guys. Problem is the damn ground's too soft if you go too far off the runway, and our bombers bog down."

"Jesus."

"No kidding."

Jack looked at Eubanks, who was still listening to O'Donnell. He grimaced.

"Maybe I'd better not bother them if they're planning a move like that."

"You're pretty smart for a second lieutenant," the captain said agreeably.

They moved forward in the line. After they got their food Jack went with Wagner to a table populated mostly by 17th and 20th Squadron pilots, all young second lieutenants commanded by not-much-older first lieutenants.

The food was good; beef patties with mashed potatoes in gravy, rolls, corn on the cob and green beans. There was apple pie for desert. The mess hall itself was hot, but fans stirred the air overhead and the building was constructed so that the windows on its side opened to create shade and let in the breeze.

Jack waited until he saw Col. Eubanks and Maj. O'Donnell pick up their trays and head for the dirty-dish stack by the exit. He picked up his own tray and went after them.

"Excuse me, Colonel Eubanks?"

The colonel and the major turned to look at Jack, who came to attention and saluted.

"A pursuit pilot, Gene," said the major. He had a florid, good-natured face with twinkling eyes. "But he knows your name. That can't be good."

The colonel rolled his eyes and returned Jack's salute. "What can I do for you, lieutenant?"

"Sir, my name is Jack Davis, and I..."

"Wait. Jack Davis? You're Charlie's brother?"

"Yes, sir. I was wondering how he is."

"He's fine, lieutenant. As far as I know. What I'm not sure about is where he is exactly."

"Is he coming here?"

"Should be. I heard he left California after he got a new engine on his B-17. I expect him any time."

Jack nodded. "Thanks, Colonel."

"My pleasure, lieutenant."

The two senior officers turned and left.

"I didn't know you moved in such rarefied circles, Jack," Wagner said behind him.

"I don't," Jack replied. "I figured if anyone would know about Charlie, it would be his CO."

"Sound enough thinking," Wagner agreed. He walked off towards the 17th's dispersal area. "How was your flight?"

"Everything looked good," Jack replied. "What d'you think, Boyd? Will the Japs come again tonight?"

Wagner shrugged. "They'll come tonight, or tomorrow night, or whenever the little yellow bastards damn well please. I'm not a fortune-teller. All I know is you and I will be waiting for them if they come. Good enough?"

"Guess it'll have to be."

Starlight and Arapaho

"Lieutenant Davis, wake up."

Jack blinked in the radiance of the flashlight. "God damn it, get that light out of my eyes," he said.

"Sorry, sir."

"Jesus, private, didn't they tell you about night adaptation?"

"Night what, sir?"

Jack sighed. "Nothing. Don't shine that light in my eyes again. You just made me night-blind for thirty minutes."

"Oh, hell. I'm sorry, sir."

"Next time turn the light out and shake me, OK? Spread the word about it, too. If you have to wake a pilot up who's supposed to fly at night, don't shine the damned flashlight in his eyes."

"Yes, sir."

"OK, I'm up. Take off."

"Yes, sir." The private left the tent. Jack swung his legs over the edge of the bunk, yawning, and fitted his feet into his boots. Working by feel he found his pistol and his helmet. Parachute pack and Mae West were sitting on the canopy rails of his P-40.

He went to the latrine nearby, relieved himself, and walked to the operations tent. Clark Field was ghostly under the stars. Jack looked overhead, estimating the cloud cover at about three-tenths.

"That you, Jack?"

"Yes, sir."

"OK. Glad to see you're early. Let's go ahead and preflight, then we'll warm up the engines."

"Yes, sir."

Jack had never preflighted a P-40 at night before. The P-40's crew chief handed him a flashlight with a red lens. He walked around the airplane with Jack, checking the control surfaces and the engine fluids, then helped Jack into the cockpit.

Wagner's airplane was next to Jack's. "Ready for engine start, Jack?"

"Yes, sir."

"OK. Wait for the go signal from your crew chief. Two red blinks from the flashlight."

"Two red blinks."

The crew chief clapped Jack on the shoulder and climbed down off the wing. Jack could just make him out, walking around the pursuit's wingtip and standing in front of the airplane.

"Ready?" a strange voice asked. Jack guessed it was Wagner's crew chief.

"Ready," said Jack's crew chief.

Jack saw two red flashes, but before he could react he heard Wagner's voice calling "Clear prop!"

Jack raised his voice. "Clear prop!"

First from Wagner's P-40 and then his own came the whine of the energizer, the labored turning of the propeller, the cough of the engine with a bit of blue fire out of the exhaust, another cough and then a series of them. Jack looked at his own engine instruments, glowing in the fluorescent lamps, as the Allison coughed one more time, then began to run as Jack advanced the throttle and the manifold pressure a little bit, standing on the toe brakes in case the chocks under the main wheels gave way.

He looked up from the instruments once the CHT and the oil temperature came up and glanced across at Wagner's airplane. There was an even blue flame winking from the exhaust pipes of Wagner's engine, and the roaring engines were nearly deafening.

Jack advanced the throttle to full power, holding the stick forward against the propeller blast, his feet firmly on the toe brakes. The airframe shook and shimmied, wanting to fly, wanting to fly, feeling the wind of the propeller blowing over the wings, fuselage and elevator. Jack felt it in his fingers, in the seat of his pants, in his feet.

The crew chief gave him two blinks. Jack pulled the throttle back, pulled the mixture to IDLE CUTOFF. The Allison spat in disgust, popped, banged, and stopped.

The crew chief climbed up on the wing next to Jack. "How'd she look, sir?"

"Pretty good. Gauges came up like normal, nothing strange."

"OK, glad to hear it. This is the one that overheated, right? We sent it down to the Air Depot at Nichols yesterday."

"That's right. I had her up to 28,000 this afternoon. Engine never gave any trouble."

"That's what it said on the Form 1. Don't mind me, lieutenant, I just like to make sure the machinery is working right."

"Sergeant, you call me Jack as long as you're working on my airplane. I like the machinery to work right too."

The man chuckled. "I'm Stan, Jack, and I'll do my best."

"Good enough."

The crew chief helped Jack out of the cockpit. Someone brought chairs out for Wagner and Jack to sit on by their airplanes.

In the big hangars work was going on.

"Tell me a little about your civilian flying, Jack," Wagner said. "You handled yourself pretty well in that little scrimmage we had."

"Friends of my Dad's," Jack said.

"Your Dad? What about him?"

"Dad flew in the Great War. He was killed in an airplane accident in 1938. I'd just gotten my license and a Waco biplane. Some friends of his used to fly with me."

"Let me guess. Some of his old squadron mates."

"That's right."

"So they taught you about watching for the Hun in the Sun and all that stuff?"

"A little."

"Good. That may be useful. Anything else?"

"Before I got accepted to the Air Corps I wangled my way in to an instrument flying course."

Wagner frowned. "How far did you get?"

"Not as far as some of the really advanced stuff like radio range landing approaches, but I can fly instruments pretty well."

"How come you didn't end up as an instructor? Or flying B-17s with your brother?"

"It was peacetime flying and civilian instructors, even if the instrument instructors work for United Airlines. Nobody asked. I didn't say. Besides, I wanted to fly pursuits."

"Like father, like son?"

"No."

Wagner was silent for a moment. Jack could see his face in profile. Wagner was looking up at the stars.

"Your family has money," Wagner said.

"We're comfortable."

The squadron commander nodded. "So again, Jack, I think I have to ask why the hell you're here. You've got money, you've probably got connections. You could have all sorts of jobs back Stateside, but here you are in the asshole of the world with the rest of us, waiting on Hirohito to decide whether or not to come south. Why?"

"This is where I was ordered, Boyd."

"If you're going to be on my wing, Jack, I want to be sure of you."

Jack hitched his chair closer to Wagner's and spoke in a low whisper. "Can you hear me, Boyd?"

"Yes."

"That was insulting. I don't think you'd ask any of your other pilots. So why are you asking me?"

"I don't trust rich guys who have things handed to them on a silver plate. They have a tendency to quit when things get tough." Wagner whispered also. He turned his face in the darkness so that he was only a few inches from Jack's.

"I had a lot of things given to me. I was born lucky. So what? I worked my ass off at Randolph and Kelly. I worked hard in the 31st. I worked hard for Ed Dyess. What's your problem?"

"I don't know you."

"Then why'd you ask for me?"

"I know you're a good pilot. I've seen you work. That doesn't mean I know you. I haven't had a chance to watch you, learn what makes you tick. I still don't know, not for sure. But you're pissed off for all the right reasons. That's good enough for me, for now, so I hope you'll accept an apology."

Wagner stuck out his hand.

Jack hesitated, just for a second. He was angry. Then he nodded and took Wagner's hand.

"No offense, boss, but I don't know you either. You don't let me down, and I won't let you down. Fair enough?"

"Fair enough." They shook on it.

The slow hours passed as the stars turned overhead and the clouds drifted on the wind. The two pilots talked off and on. Jack learned that Wagner had studied aeronautical engineering and was from a town in Pennsylvania named Nanty Glo.

"Nanty Glo?" Jack asked. "Where's that?"

"About sixty miles east of Pittsburgh. Just a little small town, but it's home. How about you?"

"Aw, Bridgeport, Connecticut, I guess, with a lot of time in New York and down in Savannah, Georgia, where Mom is from. I was at Yale for two years but I already knew I wanted to go into the Air Corps, so I took a little bit of everything. English, chemistry, physics, calculus, history, you name it."

"Think you might go back to school some day?"

"I guess it depends. You?"

"I'd like to finish that engineering degree."

The telephone rang in the Ops Shack.

"Scramble the alert section!"

Jack ran to his P-40, shrugged into his parachute harness, and climbed into the seat. His crew chief reached in, helping him with the oxygen mask and the seat harness. Then someone jumped up on the wing next to the crew chief.

"Major Grover says to stand down. False alarm."

Jack leaned back in his seat, letting out his breath in an explosive rush. "Crap."

A Ford truck chugged up to the flight line and stood idling while someone got out.

"Want me to help you out, sir?" the crew chief asked.

"No. I'll sit here for a minute, chief. If they can decide it's a false alarm maybe they'll decide it's the real thing."

"OK, Mr. Davis."

The figure who got out of the truck walked over to Wagner's P-40 and climbed up on the wing. Jack could hear them talking.

"Hey, Jack."

"Sir."

"Let's go up and have a look anyway."

"You're the boss."

They started engines. The Ford truck led them to the departure end of Clark's sod runway. They turned to face down the field, Wagner ahead of Jack, opening his engine up to check the magnetos. Ahead of them weak, ghostly blue lights outlined the runway. From the tower came a green light.

Wagner's P-40 accelerated down the field. Jack pushed forward on throttle and manifold pressure, coming off the brakes, heart beating a little fast from the adrenaline of takeoff at night on a partially blacked-out field, watching the blue winking exhaust from the right-hand exhaust stack of Wagner's engine ahead and on his left and the blue runway lights speeding by off his right wingtip. Jack lifted his tail off the runway and two seconds later he saw Wagner's exhaust flames start to rise. Jack hauled gently back on the stick, keeping formation off Wagner's right wingtip.

"Arapaho, Arapaho, this is Starlight," said Ground Control.

Wagner answered. "Arapaho Leader, go ahead Starlight."

"Make your vector zero zero zero, climb to angels ten."

Jack cleaned up landing gear and flaps. Wagner wasn't in any hurry. He started climbing at most economical climb, about 1000 feet per minute. The P-40 was heavy and well-armed; it was made to fight at low to medium altitude, not bounce up into the stratosphere like a rocket. That, Jack reflected sourly, was why the brass decided the airplane only needed a single-stage supercharger that lost half its efficiency above 17,000 feet.

Interference and static hummed and crackled over their earphones. Jack kept it tucked in close to Wagner's airplane.

"Starlight, Arapaho is at ten."

"Affirmative, ...pahoe. Hat... ."

"Starlight, did not understand your last transmission, say again."

"(*ssss*)at ten."

"Roger, Starlight, holding at ten."

Wagner started a standard-rate turn to the left. Jack stayed in tight. Once he thought he saw a pale flash in the cockpit of Wagner's airplane that might have been Wagner's face, looking back to see if he was there.

They completed a turn and started another. Jack watched the clouds and the stars; the clouds were barely visible all around them. He could tell from the lights of the towns on the plain of Luzon below them that they were drifting to the west with the wind. Manila was a soft glow on the southern horizon; Corregidor and Mariveles were evident at the mouth of Manila Bay. He looked at the clock on the instrument panel, which read 0055h.

"Arap... is Starlight. Contact. Make (*ssss-pop*) ... three zero zero for inbound."

"Three zero zero," Wagner affirmed. "Starlight, be advised, radio contact is intermittent, repeat, radio contact is intermittent. Arapaho coming to heading three zero zero for inbound contact."

Starlight's reply was lost amid the hiss and crackle of static.

They came around to due north; Wagner rolled out on a heading of three zero zero and started a gentle climb.

Jack remembered the manual for interception they'd gone over, however briefly, at Clark Field last week. The radar command was supposed to include a speed as well as a vector.

"Ours not to reason why," Jack said to himself.

Then he looked at his CHT, which had started to heat up after running fine for the last twenty minutes. It wasn't in the danger range, but it looked high for this throttle setting. It climbed a few more degrees and steadied down. Jack scanned the rest of the engine instruments, which showed normal operation.

The two P-40s were over the west coast of Luzon in moments. There wasn't a lot to see. The only way you could tell you were over the ocean was the faint lights of coastal villages suggesting a line in the darkness.

Abruptly the interference over their headphones faded.

"Arapaho, this is Starlight, come left to two eight zero."

"Two eight zero, Arapaho."

Jack followed Wagner into a gentle turn.

"Arapaho, this is Starlight. You're right on top of them."

Jack looked around. He was flying formation at night looking for another airplane that they knew was close, but not how close.

Adrenaline started up again. The thing about a midair collision at night is how very, very sudden and unexpected it is.

He looked up, but they were flying under a cloud. There wasn't a lot of cloud, about three-tenths, but enough that it made hide-and-seek a real possibility. Then they flew out from under the cloud. Above them there were only stars.

Jack wondered what he'd actually see. Evidently the intruder seen about a week ago off the mouth of Manila Bay had been flying with his navigation lights on. But that was a week ago. If the Japs were actually probing their defenses, they'd be running dark, with only the flames of their engine exhaust to give them away. That would be visible only from certain angles and from close range.

But the flame from his engine exhaust was the only sure reference he had on Wagner's airplane, and if Wagner maneuvered abruptly they'd lose contact at once. Keeping formation on a moonless night took constant attention. Jack, flying Wagner's wing, couldn't do much looking around for Starlight's radar contact.

"Arapaho to Starlight, zero contact, repeat, zero contact."

The static returned with a howl and a popping hiss like frying bacon.

"Starlight, say again."

There was a pause. "Arapaho, you (*sss-skree*) of the contact."

Jack darted a look around, back to Wagner's airplane, then another look in a different place, then back to Wagner.

"Starlight, this is Arapaho. We have zero contact, repeat zero contact."

Jack darted looks around the sky while Wagner tried to talk to ground control through the crashing, moaning static. All Jack saw was the clouds and the stars. There was a faint radiance on the eastern horizon that might be the rising moon, still under the horizon. He looked at his fuel gauge. He was good for now, but that damned cylinder head temperature was up another notch. The oil pressure and temperature looked normal, and if it was engine overheating the oil temp should be increasing too.

For the briefest moment he heard Roy Chant's voice in his head, but it was just a memory. Jack shoved it back and looked again at the shadowy outline of Wagner's pursuit and the blue flames of its exhaust.

"Arapaho Lead to Arapaho Two."

"Go ahead, Lead."

"See anything?"

"Negative, Lead."

"OK, Lead is turning to one eight zero. Follow me, Two."

"Roger, Lead."

"Starlight, Starlight, Arapaho has negative contact, coming to one eight zero. Advise contact."

Jack played the moving geometry in his mind. He didn't know that much about radar or how it worked, but a heading of 180 would take them south along the coast. That made sense if the bogey was probing the defenses off Manila Bay, maybe.

Starlight hadn't said anything, though, about what heading the bogey was on. Or maybe they had and it was lost in the static. Jack figured Wagner wanted to get some separation from the bogey. Then maybe Starlight could vector them in again.

Jack looked at his fuel gauge. They'd been up for an hour, more or less. Fuel wouldn't be an issue for two more hours. The field at Iba, where the radar station was located, was on the coast. It wasn't far off in case of an emergency.

He looked at his engine instruments again. The CHT indicator sat where it had the last time, a little high but not all that high. Jack scowled at it.

"Arapaho, Arapaho, ...light. ...to heading one seven..., one seven nine."

"Roger, Starlight, Arapaho is coming to one seven nine."

Jack looked at his gyrocompass. It showed they were on heading 180; he followed Wagner's lead, changing heading one degree to the east.

"Arapaho, ... the contact, repeat,... contact."

"Starlight, say again, your transmission garbled."

"*bbrrrsszttt...closingsssssssssstt...*"

"Arapaho Lead to Arapaho Two. Two, can you hear Starlight?"

"Lead from Two, garbled at best."

"See anything, Two?"

"Negative, Lead."

"Roger, Two, keep your eyes peeled."

Jack looked ahead and to the right; he knew Wagner should be looking ahead and to the left. All he could see was the same starlight on the barely-visible gray clouds with the radiance growing from the moon rising on the eastern horizon.

"Starlight, this is Arapaho, negative contact, negative contact."

"Underst... rapa. Continue present...."

"Starlight, you are still garbled, continuing on one seven nine, repeat, continuing on one seven nine."

Jack looked at his engine instruments.

This time there was no doubt. The CHT and the oil temperature were both climbing. He cross-checked his coolant flow gauge and manifold pressure settings.

He moved the fuel mixture to AUTO-RICH and opened the oil-cooler flaps to increase the flow of cooling air through the radiator, bumping the throttle forward a little to keep his speed up against the drag of the flaps. In theory, both of those should help cool the engine. In theory, but the temperature-indicating gauges were still climbing after a full minute.

"Arapaho Lead, this is Two."

"Go ahead, Two."

"Lead, my engine is overheating."

"Do you have an emergency?"

"Not yet, Lead."

"You check your fuel mix and oil-cooler flaps?"

"Got it in AUTO-RICH, flaps full open. Temps still going up."

"Roger that. Head for the barn, Two."

"What about you?"

"I'll stay for a little bit."

Jack bit off a curse. He looked at his gauges again; the temperatures were still climbing and he thought he heard something a little rough in the engine's note.

He didn't want to leave Wagner alone.

"Watch yourself."

"Scram, Two."

Jack retarded the throttle, put the nose down, and turned to the east. He and Wagner had climbed to twelve thousand feet and Clark was less than forty miles away. Jack did some quick mental arithmetic and set up a rate of descent at five hundred feet per minute with an indicated airspeed of 260 mph. He switched radio frequencies to contact the tower at Clark Field.

That frequency had a lot of static as well. Jack figured he might not be able to contact the field until he was closer but there was no harm in trying.

"Clark Tower, Clark Tower, this is Army Four Zero Four, come in, over."

Nothing but static.

Jack waited, looking at the lights of small towns and villages below, sweeping an eye over his instruments. Airspeed and rate of descent looked good but the engine temperatures were still climbing.

When an engine overheats past a critical temperature the fuel-air mixture in the cylinders begins to detonate instead of burn, and the viscosity of the lubricating oil breaks down. Cylinder sleeves blow out, cylinders freeze inside the sleeves, the cylinder shaft seizes, breaking the crankshaft, fuel lines rupture, the propeller shaft shears; an engine fire is a very real possibility. All of those pictures were playing in Technicolor inside Jack's mind, building on the adrenaline and the rapid beating of his heart.

It pissed Jack off. *It's not just for me*, he told his fear. *I'm flying for two*.

The adrenaline stayed along with the rapid heartbeat, but he looked around the cockpit and the surrounding night sky and realized he had everything under control that could be controlled. He debated opening the canopy in case he needed to bail out quickly, but decided that if a fire started the air over his canopy would suck the flame into the cockpit. Better to wait until he was on approach.

He keyed the radio again. "Clark Tower, Clark Tower, this is Army Four Zero Four, come in, over."

The reply was rough with static but clear enough: "Go ahead, Army Four Zero Four, this is Clark."

"Clark, Four Zero Four is inbound with an overheating engine."

"Roger, Four Zero Four. Estimate your position."

"Four Zero Four is ten miles west of the field at five thousand feet. I should be in the pattern within five minutes."

"Understood, Four Zero Four. We'll light the runway."

"Roger, Clark."

At one o'clock in the near distance light stabbed down the runway at Clark, picking out the silver B-17s parked along the runway.

"Four Zero Four has the runway, Clark."

Jack looked back at his engine instruments. The CHT and oil temps were edging into the danger zone. He looked back at the light illuminating the runway and then at his altimeter.

"Clark, say your altimeter."

"Four Zero Four, altimeter is two niner niner five, wind from the east at 5 mph."

"Two niner niner five."

Jack reached out and set his altimeter for the barometric pressure at ground level at Clark Field. He had to think for a minute to remember the field elevation varied from 500 feet near the hangars to 430 feet at the north end with a hump in the middle of it.

The engine rumbled and started to vibrate, hard.

Jack pulled the throttle all the way back and pulled the mixture to IDLE CUT-OFF, then hit the prop feathering control. The propeller spun to a stop, the blades turning knife-edge into the wind to reduce the drag to a minimum.

"Clark from Four Zero Four, my engine just quit. Entering the downwind."

"Affirmative, Four Zero Four. We'll roll the equipment."

Jack looked at his airspeed. He was still above 210 mph indicated with a 700 fpm rate of descent. He was good for altitude. As the airspeed bled down below 160 mph he hit the gear switch. The whine of the electrically-driven hydraulic pump was reassuring. Nose down a little to keep the speed up, flaps down below 150 mph with the hand poised above the lever for the emergency pump, but the electrical system worked fine. The flaps came down, the position indicator on the panel mimicking their movements. He checked the landing gear position indicator; green lights on the mains and the tail wheel.

He turned crosswind, and the big floodlight went out, leaving the blue lights outlining the runway. Jack abbreviated his crosswind and turned final, but it looked OK, he was lined up in the center of the runway, and the blue lights gave him adequate depth perception.

The main gear kissed the sod and began their bumpy rumble. Vague blurs of B-17 bombers flashed by. Jack kept the tail up as long as he could until the speed bled off and the tail quit flying of its own accord. He let the P-40 coast until it came to a stop, shut off the master switch, released his harness, and climbed down out of the cockpit.

The fire truck and the ambulance drove down the runway towards him. He looked at the cowling of the P-40's engine. There was just a little smoke coming out of it, visible in the headlights of the oncoming vehicles. Jack decided to walk away from the airplane. If it wanted to catch fire now it could do so without him standing nearby.

The fire truck stopped next to him.

"You need us, lieutenant?" the driver asked.

"There's a little smoke coming out from under the engine cowling," Jack replied. "Might just be hot oil."

The driver nodded. "Maybe we'll just give her a few minutes. If she catches fire right there she won't do any harm. It'll take that long for the airplane tug to get here."

The ambulance pulled up next to the fire truck. "You look pretty good to me, sir," the medic next to the driver said.

"I'm OK," Jack told him. "I'll wait with the firemen until the tug gets here."

The medic nodded and motioned to the ambulance driver, who reversed the vehicle and drove back down the runway.

Jack pulled off his helmet and ran his hand through his sweat-soaked hair. The stars cast a vague light over the parked airplanes, that gleamed silver where they hadn't had camouflage paint applied.

The tug drove up. Chief Willis was riding with the driver.

"What happened, Mr. Davis?" Willis asked.

Jack described the incident in a few words. The Chief nodded and grimaced.

"Sounds like the engine's gonna be good for spare parts and precious few of those," the Chief growled. "Well, at least you got the airplane down in one piece and didn't crack it into one of these here B-17s."

"I'll settle for that," Jack said.

The 17th had a field radio to listen in on the tower and Starlight frequencies. Jack tossed his gear on a chair and sat down next to the private who was listening in.

"Heard from Lt. Wagner?" Jack asked.

"Yes, sir. He never saw a thing. On his way back now."

Jack nodded. Then he yawned. "Where can a fellow get a cup of coffee around here, private?" he asked.

"Chief Willis has a pot going in the line shack, sir, if you ask polite."

"Guess I'd better ask real polite-like, after bringing back one of his airplanes with a dud engine."

"Chief won't mind that so much, sir. You got it down in one piece, and the Chief is always cussing those Allison engines."

"Thanks."

Jack walked over to the line shack, which was another tent, and knocked on the post beside the door.

"Who the hell is that? Quit knocking and come in"

Jack pulled the tent flap aside and stepped inside the tent. Outside it was still dark. Inside the tent was brilliantly lit by a battery of electric lights, shining on a work bench. On the work bench were laid out some shiny, oily parts Jack presumed came from an engine.

The Chief was glowering at the parts on the bench, but he looked up when Jack entered.

"What can I do for you, Lt. Davis?" he growled.

"I heard a rumor a man might get a cup of coffee if he asked politely," Jack replied.

"Well, you heard right. My own brew. Eat your stomach lining out if you drink it long enough." The Chief turned, examined a collection of purloined Army coffee mugs, picked one, and poured coffee from a percolator sitting on an electric coil.

"Here you go," he said. "That'll put hair on your chest."

Jack took a sip. He was inclined to agree with Chief Willis. The brew started out strong and had gotten stronger as it sat on the coil.

Jack took a second sip. "Well, if it don't put hair on my chest it might make my toenails curl at that," he said.

The Chief stuck a cigar in his mouth and lit up. "Know what these are?" he asked.

"Something out of an engine. Gears and a drive shaft. Drive shaft fractured and the gears stripped. Hell, is that out of my airplane?"

"Not bad for a pilot. Yes, it's from your airplane. That's from the coolant pump. I don't know what caused that damned Allison engine to start overheating but this is what ended up happening, and I don't know why. Now, Lt. Davis, engines are still a little more art than science, but I like to think I know something about them. You know what I suspect?"

"Nope."

"The depot down at Nichols put a bunch of P-40s together before we found out we didn't have any Prestone. Had about a dozen of them, sitting out on the flight line, nice and pretty and useless as tits on a boar hog. You can't fly a liquid-cooled engine without Prestone, and sitting out in the tropical sun ain't good for an airplane. I think something got in the cooling system, made itself at home, and didn't flush out when we replaced the coolant after it overheated the last time."

"Could be," said Jack.

The Chief shrugged. "Just a suspicion. I got no real idea. Lots of reasons the cooling pump drive-shaft might've fractured. And here comes the skipper."

There was the humming drone of a P-40 entering the pattern. Jack took another sip of the coffee. "Thanks for the joe," he told the Chief.

"Anytime, lieutenant. Keep the cup. I always forget to take 'em back to the mess hall."

Jack took the cup with him and walked back out to the 17th's flight line.

Wagner taxied up to his parking slot with an airman waving him in with hand signals. The squadron commander shut the airplane down at the "cut" command and sat in the cockpit for a moment. The crew chief climbed up on the wing root, conferred with Wagner, then handed him a clipboard. Wagner signed the Form One and stood up.

"Hey, Jack," he said. "Down in one piece, I see."

Jack nodded. "Heard you didn't see anything."

Wagner climbed out of the cockpit as Jack walked over to him.

"I wouldn't say that, exactly. I saw a lot of sky, a lot of cloud and some really pretty stars. I always like those. What I didn't see was whoever or whatever is flying around our airspace."

Wagner nodded at the cup. "Chief Willis gave you some of that battery acid he calls coffee?"

"I asked him nicely."

"Jiminy. Let's go get some breakfast and talk about the flight. I think the mess hall has better coffee than that."

They sat down to ham and eggs and coffee and ate for a few minutes before speaking again. Joe Moore from the 20th Pursuit came and sat with them, then they were joined by Major Grover and Major Maverick from 5th Interceptor Command.

"Rough night," said Grover. He looked at Jack. "Nice landing, by the way, lieutenant. I heard you brought your P-40 in dead stick."

"It was that or hit the silk, Major, and I'm too chicken for that," Jack replied.

Grover grinned. "What did you think of the exercise?"

"Sir, I'm not an expert on night interception, but I felt pretty useless up there."

"You personally, or the mission as a whole?"

"Me personally, I spent most of my time trying to stay with Lt. Wagner. Seemed to me that if I took my eyes off him for more than a few seconds I stood a good chance of losing touch with him. Then trying to find him we might collide with each other. I also got the impression that Lt. Wagner was concerned over the same thing."

Wagner raised an eyebrow. "Actually, Jack, I was, the way you were wandering all over the sky back there." The squadron commander grinned. "Just kidding. Jack stuck tighter than the proverbial burr. But he raises a good point. We're risking too much sending more than one airplane up at a time."

Maverick nodded. "That's the way the RAF does it. One airplane at a time."

Grover looked at him. "You been reading intelligence reports again?"

Maverick shrugged. "We'll have to learn to fight at night sooner or later. We have to work with what we have, but our radar isn't close to what the Brits use."

Wagner nodded. "If we knew height as well as direction that would be useful. As it is, we're stooging along in the dark. It would take some luck to come across a Jap bomber with this setup."

"You think we ought to stop trying?" asked Maverick.

"No, sir. We might get lucky." Wagner shrugged. "I'm not sure this is the best use of our resources, though."

"What d'you mean?"

"Jack here is a pretty good pilot. We don't have a lot of good pilots, and we don't have a lot of airplanes, either, not to mention .50-cal. ammunition. Luck can break both ways. What if Jack's engine had caught fire instead of lasting long enough to get him back to base? What if we'd found that intruder the hard way, by crashing into him? We stand to lose good pilots and good airplanes, to no good end."

"You don't think we should shoot the Japs down if they're probing our airspace?"

Wagner grimaced. "That's our job. We aren't really equipped to do it at night, though. When the Japs come for real they'll do it in the daytime. We might wish we had the people and airplanes we lose trying to run night interceptions when the real show starts."

Grover nodded. Maverick frowned. "Guess we'd better talk to Colonel George about it," Maverick said. He nodded towards Jack. "Boyd, you have another airplane for this young man?"

"No, sir. I doubt Chief Willis is going to be able to resurrect the engine in that P-40. We'll have to get one from the Depot."

"Maybe you should send him back to the 21st. That would make Ed Dyess happy."

Wagner looked at Jack. "What d'you think, Jack?"

"I go where I'm sent, sir."

Wagner looked at Maverick. "The deal was I got to keep Jack until the balloon goes up. Then we send him back to the 21st."

Maverick nodded. "You'd make a pretty good lawyer back in Texas, Wagner. Tell you what. It's too crowded for you guys and the 20th here at Clark. Take your squadron back to Nichols in the morning. You can get a new P-40 for Lt. Davis from the Air Depot. I'll call Ed Dyess and smooth his feathers a little."

"Thank you, Major."

The two majors left, taking their trays. Wagner sipped his coffee and looked at Jack.

"You want to stay with my squadron," Wagner stated.

"Yes, sir."

"Why? Ed struck me as a pretty good squadron commander. Maybe as good as me. He's got a pretty good outfit, too. Truth is, most of my guys are about as green as most of Ed's guys, after all the shuffling and moving around."

Jack shrugged. Then he leaned forward. "You know I lost a friend."

"Roy Chant. I know."

"It's a little easier with people that don't know you and don't give a crap about you until you earn it. Does that make sense?"

Wagner nodded. "OK. Welcome to the 17th Pursuit, Lt. Davis."

CHAPTER ELEVEN
Communications

Colonel George Lays It Out

Jack filed into the post theater with the rest of the 17th
Pursuit. He waved at some of his squadron mates from the 21st.
He saw Ed Dyess, but Dyess was talking to another pilot Jack
didn't know.

They found seats. The theater was abuzz with conversation,
the air was thick with heat, humidity and cigarette smoke.

Major Maverick came on stage. "'Ten-hut"

The pilots in the audience came to attention. Silence fell
immediately.

Colonel Hal George came onstage behind Maverick.

"Rest, gentlemen," said Colonel George.

Jack looked curiously at the CO of Fifth Interceptor
Command. He saw a man about the age his father would have
been. He had heard that Colonel George, like his father, was an
old-time aviator, had flown in France in the last war, and was an
ace with five kills.

There was a quiet murmur as the pilots of the two squadrons
took their seats. George stood in front of them with his hands

behind his back, looking slowly around the theater. Jack saw George's scan stop here and there, as if he were marking the presence of someone he knew. It stopped at Boyd Wagner, two seats down from Jack, and then passed over Jack with the briefest of glances.

After perhaps a minute there was utter silence in the room except for the occasional cough.

Then George began to speak.

"You all know that we pursuit pilots are here to provide for the air defense of the Philippines," George said. "The decision to reinforce the Philippines was made in Washington only last May. That may account for some of the, ah, somewhat hasty and impromptu nature of things in the Far Eastern Air Force."

There was a derisive snort from somewhere in the audience. George nodded.

"I feel the same way," he continued. "Now, we all know that out here in the Orient there are only a few major players. The British are in the west, in Malaysia, Burma and India. Holland was occupied by the Germans last year, but the Dutch colonies in Java and Borneo are south of us. I'm informed they are very serious indeed about holding on to what they have. Besides, to the best of my knowledge, the Dutch and the British are both friendly nations who have every reason to want to stay friendly with Uncle Sam."

George paused again, looking slowly over the audience.

"So that's the west and the south," he said. "To the southeast there's Australia, also a friendly nation, part of the British Commonwealth, who also has every reason to stay friendly with us. To the east of us there's nothing but a hell of a lot of water and a few small islands for thousands of miles. Then there's our charming neighbor to the north, and I'm not talking about China. I'm talking about the Empire of Japan.

"Most of you know that since November 27 there have been reports of unidentified aircraft in or uncomfortably near the Philippine air defense zone. These incursions have all been at night. We attempted to intercept the intruders without result, and until we have a radar warning system that consists of more than one radar set, it seems unlikely we will make a successful interception absent the purest luck. Luck, however, is something upon which no man may count.

"Most of you know that the Japanese seized Vichy French possessions in Indochina last October. That puts a sizeable portion of their navy at a place called Cam Ranh Bay, about 800 miles west of here. Then, 500 miles north of us, is the island of Formosa."

George paused again, deliberately.

"I'm told there may be as many as three thousand Japanese military or naval aircraft in Formosa."

Jack blinked.

Three thousand?

Against maybe 90 P-40s and 35 P-35s?

"Jesus," someone muttered close by. "And the RAF thought they had it tough last year against the Krauts."

George let the noise level of comments rise for a moment before lifting one hand for quiet.

"I don't believe in sugar-coating things," George said. "This isn't a suicide squadron here, at least not yet. But all of you got through flight school, and that means you can do arithmetic. The best I can say about the odds is that they aren't in our favor. The rest of it you can figure out for yourselves."

In the audience there was now total silence.

"We could be at war at any time, and by that I mean next week, tomorrow, even an hour from now. You must, each of you, prepare yourself mentally. For make no mistake, we will fight. Each of you, I know, will fight. Here is the best advice I can give you.

"First, listen to your squadron and flight commanders. They are good, seasoned men, among the very best pilots in the Air Corps. I could not ask for better.

"Second, trust each other. We found in the Great War that air combat wasn't about individuals. There were some great pilots who made a lot of kills as lone wolves. Less than a handful lived through the war. Teamwork is the key. If you work together you will be far more effective at protecting each other and killing the enemy.

"Third, understand that you must, you will, kill the enemy. No sane man likes the idea of killing another man. Understand,

218

though, that the enemy *will* kill you if you give him the chance. With the odds against us you have no choice but to be ruthless and tough. There's nothing pretty about killing. There's certainly nothing pretty about being killed, so work hard at being killers. That's the best way you can serve your country and yourselves.

"Finally, a practical matter. You all know the orders the Minutemen were given at Lexington and Concord. 'Don't fire until you see the whites of their eyes.' That's a good rule for air fighting too. The closer you are, the less likely you are to miss. Get in close, then get closer. Stick your guns in their cockpits before you pull the trigger, and you won't miss."

George looked around for a moment longer.

"That is all." He turned and left the stage.

Major Maverick called the room to attention, but by the time the pursuit pilots had snapped to attention the Colonel was gone.

Jack looked around the theater.

The pilots were talking to each other in low tones. He couldn't blame them. Anyone with any brain matter whatsoever already knew they were in a tough spot, but Colonel George had spelled it out in language anyone could understand.

A *suicide squadron*? What the hell was that supposed to mean?

There was a slow movement towards the exits. Eventually Jack stood in the sunshine, adjusting his cap on his head and looking around. He saw an enlisted man trot up to Lt. Wagner. They exchanged a few words, then Wagner beckoned to Jack.

"Jack, I'm told you have a present waiting for you at the Air Depot," Wagner said. "You up for a little flying?"

"Hell, yes," Jack replied.

"Then remember what we just heard. Keep in touch with 5th Interceptor Command. You never know."

"Yes, sir."

Unidentified Aircraft

Darwin was 2000 miles behind them. After nine hours in the air Charlie was ready to land, stretch his legs, grab a shower and some chow and some sleep. He was quite sure that everyone in the airplane felt the same way.

219

"Pilot, navigator."

"Go ahead, navigator," Charlie replied.

"That's the Verde Island Passage on the left and the coast of Luzon ten miles ahead. Make your heading 339. ETA Clark Field forty-five minutes."

"OK, Al, good work. Radio operator, pilot."

"Radio operator here, sir."

"See if you can contact Clark Field, Dobbins. Send them our position and ETA."

"You got it, skipper."

The B-17 coasted over the beach. Charlie looked down at the dark green land below him, remembering what it had looked like three years ago from the porthole of the China Clipper.

"Pilot, radio operator."

"Go ahead, Dobbins."

"Skipper, Clark acknowledges our ETA. Get this, there's an unidentified aircraft in this area."

"Unidentified?"

"That's what they said, sir."

"Is it Japanese?"

"I asked if it was friend or foe, sir, but all they said was it's unidentified."

"OK. Thanks, Dobbins. Pilot to crew, you heard Dobbins. Be on the alert for that unknown aircraft."

A chorus of "Rogers" came over the interphone.

Bob Payne leaned over from the co-pilot's seat and tapped Charlie on the shoulder. "Think we ought to load the guns, skipper?"

Charlie thought about it. Almost certainly any lone intruder, unless it was a misidentified aircraft, was a Japanese photo-reconnaissance ship. Any such intruder would be flying at 25,000 feet or more.

The B-17 was flying at 8,000 feet. Even if the intruder were at low altitude Charlie doubted it was much of a threat.

Still...

"Oh, what the hell," said Charlie. "Good practice for the crew."

Charlie keyed his intercom. "Pilot to crew. Load your weapons. I repeat, load your weapons. But keep your fingers off the triggers until I give the word. No accidents."

"Navigator to pilot, unidentified aircraft at ten o'clock high!"

Jack had read and reread the pilot's manual for the P-40 in the last two weeks. Nevertheless he got the crew chief, Warshowski, to walk around the airplane with him. The mechanics knew things about the airplanes that weren't always in the manuals, and this one was fresh out of the Nichols Depot.

"Looks like a good airplane, Mr. Davis," Warshowski said when they completed their preflight. "I got the word about the ammo and you've got 700 rounds per gun. I'm pretty sure we even got all the cosmoline out of the barrels."

Jack nodded. "Have the guns been bore-sighted?"

"No, sir. We'll do that when you get back."

"OK. Tracers?"

"Every fifth round. Why?"

"Nothing. Something I heard once."

"Oh, you mean about leaving the tracers out, so if you miss, the guy you're shooting at doesn't see them go by?"

Jack nodded.

"If you want, sir, I'll have a word with the armorer and have the tracers taken out. That sort of thing is pretty much up to you."

Jack nodded and got in the airplane. The crew chief helped him buckle in. The big in-line Allison engine started with minimal persuasion, a little gray smoke wafting out of the exhausts to be blown to rags by the slipstream from the propeller. The crew chief watched the gages with Jack until the oil pressure and engine temperature came up into their operating ranges.

"Good luck, Mr. Davis," the crew chief said, speaking in Jack's ear to be heard over the rumbling engine, and climbed down from the wing.

Thirty minutes later Jack was above 20,000 feet with the cockpit heat going full blast. He shivered a little in the cold and wished he'd brought more in the way of clothing than his leather flying jacket. He leveled out to admire the view.

Nichols Field was below him to the southwest as he circled between Norzagaray and Angat Lake. Manila was only a little to the north of Nichols, and the great stretch of Manila Bay was visible all the way to the Bataan Peninsula in the west, and to the east he could see Lamon Bay. There were white clouds puffing up to his altitude, and what was that to the south?

It was a glint of sun on aluminum.

Jack switched his radio to the Interceptor Command frequency. Repeated calls brought no response save howls of atmospheric static. Jack tried the operations frequency at Nichols Field and heard someone talking but apparently it was an airplane or airplanes in the pattern. No one answered his calls.

"God-damn radio," he said to no one in particular. The tropics were hard on radios and the Philippines seemed to add its own difficulties.

Jack checked his fuel and looked all around him. Except for himself and the unidentified aircraft there appeared to be nothing else in the sky.

He looked at the dot, thousands of feet below and still five miles to the south. It was an unlikely direction for the Japs to come from, but not unlikely to be an aircraft coming from Australia, or even from the Dutch colonies in Java.

It might be Japs, one of the big four-engined flying boats flown by their Navy, maybe. The intruders had been coming at night, but sooner or later they'd try by day. They could figure that the FEAF would be looking to the north, which was the most likely direction for a Jap attack to come, and if they came from the south they'd be over Manila and Manila Bay before anyone knew what was happening.

Yeah. Maybe.

Jack turned his gunsight to full bright and armed the six machine guns. He debated firing his guns but decided against it. The bright stream of tracers might alert the Japs.

If they were Japs.

Jack changed heading and began a gentle descent. Every few minutes he tried Interceptor Command on the radio, but other than a scraping, screeching noise over his earphones, there was no reply.

Charlie leaned forward and peered up through the narrow windscreen of the Fortress. The little speck was still there, but it had changed heading and seemed to grow slightly. He felt something prickle on the back of his neck and realized it was the hairs there.

"Radio operator, anything else from Clark about an unidentified aircraft?"

"No, sir. There's a hell of a lot of static on the air just now, skipper. Might be the Japs, jamming our frequencies."

"OK, keep trying. And don't get carried away just yet." A thought struck Charlie. "Dobbins, what's the frequency for Radio Manila?"

"One second, skipper... Here it is. It's 407.3 kilocycles."

"Thanks."

Payne raised an eyebrow as Charlie leaned forward to the radio direction finder.

"Radio Manila ought to be raising hell if we're at war, right?" Charlie said as he set the frequency on the RDF.

"Oh, right," said Payne.

"Waist gunner to pilot."

"Go ahead, Lefty."

"Skipper, there's only one guy up there. Single engine, looks like a monoplane. He dipped his wings a second ago and changed heading."

"Thanks, Lefty. Keep your eyes on him. If this guy attacks it'll happen fast."

"Huh," came the reply. "I been tracking that S.O.B. for the last three minutes, Skip. If the little slant-eyed bastard wants to play we'll give him more than he wants."

Charlie started to say they weren't sure it was a Japanese aircraft. They weren't sure of anything but that their stalker was right where any pursuit would want to be.

Radio Manila came up on the RDF. A female voice crooned something in a language Charlie didn't recognize.

"Sure doesn't sound like they're too concerned," said Payne.

"No, it doesn't," Charlie agreed. But he looked up at the tiny cross-shape above them, now heading to come in from their six o'clock.

The classic attack from the rear, in the blind spot where the B-17D had no tail guns.

Jack tried to call Interceptor Command once again and swore in disgust when his headphones produced nothing other than screeching, howling, and a hiss-pop that sounded like bacon frying.

By now he was fairly sure that the airplane below him was an American B-17. He'd been watching them from below for the last two weeks as they sailed along on their high-altitude training exercises, so he was familiar with the silhouette.

That bomber guy, Eubanks, said Charlie and his crew might be along. He didn't know when, though, and no one had said anything about B-17s coming in from Darwin or wherever, and at this height one four-engined airplane looked a lot like another.

He would have to get close enough to be sure. Almost surely by now the crew of the other airplane knew he was here. Without surprise the only card he had to play was speed.

Jack tugged on his restraints, then tugged again to be sure they were as tight as he could manage. He didn't want to be thrown around during violent maneuvers.

Then he pulled up into a half-roll with a split-S at the top, straightening only when he had the small image of the unknown aircraft in his gun sight. He felt his finger creep over the trigger on the control stick. He deliberately relaxed but a moment later it crept over the trigger again.

He'd been airborne for less than an hour. Could the word have been passed and war declared since then?

Screw it. Jack concentrated on holding the P-40 steady as the speed built up and the unknown four-engined aircraft grew in his sights.

He grinned, hard and tight.

"Jesus, skipper, he's coming down, that bastard's coming down, seven o'clock high!"

Fear shot over the electrical circuit of the intercom, through Charlie's headset, and opened the adrenaline valves into his bloodstream so hard and fast his heart skipped a beat and he gasped for breath. It was only a fraction of a second.

"Keep the line clear!" Charlie ordered. His own voice sounded higher than he liked. He took a deep breath. "Call the bandit!"

Stern's voice came up on the intercom.

"Bandit, seven o'clock high, coming down fast," said Stern. His voice too was jerky and high pitched, but the report was correct and to the point. "Left waist, top gunner, do you see him?"

"Roger Roger, got the bastard in my sights!"

"Track him, boys, track him, but let him get close before you open up."

She was silver all over but there were red meatballs on the wings. But that silhouette was all B-17! Then he saw the white star and blue field surrounding the red ball.

It was the same national insignia on his own wings.

Jack kicked right rudder and broke away in a diving turn. He leveled out and looked up to see "U.S. ARMY" written on the lower wings of the bomber. He zoomed away from the other airplane, letting his speed bleed off, before climbing away.

He wasn't happy, not just yet.

"Bandit breaking away," Al said. "Ah, skipper, that's a P-40. One of ours."

"I see a red meatball on the fuselage," said Lefty.

"Hold your fire, hold your fire," said Charlie. "Look again. He didn't shoot at us when he had the chance, after all."

"Top gunner to pilot. Hard to be sure, skipper, he's tail on. Wait, he's turning – yeah, that's a P-40. Seen plenty of 'em back in the States."

"OK, OK, pilot to gunners. Let's take a deep breath, but keep an eye on this guy."

Again the chorus of "Rogers" over the intercom.

"Can you see him, Bob?" Charlie asked the co-pilot.

"Yeah. He's leveled out at our altitude, looks like he's coming in nice and slow. Yeah, look at that. He's flipping up his wings. Ha. He's Air Corps, skipper. It says US ARMY on the underside of his wings."

Something buzzed and crackled over Charlie's earphones. The fear left him abruptly and was replaced with anger. He was tempted to have his gunners hose off a few rounds at the sonofabitch just to teach him some manners.

After a few seconds of flying at their level the P-40 peeled off in a long graceful turn to the north, towards Manila and Nichols Field.

"Well, welcome to the Philippines," said Payne over the intercom.

Jack continued calling Interceptor Command and Nichols Field over the radio but got no response. Once he got to Nichols he circled at pattern altitude, the procedure followed when unable to use the radio, until he saw the tower blinking a green light at him in the signal to land.

He opened the canopy. The rush of wind through the cockpit pulled dust and one or two bits of trash from their hiding places. Throttle back to 1000 RPM, propeller to flat pitch, cowl flaps open, wheels down, full flaps, a nice satisfying thump as the gear locked into place. Jack turned on final and lined up the bare spot on the sod runway. Just above the runway he began his roundout, throttle all the way back; the mains touched with the slightest of bumps and a rumble of the main wheels on solid earth. Stick back, back just a little more to keep the tail up as the as the speed dropped, then the slight thump as the tail wheel came down. Jack brought the stick back into his lap and hit the brakes gently, then a little harder until he was down to taxiing speed. His crew chief ran out onto the apron, holding both hands up, and guided Jack to his shut-down spot.

Jack ran up the engine to clear the cylinders, then closed the throttle and the mixture. The propeller changed from a barely visible spinning blur to individual blades that slowed, stopped, ticked over once more, rocked back and stopped.

The crew chief climbed up on the wing. "How'd she run, sir?"

"The airplane's great, chief. Smooth as silk. Got a problem with the radio, though, all I can hear is static."

The crew chief nodded and reached down to help Jack out of the restraints. "Write it up, sir, and I'll get the electrical shop to have a look at it."

"Will do, chief."

Jack climbed out of the cockpit and off the wing before shrugging out of his seat-pack parachute and slinging it over his shoulder. The heat hit him and he unzipped his jacket, shifting the parachute around so he could sling jacket and parachute over his shoulder as he walked into the operations shack to report the B-17.

Wagner stepped into the doorway of the shack as Jack walked up the steps.

"Good flight?" Wagner asked.

"Yes, sir, except my radio packed up. Couldn't get anything out of it but static. And, skipper, I need to report sighting a B-17."

"We see 'em all the time, Jack. What's the big deal?"

"It came out of the south, Boyd."

The squadron commander frowned. "Well, they sent us down here to make room up at Clark for the 7th Bomb Group. And you know the 19th sent half their airplanes down to Mindanao early this morning. Maybe that was one of theirs, coming back for some reason."

"Could be. Probably is. Do you know of any B-17s that are supposed to be where I saw this one?"

"Nope."

"Well, there you are."

Wagner nodded. "What happened?"

Jack started to report his encounter with the B-17, but after a few words Wagner held up his hand. "You know, maybe we should make this official. Probably a communications breakdown, but if so, we should kick it upstairs," Wagner said.

Jack followed his squadron commander into the relative coolness of the operations shack.

There was a lieutenant seated at a desk who looked up as they came in. The placard on his desk read "Duty Officer."

"Cameron, Lt. Davis here has to make an intercept report," Wagner told the man at the desk. "Help him out, will you?"

"Yes, sir," Cameron replied, reaching into a drawer and pulling out a form. Wagner leaned against the wall and lit a cigarette, watching Cameron.

Jack ran through it all with Lt. Cameron, position when first sighted, time when first sighted, altitude, type aircraft sighted.

"I kept trying to call Interceptor Command to verify the identity of the aircraft, but I couldn't reach anybody," Jack concluded. "So I made a run on the aircraft and determined it to be a B-17D, with red and white alternating stripes on the rudder, tail number 64 on the vertical stabilizer."

"You made a run on the aircraft?" Cameron repeated. "As in, you attacked it?"

Jack looked at the man. He noticed Cameron didn't wear wings, marking him as a non-flying officer.

"No," Jack said. "I didn't know if it was hostile when I began the run and had not certainly identified the aircraft as a B-17. I wasn't going to give up any more advantage than I had to, considering the possibility that it might be an enemy. So I set up an attack pass, yes, but I didn't fire on the other aircraft, so I can't actually say I executed the attack."

Cameron looked up at Wagner, who stared back as he took a puff from his cigarette.

"OK," Cameron said. "I'll call Interceptor Command and get this logged in."

Wagner nodded. "Jack, come out on the porch with me."

Once they were out on the porch Wagner gestured for Jack to sit down.

"Seriously, Jack, you made a diving attack on a B-17? Might've been a little dangerous. Those guys might have thought you were a Jap. We had a report of an unidentified aircraft over Luzon from the Raid Warning Net just after you took off. We tried to call you to check it out, in fact, but couldn't raise you on the radio."

Jack nodded. "I reported the radio malfunction to my crew chief."

Wagner nodded in reply. "Well, radios don't do too well in the tropics. The damp and the heat and all that. Plus you were in a brand-new, just-assembled airplane. Bound to be a few bugs. Better the radio than the engine or the fuel system."

"Yes, sir," Jack said.

"You arm your guns?"

"Yes."

Wagner nodded again and stubbed out his cigarette. "OK. You did the right thing. Probably made those poor bastards in the B-17 wet their britches when you rolled in on them, though, so we might get some grief from FEAF over it. Don't worry about that. Go get some rest and some chow or whatever."

"Yes, sir."

CHAPTER TWELVE
The Spice of the Orient

Landing at Clark

Charlie Davis and his crew landed at Clark Field late in the afternoon. Like Hickam, Midway, and Wake the field was a bedlam of construction activity, but the main runway was still sod and from the landing pattern he could only see one revetment built. There was a B-17 in it, but the rest of the big silver bombers were parked close to the runway, dangerously close, in Charlie's opinion.

"Jeez," said Bob Payne. "How come they don't move those Forts back a little?"

"Probably drainage," Charlie said. "Ground's too soft to take the weight of a Fort. They haven't gotten around to making a proper airfield out of Clark yet. If they move 'em too far back from the runway it'd take a bulldozer and a platoon of engineers with steel mats and shovels to get 'em out."

They were cleared to land. Charlie was surprised to see the hump in the runway, behind which the admin buildings and hangars sank out of view as he touched down, rolling uphill and slowing radically as he did. An elderly Ford truck with a

FOLLOW ME sign on it turned and raced in front of him, guiding him to a slot on the tarmac apron in front of the hangars.

There was a moment of silence when the engines shut down and the propellers slowed to a halt. Charlie thought of it as the moment of transition. They had flown halfway around the world, alone, and only two months ago aviators who accomplished that feat received the Distinguished Flying Cross. For now it meant one adventure was over. The next had yet to begin.

Ten hours in the pilot's seat of a Fort was enough for anyone's backside, however supposedly young and allegedly supple. He stood up slowly from the seat, making his way past the throttle quadrant and instrument controls, and back through the bomb bay and the radio compartment to the waist, where the gunners opened the door and climbed out of the airplane.

Charlie went out after the waist gunners and stood on the tarmac stretching. He smelled the familiar odors of any airfield, oil and gasoline and hot metal, but here there was more, the not so exotic smell of nearby rice paddies fertilized with the excrement of humans and water buffalo.

"Ah, the spice of the Orient," Charlie muttered to himself.

A jeep came tearing up, driven by a sergeant with a major in the seat beside him. Charlie came to attention and saluted as the jeep screeched to a halt beside him.

"Charlie, where the hell you been?" the major inquired, after returning his salute.

"Aw, Lee, we took the scenic route."

Major Lee Evans was Charlie's squadron commander. They shook hands.

"Damned glad to see you in one piece, Charlie. Last I saw you were trailing fire and losing altitude."

"Well, that was a long time ago and half a world away. What's the drill, skipper?"

Evans looked at the men emerging from Charlie's Fort. "Jeez, Charlie, what happened to your crew? I don't know half these guys."

"Personnel sergeants at Hamilton."

Major Evans snorted. "Yeah. I see Bobby Smith is gone. Who's your navigator?"

"Hey, Al!"

Stern came over when Charlie beckoned to him. Charlie introduced him to Major Evans, who looked dubiously at Stern.

"Forgive me for asking, lieutenant, but how long have you been out of navigator's school?"

Charlie put a possessive hand on Stern's shoulder. "About three weeks, Lee, but Al here got us all the way across the Pacific without a hitch."

"Yeah? You lucked out, then, Charlie. You better be careful. I hear Gene Eubanks is looking for a new navigator."

"If it's all the same to you, Major, I'd rather stay with this bunch of bums," Stern said. "We kind of got used to each other."

Evans looked from Stern to Charlie and back again. "Fine by me. Tell you what, Charlie, leave the airplane with your copilot, and hop in the jeep. When the tower called saying there was a Fort in the pattern Gene wanted to know who the hell it was. You've been on his mind for some reason."

"Yes, sir." Charlie turned to Stern. "Al, tell Bob to make sure the airplane is serviced and bedded down for the night, then have him see about quarters and some food for everyone."

"Roger that, skipper."

Charlie nodded and climbed into the jeep. The driver tore off in a half-circle that nearly threw Charlie out before he settled in.

There were B-17s with mechanics swarming over them inside the hangars and two more on the tarmac, evidently waiting their turn for servicing or modification. Off to one side, like so many poor relations, stood a collection of P-40 pursuits. Charlie's mouth hardened as he looked at them.

"Say, Lee, where do I file a complaint?"

The major smiled at him, holding his hat on with his left hand against the wind of the jeep's passage. "You haven't been here long enough to complain about anything, Charlie. Wait a few days. Then you'll see how screwed up things really are."

"Lee, we got jumped by some idiot in a P-40 over the Luzon coast. That was after our call to Clark with a position report. They passed us a warning about unidentified aircraft. My gunners almost shot the bastard down."

"I think maybe that's what Gene wants to talk to you about," Major Evans said. "The Warning Net picked up information about an unidentified aircraft over Luzon about the time you crossed over the coast."

"You mean, me? But I've had clearance every step of the way."

"I don't doubt it, Charlie. I know you pretty well. The point is, though, FEAF had no idea you were inbound until you contacted Clark Field over Mindanao."

"Are things that screwed up out here?"

"Like I said, wait until you've been here a few days. You'll see for yourself. But yeah, things could be a hell of a lot better."

Charlie nodded. "Fair enough, Lee."

The jeep screeched to a stop in front of a building bearing the legend "19TH BOMB GROUP OPERATIONS." Like most of the buildings on the base, it was new, built of raw lumber, and surrounded by shutters to keep the frequent tropical rains out. Inside fans turned overhead and it was, at least, out of the sun. Charlie and Major Evans walked down a row between desks manned by enlisted typists to a space at the back, set apart by screens, with a sign that said "COMMANDING OFFICER." Evans knocked on the flimsy wood holding up the screen.

"Come in," someone said from inside.

Inside the office was a desk. Behind the desk sat a man in undress khakis with the silver oak leaves of a lieutenant colonel on his shoulders. There was a name plate on his desk that said "LT. COL. EUGENE E. EUBANKS." Charlie and Major Evans came to attention and saluted.

"Rest, rest," said Eubanks. He stood and offered his hand. "So, Charlie, you're the mysterious phantom aviator, eh?"

"One of them, maybe, sir," Charlie replied.

"I'm glad you made it out here, Charlie," Eubanks said. "Usually I'd be a little more cordial, but things are kind of busy right now. I had to send half the boys down to some pineapple field in Mindanao. In fact, after you rest up a little tonight I'm going to send you down there to join them. I'm sure you saw for yourself that this field is bursting at the seams."

"Yes, sir, I did."

Eubanks nodded. "To cut straight to business, Charlie, I've been on the phone for the last twenty minutes trying to find out why you had all the appropriate clearances but were still reported as an unknown by 5th Interceptor Command. Needless to say the net has some bugs still to be worked out. Tell me about your flight from Darwin."

Charlie gave Eubanks a brief, succinct description of the flight from Australia, with times, altitudes, coast-in points and other data.

At the end Eubanks nodded. "That sounds pretty much in accord with everyone else who has come along that route. I've always wondered what might happen if the Japs try to slip in someone behind one of our ferry flights."

Charlie was puzzled for a moment. Eubanks looked at him without expression. Charlie said, "You mean, you expect the Japanese to attack without declaring war?"

Eubanks nodded. "I think the first we'll know about it is when the bombs start falling."

The phone on the colonel's desk buzzed. Eubanks picked it up. "Eubanks. OK, put him on."

Eubanks covered the mouthpiece. "Interceptor Command," he said quietly. "Let's see what they have to say about an unauthorized flight."

Officers and Gentlemen

The sun was low in the west when Charlie Davis and Col. Eubanks drove up to the sentry post at FEAF HQ at Neilsen Field. They were waved through after a brief inspection by the guard. The sentry directed them to HQ Operations.

"Aw, crap," said Eubanks. "That means Brereton himself wants in on this."

"General Brereton?" Charlie asked.

"Yep," said Eubanks. He straightened his tie and looked critically at his uniform cap. Charlie didn't even try to straighten up his flight suit. He'd practically lived in it for the last three days. He knew he was a little ripe and did not present the most military appearance, but he didn't care. They'd been ordered to report to FEAF as soon as possible, and that was what they had done.

A jeep screeched up behind their staff car and two young pilots got out. One was a first lieutenant, the other a second lieutenant. Both of them were clad in flight suits, leather jackets, and crush caps and looked as if they'd stepped right from their airplanes into the jeep.

The second lieutenant looked familiar.

Evidently the second lieutenant thought he looked familiar too, because he took a second glance as he and the first lieutenant came to attention and saluted them.

"Oh, hell," said Charlie. "Bad pennies and little brothers. You never know when they're going to turn up."

"Hey, Charlie, how the hell are you?" said Jack.

The two brothers shook hands, smiling.

Wagner looked from Charlie to Jack to Eubanks and shook his head.

"Oh, Boyd, don't tell me," Eubanks said wearily. "Tell me it was you."

"Wish I could, Colonel," Wagner replied. "But I can't."

Charlie stepped back and looked at Jack, who blinked and looked supremely puzzled.

"Aw, hell," Charlie said. "It was you, wasn't it, Jack?"

"Me what?" Jack asked.

"You that buzzed my airplane this afternoon, that's what."

"That was your B-17?"

"Hell, yes, that was me! God damn it, Jack, you came too God damn close! And you might've gotten yourself shot all to hell."

"Captain," Colonel Eubanks said drily. "Do I gather correctly that this is your brother and that he's the one that buzzed your Fort earlier today"

"Sir," Jack said hotly, "With respect, I did *not* buzz Charlie's airplane. I had a report of an unidentified aircraft in the area. I made numerous attempts to contact Interceptor Command and..."

"OK, OK," said Eubanks, holding up a placating hand. "Boyd, can I talk to you for a second?"

"Of course, Colonel."

Eubanks and Wagner walked away a half-dozen paces and conversed in low tones.

"You scared the shit out of my waist gunner," Charlie said quietly. "He thought you were going to shoot and shoot to kill."

"I was ready to, if I couldn't make a positive ID," Jack said. "You heard about the war warning and all that."

"Yeah."

"Charlie, look, it wasn't a buzz job. I knew you had to know I was there. If you were a Jap I'd already given you way too much advantage, just by looking you over. Your gunner was right. That was a gunnery pass, and I was ready to shoot if I thought it was necessary."

"What happened to your radio?"

"Some kind of short. Our radio guy fixed it, but all I could hear at the time was static."

"We thought you were a Jap recon plane. There was a report of an unidentified aircraft over Luzon."

"I know. I got the same report before my radio packed up."

Charlie nodded and then sighed. "Christ. What a can of worms. I'm sorry I got you in trouble, Jack."

Jack shrugged and grinned lopsidedly. "Seems to me I remember someone telling me that second lieutenants spend their lives in trouble."

"Yeah, I guess I did say that, didn't I? Look, I don't know your CO – and anyway, what's a first lieutenant doing commanding a pursuit squadron? That's a major's slot."

"Well, Buzz is sort of a law unto himself. He's a real hot pilot."

"Is he on your side?"

"I think so."

"Then my advice is let him do the talking."

"You're a pal, Charlie."

"Aw, what's a big brother for?"

At that moment Eubanks and Wagner walked back to the two brothers.

"Lt. Wagner has convinced me that Jack here is a conscientious pilot who was simply trying to do his duty," Eubanks said. "Do you concur, Charlie?"

"I had a chance to talk to Jack myself, Colonel. He can be a little reckless, but it sounds like a communications mixup to me. Nobody's fault."

Eubanks nodded. "Pretty much. We'll try to handle it that way. Lieutenant Davis, my advice to you is to let your elders do the talking, speak only when spoken to, and if you're asked any questions at all, volunteer nothing beyond what you're asked. Understood?"

"Understood, sir."

"Follow me, then."

As they turned to enter HQ Operations Charlie whispered to Jack, "I'm impressed. You sounded like a real live Army officer there, Jack."

Jack started to give Charlie a wet, juicy Bronx cheer but remembered he was an officer and a gentleman just in time. Charlie smothered a smile.

You Aren't Far from the Japs

Charlie thought General Brereton looked tired. His eyes were alert and he sat erect behind his desk, but the ashtray at his right hand was full of cigarette butts and his "IN" tray was overflowing. After salutes and introductions Brereton bade them all be seated.

"Gentlemen, before we begin I want to make something clear," Brereton said. "I don't have enough pilots or airplanes to lose either to foolishness. And I know pursuit pilots pretty well. They like to show off how good they are. Are you a good pilot, Lt. Davis?"

"Yes, sir," Jack replied.

"How about you, Captain Davis?"

"Yes, sir."

"Davis. Wait. Are you two brothers?"

Jack looked at Charlie. *You're the eldest and a captain, you talk to the big bad fire-breathing general*, the look said.

"Yes, sir," Charlie replied.

"Oh my God. Don't tell me. You're Frank Davis' boys, aren't you?"

"Yes, sir," Charlie said again.

Brereton leaned back in his chair and sighed, rubbing his eyes. "Frank was a good man. My condolences, very much after the fact, but my condolences nonetheless. Now," said the general, sitting up and looking sharply from one brother to the other. "You, Captain, tell me what happened."

Brereton quizzed both brothers, then nodded, sat back, and lit a cigarette after offering the pack around. "OK. I suspected it was a communications foul-up, mostly because the communications network is all fouled up. But it was necessary to be sure that Lt. Davis wasn't playing the hot dog and that Capt. Davis wasn't prone to, shall we say, nervousness under attack. I hope you gentlemen will pardon the necessities of command."

"Of course, sir," said Charlie.

Jack nodded. "Yes, sir."

"Lt. Wagner, Col. Eubanks, you gentlemen are the relevant commanding officers. What do you gentlemen think? Wagner?"

"Jack's a good pilot, sir," said Wagner. "I'd bet on him."

"I'd say the same about Charlie," Eubanks said.

"OK. Thank you for coming, gentlemen. We'll let the matter drop. I'll have a word with Hal George at Interceptor Command. Go back to your stations and get some rest."

Once back on the sidewalk in front of the Operations building, Eubanks took a deep breath and let it out slowly.

"That went better than I might have expected," he said. "Look here, Charlie, I'm sure you're tired and would like to get back to Clark and rest up, but..."

"Give me a minute with Jack, sir," Charlie said to Colonel Eubanks.

Charlie took Jack by the arm and led him a few paces away. "How you doing, Jack? Really?"

"I'm OK, Charlie. How about you?"

"I'm fine. Tired. Oh, before I forget, come with me."

Charlie led Jack back to the jeep. Before they left Clark for the drive down to Neilsen Charlie threw his B4 bag in the jeep.

"Got something for you, little brother."

Charlie handed Jack the manila envelope he'd carried all the way across the Pacific.

Jack took it and blinked when he saw the handwriting on the envelope.

"You saw Irina?"

"Sure did. She came out to Hamilton, looking for you, and gave me that herself. About ten minutes before I took off for Hawaii, actually, so you're lucky to have that."

Jack ran his finger over the seal of the envelope.

"OK, kid brother, stop drooling. Irina said to be careful when you opened that. Let's see." Charlie summoned up a mental image of the scene and spoke in a passable, if somewhat masculine, imitation of her voice: "Please put this in Jack's hands yourself. I should blush for anyone else to see it."

Jack grinned. "Thanks, big brother. You're OK for a bomber guy."

"I wish we could get together for a couple of drinks or something, but I have to be somewhere first thing in the morning. You know how it is."

Jack nodded. "Yeah. We're on leaves-canceled and everyone stick close to base alert ourselves."

"It's that bad?"

"Probably worse. We got a hell of a talk from Colonel George this afternoon. He says there's three thousand Jap airplanes up in Formosa, all ready to fly down here and give us what-for."

Charlie whistled. "Jesus. Look. This squadron commander of yours, Wagner? If he's the hot pilot you say he is, you listen to him and do the smart things, not the crazy ones."

"I'm a pursuit pilot. We're crazy by definition."

Charlie shook his head slowly and then threw a slow roundhouse at Jack's head. Jack ducked it and threw a punch to Charlie's gut. The blocks and punches and counterpunches got faster and faster until they both backed off, grinning.

"I'd'a had ya," said Charlie.

"Maybe," said Jack. "Keep dreaming. Be careful up there at Clark, Charlie. You aren't that far from the Japs if they decide to come south."

Carry Out the Mission

Lt. Wagner had Jack drive back to Nichols Field from Brereton's HQ. The road was paved mostly with good intentions. Above them was the tropic sky, the deep black of it so clear the faraway stars seemed to reveal their distance from a troubled planet.

When Jack braked to a stop in front of the 17th's Operations shack, Wagner beckoned him to follow and walked in. They went back to Wagner's office, little more than a desk behind bamboo screens. Wagner opened one of the desk drawers and pulled out a bottle of whiskey and two glasses. He poured an inch into each glass, gestured at Jack to sit, and sat behind his desk.

Wagner raised his glass. "If you don't mind, Jack, I'd like to drink to your dad," he said. "He was kind of a hero of mine, when I was growing up."

"Sure thing," Jack replied.

"Well, then, to Frank Davis," Wagner said, and drank off the whiskey in his glass. Jack raised his glass but only sipped. Wagner raised an eyebrow.

"I say something wrong?"

"Not at all, sir. I'm not much of a drinker."

"No? Probably a good thing. College athlete?"

"Yes, but that's not the reason." Jack grinned, a little sadly. "Dad brought us out here, Charlie and I, to the Philippines, back in 1938 on the Pan Am China Clipper. I was only 18. When we were in Honolulu Dad conned the bartender at the Royal Hawaiian and got me loaded on rum drinks. They said I tried to dance the hula with the native girls. All I really remember is a hell of a hangover, and I've not been much of a drinker since."

Wagner smiled. "You get to see your brother much?"

"Aw, we've both been pretty busy. You know what it's like, Stateside, just now."

The squadron commander grimaced. "Yeah. We're building a modern air force from scratch. And a modern army, too."

"And Charlie being West Point and good at his job, and me being in college and then flight school, well, there you are."

Wagner nodded. "By the way, that exercise this afternoon. You stuck pretty close to Fernandez. Good job, but what did you think?"

"Bluntly?"

"That makes it plain your opinion isn't good, Jack, so go ahead."

"Noyes sent Yellow Three and Four down to spoil the escort's attack. They did. But our mission wasn't to get in a scrap, it was

240

to intercept an enemy bombing raid. With all respect to Lt. Noyes, he should have ordered whoever could to break away from the dogfight and go after the bombers."

Wagner looked at the trace of whiskey at the bottom of his glass and poured himself another, smaller drink. He offered the bottle to Jack, who shook his head.

"Even if it was only one pursuit that could get away?"

"That one airplane would force the rest of the bomber's escort to come down and fight. Anyone who could break free of the escort after that could attack the bombers."

"Might be sort of hard on the one guy, though."

"Yes, sir. Might be." Jack took another sip of the whiskey in his glass.

"So what do you think I should do, next time we run this exercise?"

"Stress the actual mission. It's fine to shoot down enemy pursuits, but if the bombers clobber your airfield, who actually won the fight?"

Wagner was silent for a moment, looking at the whiskey in his glass. "Where'd you learn to think like that, Jack?" he asked.

Jack shrugged. "Hell, it's what they taught us back in basic cadets," he replied. "You know, learn your mission, carry out your mission, all that stuff."

"Yeah," Wagner said. "So tell me. How do you see our mission, here in the Philippines? After what Colonel George had to say?"

It was Jack's turn to be silent. Then he took a slug of whiskey and looked Wagner in the eye. "Well, skipper, it seems that the Japs, someday soon, will come south. When they do, I think our mission will be to make it as expensive and lengthy a process for them to take the Philippines as we can."

"You don't think the Navy will come help us?"

"They might. The Jap Navy might have something to say about it. Who knows how that will go?"

"So you think it's our job to die for our country?"

Jack scoffed. "Hell, no. It's our job to make the Japs die for their country."

Wagner nodded slowly. "Good. That's exactly right. Go get some sleep, Jack. We'll be on alert again dawn tomorrow."

Jack grinned and drained the whiskey from his glass. "Yes, sir."

A Drink in the Dark

Eubanks' driver dropped Charlie off in front of a tent identical to a half-dozen others along the dirt path. The base was partly blacked out as an air-raid precaution and Charlie couldn't see a thing except the vague outline of the huts against the stars in the black sky.

There was a cranking whine, a belching cough, and an uneven roar in the distance as someone started a Wright radial engine. Charlie looked in that direction. There was a glow from the lights in the hangar. If Jap night bombers came to visit them that glow would mark the hangars as well as a searchlight.

Carefully, in the dark, Charlie put his feet on the steps up to the shack, pushed aside the mosquito-netting door, and walked in. Someone shone a shielded flashlight in his face.

"Jesus!" Charlie said, holding up his hand to shield his eyes.

"Sorry," said a voice. "Had to make sure you weren't a Jap saboteur."

"Al?"

"That's me. Hi, Charlie." Charlie's eyes were night-adjusting. A vaguely man-like shape stood up out of the darkness. "We saved you a bunk and put your bags underneath it. You hungry?"

"Eubanks fed me."

"Want a snort? The BX had some sort of rotgut whiskey."

"Not much of a recommendation, Al."

"Well, it's been a long day."

Charlie sat down on the nearest bunk, which, from the hard lump and the sleepy protest, was occupied. Charlie stood hastily.

Stern chuckled. "You're two bunks down. I'll get the booze."

Charlie felt his way along the dark aisle until he found the empty bunk Stern indicated. He sat down on it, feeling the rough scratchy army wool blanket. He took off his cap and felt at the head of the bunk until he found a little post, where he hung his cap. After that he ran his fingers through his hair and wondered about a shower. He'd been sweating freely and didn't really want to climb sweaty into the clean sheets on the bunk. Sleeping in his gamey flight suit wasn't an appealing notion, either, but he was considering it when Stern came back.

There was the clink of glass on glass and a gurgle. A faint sweet tang of alcohol floated into his nostrils. The navigator handed him a glass.

"Here's how," Stern said, and drank.

"Chin chin," Charlie replied, following suit. It was some sort of raw cheap stuff all right, and it made Charlie gasp. "Damn. What the hell is that, panther sweat?"

"You don't like my booze, I'll take it elsewhere."

"Aw, now, don't get sensitive, Al."

The navigator chuckled. "If I were sensitive I couldn't drink this horse piss."

Charlie took another sip. The stuff had claws but it felt warm in his belly, and he could feel relaxation spreading through him. He took a deep breath and sighed, drinking again.

"Thanks, Al," he said.

"You're welcome, skipper. Do you want to hear about your chicks?"

"Yes."

"Bob's the one you sat on, and as you can tell he's sound asleep. The gunners are all in the enlisted quarters with Sergeant Frye. They had some chow and a couple of beers and the last I saw of them they were all tucked in and sleeping sound."

"Good. How's Lefkowicz?"

"Fine. A little shook up, still. By the way, did you file that complaint?"

"Well, a hell of a thing, that. Turns out the crazy P-40 pilot is my brother Jack."

"Your brother?"

"I maybe never mentioned him. He's two years younger than me. Last time I talked to him he was about to graduate from flight school and get his wings. Then we got involved with bringing B-17s across the water and I sort of lost track of him."

"Guess you were surprised," Stern said drily.

"Well, you might say so. Here Col. Eubanks and I pull up at FEAF HQ where we're about to report on this little incident to General Brereton himself, and up pulls a jeep with these two pursuit types in it. Out they jump, and one of them is Jack and one of them is his squadron commander, who's a 1st lieutenant."

"A 1st lieutenant squadron commander?" Stern asked.

"That was my reaction. But the guy impressed me. Seemed like one of those old Wild West gunfighters you hear about, you know, quiet, watching everything, missing nothing."

"You ever want to be a pursuit pilot?"

"Me? Hell, no. I'm the methodical type."

Stern leaned forward. "Your brother sure scared the shit out of Lefkowicz."

"Why, I wonder? We've had pursuits dive on us before in training."

Stern hesitated. "Truth is, Charlie, I was scared myself. I mean, back in the States, it's all good fun, right? Everyone goes home at the end of the day unless someone does something stupid and cracks up." Stern tipped up his glass and drained it. "But when that guy made that pass on us, it was like he knew something we didn't. Like maybe something we ought to know."

Charlie nodded. He thought about how Jack looked when he got out of the jeep with Lt. Wagner, the expression of his eyes and his mouth, familiar somehow, and then he remembered, it was the same look their father Frank had sometimes, talking about a tough moment flying. But it was always something that happened during an air race or some sort of record-setting attempt. Their father, who had seven kills in World War One, had only talked about his war experiences that one time, three years ago.

Charlie held his glass out to be refilled. "Maybe you're right, Al," he said.

"So you met Brereton? What's he like?"

"Just another general. He looked tired. Big bags under his eyes. Said something about not having pilots or airplanes to waste."

"And he doesn't, either," Stern replied. "Far Eastern Air Force, sounds pretty impressive, doesn't it? You know how many aircraft in the FEAF?"

"Nope."

"Thirty-five ships in our outfit, the 19th Bomb Group. That's the striking force. I heard a rumor the 7th Bomb Group might start arriving in a few days, so that would be another thirty-five. They're supposed to have the new B-17s, the E-model with the tail guns. Then there's some B-18 Bolos, which aren't worth a shit, and some B-10s which I think belong to the Philippine Commonwealth Air Force, and really aren't worth a shit."

"Air Corps hand-me-downs," Charlie muttered.

"Yup. The PCAF even got the P-26 Peashooters the Air Corps used to fly out here. I heard FEAF has about a hundred P-40s, some B models but mostly the new E model, dispersed all around Manila and Manila Bay. Oh yeah, and some Seversky P-35s."

Charlie nodded. A hundred modern P-40s could surely put up a fight against whatever the Japs could throw at them, and the P-35s were at least fairly modern if not top of the line.

Suddenly, though, in the dark night of an advanced base with a potential enemy 500 miles north of him who might strike at any time, he wondered about that, and about what Jack said about 3000 Jap bombers in Formosa. Charlie knew a hell of a lot about bomber operations, but he realized he had absorbed the conventional wisdom in the Air Corps that the "bomber would always get through." Massed formations of bombers with interlocking defensive fields of fire, thundering along at high altitude above the effective reach of fighters and anti-aircraft artillery, that was Air Corps doctrine and had been for at least a decade. But all that was just words, words in a book, words from a classroom lecture. It was an article of faith, which might or might not prove factual.

Very soon, Charlie now understood, he might witness the actual effectiveness of this doctrine – this unproven doctrine – in a shooting war.

Thank God it was against the Japs and not a first class air force like the Kraut *Luftwaffe*. Hell, the Japs were still flying a Mitsubishi pursuit that looked like the Boeing P-26. He'd read Air Intelligence reports on that airplane, the Mitsubishi Type 96. It could all but turn inside its own wingspan but it carried two 7.7-mm machine-guns for armament and had an open cockpit and fixed landing gear. The P-40 surely ought to be able to chew the Type 96 up, if the Japs brought them this far south, like maybe on an aircraft carrier.

Of course Charlie knew that renegade in China, Claire Chennault, issued warnings about some kind of Jap super-fighter, but the Air Intelligence types Charlie knew discounted Chennault. "He retired as a captain," they pointed out. "And he's in the pay of the Chinese, who've been over here with their hands out begging for airplanes, rifles, machine guns and artillery pieces ever since the Japs started kicking their asses back in 1937. There's no Jap super-fighter. That's Chennault blowing hot air for his boss Chiang Kai-Shek. Either that or the poor old bastard's gone totally Asiatic."

"So what do you think, skipper?" asked Stern in the darkness, as he poured them another drink. "Since it's basically us and the P-40s to stop the Japs if they come."

"The only thing we need to worry about is a surprise attack," Charlie said. "I hear they've got radar out here, so maybe we'll have enough warning to scramble the P-40s and get the B-17s out of harm's way."

"Yeah. Clark's the only field in the Philippines that can handle a B-17 until they get that field down in Mindanao ready. Talk about having all your eggs in one basket."

Charlie saw the glint of Stern's glass as he upended it, draining the last of his whiskey.

"You want another shot?" Stern asked.

"Nah, I'm good. I want to be halfway awake tomorrow morning. And by the way, Al, that field down in Mindanao? Guess where we're going tomorrow?"

"Aw crap. Are you serious?"

"Yup. That's straight from Gene Eubanks."

"Who's he?"

"Your boss and mine, Al. He runs the 19th Bomb Group. So get some rest, you're going to have to find us a nice pineapple field tomorrow."

Stern chuckled. "Swell. G'night, then."

He moved away into the darkness, among the bunks occupied by sleeping pilots and navigators.

Charlie finished the last of the whiskey and stretched out on his bunk in his sweaty, smelly flight suit. Fatigue and alcohol reached up from his subconscious and dragged him down into deep sleep in moments.

CHAPTER THIRTEEN
Tension

<u>It's Going to Be a Hell of a Show!</u>

Jack woke up and looked at the blue sky and the orange clouds of dawn, just visible through his shuttered window. It was early but even on Sunday morning the smell of coffee wafted along the hallway.

He swung out of bed and threw a robe on over his skivvies. On the desk he saw the manila envelope from Irina. He went to the desk and pulled the picture from the envelope.

Irina smiled up at him from the picture. It was a demure smile, but there was very little demure about the picture. His fiancée wore some sort of negligee that was light-colored and diaphanous. It hinted at curves and lines; it hinted at mysteries that made his breath run short and the blood rush to his groin.

Painfully.

It was hard to look away from that picture. He could remember the way her skin smelled, the softness of her lips under his, her arms around his neck. He'd spent a long time last night remembering those things. Jack sighed and put the picture back in the envelope. Then he looked down.

There was no way he could go out in public in his skivvies, not like this. He put on a pair of khaki pants and a t-shirt, then he went down the hall to the kitchen.

Ramon sat at the table in the kitchen, drinking coffee. There was a plate of sweet rolls on the table in front of him. Jose was at the stove, and as Jack came in he put bacon on a skillet on the stove.

"Good morning, Mr. Davis," Ramon said gravely. "Did you sleep well?"

"I slept," Jack replied. "It was a restless night."

"I see," said Ramon. "Coffee?"

"Please," said Jack.

Ramon handed him a cup. Jack poured from the carafe on the table.

"Ramon, if you ever want to come to the States and start a business there, you let me know. I might be able to help. With recommendations if nothing else."

"Why would you do that?"

Jack saluted Ramon with his coffee cup. "You make a hell of a cup of coffee. My mother would approve and so do I."

"The Senora Davis?" Ramon asked. He considered for a moment. "She is your mother, but what sort of woman is she?"

"Very strong. Formidable. You know of the American South?"

"Indeed."

"I may say she is a Southern belle."

Ramon nodded. "I thought your mother and your father must be people of estimable character. I know that your father and Colonel Miller were, what is the English phrase? Compadres?"

"Comrades in arms."

"Just so. Seldom are such friendships trivial. If I may say so, you yourself strike me as a person of character. There are overtones to you which tell me some, at least, of your strength comes from your parents."

Jack considered that, sipping the delicious coffee. "Thank you, Ramon. I shall pass that compliment on to my mother. She will appreciate it."

"Please do. And now, may I ask a delicate question?"

"Of course."

"When will the war start?"

Jack sighed. "You understand I am a junior officer and know very little."

Ramon nodded.

"It might be soon. Today. A week. But soon."

Ramon sipped his coffee. Jose finished the first batch of bacon and laid it on the table before them.

"Many of my friends have sons or brothers in the Army. I know you are a pilot and not an infantryman, but if the Japanese should invade..." Ramon hesitated.

Jack looked his host in the eye. "You're right. I'm a pilot, not an infantryman. The Army expects to stop the Japanese if they do invade."

"I'm sure that is so. What about air raids?"

"You should have a shelter prepared. Even a slit trench would be useful. Dig it deep enough that you can sit in it easily, with your head well below the ground. It will protect you from shrapnel and flying debris, but not a direct hit."

"It sounds like a grave."

"Yes. But it may also save your life, and those in your house."

"Thank you," Ramon said. "That seems like good advice in times such as these."

Jack nodded. "You will understand that there is not much else I may say."

"Of course."

They sat for a moment, sipping coffee and eating bacon. Jose took toast from the oven and laid it next to the bacon.

"Eggs scrambled?" Jose asked Jack.

"Please," Jack said.

"What shall you do today?" Ramon asked.

"I must go to the field shortly," Jack replied. "We are on duty."

"You expect visitors?"

"It may be."

"To be bombarded from the air, as the Chinese and the English and the Poles have been, must be a terrible thing."

"As you say. My friends and I will try to prevent that."

"Indeed. Then I will pray for your success, you and the other pilots." Ramon sipped his coffee. "And I shall dig a slit trench."

"Good. Thank you, Ramon."

Jack went back to his room, shaved, dressed, called a cab. He waved good morning to the other pilots, who were stumbling in for breakfast as he left. The cab took him over the rickety bridge and dropped him off in front of the 17th's Operations Shack.

Jack nodded to the Officer of the Day. "What's going on?" Jack asked.

The OD shrugged. "It's Sunday morning. We're on alert. I guess if you want to wander over to the Air Depot they've got a P-40 that needs its engine slow-timed. Other than that, stick around where you can get back fast."

Jack nodded and drew his flying gear, then walked over to the Air Depot. There were indeed a pair of P-40s sitting to one side. Jack asked an airman where the line chief might be.

"Chief Jones? Probably with his head stuck inside an engine mount, cussing a blue streak," the airman replied. "Try Hangar 2, sir. I saw him there about ten minutes ago."

Chief Jones was indeed cussing a blue streak when Jack found him, but his head wasn't in an engine mount. He was looking at the machine guns mounted in a P-40 being assembled. The chief was addressing his remarks to a pair of frightened young airmen in greasy coveralls and fatigue caps, who stood at rigid attention.

Jack knew better than to interrupt a line chief in full flow, so he hung back and listened.

Sorting the profanity from the details, Jack gathered that the machine-guns, prior to installation in this aircraft, were not properly cleaned of the Cosmoline preservative they had been packed in for shipping. That concerned Jack. Machine-guns not properly cleaned were liable to jam. The problem with a jammed machine-gun was that you only fired one, or tried to fire one, when you needed to badly.

"Now get to work and clean these god-damn guns proper!" Chief Jones finished.

"Yes sir! Yes sir !" chorused the two young armorers, who immediately turned to.

Jack waited a moment before clearing his throat.

"What can I do for you, lieutenant?" the Chief said.

"I hear you might have an airplane that needs to be slow-timed."

"That I might, sir, and who might you be?"

"Jack Davis. I'm with the 17th."

"That's right. I've seen you around, but I thought you were with the 21st."

"So I was, until a few days ago."

Chief Jones nodded. "Those two over there are ready to go. Fresh out of the crates, put the last touches on 'em and buttoned up the panels this morning. Ammo trays are full."

"What's this about the machine-guns?"

"Well, them two boys over there got a little enthusiastic. Figured they'd cut some corners and a little grease wouldn't matter. Problem is, sir, a little grease can cause them guns to jam. Then you got a real problem, because you can't clear that jam in the air."

Jack frowned. "What happened to the hydraulic charging system?"

"Got a tech order from Wright Field. Seems they think charging the guns in the air will cause the pipes in the hydraulic system to burst. We put a P-40 up on jacks and cycled the hell out of the landing gear and the gun chargers and it worked like a charm, every time. But we can't get that order rescinded, and until we do, my orders are to plug the system. That means you have to charge the guns on the ground."

"Jesus. Taxi around with live guns?"

"I hear we're on war alert, lieutenant."

"OK. Well, maybe you better have someone charge the guns in Number 44 over there. Just in case."

"Sure thing, lieutenant."

Slow-timing the engine meant flying around with reduced throttle settings after takeoff to let the moving parts work in and get acquainted with one another. Jack climbed to two thousand feet, leveled off, and did a leisurely race-track tour of Manila, staying within a few miles of Nichols Field and Neilsen Field in case the engine gave trouble.

Chief Jones was waiting with the Form One when Jack taxied in.

"Any problem, Mr. Davis?"

"No, Chief. Purred like a kitten the whole time."

"OK, good. Thank you."

251

"My pleasure. Got another one ready for after lunch?"

"It's Sunday, lieutenant. We might take the afternoon off."

"You might?"

"Or we might not. In fact, we'll have something for you to fly if you want." The Chief grinned.

"Thought you might," Jack said. "I'll be back in a little bit."

The mess hall was crowded, noisy and hot. Jack got in line behind another group of lieutenants, one of whom turned to look at him.

"Jack! Jesus Christ, is that Jack Davis?"

Jack had to think for a minute, remembering that last night aboard the *Coolidge*, nearly three weeks of eternity ago.

" Tim Clement," Jack said. "How are you?"

"Oh, swell. We heard a rumor that there were A-24s being assembled down here, so we thought we'd check."

"Hell's bells. You guys in the 27th still don't have airplanes?"

"Airplanes? Har-har-har," Clement laughed sarcastically. The other lieutenants shook their heads in disgust. "I don't think I've gotten enough flight time since we got here to qualify for flight pay. We're still living in tents up at Neilsen Field. How about you? What's the 21st Pursuit doing? You guys got some airplanes, at least?"

"Finally," Jack said. "But I'm with the 17th Pursuit now. The guys in the 21st started getting P-40s the day I was transferred."

The mess attendants loaded their trays. They found a table in the corner and sat down.

"So what the hell have you guys been doing without airplanes?" Jack asked.

"Not much," Clement said. "I got some time in that piece of crap B-18, but at that I guess it's better than nothing. Bains here has been flying an O-52, if you can believe that. Mostly we've been trying to keep from going Asiatic and staying out of the way of silly work details the Regular Army types dream up."

"Supervising privates whitewashing rocks outside the Neilsen Field Officers Club," Bains said darkly. "Crap like that."

"But change is in the wind," Clement said. He winked at Bains, who grinned. "We got something special planned for tonight."

"Oh? What's that?" asked Jack.

"We've got a hell of a party going on at the Manila Hotel."

"What kind of party?"

"The kind you don't write home about, especially to your mother," Bains said.

"You better believe it" Clement exclaimed. "My God, we've got some real operators in the 27th Attack. Major Conrad, one of our squadron commanders, was stationed out here in the Philippines before and made some calls. Then our group intelligence officer was in Hollywood and knows some people too. Man, let me tell you, this show tonight is supposed to be hot! They've got a hell of a good band, out here on tour from the States, and some of the best strippers anywhere, white girls to boot!"

"You're welcome to come if you want," said Bains. "We even invited General Brereton."

Jack thought of the tired-looking man he'd met the night before, whose in-box overflowed with trouble.

"He could use a laugh," Jack said. "I'd come but my squadron is on alert."

"Oh, what the hell, Jack. Sneak out for a bit. Who'd know?"

Jack thought of the picture Irina sent him. Compared to the promise of that picture the thought of watching some girl he didn't know cavort half-naked around a stage to the drunken encouragement of a room full of young pilots held little appeal.

"Maybe next time," he said. "You guys have fun, though."

Clement suddenly grinned and elbowed Bains. "George, I bet it's a girl. Yep, I bet that's it. Jack here has him a girl and you know how some of them are, they don't like it when a man drinks too much and especially they don't like him looking at other women. That's it, ain't it, Jack?"

Jack shook his head. "You're too quick for me there, Tim."

"So what's she like?" Clement leaned forward eagerly.

"Tim, Tim, what good does it do to know? You'll just be heartbroken, and then spend the rest of the night drunk and frustrated, watching women strip and dance naked except for a G-string."

"Aw, c'mon, Jack, be a sport."

Jack shook his head.

"Yeah, c'mon, Davis," said Bains. "Clement here ain't had any since I knowed him."

"If that's true I shouldn't say anything," Jack said. "Is that true, Tim?"

Clement rolled his eyes, scowling at Bains. "You shouldn't believe everything you hear, Jack, especially coming from this joker."

"Oh, is that so? C'mon then, Tim, name one, just one."

"A gentleman doesn't tell," Clement replied loftily.

"Yeah, and a gentleman don't get any, either," said Bains. "Except maybe for Jack here."

Clement snorted. "How would you know, Bains? You saying you aren't a gentleman and you get all you want?"

Jack stood up and took his tray. "You boys enjoy yourselves tonight. Sounds like a swell party."

Sitting In the Pineapple Fields

Charlie looked out the window at the ocean below. They flew over green islands set in a blue sea – the Bohol Sea, as Al Stern announced in his last position report -- and some of the islands were big enough to have rice paddies and small towns on them. Dead ahead lay the bay-indented coast of a larger island he suspected to be Mindanao, with hills rising up from the north shore, and about damned time. It wasn't as bad as the trip across the Pacific but four hours straight and level with nothing to do but keep an eye on the instruments and the autopilot was plenty.

"Pilot, navigator," Stern called over the intercom. "That's Mindanao up ahead. We're entering via Macajalar Bay. That island to port is Camiguin Island. Keep this heading. We should be twenty minutes from Del Monte."

"And we look for a dirt strip in the middle of a big pineapple field, right?"

"Pretty much, skipper. They're supposed to be on the lookout for us. What's a pineapple field look like, anyway?"

"If you figure it out, Al, let me know and there'll be a pair of us."

A dirt strip carved out of a pineapple field, when no one even knew what a pineapple field looked like. Charlie had seen more foul-ups in the last twenty-four hours than he'd seen in the last two years. It made him wonder how many other things might be screwed up or incomplete in the preparations for war in the Philippines.

Did whoever was in charge at Del Monte even know they were on the way? Was there anything in the way of antiaircraft defense at the airstrip? Eubanks told him it was barely long enough for a B-17 and hadn't much in the way of amenities or supporting services, so surely they wouldn't have antiaircraft guns set up yet. "No amenities" meant they would fill their airplanes out of hand pumps and 55-gallon drums, probably, and that was unsettling. Del Monte was supposed to be a relief field for Clark, but both fields were the product of an air force expanding too quickly and without the base structure needed to fight in the Twentieth Century. B-17s weren't horses and an air force wasn't airborne cavalry. Trouble was most of the Army generals were raised in an era when airplanes were considered machines whose best use would be in frightening the horses drawing the enemy's artillery or supply wagons. It was hard for those generals to even understand the uses to which the internal combustion engine could be put, much less how to employ a flying machine. Charlie snorted. A lot of those generals had opposed the development of tanks and wanted to keep their precious horse cavalry.

The B-17 passed over the coast and the low range of hills behind it. There were small towns on the coast with fishing boats and other small craft in the bays or harbors. In ten minutes the hills stretched down to a plain of obviously cultivated fields.

"Radio operator, pilot," Charlie called over the intercom. "Has Del Monte come up yet?"

"No, sir," the radio operator replied. "Been calling for the last fifteen minutes. Can't raise them."

"OK. Are you still in contact with Clark?"

"Yes, sir, off and on."

"Very well. Let them know we're approaching Del Monte but can't raise them on the radio."

"Roger wilco, skipper."

Then below them and slightly to the left Charlie saw the glint of sun off aluminum, and with that clue he made out a faint skinny rectangle in the fields, and the figures of B-17s parked along the airstrip.

"Hey, Bob, look over there at eleven o'clock," he said. "That's it."

Payne nodded. "Landing checklist?" he asked.

"Get it ready, but let's see if Sparks can raise someone on the radio now that we're overhead."

They were flying at 8000 feet and Charlie began a slow circle over Del Monte.

"Sparks?"

"Still no go, skipper."

"OK. Al, what's the field elevation at Del Monte supposed to be?"

"Nineteen hundred twenty, skipper."

"OK." Charlie turned to his co-pilot. "Bob, we'll descend and make a pass over the field at 2300 feet. That should wake them up down there."

Charlie was tempted to do a little more than make a sedate pass at 2300 feet. He was tempted to take his big four-engined airplane right down on the deck and buzz the hell out of the little dirt strip. He shrugged, surprised at himself. That was something his dad or his brother Jack might do.

"Hey, Skipper, it's Sparks. Del Monte finally came up on the Morse key. They say their altimeter is two-niner-niner-seven, wind 5 from the west. Pattern is clear and we're number one to land."

Payne reached forward to set the altimeter.

Charlie grimaced. "OK, Sparks, tell 'em we got that and we're coming in."

"Yes, sir."

They landed. Another jeep with a hastily-painted "FOLLOW ME" sign attached to it led them to their shut-down spot amid some crushed pineapple bushes.

"Wow," said Payne. He looked out the windows of the Fort. The other bombers were parked in the open along the runway. The only accommodations appeared to be a collection of tents off the south end of the runway. "I thought Seven-Mile was bad. This place really is the back end of nowhere."

"No kidding," Charlie muttered. The "Follow Me" jeep raced off after directing them to their parking spot. The cloud of dust it left pointed to the cluster of tents.

Kit Smith, the sergeant-bombardier, came up from the nose. "Just gonna recheck the pins in the fuzes on the bombs, skipper," he said. "Make sure they're secure."

Charlie nodded. The Ordnance people at Clark loaded the bombs this morning. Del Monte had no ordnance supplies. The bombs were aboard against the eventuality of war. Along with the top-secret Norden bombsight, the bombs were the special responsibility of the bombardiers.

Usually Charlie deplaned through the crew door in the aft fuselage, but this time he and Payne went out through the nose hatch. Al Stern sat at his tiny desk, stowing his charts and navigational equipment.

"I think we were thirty seconds off your estimated arrival time, Al," Charlie said.

Stern sniffed. "Twenty-eight, by my reckoning," he replied. "But only because you extended that circle over the field when we came in."

Charlie clapped Stern on the shoulder and let himself out the nose hatch. Payne followed him. They stood looking around as Stern levered himself out of the hatch to join them.

"Looks kind of like the San Joaquin Valley in California," Payne observed. "You know, hills in the distance, lots of farms. Hot."

Charlie looked around. "Damn. Wonder if they've got a shower rigged up yet?"

"Oh, was that you, skipper? I wondered what that stink, I mean, that extremely original aroma was, the last few hours."

"That's insubordination, Lt. Payne," Charlie said in his severest tone. "The penalty for that might be death by boredom."

"Looks like we've come to the right place for that," Stern observed.

A jeep started up from the cluster of tents and came their way. With the driver was a major Charlie recognized.

"Hey, Charlie, how you doing?" the major asked.

Charlie saluted. He was aware of Bob Payne and Al Stern coming to attention and saluting beside him.

The major returned it casually. "At ease," he said.

"Good to see you again, Major O'Donnell," Charlie said.

"Jeez, what did you do, pick up a whole new crew? Payne here is the only one I recognize."

"Had a little trouble with the personnel sergeants."

O'Donnell scoffed. "OK. Well, pretty obviously, you aren't Japs or Krauts or Polynesian dancing girls. But I told Gene yesterday we don't have room for more airplanes down here until we get those bulldozers back and clear some more of these damned pineapples away, and the Del Monte people grumble when we do that."

A truck rumbled up and stopped, idling. "All aboard for the Del Monte Hilton!" the driver called out.

"Take the gunners to the mess tent and get them some chow, will you, Hastings?" Major O'Donnell called to the driver. "Then you can show them where to leave their gear."

"Yes, sir," Hastings replied.

"As for us, we're going to have a meeting of all officers in about an hour," O'Donnell continued. "Perhaps you gentlemen would like to freshen up a bit and grab some chow yourselves?"

"Lead the way, Major," Charlie said.

CHAPTER FOURTEEN
Pearl Habor and Clark Field

Warm Your Engines

Jack woke up. He blinked in the darkness and looked out the window. The sky was dark and a few stars were visible. Then he heard a knock at a door down the hall. The knocking was urgent and rapid, quite unlike Ramon's usual courteous, discreet knock. There was a moment's muffled discussion and a startled oath. Quick steps came down the hall and the rapid knocking repeated.

Jack sat up, turned on the light and started to get dressed.

By the time Jack had his socks on the knocking reached his door.

Private Jelabin poked his head in. "Mr. Davis?"

"What's up, Jelabin?"

"Don't know, sir. Mr. Dyess, he said come down here and get everyone down to the field and right damn quick. Somethin' comin' in over the radio what's got everyone pretty excited down at Nichols."

"Well, you know I'm with the 17th now, but maybe I could hitch a ride with you anyway?"

"Sure thing, sir. Don't forget your .45. I got a feelin'."

Jack thought about Colonel George's speech and nodded. He picked up Irina's last letter and fitted it into his B4 bag, checking quickly to see that the essentials were there.

Five minutes later Jack joined the other pilots filing out of the front door. From nowhere Ramon had appeared, standing by the door, briefly shaking hands with each man as he passed.

"Vaya con Dios," Ramon told them.

"Vaya con Dios, Ramon," Jack replied.

Jelabin broke his own record driving down Rizal Boulevard and over the rickety, shaking bridge onto Nichols Field. The 21st's P-40s were dispersed among the trees at the south end of the old runway at Nichols; the 17th's pursuits were at the east end of the new concrete runway. Jack had Jelabin drop him off near the entrance.

"I'll walk the rest of the way," he said. "If it's war, fellows, good luck."

The truck drove off into the darkness of the blacked-out field, its occupants shouting good luck to Jack in a ragged chorus.

Jack started walking. There was enough starlight to see the road and be sure he wasn't walking into someone.

The field was a beehive of activity. Men were being roused up out of tents. An Allison engine started up, then another, and another. Jack started running towards the 17th's Operations Shack.

A dozen pilots already stood outside the tent, smoking cigarettes and talking.

"Where's Wagner?" Jack asked.

"Over talking to Major Maverick, trying to find out what the hell's going on," the man replied.

"Well, what the hell is going on?"

"Pearl Harbor's been bombed."

"Bullshit."

"That's what they're saying on the radio."

"Who?"

"Jesus, Jack, I don't know. Some guy has a Trans-Oceanic shortwave radio and heard it, someone else got a message from 5th Interceptor Command who heard it from someone else. We've got orders to stand by."

"Not anymore," said a new voice. Jack recognized Wagner. "We don't have any orders right now. You fellows go back to your quarters and get some rest. You might need it."

The rest of the pilots dispersed. Jack looked at Wagner, put his B4 bag by one of the chairs in front of the tent, and sat down.

"Not sleepy, Jack?" Wagner asked.

"Guess I'll catch a few winks right here, boss," Jack replied.

"You know something I don't?"

"Has Pearl Harbor really been bombed?"

"Sounds like it. Major Maverick is on the phone to FEAF, trying to find out for sure."

"Then I guess I'll stay here. I'll bet you we're going to be busy at first light."

"No takers." Wagner picked a chair and sat down. "Moon will be up a little before 0500. Maybe we'll know something by then."

It seemed like seconds only. Someone shook Jack by the shoulder.

"Wake up, lieutenant," said an unfamiliar voice.

"OK, OK," Jack said. "I'm awake. What's going on?"

In the east the moon rose over the horizon.

"I don't know, sir. Lt. Wagner got called over to Base Operations. He asked me to get you up and tell you to start warming up the airplanes when some of the other pilots get here."

"OK," said Jack.

The man walked into the tent. Jack heard voices from inside. A truck drove up and pilots started climbing out.

"Where's Wagner?" someone asked.

"Base Operations," Jack said. "He wants us to start warming up the ships."

Jack started walking towards the dispersal area.

"What, are you in charge?" someone asked.

"No, but I reckon you better come along anyway," Jack said. "If the Japs really are coming you might wish you had a P-40 ready to go."

"Where are we going?"

"When you find out, you tell me. Then we'll both know."

Charlie was awakened in the early morning darkness by someone shaking him.

"OK, OK, I'm awake," he said. "What the hell is it?"

"Not sure, sir. Major O'Donnell wants everyone at the operations tent."

"OK. Is this all officers?"

"Yes, sir. I'll wake up your copilot and navigator. The Major wants everyone soonest."

Charlie swung his legs off the bunk, groped for a match, and struck it. There was a stub of candle by his bedside. He lit the candle. The tiny amber flame flickered inside the canvas tent. Charlie dressed quickly, stuck his feet in his boots and blew out the candle.

In the east the dawn pinked the silhouette of the hills and overhead the stars faded. There was barely enough light to see the tails of the B-17s marching off into the distance along the airstrip. A hint of breeze brought the smell of earth and growing pineapple to his nostrils.

A kerosene lantern lit the operations tent. The interior of the tent was dense with cigarette smoke. Charlie found a seat on a crude wooden bench. In a minute he was joined by Bob Payne and Al Stern, both of them yawning.

"What's going on?" Payne asked sleepily.

"Don't know," Charlie replied.

"'There shall be wars and rumors of wars,'" Stern said. "Five'll get ya ten it's one or the other."

Major O'Donnell stood up in the light of the kerosene lantern. The buzz of talk in the tent died away when he raised a hand for silence.

"Gentlemen, three hours ago the Japs attacked Pearl Harbor," he said.

The silence erupted into a clamor of surprise and disbelief. O'Donnell waited for a moment and called for quiet.

"We don't have any details as to the extent of damage or casualties," O'Donnell went on. "I know we here in the Philippines thought the Japs would strike us first. There's some speculation that the attack on Pearl Harbor was some sort of feint. But that's just speculation."

O'Donnell paused and looked around the tent. "What isn't speculation is that FEAF has issued orders placing us on full alert. No one knows what the Japs will do next, but sooner or later they will, they must strike here in the Philippines. In effect, gentlemen, we must consider ourselves at war with Japan. The possibility of sabotage becomes immediate and real. I am posting sentries armed with rifles loaded with live ammunition. Anyone approaching the airstrip, the airplanes or any of our installations here will be challenged, and, if they don't give a satisfactory counter-sign, will be fired upon. Are there any questions?"

Someone asked, "What's the challenge and counter-sign, sir?"

"The challenge is 'lollygagger' and the countersign is 'loyalist,'" O'Donnell said at once. "Most Japs can't make an 'ell' sound, so if you hear someone say 'royarist' it's time to start shooting. Any more questions?"

Charlie said, "Major, I've got a load of 600-lb. bombs on board my ship. Any plans on using them against the enemy?"

That question raised a growling buzz of approval. O'Donnell nodded. "That's a good question, Charlie, and the answer I have is, I don't know. I don't even know if it would be smart to arm the other Forts, for the simple reason that we might be sent on anti-shipping strikes, or stage north to Clark Field to join up with the rest of the Group and bomb Formosa. I don't have any orders from Col. Eubanks or FEAF, but you guys know what these Forts are built to do and how they should be employed. As soon as I know something you'll know, likely because I'm giving you orders to go and do it. For now, preflight your airplanes and warm up your engines. Be ready to go as soon as we get orders."

O'Donnell looked around for a moment. "Dismiss."

Pepsodents on Patrol

The sun broke over the hills east of Nichols Field as Wagner led the 17th Pursuit off the ground. Jack followed him off as an element leader in Wagner's flight of four, taking off in the dust raised by Wagner and his wingman. Then Jack was up, retracting undercarriage and trimming for the climb off Wagner's right

263

wing in echelon formation. He looked back at the airstrip, where the next pair of P-40s was taking off.

"This is Pepsodent Blue Leader," Wagner called over the radio. "Execute Bravo. Repeat, execute Bravo."

Jack reviewed the details of the signal "execute Bravo" as he checked his position and that of his wingman. The 17th Pursuit, acting under orders of Fifth Interceptor Command, had orders to climb to 17,000 feet and patrol the northern edge of Manila Bay, there to intercept Japanese bombers breaking through the defensive barriers of the P-40s at Clark and Iba Fields.

Jack felt uneasy about that. There wasn't anything of any real military value in Manila, so what was the point to striking it? If the Japs were going to hit somewhere on Luzon they were going to hit the airfields first, and they'd come straight down from the north from their bases on Formosa. Those bases were at least 500 miles away. At that range the Japs wouldn't try anything fancy, just come straight in and hope to come straight back out.

Jack checked his fuel gage. He and the rest of the squadron had 52-gallon auxiliary fuel tanks slung under the fuselage, but they'd burn that climbing to 17,000 feet. After that they could set the engine for 2100 RPM and loiter about at just under 200 mph, giving them about two hours with onboard fuel. After that they'd better head for the nearest gas station. A gas-thirsty 1100-horsepower Allison engine wouldn't run on fumes.

He looked all around him, taking in the squadron strung out in flights of four behind them and the sky all around them. The sun was a little above the horizon, throwing shadows across sleepy Luzon below, making a gorgeous tropical show of pink and red and yellow on the towering cumulus clouds forming over the land. The clouds were already up above 5,000 feet, and would get higher still as the sun warmed the land, making water vapor rise and feed further cloud growth. Just in the seventeen days he'd been here in the Philippines he'd seen those clouds reach 20,000 feet easy and spawn some truly powerful thunderstorms. That, he was told, was normal for the tropics.

When they reached their assigned altitude of 17,000 feet they couldn't see much of the ground but there was still good visibility on top of the clouds.

"Pepsodent Blue Leader to all Pepsodents, go to max conserve," Wagner radioed.

Jack set his engine controls for 2100 RPM at 27 inches of manifold pressure. He leveled out as Wagner did. Their airspeed increased a little, from about 140 mph in the climb to about 190. Jack looked around again. White and Red flights were on their left, Yellow flight on the right, at slightly different altitudes, spread out in a loose vee.

Gradually the adrenaline of the full-throttle climb faded out of his system, and gradually the boredom crept in, because nothing happened. An hour went by, then another, and they flew back to Nichols to refuel.

The Japs Played Hell at Pearl

Charlie oversaw the fueling and checking of his Fort. When it was over he went back to the operations shack. A corporal coaxed Radio Manila out of the radio, and Dave Bell's excited monologue wavered in and out of audibility.

Major O'Donnell sat nearby, smoking a cigarette. When Charlie came in O'Donnell beckoned to a seat by him.

"We're ready to go, sir," Charlie informed him. O'Donnell nodded.

"That Dave Bell guy says Radio Honolulu reports Pearl Harbor took a major pasting," O'Donnell said quietly. "The whole damn harbor's on fire, warships exploding, Jap airplanes flying down the streets strafing anything that moves. Ford Island and Hickam Field are hidden by smoke clouds. Or so Bell says Honolulu says."

Charlie nodded. O'Donnell offered him a cigarette, and when Charlie took it, O'Donnell produced a Zippo lighter.

"Thanks," Charlie said, taking a deep drag. "We hear anything from Eubanks or FEAF?"

"Sit tight."

"That's it?"

O'Donnell nodded, taking a drag on his own cigarette. It burned down to a stub, and O'Donnell put it out and lit another.

"What do you think, Charlie?" O'Donnell asked.

Charlie shook his head slowly. "It sounds like the Japs played hell in Hawaii. Why haven't they hit us? You'd think they would have tried to hit Clark Field, at least, right at dawn. It's not like they don't know exactly where it is."

"Eubanks got all the B-17s off at dawn, thinking just that," O'Donnell said. "We found that out a little while ago."

"Well, they can stay up most of the day if they need to, or head here. That's about the only alternatives they have."

"Christ, if they come here, where the hell would we put them? We'd have to park them in the pineapple fields, and most of them would bog down in the soft dirt. We'd be days digging them out and vulnerable to any kind of attack."

"How is it that no one thought of this months ago, sir?" Charlie asked quietly.

"Because it wasn't until last spring that the War Department figured we should hold on to the Philippines," O'Donnell replied, in the same tone. "In part that was because General Arnold sold the White House, Congress, General Marshall and anyone else who would listen on how the B-17 Flying Fortress was the answer to all our problems. The way I heard it, Arnold told the President that if we had a hundred B-17s out here we could thumb our noses at the Japs."

"But we barely have a hundred B-17s in the whole Air Corps," Charlie said. "And we don't have a hundred B-17s to defend the Philippines, we've got what, thirty, thirty-five?"

"Thirty-five, and half of them are sitting down here in this pineapple field," O'Donnell confirmed. "All together that's about one-quarter of the entire heavy bomber strength in the entire Air Corps."

Charlie took a deep breath and let it out slowly before taking a last drag on the cigarette O'Donnell had given him. He started to open his mouth and then shut it, shaking his head instead.

"Yeah," O'Donnell said. "You might say we started too late and we've got too little, and we're going to have to fight anyway."

Gone

Jack followed Wagner back to Nichols with the rest of the 17th. Almost as soon as he shut the engine down the fuel trucks drove up and started filling tanks. The pilots gathered around the Operations tent to grab a sandwich and some coffee.

"Listen up," said Wagner. "The Japs may have tried a probe. The 3rd Pursuit at Iba got vectors on a radar contact somewhere over the South China Sea early this morning. They didn't find anything but there was something on radar."

Jack wondered what it was like chasing a radar ghost in daylight instead of darkness. Maybe Interceptor Command would get the finger out and pass on the information in time for them to act on it.

The telephone in the Ops tent rang. Wagner picked it up before the private behind the desk could.

"17th Squadron, Lt. Wagner speaking."

The squadron commander nodded, reaching for a pencil and jotting notes.

"Yes, sir," Wagner said. "We'll go as soon as we've finished fueling."

He put the phone down. "That was Interceptor Command. You guys finish those sandwiches, we're going back up."

An hour later Jack was in his slot as Wagner's element leader, orbiting over the northern edge of Manila Bay. He listened on the radio but there was nothing, nothing but a droning, hissing static that made it difficult to hear even the close-range transmissions of his squadron mates. Jack heard Wagner call Interceptor Command every five minutes, without any reply. The minutes ticked by into hours as the engines sucked their fuel tanks dry. Jack scanned the sky and watched his instruments.

He didn't think it would be like this, but he didn't know what it would be like, anyway. All he'd ever heard were stories, stories from his father and his friends, stories he'd read in books. Now around him was the blue sky and the clouds and the sun. He held up his finger to block out the direct light of the sun, a trick his father told him once, to look for the Jap in the sun.

There was nothing. The sky was empty except for the 17th, and the radio screeched and howled with static, until Wagner rocked his wings in the signal to turn for home.

A jeep waited next to the Ops tent when they got taxied in. A colonel sat beside the jeep's driver. Jack shut down, watching as Lt. Wagner did the same and got wearily out of his airplane. The colonel beckoned Wagner over, and something strange happened.

The colonel spoke a few sentences to Wagner, who wilted as if he'd suddenly had the weight of three men put on his shoulders. The colonel got back into his jeep. The driver put it in gear and drove out the gate towards Manila.

Wagner still stood there, staring at the ground, closing and opening his fists, shoulders hunched.

Jack walked up to him and stood at Wagner's shoulder. The squadron commander didn't notice him until Jack said softly, "What is it, Skipper? What's wrong?"

Then Jack saw that Wagner's eyes were screwed shut. A tear leaked out of the near eye.

By ones and twos the other pilots gathered around.

"Clark Field," Wagner said finally. He took a deep breath and opened his fists. He took off his flying helmet and rubbed his face and hair with his hands, finally combing his hair back and putting the helmet back on.

"What about it?" Jack asked.

"Gone," Wagner replied.

The pilots looked at each other in confusion.

"Gone," Wagner repeated. "While we were orbiting above Manila Bay, forty miles away, just forty miles, ten minutes flying time, the Japs came in and caught every B-17 and P-40 at Clark Field on the ground like so many sitting ducks and blew them into scrap along with no one knows yet how many men. Hundreds, maybe."

"What about the radar at Iba?" Jack asked.

"Gone," Wagner said. "Same as Clark. The Japs caught all but a handful of P-40s on the ground and bombed the place all to hell." He took another deep shuddering breath. "You guys go and pack some clothes for a few days stay. We're going to Clark Field."

Oh my God, Jack thought. *Charlie. Charlie's at Clark.*

Holes the Size of a Man's Head

At Del Monte the morning wore itself into a long hot anxious afternoon. No orders came. The sentries O'Donnell posted paced their lines, weapons unslung, peering suspiciously into the waist-high pineapple bushes as if a horde of Jap paratroopers might jump out at any moment. One of the crew chiefs improvised machine-gun nests with spare machine-guns, useful against infantry or low-flying aircraft. The men manning the guns scanned the sky with wide eyes, training their weapons on circling hawks until a look through binoculars identified the birds as birds and not marauding Jap bombers. Charlie, like the other aircraft commanders, checked over his airplane again. He and Payne started the engines, running them up to full power and watching the gauges while the flight engineer and a crew chief stood behind them, alert for any misbehavior. Then they topped off the fuel tanks, secured the flight controls, and went back to waiting. Charlie tried to nap, propped up against one of the main wheels of the airplane, but gave it up.

Charlie was at the operations tent when a garbled, static-filled message squealed out of the radio. Major O'Donnell bent close to the speaker, listening.

"Someone's coming in," O'Donnell said, straightening up. "Sounds like they're in bad shape."

O'Donnell and Charlie looked to the north. A sergeant came out of the operations tent and handed the major a pair of binoculars. After a moment's scan O'Donnell steadied. Then, slowly, he handed the binoculars to Charlie.

Charlie looked in the direction O'Donnell pointed out. A mote swam in the field of view of the binoculars, a silvery mote with a halo around it.

Charlie realized the mote was an airplane, and what looked like a halo was smoke. In a few moments the mote grew wings. The smoke came from the No. 4 engine.

O'Donnell stood there, looking at the airplane that was now visible to the naked eye.

"Sir, do we have a crash truck? A doctor, or even a medic? There might be wounded men aboard."

"A doctor?" O'Donnell shook his head. "I'll call the Del Monte people. They have a doctor. Find Chief Ames. He's got a crash truck, sort of."

Charlie found Chief Ames assembling the crew of the crash truck. On a base stateside, or even at Clark Field, a crash truck would have a man in an asbestos suit, large and small fire extinguishers, stretchers, and other equipment to pull men from burning aircraft. There'd also be a fire-fighting truck. Here at Del Monte they had a couple of crash axes, two fire bottles that looked like the ones carried in the B-17s, and a larger fire extinguisher stenciled "DEL MONTE PINEAPPLE" on its side.

Chief Ames saw his look. "The Del Monte people had a little airstrip here for light planes," he told Charlie. "We sort of inherited their equipment. It's better than nothing."

Charlie realized he had been about to say something about how non-regulation the civilian fire extinguisher was. But it was the best they had and if it would save an airman's life who cared?

"Mind if I ride with you?" he asked.

"Hop aboard, sir," the Chief invited.

By this time the B-17 was overhead. The smoke from the No. 4 engine was thick and black. The propeller on No. 4 was feathered.

There were holes the size of a man's head in the metal skin of the wings and the fuselage, and the right waist gunner's window was a collection of shattered, jagged Plexiglas. The fabric of the rudder was burnt and blackened in places, with the underlying aluminum ribs visible.

"What the hell?" Charlie whispered.

"Cannon," the Chief said in a grim voice. "Light cannon, 20-mm stuff. I seen some pictures of RAF Spitfires hit with Kraut 20-mm cannon. Looked about like that."

They drove the crash truck out to the end of the runway and parked, engine running, as the damaged Fort lined up on final approach. Charlie sighed in relief as he saw the main gear and the flaps come down. The Fort's pilot babied her down on the approach, and Jack realized from the note of the engines that he was holding power back on at least one engine and pushing the other two. Charlie nodded, it made sense: the rudder's effectiveness was reduced, so it was less useful fighting the drag of the shut-down No. 4 engine. Reducing the power on the No. 1 engine and carrying more on Nos. 2 and 3 avoided asymmetrical thrust.

The pilot came back on the power as the mains touched, sending out puffs of dust. The pilot held the tail off until his airspeed bled down and the tail wheel touched. A moment later Charlie heard the squeal of brakes, and the "Follow Me" jeep raced the crash truck out to meet the newcomer.

The pilot didn't even try to find a good spot. He guided his airplane to the end of the runway, braked to a halt and shut down as the crash truck drove up.

Charlie got out and ran to the entrance door. He reached for the handle but someone turned it from inside.

A sergeant-gunner stood in the door. His eyes looked around, then focused on Charlie and the captain's bars on the shoulders of Charlie's jacket.

"Sir, you got a doctor here?"

"We've sent for one, sergeant."

The sergeant nodded and climbed down from the airplane. He sat in the dirt next to the airplane as if someone cut the tendons to his legs and stared up at the sky.

Charlie went up the ladder into the interior of the Fort.

Powerful odors smashed into his nostrils: the familiar reek of cordite propellant from .50-cal. machine-guns and another odor, a combination, a coppery sort of smell overlaying the stink of an open sewer. Hundreds of brass shell casings littered the deck of the Fort's waist section.

A man in a flying suit and ball cap lay on the floor. The flying suit was torn and bloody. One leg was nearly severed and lay at an angle across the other leg. There was a tourniquet above the wound on the leg – someone's belt, twisted with a wrench handle. There was a puddle of drying blood under the man, whose eyes stared up at the overhead of the fuselage without blinking. His lips were slightly parted.

"Get out of the way, sir," said a voice behind him.

Charlie moved forward, slipping on the mix of shell casings in the puddles of drying blood, and moved forward to the top gun

271

position and the radio compartment. He moved past holes the size of a man's head blown in the skin of the fuselage, little holes about the size of a pencil's width punched in the fuselage, letting rays of light in. The radio operator was slumped over his desk, dead, the radio riddled with bullet holes and splashed with the operator's blood and brains.

He hurried past, down the narrow walkway in the bomb bay, to the cockpit. The pilot, he saw, had half risen out of his seat. The copilot's head lolled to one side. The pilot turned to Charlie.

"Christ, help us!" the pilot said. "Help get Sammy out of his seat, he's hit bad!"

"Get his seat harness loose," Charlie said. The pilot reached over the throttle quadrant and fumbled with the release mechanism.

Charlie was shoved abruptly behind the pilot's seat.

"Excuse me, sir," said Chief Ames. The pilot got the seat harness loose.

Ames was a large, powerful man. He picked the copilot's body up under the armpits and straightened, pulling the man up and out of his seat. Charlie moved forward and caught the man's legs as Ames continued straight back out and down the fuselage the way they came in, carrying the unconscious copilot, lifting him by main strength over the girders flanking the bomb-bay walkway.

Charlie saw a nasty crease on the side of the copilot's head. There was a bloody compress bandage on the man's shoulder. If he'd been conscious the copilot would be screaming in agony from the way Ames pulled on him but there was nothing else to be done.

As they handed the copilot's unconscious body out of the airplane a civilian car braked to a halt on the airstrip. A medium-sized man in a dusty white suit and panama hat jumped out, carrying a black bag with him.

Charlie and Chief Ames laid the copilot on a stretcher from the crash truck. The doctor knelt beside the stretcher, turning the copilot's head to look at the wound there, looking in the man's eyes, opening his flight jacket and frowning at the red-soaked compress bandage over the wound in the copilot's shoulder. Then he felt the man's pulse and his frown deepened.

The doctor looked at Charlie. "You fellows got anything like a surgery?" the doctor asked. "I can't do much for this man right here."

Chief Ames said, "Doc, what we have is a nice steady table in the mess hall we can stretch him out on."

The doctor nodded. "That'll have to do. Got any blankets?"

"Yes, sir."

"Good. Wrap this man in them, he's in shock. Take him to your mess tent. Have your cooks start boiling water, lots of it. Have them clean the table off and get some clean sheets and spread them over the table. Can you do that?"

The Chief nodded. "Yes, sir."

"Good, go to it."

The Chief motioned to the stretcher men, who loaded the copilot onto the crash truck and drove slowly towards the mess tent. Chief Ames jumped into the "Follow Me" jeep, whose driver sped ahead of the crash truck.

The doctor looked at Charlie. "You all right?"

"Yeah. Yes. I wasn't on this airplane."

The doctor nodded and moved to the sergeant gunner who was now half-sitting, half-lying in the dirt beside the entrance ladder. As he looked the man over he asked Charlie, "Anyone else injured aboard this airplane?"

"Two men dead. I don't know who else is aboard."

At that moment the hatch in the nose compartment opened. The bombardier levered himself down out of the hatch and stood there, a little wobbly on his feet. The pilot appeared in the waist entrance. There was another man behind him, a sergeant gunner.

"We're OK," the pilot said.

He started down the ladder, stumbled, caught himself, and made it the rest of the way down. He looked at Charlie.

"Who are you?" he asked.

"Charlie Davis," Charlie replied.

"Kennedy, Walt Kennedy," the pilot said. He pointed at the crash truck. "That's my copilot, Sammy Bensen."

"What happened?" Charlie asked. "Were you at Clark?"

"Sort of," Kennedy replied. "We tried to get in about the time the bombs started falling. That was bad, but the Jap fighters were worse."

"Jap fighters? How could a Type 96 do all that to you?"

Kennedy shook his head. "These weren't Type 96s. Don't know what they were except fast and maneuverable and well-armed. Machine-guns and cannon. Most of them were down on the deck strafing the field when we got there, but a couple came up after us. They just sort of hung on their props and climbed straight up."

Charlie figured that was exaggeration, but even if exaggerated this new Jap fighter must be bad news indeed.

"Come on," Charlie said. "Let's get you to Operations. I'm sure the Major wants to talk to you."

"O'Donnell still in charge here?"

"Yes."

Kennedy nodded and started walking. The sergeant gunner with him sat with the other gunner by the airplane. The bombardier and the navigator fell in behind them.

Take a Good Long Look

Clark Field was burning.

As the 17th entered the traffic pattern for Clark's single bomb-cratered runway they flew through the smoke. Alongside the runway nothing remained but smoldering wrecks, the wrecks of the B-17 Forts of the 19th Bomb Group and the P-40s of the 20th Pursuit. Jack gave up counting destroyed B-17s after twelve because he couldn't tell if some of the burning spots were one or two airplanes.

The hangars burned along with almost every other building on the field. They'd seen the smoke all the way from Nichols Field.

Jack turned on final approach and cranked down the flaps and landing gear. He saw Wagner flatten his glide to land further down the field where the runway was less damaged. Jack wasn't sure he would have tried landing on that cratered piece of sod but Wagner seemed pretty determined about it.

It didn't surprise Jack.

Jack tightened his restraint harness as he rounded out, leading his wingman, Jimmy Vaughan as Pepsodent Blue Four, over a bomb crater big enough to swallow a P-40 whole. Jack gave the engine a touch of throttle and then pulled all the way back, cutting engine power completely to land just beyond the crater. Jack craned his head to see past the P-40's long nose as the tail came down. He kicked rudder and applied the toe brakes as his airplane danced on the lip of another crater, then whipped his head to the other side, avoiding a third crater. Then they were past the worst of the damage, following Wagner and his wingman in S-curves along what was left of Clark's single runway. Jack had no idea where Wagner was headed. Finally Jack recognized what was left of the apron amid the hulks of burned-out P-40s and other wrecks unrecognizable.

As soon as his propeller kicked to a stop the smoke eddied into his cockpit. Jack coughed, inhaled at the wrong moment and got a good lungful of the nasty choking stuff. He coughed again, nearly doubling over in his cockpit. He hated smoke, didn't even like being in a room full of smokers. When he got his lungs more or less clear his eyes were streaming and felt swollen and inflamed.

That was when he became aware of the smell.

The stink of burning aluminum and magnesium bit into his nasal passages. Heat wafted over him in wind eddies, bringing with it black smoke from burning oil. Jack kept coughing until a shift of wind cleared the air. He wiped his streaming eyes with the edge of his scarf and climbed out of the P-40's cockpit.

Another wind eddy brought the smell of burning, carbonized meat. Carbon burns at an even higher temperature than most metals and produced a worse smell as far as Jack was concerned. That burning carbon smell was what was left of B-17 and P-40 airmen trapped in their airplanes during the attack, or caught in the flames of exploding gasoline.

Charlie, thought Jack. *Where can I find out about Charlie?*

Jack gathered up Jimmy Vaughan with a look and a gesture with his shoulder. They joined the pilots gathering around Wagner. Jack saw parties of men helping the wounded, or gathering the dead, or trying to extinguish the flames. Fire bottles and larger fire extinguishers lay here and there, empty, abandoned, silent testimony to attempts to put out burning airplanes, or perhaps only to beat the flames back enough to enable the rescue of trapped and burning men.

Jack reached Wagner and stood beside him in silence with the rest of the 17th.

Finally Wagner spoke. "Take a good, long look," he said, loudly enough to be heard over the flames and the roar of passing vehicles. "Take a God-damn *good* look. What happened here today is partly our fault. We are pursuit pilots, and it's our job to prevent things like this. Maybe there's not a lot we could have done. But the truth is we didn't do a damned thing." Wagner paused.

Jack found himself looking at the ground with his fists balled up so hard he could feel his fingernails cutting into the flesh of his palms. Wagner wasn't right, he knew that, it wasn't their fault, it wasn't *his* fault, they'd only being doing what they were told. But Jack also knew that while he and every other pilot of the 17th had been doing what they were told, American airmen were being machine-gunned on the ground by Jap fighters. His own brother might be lying out there somewhere, blown apart or burned beyond recognition.

For whatever reason, the 17th had orbited, fat, dumb and happy, vigilant as all hell and seeing nothing at all, while the Japs burned Clark Field to the ground.

"We didn't do anything today," Wagner continued. "But that doesn't mean a damned thing about tomorrow. You men listen to me. You're Americans, and you're standing here looking at what the Japs have done to other Americans. I know you're angry, but don't give in to that anger. Don't believe anger makes you invulnerable. A bullet doesn't care how right you are. Just remember this. Our duty isn't to die for our country. Our duty is to make those little yellow bastards die for *their* country. You boys got that?"

It took a moment. Then Jack heard a low growl and realized it was coming from his own throat. But it sounded oddly resonant, and then he understood all of Wagner's pilots were doing it.

"Just remember that," Wagner said. "I have a feeling it's going to be a long damned war. We're going to need every pilot, ever airman we can get to win it."

Late that afternoon Charlie went to Major O'Donnell's tent. A captain sat there, a young-looking guy with dark wavy hair. It took Charlie a minute to place him, then he remembered the captain's name was Colin Kelly.

"Charlie, you remember Colin," O'Donnell said.

"Sure." Charlie shook hands with Kelly, who nodded.

"Good to see you again, Charlie," Kelly said. "Heard you made it all the way across the Pacific by yourself."

"I have a good crew."

Kelly smiled.

O'Donnell said, "OK, here's the deal. You guys ready?"

"Yes, sir," said Kelly.

"I managed to get Col. Eubanks on the line. Clark is closed to B-17s until they can clear the runway, which, best guess, won't be until sometime tomorrow."

Kelly grimaced. "I talked to Walt Kennedy before I came in. Sounds like the Japs did a real job up at Clark."

O'Donnell nodded grimly. "Gene sounded like he aged twenty years since I talked to him yesterday. He had fifteen B-17s at Clark this morning, and he said he'd be lucky to get two of them back in commission."

"Jesus," Charlie said.

"Right. Gene also told me he spent most of yesterday morning trying to get MacArthur's headquarters to agree on a mission to bomb the Jap airfields on Formosa."

Charlie exchanged a look with Kelly, who turned to O'Donnell. "Pardon me for asking a dumb question, Rosie, but why was there even a question about bombing Formosa?"

"Captain, I won't presume to comment on the doings of higher beings," O'Donnell said. "But I'm sure you grasp this is only the opening act, and I'm sure the Japs have other things up their sleeve for us."

"Invasion?" asked Charlie.

O'Donnell nodded. "I've got word from FEAF that there's an invasion fleet, headed for somewhere on the northwest coast of Luzon. I'm to send a squadron north to help deal with that, and you're going. Kelly here will be in charge."

Charlie looked at Kelly. "OK. What's the plan?"

O'Donnell made a hand-off gesture to Kelly, who nodded. "If they can get the runway at Clark clear by tonight, we'll take off here in time to be over Clark at first light," Kelly said. "Charlie,

277

you've already got bombs aboard, so once we land and refuel at Clark I'm going to send you north to reconnoiter from the Babuyan Channel in the north, and then south to cover the northwest coast as far as Lingayen Gulf. You'll attack targets of opportunity but your primary mission will be reconnaissance. As soon as I can get refueled and rearmed I'm taking the rest of the squadron into the air to avoid..." Kelly coughed and looked away.

Charlie nodded. "I get it," he said.

"One reason I picked you for this is you've got a pretty new airplane," Kelly said. "At least, so Chief Ames tells me. Take your Fort up to 30,000 feet. That should keep you above the Jap fighters."

"OK. Let me suggest you might want to send me on about a half-hour earlier than the rest of the squadron. If I can get in and refuel at Clark at first light I'll be in position that much sooner."

Kelly said, "That's a pretty good idea, Charlie. Vigan Bay is only about 160, 170 miles north of Clark. If you can get off before dawn you can be over the Babuyan Channel by the time the sun's up."

"Can do," said Charlie.

Any News of Charlie?

Jack stood in line at the mess hall at Clark Field that evening when he heard the Japs were landing at Vigan Bay and Aparri on the north end of Luzon, less than 170 miles away.

Except for windows shattered and denuded of glass by blast shock, the mess hall was intact. The Filipino cooks swept the glass into glittering piles in the corners, wiped the tables free of dust, relit the stoves and started turning out hot meals.

"Is that a rumor, or the straight skinny?" he asked the officer discussing it with the man next in line to him.

That officer, a captain, looked at Jack, who was in his flight suit, leather jacket and flying boots. All his other clothes were still stowed in the tiny luggage compartment in his P-40. Jack wore his officer's cap and had his flying helmet stuffed in the map pocket of his coveralls. The captain was some sort of non-flying officer. His uniform was dusty and singed. He wore a bandage on one hand.

"I work at Base Operations," the captain said. "As far as I know, it's straight. At least, everyone seemed pretty agitated over it. I heard Eubanks say he was going to put some bombers up in the morning, as soon as they can get up from Mindanao, and hit the Japs with them."

Jack nodded. "I've got a brother with the 19th," he said. "Who would I see about finding out if he's accounted for?"

The captain was quiet for a moment, looking thoughtfully at Jack. "I don't think they've gotten as far as putting a casualty list together yet," he said quietly. "What's your brother do?"

"B-17 pilot."

"They'd know about pilots, or any of the aircrew, for sure. I'd go up to the 19th's Operations office and ask. Worst they can do is tell you to get lost."

Jack hardly tasted the ham sandwich and coffee he was handed. As soon as he was finished he handed in the plate and the coffee cup and went looking for the 19th BG's Operations office.

19th BG Ops was now a hastily-erected tent with a hand-lettered sign Jack missed as he walked by. Jack would have kept walking if a jeep with Col. Eubanks in it hadn't pulled up.

Eubanks got out of the jeep, looked at Jack without recognition, and started to go inside the tent.

"Excuse me, Col. Eubanks," Jack called. When Eubanks turned to look at him Jack came to attention and saluted. Eubanks returned the salute, his face without expression and looking as if he had aged twenty years in the two days since Jack met the colonel in General Brereton's office.

"I'm Lt. Jack Davis, sir. We met at General Brereton's office Saturday evening. Can you tell me anything about my brother, sir, Captain Charles Davis? He's one of your pilots."

For a second Eubanks looked at Jack as if he had spoken in some unknown foreign language. Then the colonel blinked.

"Captain Davis? Charlie Davis?"

"Yes, sir."

"He wasn't here this morning, if that's what you're asking, Lieutenant. He and his crew are down in Mindanao. Didn't have enough room for them up here." Eubanks cracked a half-second's worth of deathly smile. "Guess we don't have to worry about that now. The airplanes down at Del Monte are what I have left for a bomb group." Eubanks started to turn away, then turned back and said, "Your brother will be up here very briefly in the morning, Lieutenant. I'm not sure when, and I can't say why."

Jack started to blurt that he'd heard about the Japs landing but thought better of it.

"Thank you, sir," he said.

Eubanks nodded and went inside the tent.

CHAPTER FIFTEEN
Invasion

<u>Clark Field</u>

"OK, Skipper," said Al Stern over the intercom. "We're passing over the north coast of Manila Bay now, on heading for Clark Field, ETA fifteen minutes."

"Right, thanks, Al. Sparks, raise Clark, tell them our ETA."

"Roger, Skipper."

Charlie looked over the nose of the B-17 into the pre-dawn darkness. According to his briefing before leaving Del Monte three hours ago the runway craters were filled and a flare path for landing laid out.

"It's liable to be nothing more than some torches, or maybe some guys shining jeep headlights down the runway," O'Donnell told him during the preflight briefing. "When you figure you're in the vicinity shoot off two red flares. That's the agreed-upon recognition signal."

Charlie keyed his intercom. "Al, let me know when we're five minutes out."

"Roger, Skipper."

"Skipper, it's Sparks. I've got a signal from Clark Field. They acknowledge we're inbound and urge caution on landing."

"I guess they didn't say why."

"No, sir."

"OK, thanks, Sparks."

Charlie looked over at Bob Payne in the dim light from the instrument panel. "What do you think, Bob?"

The copilot shrugged. "Who knows? At least they aren't under attack. Probably they didn't get those holes in the runway filled in all the way."

Charlie nodded, looking ahead into the moonlit night. The waning moon gave dim light on the country below, gleaming off rice paddies and streams, seven thousand feet below them.

"Bob, you got the landing checklist?"

"Ready to go, Skipper."

"OK. Let's start descending. Make it 500 feet per minute."

Charlie came back on the throttles and RPMs. Payne set the elevator trim for a 500 feet per minute rate of descent.

"Five minutes out, Skipper," Stern called over the intercom.

"Roger, Al. Sparks, you got those flares loaded?"

"That's affirmative, Skipper."

"OK. Double check that they're both red."

There was a moment of silence over the intercom. "Two red flares as ordered, Skipper."

"Thanks, Sparks. Just being careful."

There was a chuckle over the intercom. "No problem here, boss. Hard to be too careful in a situation like this."

The B-17 descended through four thousand feet. As they did Al called, "They can't be too far ahead of us, Skipper."

"Roger that. Sparks, fire those flares."

"Roger." From aft came the faint chug-chug as Sparks fired off the red flares.

"Reload with two more red flares, Sparks, in case we need to convince them."

"Roger, Skipper."

"Pilot, navigator, we should be right on top of Clark."

"OK. Pilot to crew, anybody see anything that looks like a flare path?"

The bomber droned on through the night.

"Uh, Skipper, right waist."

"Go ahead, Lefkowicz."

"Look out about three o'clock, maybe a mile away."

Charlie dropped the right wing. Payne looked out his window, craning as far over as he could.

"I got something, Skipper, but it isn't much. Not sure what it is. It's a glow of some kind, though."

"OK. You take the airplane."

"Roger, copilot has the airplane."

Payne banked the Fort to the right and lined up on the faint glow he had seen. When he leveled out Charlie saw it himself, the faintest glow barely above the nose. Then, as he watched, the glow increased, as if another set of lights had switched on.

"OK, Bob, let's go down for a look. I've got the airplane. Lower the landing gear when we slow below 150 and stand by with flaps."

"Roger, pilot has the airplane. Landing gear coming down."

The bomber slowed with the drag of the landing gear.

"Bob, let's have half-flaps."

There was a rumble and a vibration in the airframe as the flaps came down. Charlie fed in a little nose-down elevator to compensate for the nose-up effect caused by the flaps. He gave the engines some throttle as well and checked their descent at 2000 feet. Clark Field's elevation was 475 feet above sea level, and just in case there was a good reason to run for it Charlie wanted some extra altitude to dive while he cleaned up the flaps and gear.

"Pilot, navigator, I can see the runway pretty well. I think it's the runway. Holy Mother of God."

"What is it, Al?"

"There's a burned out Fort right next to the runway," the navigator replied.

"We knew there would be," Charlie replied grimly. By now he could see the runway himself.

"Skipper, it's Sparks. Clark says altimeter two niner niner three, wind calm, but they advise landing at the northeast end of the field."

"Roger that, Sparks." Charlie saw that, without waiting for instructions, Payne was resetting the altimeter.

He looked at the altimeter. Thirteen hundred feet was good enough for the downwind approach altitude. He turned the Fort a little, heading 045, and began to set up the approach.

Don't Be Dumb

Jack awoke when someone shook him.

"Mr. Davis," the someone said. "Mr. Davis, wake up."

"What is it?" Jack mumbled.

"Pilot's briefing in thirty minutes. You got time to shit and shave, sir, and if you hurry up about it, maybe grab a cup of coffee. Oh, and there's a Fort in the landing pattern. Probably on the ground by now."

"OK. Thanks."

Jack swung out of the cot, becoming aware again of the odor of soot and burnt metal as he reached for his flying boots. Around him in the darkness other pilots of the 17th were awakened.

Then he heard the low rumble of radial engines, gradually growing in intensity. He stomped his feet into the boots and walked to the door in time to see the silhouette of a Fort, jeep headlights gleaming on its propeller blades as it taxied by.

Jack trotted after the Fort. A fuel truck pulled up to the B-17 as its engines shut down. A jeep drove past. Jack recognized Col. Eubanks in the passenger seat of the jeep.

The entrance door in the B-17's waist opened. Charlie and another guy, both in flight jackets and wearing crush caps, climbed out of the airplane.

The colonel's jeep stopped beside the fuselage of the Fort. Mechanics climbed up on the Fort's wings to open the caps over the bomber's gas tanks. Charlie and the guy with him saluted the colonel. They started a conversation, which seemed to consist of the colonel doing most of the talking, and Charlie doing most of the nodding. Another guy climbed down from the Fort. He saluted the colonel and shook hands with him.

Jack guessed the two guys with Charlie were his copilot and navigator, and from the dead-serious looks on their faces Colonel Eubanks was briefing them for a mission. The two Forts surviving yesterday's air raid weren't fit to fly, not yet. So Charlie was an advance scout for the Forts down in Mindanao. Col. Eubanks was sending them to hit the Jap invasion fleet from high level while the P-40s went in low to strafe whatever was on the beach.

A minute later Eubanks shook hands all around, got in his jeep and left.

"Hey, Charlie!" Jack called.

Charlie looked up when his name was called. Jack walked forward with his hand out. Charlie took his hand and clapped him on the shoulder.

"Holy Hannah Mother of God, Jack, I'm glad to see you," Charlie said. "Are you OK?"

"So far," Jack said. He nodded at Charlie's B-17. "I gather you guys are going up for a joyride?"

Charlie grinned. "Yeah. I guess you could say that. Looks like your guys might be headed the same way."

Jack shrugged. "Probably. And neither one of us can ask for details."

"What's the point? Besides, I'd just have to shoot you." Charlie stepped back. "Look, let me introduce you to my crew. This is Bob Payne, my copilot, and Al Stern, navigator."

"You get to tell this guy where to go?" Jack asked Stern as they shook hands. "Damn, I've wanted to do that once or twice."

Stern smiled. It wasn't much of a smile.

"Look, Jack..."

"I know. Me too. Briefing."

"Yeah. Sorry there's no more time."

"That's OK. Don't do anything stupid out there today."

"This from a pursuit pilot?" Charlie squeezed his shoulder. "Don't do anything dumb yourself. You know how pissed Mom would be if one of us got killed."

50 JAP SHIPS

Charlie planned on climbing to 20,000 feet over the South China Sea on a heading of 270 when he left Clark Field. That would put him about ten miles out to sea when he turned to a heading of 010 for the climb to 30,000 feet.

285

When they got to 20,000 feet and turned to 010 Charlie, looking out over the right wing, saw a band of pink on the horizon. The moon was off the left wing. There was enough light from the moon to make out the ocean below and the darker, nonreflective line of the land.

"Pilot to crew, be careful of your oxygen," Charlie said over the intercom.

For now, everything seemed to be running fine. He and Bob had managed the switch over to the turbo-superchargers as they climbed above 15,000 feet without mishap, and so far the engines ran exactly as they should.

"Pilot, bombardier."

"Go ahead, Kit."

"Skipper, I see something in the water, about eleven o'clock. Might be ships. I'm trying to count wakes."

"Roger, Kit. Al, what's our position?"

"We're due west of Vigan Bay, skipper."

"OK. Al, work up a position, then figure an estimated heading and speed on those ships. Get the wake count from Kit and pass it to Sparks. Got it?"

"Affirmative, skipper."

"Pilot to crew, keep your eyes open for Jap fighters. I don't know if they can reach us but let's keep our eyes peeled. We don't need any more surprises."

The band of pink along the horizon expanded and deepened into red and orange. In the growing light below them the wakes of dozens of ships appeared, heading southeast towards Luzon.

"Radio operator, navigator. Sparks, I'm coming back with a position report and count for you."

Stern came up through the crawlway access aft of the pilot's seat breathing from a jump bottle. He tapped Charlie on the shoulder and showed him what he'd written:

50 JAP SHIPS
HEADING 160
SPEED 15
18 MILES NORTH OF VIGAN BAY
TIME 0545

Charlie nodded. The bomber continued on heading. Down below were reasonable targets for their bombs, the four 600-lb. weapons they'd been lugging around from Clark to Del Monte and back to Clark and now all the way up to northern Luzon. On the other hand the Jap fleet was a moving target, and those four bombs weren't going to stop it.

"Pilot, bombardier."

"Go ahead, Kit."

"Skipper, I've got a nice line on some kind of big ship. It's got a lot of turrets and guns and stuff. I reckon it's a battleship."

"Kit, wouldn't you rather drop bombs on something standing still? It'll take us about an hour to get up to Aparri and back. By then those ships will be at anchor in Vigan Bay."

"Er – OK, Skipper."

Charlie grinned under his oxygen mask.

Stern came back on his way to his navigator's position, clapped Charlie on the shoulder and gave him a thumbs-up.

"Radio operator to pilot. Contact report sent to Clark, message acknowledged."

"OK. Thanks, Sparks."

Charlie couldn't see the invasion fleet now. They were directly under him. He wondered if the Japs had seen them.

"Skipper, belly gun, we got flak bursts below us."

"Roger, belly gun. How far below us?"

"Not far. Two, three thousand feet."

"OK. Let me know if they start reaching any higher."

"Affirmative, Skipper."

"BANDITS!"

The shout nearly overtaxed the intercom. Before Charlie could ask where and how many, the voice came back, still high pitched but much more under control.

"Bombardier to crew, bandits, bandits at 12 o'clock, a little low! Look like they're climbing up to us!"

Charlie deliberately slowed his voice even as his heart rate raced into high gear. "Rrroger, Kit, let's keep those calls to the point. Good eye, though. I see 'em."

Charlie increased the RPMs on the turbos and put in some up trim on the elevator. The rate of climb indicator showed 500 feet per minute. The B-17D had a service ceiling of 35,000 feet. He didn't really want to climb that high because it increased the risk of engine failure, along with the increasing risk imposed by colder outside air temperatures and the danger of hypoxia to his crew.

Contrarily, if he could climb above those Jap fighters that would be a good tactical move.

"Bob, watch those engine gages," Charlie said to his copilot. "Let me know about as much as a twitch."

"Roger, skipper, but we may not even get that much."

Charlie nodded but didn't reply. Payne was right. Their first warning of a malfunction might be the impeller wheel of a turbosupercharger, turning at 30,000 RPM, coming apart and sending bits of metal flying in all directions.

Charlie leveled off at 34,000 feet. He could see the enemy fighters clawing up at him. As he watched one of them fell off into an uncontrolled tumble. Either the pilot lost control of his airplane in the thin air or the pilot's oxygen equipment failed with resulting loss of consciousness. Another of the Jap fighters pulled up, falling off into a spin almost immediately, but even as he did he fired his guns at the Fort. Red and white tracers licked up at them, whipping in a wild arc mirroring the movements of the Jap fighter.

"Navigator to crew. Those are Jap aircraft, see the meatballs? Definitely not A5Ms, the canopy is enclosed and they've got retractable gear."

Charlie turned gingerly to the right, back towards Luzon. He fed in some nose down trim, backing off gently on the turbo settings. Beside him he could feel Payne's slight relaxation. Gravity took over from the engines and the bomber accelerated away from the Jap fighters.

"Pilot to crew, don't think they'll all be that easy. We have to come down from the mountaintop sometime, after all," Charlie said over the intercom. "Al, when do we change heading to pass over Aparri?"

"Give it another ten minutes, then come right to zero eight zero."

"Roger that," said Charlie.

A Good Account

Jack sat with the other pilots of the 17th near a slit trench. One flight was aloft over Clark as a guard against air raids. The other three flights, twelve pilots in all, were in readiness to attack the Jap invasion fleet at low level as soon as they were reported.

A jeep roared up, spilling Lt. Wagner and some ground-pounder major wearing one of those silly-looking "Kelly" helmets as the driver braked to a stop. Jack stood with the other pilots and gathered around Wagner.

"Gentlemen, we're going to attack the Jap invasion fleet at Vigan Bay," Wagner said without preamble. "That's about 170 miles north of here. The Japs are landing in force and we can expect enemy fighters over the beach." He indicated the major. "This is Major Sinclair. He's here to brief us on places to avoid, since our own people are defending the beach."

"Thank you, Lt. Wagner," the major said. He unrolled a map from under his arm, knelt down and spread it on the ground. "This is a map of the Vigan Bay area. Judging from the confused and fragmentary reports we're getting from the area I can't tell you exactly where our units are likely to be when you arrive at the beachhead. However, any stores, artillery pieces, landing craft, troop concentrations, anything actually on the beach itself or in the water is going to belong to the Japs. Hit the little yellow bastards with everything you've got. Take a few minutes and familiarize yourselves with the map. It's the only one I've got."

Jack frowned. He thought the regular Army, the people concerned with artillery pieces and marching infantry and cavalry charges and things of that sort, were constantly collecting maps and so had maps to spare. But this Army major evidently had only the one map.

Then he bent to examine the map.

It wasn't much of a bay, just a shallow indent on the coast with a little fishing village and some hills behind it. A road led east to another road leading south down the center of Luzon – leading to Clark Field. Jack nodded. Clearly the Japs had their own maps and knew exactly what they were doing.

"Little slant-eyed bastards," one of the pilots muttered. "We'll run right over them."

"That's the spirit," said the major. "Lt. Wagner, you have a fine bunch of men here. I'm sure they'll give a good account of themselves today."

The major's words sent a chill down Jack's spine. He'd read words like that in history books, as in, "Hooker's V Corps gave a good account of itself but was unable to take the strategic heights above Chancellorsville from Lee's army."

If you dug a little deeper that phrase "gave a good account of itself" usually meant they'd had the shit shot out of them to no purpose.

The major saluted them, did an about-face, got into the jeep and drove off. Wagner stood for a moment looking after him before turning to face his pilots.

"Just another thing, gentlemen, before we take off. As you know the Japanese do indeed have a new fighter. We know its combat radius is at least 500 miles, since the fighters that hit us on the 8th came from Formosa. I got a report a few minutes ago that the B-17 on reconnaissance got higher than the new fighter, but not by much, only a thousand feet or so, and at that altitude might have been about as fast as the new Jap fighter. So there, gentlemen, we already know that the Japs have a better service ceiling than we do and about the same top speed. Don't expect to have the altitude advantage and be very careful how you engage until we know more about them." Wagner looked at each of them for a moment. "As far as I'm concerned if you go, hit the target, and come back more or less in one piece, you'll have given that good account of yourselves. Don't take any stupid chances. I don't want any heroes or any of this do or die glory crap. We don't have enough airplanes or pilots for that. Does everyone understand?"

Jack nodded, and so did everyone else, but he wondered how many of them actually listened to what Wagner said.

As they went to their P-40s Jack took his wingman, Jimmy Vaughan, aside. "Jimmy, you keep your neck on a swivel the second we're off the ground, you hear me? Don't worry too much about flying formation. Just keep your eyes open and keep looking around. We'd better see the Japs before they see us if we want to have a fighting chance."

Vaughan frowned at him. "What the hell kind of talk is that, Davis? You got the wind up or something? Those little bastards might be OK when they take you by surprise, but we'll show them what it means to get into a stand-up fight. Just you be sure *you* don't run out on *me*."

Vaughan walked away and Jack watched him go, feeling he should do something, say something, but then there was the falling whine of an inertial starter as an Allison engine started. Jack started running for his airplane, and as his crew chief helped him buckle in engines were starting up and down the line.

Fighters Coming In

Charlie and his crew flew towards Aparri and the Babuyan Channel as the sun came over the horizon. Charlie maintained a slight descent, trading altitude for airspeed, indicating 280 mph at 27,000 feet. There was another Jap fleet off Aparri, this one within a mile or so of the beach, where he could see smoke and dust rising along the shoreline as Jap warships bombarded the beach.

As much as the wrecked, burned-out bombers at Clark Field, as much as the Zeros trying to shoot them down, seeing foreign warships fire on American territory brought home to him a simple shattering truth.

They were at war.

Within moments the dark puffs of AAA fire burst around them while Al Stern put together another position report for Sparks to send off. That done, Charlie turned back for the beach.

"Pick the biggest ship you can find, Johnny, and drop on that," he told the bombardier.

"Bandits! Bandits, Japs at two o'clock level"

Charlie advanced the throttles and leveled out. He could see the little specks that were Japanese fighters out of Payne's side window.

"Roger. All right, gunners, we're setting up our bomb run. Keep those Japs off us until we drop."

The bombardier's voice came up on the intercom, fast and excited. "Got a target, skipper, come left about five degrees."

Charlie eased the big bomber five degrees to the left.

The right waist gun fired a series of jackhammer bursts that shook the airframe. Out of the corner of his eye Charlie was aware of the sparkling guns in the nose and wings of the Zeroes.

"A little more left, skipper."

Machine gun bullets and cannon shells raked across the wing and the fuselage in a series of *pings* and *WHAMS!* A cannon shell exploded against the fuselage skin behind the cockpit. A sudden howl of wind screamed through the resulting hole. Charlie raised the wing, coming a little left. The left waist gun started to fire.

"Pilot to crew, sound off!"

"Bombardier OK. Steady as she goes, skipper. Opening bomb bay doors."

"Navigator OK."

"Copilot OK."

"Radio operator OK."

"Bottom gun OK."

"Left waist, I got nicked but I'm OK."

"Right waist OK. I think I got a piece of one, skipper."

"Good work. Get the whole one next time, Lefty. OK, everyone stay sharp, those little bastards will be back."

"Pilot, bombardier, thirty seconds to drop."

"Roger, bombardier, thirty seconds."

Charlie concentrated on the airplane, on what the four-engined beast told him as its engines sang their one-note roar, at the scream of the slipstream over the new ragged holes in the wings and fuselage, the feel of the controls through his cold gloved fingers and the tips of his booted toes on the rudder.

"Fifteen seconds," said the bombardier.

"Left waist, fighters coming in! Sparks, they're coming in a little higher, be ready on the upper guns!"

"I'm on it," said Sparks.

The fighters opened up on them as Smith called "Bombs away" over the intercom. The Japs came from eight o'clock and a little high. The Fort's gunners opened up and something smashed into the wing, hard, and the No. 1 engine belched fire and black oily smoke. Charlie fed in rudder before the airplane could start to yaw. Hornets suddenly buzzed and whined through the cockpit, smashing into the Plexiglas windshield and the instrument panel. Charlie felt searing pain across his left

292

shoulder. Something exploded against the armor plate on the back of Payne's seat, tossing him like a strapped-in rag doll. A fighter trailing a long streamer of flame behind it howled just over the cockpit, which for a moment was enveloped in black oily smoke.

Payne slumped bonelessly in his seat.

Charlie feathered the No. 1 engine and activated its fire extinguisher. Behind him he could hear the whine of the bomb-bay doors closing. He pushed the throttles on the remaining three engines forward and went into a diving turn to the left.

"Al, when you get a minute, let's have a heading for Clark Field," Charlie called. "And Kit, get up here and give me a hand with Bob, he's been hit bad."

The airspeed crept back up to nearly three hundred miles per hour, even with the dead engine. They were losing 800 feet per minute. He'd set up a heading of 180 for now and hope everything held together.

"Left waist, fighters coming in!"

The B-17 shook as the guns fired.

Targets at Vigan Bay

Red Flight carried 25-lb. bombs under their wings. They went in low, at 1000 feet. The rest of the squadron stayed above them at 10,000 feet. Fifteen minutes after they reached 10,000 feet Jack saw smoke rising from the direction of Vigan Bay.

"This is Pepsodent Leader, we're in Indian Country, keep your eyes peeled. And keep the radio clear until you see something. Lead out."

Jack looked up to the north, then all around them.

At first he saw nothing. Then, at ten o'clock high, four specks.

"This is Pepsodent Blue Three, bandits, ten o'clock, I count four, no, make it six."

"Roger that. Pepsodent Red Leader, you copy?"

"Affirmative, Leader. We're ten minutes from the beach."

"Lead from Blue Three, bandits coming down."

"Roger, Three. Keep 'em off Red Flight, boys, and follow me."

293

Wagner turned and began to climb into the diving Japs, but as they came down the six Japs split into two elements, three each going right and left, still diving but at a shallower angle.

"Yellow and White, take the eastern guys," Wagner radioed, and he turned, still climbing after the three Japs to the west.

Jack took his attention off the three Japs to the east and locked on to the western flight. He got a good look at them, kind of a pretty airplane, really, a slender, aerodynamic fuselage with an odd triangular tail and a bubble canopy with a radial engine. It was painted gull gray overall with that bright red meatball halfway between the trailing edge and the horizontal stabilizer, and some sort of stripes and markings he couldn't make out.

Abruptly the Japs steepened their dive angle and turned north.

There was confused shouting over the radio as Yellow and White flights engaged the Japs.

Wagner turned after the Japs heading north. Jack, looking ahead and down, saw the four P-40s of Red Flight almost at treetop level, nearly to the beach at Vigan Bay.

"Three, edge out a bit to the right, we'll catch them in a crossfire," Wagner radioed.

"Roger, Lead," Jack replied.

One thing the P-40 did was dive and Blue Flight caught the Jap fighters diving in on Red Flight.

"Pepsodent Red Leader, watch your six," Wagner radioed.

Jack thought he sounded calm, almost bored, and realized suddenly that was deliberate.

"I see 'em I see 'em! Keep 'em off us, Lead, we're almost there!"

Then the Zeroes did something Jack would have sworn was impossible. They pulled up, seemed to stand on their props for a second, then kicked rudder and began to fly to the east, still climbing. The P-40s built up momentum in the dive and the Japanese maneuver caught them by surprise. Wagner, in the lead, rolled right and came back hard on his stick. His wingman tried to follow him into the maneuver and overshot outside. Jack stayed with Wagner through the turn but when he looked around for his own wingman, Blue Four, Vaughan was nowhere to be seen.

Wagner held his P-40 at the very knife edge of an accelerated stall, and Jack knew that because he could feel the adrenaline edging into his system and his heart rate increasing as he called up everything he had, every bit of finesse on the controls, every bit of skill, and guided the P-40 along that vanishingly thin line between controlled flight and a stall that would send him spinning out of control with the Philippine jungle only five thousand feet below, probably, very probably not enough room to recover from a spin if he lost it. Then they were around and the Japs dove on them, nose and wing guns winking, and Jack picked one that swelled in the ring and post gun sight. He waited as Jap tracers danced around him and slammed into his wing and flashed past his canopy, he waited until he saw the cylinders of the Jap's radial engine and then he squeezed the trigger. The six machine-guns hammered and roared and tracers streaked into the Jap at nearly point-blank range, chewed the engine into bits and suddenly the Jap dissolved into flames and exploded. There was a WHAM as Jack flew through the debris and the P-40 shuddered, shook and straightened as if nothing had happened. Jack looked to the right and saw Wagner, ruddering over into a diving turn after the third Jap. There was a greasy ball of smoke in the sky below Wagner and bits falling away.

Jack kicked his rudder and checked his tail, then dove down after Wagner, who was after the third Jap. He looked to the east and saw three Japs still tangled with P-40s, probably Yellow and White flights. Smoke trails led down and away from the fight.

"Blue Four from Blue Three, Blue Four from Blue Three, come in," Jack called as he dove. Then Jack saw Wagner, closing on the third Jap, who was closing on a P-40 who in turn was trying to turn away from the Jap.

Jack saw at a glance that the P-40 wasn't going to make it. The pilot could not or was not turning hard enough. He bled airspeed in the turn and the Zero was way inside him, almost enough to pull lead for a deflection shot. Jack saw the flash of the Jap's guns, the tracer licking out into the P-40, the winking *flashflash* of the 20-mm cannon shells exploding across the nose of the P-40. A streamer of fire and smoke erupted from the engine. The canopy came off the P-40 but the Jap kept firing as the pilot tried to get out. The Jap's bullets caught the pilot half-in and half-out of the airplane. The pursuit gyrated out of control, throwing the pilot free as the P-40 fell towards the earth.

The Zero turned and pulled up, doing that straight-up vertical climb the Zeros had done earlier. Wagner overshot and the Zero kicked over onto Wagner's tail.

Wagner had the speed but the Zero was turning, turning tight at what had to be a speed so slow the P-40 would stall regardless of pilot skill, and came around onto Wagner's tail. Wagner pulled up, momentarily drawing away from the Zero, then the Zero started to catch up in the climb.

Jack's speed was still high and he horsed back on the stick, holding the throttle all the way forward, drawing up on the Zero until, again, he was close enough to count the rivets and opened fire, the sparks from the bullet strikes climbing across the fuselage and into the Jap's cockpit. Abruptly a puff of red coated the inside of the canopy. The Jap fighter pulled up and fell off on its right wing, spinning down to the ground below.

"Pepsodent Leader from Blue Three, have you seen Blue Four?"

"Negative, Three. That was Blue Two that just bought it."

"This is Red Leader, anyone in the vicinity of Vigan Bay, we got plenty of targets!"

"Blue Three, this is Lead, you're with me," Wagner radioed. "Yellow Leader, White Leader, come in."

There was silence on the radio. Jack formed up with Wagner, looking, always looking, clearing his tail and watching Wagner's. To the east there were some confused smoke trails but not much else. He saw no airplanes. Either Yellow and White flights were down or the survivors were headed back to Clark.

"Red Leader, where are you?" Wagner radioed.

"Six miles south of Vigan Bay with two. Lost Billy over the target. We're all shot up pretty good. Three Zeroes chasing us."

"Buzz, it's Jack, I see them at nine o'clock low."

"OK, Jack, got 'em. Follow me."

Jack looked around as Wagner pushed over and dove down on the Zeroes chasing the P-40s.

"Lead, we have six bandits at six o'clock high," Jack warned.

"Roger, Jack, keep an eye on 'em."

The P-40s stayed ahead of the Jap Zeroes, running at what Jack was sure was full throttle. Jack looked over his shoulder as the Zeroes above them started down.

Wagner pulled out of his dive, avoided an overshoot, coming back up and shooting at the left rear Zero from below. Jack caught the right wingman as he broke right and away from Wagner, but only got a piece of him. The Zero went down on the deck, pieces flying off his left wing. Wagner's Zero spouted flames and shed a wing, spinning down to the deck.

"Just keep going, Red Leader, and don't look back," Wagner radioed.

He pulled up into an Immelmannn turn to face the Zeroes coming down at them.

Jack was with him, scanning his engine and fuel gages. After all the climbing and throttle jockeying and full speed maneuvering fuel was low. He looked at his ammo. About half a load left.

Then the Zeroes arrived.

A Rough Landing

Charlie felt something warm and wet drip down his right arm. He'd been hit in the right shoulder when the cannon shell exploded against Payne's armored seat back and hadn't known it. Kit Smith, the sergeant bombardier, had come up from the nose. When Smith pulled Payne out of the seat the copilot's insides came out of the hole blown from his ribcage to his hipbone. Smith recoiled and froze for a second before getting Payne's body the rest of the way out of the seat. The Jap fighters made one more pass and then peeled off to the west, towards Vigan Bay.

Now Smith looked over at him. His eyes were worried over his oxygen mask.

"You OK, Skipper?" he asked.

"I'm fine. Al, it's Charlie, where the hell are we?"

"Fifty miles north of Clark."

Charlie looked at the engine gages. No. 1 was dead but the fire was out. He'd left the other engines at full throttle, trying to outrun the Zeroes, and they had come damned close to doing that. The Zeroes caught up, made passes, and in turning away lost a mile or so which took them thirty or forty seconds to get in position for another attack. As the waist gunners called the attacks he yawed the Fort one way or another to give them the best shot.

At least two Zeroes peeled off trailing smoke, and another came apart in midair. That left six still in the fight when they broke it off.

"Did we lick them?" Smith asked.

"No. Probably got news the other guys were attacking at Vigan Bay."

Smith nodded. "What do you want me to do when we land?" he asked.

"Handle the flaps and the landing gear." Charlie showed him the controls. "I'll do the rest."

"Skipper, it's Sparks. Clark says they're clear, altimeter two niner niner niner, wind calm."

"OK, thanks, Sparks."

He could see Clark now, just ahead of them. "Sparks, get the flares ready."

The field was still marked by burned-out aircraft and a haze of smoke. Charlie ignored the pain in his shoulder and made his approach, careful in the turns with the drag of the dead engine.

"OK, gear down," he told Adams. "Flaps down, all the way down."

The gear whined, hydraulic pumps groaned. Once the flaps were down and he was lined up on final he cut No. 4 engine back to idle. The green light showing the left main down and locked winked on, but the green light on the right main remained out.

"Pilot to bottom gun, can you tell if the right main is down?"

"It's down, Skipper, but it doesn't look quite right. The locking strut doesn't look straight."

"Sparks, see if you can crank it down. I'm going around."

Charlie fed power back to the No. 4 engine and brought the other two up. He flew down the runway, gathering speed and climbing out to the left to get back to traffic pattern altitude.

"Skipper? It's Sparks. We tried to crank the gear down. It just sort of cranks without coming to a stop."

Charlie nodded to himself. He could baby the Fort down all he liked but when weight came on that wheel it would collapse and he would skid off the runway. He thought for a moment about coming in with both wheels up and making a belly landing in the soft ground by the runway.

He shook off the indecision. "OK, pilot to crew, take stations for crash landing. Sparks, let Clark know we're coming in with one wheel likely to fold."

"Roger, Skipper."

Charlie lined up on the runway again and came down, holding a bit to the right of center, not wanting to edge too far and catch a wingtip on one of the wrecks on the edge of the runway. He had to pick his landing spot and hold off until, when the wheel collapsed, it would carry him off into a spot unlittered by wreckage.

He came off the power and the roar of the engines died to a muted rumble. The Fort floated down and touched, Charlie lifting the right wing to keep as much weight as possible off the right main, and closed the throttles on the three good engines. The right main touched the sod runway, ran for a hundred feet and collapsed. The right wing tip dug into the ground. Charlie slammed on the left brake and the left rudder. The Fort swung off the runway into the soft ground beyond, lurching and sliding as it came to a stop.

"Everybody out!" Charlie called. He disconnected himself from the seat and oxygen line, gasping as pain lanced up from the wound in his right upper arm. Smith did the same. They climbed out over Payne's body. Stern scrambled up from the nose and the three of them ran down the narrow aisle over the bomb bay and out the waist entrance of the bomber, where the gunners were already pelting away from the aircraft. At a safe distance they all stopped and stood by the side of the runway, panting and breathing deeply, as the ambulance drove up with a clang of bells.

"Lefty, were you wounded?" Charlie asked.

The gunner grinned. "Looks like you got it worse, sir. I just took a crease. Probably won't even put in for a Purple Heart."

"Well, let the medic look at it anyway."

Lefty nodded.

Stern put a hand on Charlie's unwounded shoulder. "What happened to Bob?" he asked.

Charlie sighed. "Cannon shell, I think. Something creased me over the shoulder and something else slammed into the side of his armor plate. When it exploded it peppered me with shrapnel and blew a hole in Bob's side that..." Charlie looked away.

When he looked back Stern nodded. "Bob's dead," he said.

"Yeah."

A jeep drove up. A medic opened Charlie's shirt to look at the wounds on his shoulder. Charlie winced and looked away. In the jeep with the driver was Major O'Donnell.

"Hellfire, Davis, are you all right?" O'Donnell asked.

"It's just a scratch, sir. But I lost my copilot. Most of it is his blood."

"Damn. Lt. Payne, right?"

"Yes, sir."

O'Donnell bowed his head for a moment before looking up and asking, "Hit anything up at Aparri?"

"I don't know, Rosie." Charlie gestured to Kit Smith. "This is my bombardier, Sgt. Kit Smith."

Smith jumped to attention. "Rest, sergeant," Major O'Donnell said. "How did you do?"

The sergeant grimaced. "I lined up on the biggest ship I could see and dropped my eggs, sir. The lineup looked pretty good. I don't know if I hit anything. Maybe..." Adams gestured at the gunners.

Lefty spoke up. "Sir, we got jumped by Jap fighters during the bomb run. I looked down but all I could see was smoke."

O'Donnell sighed and nodded. "OK. Well, the 17th Pursuit hit Vigan Bay ten minutes ago, then radioed they were under attack. I guess they'll be back soon."

"Did you hear anything about the P-40s, sir?" Charlie asked.

"That's right, your brother's with them, isn't he? But no, I haven't heard anything about them. Kelly and his boys got jumped by Jap fighters the same way you did and they took a lot of damage over the target. There was a lot of confused radio chatter." O'Donnell shook his head. "The Japs must have a hell of a lot of fighters on Formosa."

CHAPTER SIXTEEN
A Good Account

One Pass and Come Home

Jack ignored the just-audible ragged sputter coming from his engine, looking back over his right and left shoulders. He was barely above the treetops and the Jap Zeroes were right behind him, moving up until they closed the range and taking potshots at him, losing speed and falling behind out of range.

Wagner was ahead of him on his left. A thin skim of smoke came out of Wagner's exhausts and Jack knew their lifetime was going to be measured in minutes, or seconds, unless one of them had a brainstorm.

"Jack, on my mark, chop your throttle," Wagner radioed.

Jack hesitated a half-second. Speed was all they had.

"Roger, Lead," he replied. "On your mark."

He was amazed at how calm he sounded. His heart beat fast and hard enough he was sure it was about to jump right out of his mouth.

The Zeroes closed in behind, closer, and the machine guns winked as they began firing.

"Now!" Wagner radioed, and chopped his throttle.

Jack was a little bit behind obeying the command and got a nose ahead of Wagner's airplane. The Zeroes behind them overshot. Their tracers blazed over and ahead of the P-40s and there they were, six beautiful, *beautiful* targets, and Jack didn't need to think about it to hold down his trigger. He kicked the rudder and .50-cal. slugs sprayed across two Jap Zeroes. Pieces flew off the enemy fighters, who flicked in a tight roll to the left and began climbing. Jack held on one of them for an extra half-second, saw the sparkle of strikes along its wing, and then it climbed away from him.

He advanced the throttle on his faithful, ailing Allison once more and looked around for Wagner. Jack looked just in time to see Wagner's tracers slicing into a Zero, whose right wing came off. The Zero tumbled to the ground and exploded.

They were alone in the air.

"Boyd, how's your fuel?" Jack radioed.

"Fumes. How's your engine?"

"Don't like the sound of it. Let's get the hell out of here."

They stayed at low level all the way back to Clark. This time they didn't make a fancy show of coming into the break on downwind, not with shot-up airplanes, not with the all too real possibility of Jap fighters attacking the strip without warning. Instead Wagner landed with Jack right behind him, just far enough behind not to pile into him if Wagner cracked up.

As Jack taxied down the runway he saw the B-17 off to one side, standing on its left main with the right collapsed under it. The wings and fuselage were decorated with big holes from 20-mm cannon fire. A group of mechanics stood under the No. 3 engine, looking up into the wheel well of the right main gear. The No. 1 engine and the wing behind it were black with soot.

Jack followed Wagner to the ramp, where a group of mechanics and ground crew waited to push the P-40s under cover. Jack climbed from the cockpit. He wasn't prepared for his knees to collapse under him, but one of the ground crew who helped him out of the cockpit caught him.

"You OK, sir?" the man asked.

"I think so," Jack said. "I don't remember getting hit or anything."

Wagner came over. "Jack, you all right?"

"Hell yes, boss, I just can't seem to stand up on my own."

Wagner shook his head. "I'm feeling shaky myself."

Jack put weight on his knees. This time they took his weight and the airman backed off, hovering a little.

"I think I'm OK now," Jack said to the airman. "Thanks."

"You're welcome, sir." The airman trotted away to help push Jack's P-40 under some camouflage netting.

"Come on," said Wagner. His face was grim. Jack followed him on wobbly legs into a tent rigged under another camouflage net.

Inside the tent were a half-dozen pilots. Jack recognized the three survivors from Red Flight. Lt. Ames, the flight leader, looked up and rose to his feet when they walked in. He came forward and shook Wagner's hand.

"Thanks, Boss," he said.

Wagner nodded.

For a moment the eight pilots were silent. Jack knew they were thinking exactly what he was thinking: *Is this it? Are we all that's left?*

Finally Wagner said, "OK. First of all, anyone make it back that isn't here?"

Ames said, "Willy Heisman from Yellow Flight got hit pretty bad in the leg. Brought his ship in but couldn't get out of the cockpit. Blood everywhere."

"OK, that's one. Anyone else?" Wagner looked around. "What about Dodo Phillips? Chuck Haynes?"

"I saw Dodo go down," said one of the pilots. He gestured at the man sitting next to him. "Walt and I are all that's left of Yellow Flight."

Wagner looked at a pilot sitting off a little by himself. He sat hunched over, rocking a little. "Matt," Wagner said. When the man didn't look up Wagner barked, "Lt. Parker!"

The man jumped and looked up. He was the only pilot from White Flight in the tent. "Matt, you were White Four," Wagner said quietly. "What happened?"

"I don't know, Boss," Matt whispered. He seemed to hunch down into himself. "We went after those Zeroes but they were just all over us. We couldn't turn with them, we couldn't climb with them. And then I was all by myself with one of those bastards on my tail."

"How did you shake him off?"

"I put the nose down and didn't pull out until I was about sure it was too late. Ran away from the bastard. That's what I did. I ran away."

"What did you do next?" Wagner asked.

"Looked around. Couldn't see anyone except some more Zeroes, up high, towards Vigan Bay. Called on the radio for the other guys." Parker looked down. "Nobody answered, so I went back to Vigan Bay, made a strafing run along the beach, and got the hell out of there. Ran away again."

"Bullshit," said Wagner. He put a hand on Parker's shoulder. "Bullshit. Whatever else, Matt, you attacked the enemy. Did you hit anything?"

"I don't know. It happened pretty fast. Tracers everywhere. I could hear bullets hitting my ship. I think I hit a barge or something, right at the waterline. Made a lot of Jap infantry eat sand. Something hit the engine and I didn't much like the way it sounded so I came home."

"You did fine, Matt."

Wagner looked at Lt. Ames. "You guys had the bombs. How did it go?"

"No Zeroes until we were off the target. I dropped my bombs on some kind of ship just off shore, had a bunch of barges or small boats around it. But like Parker said, there was an awful lot of AAA and machine-gun fire. I took hits, nothing serious, but..." Ames took a deep breath. "Anyway, Billy Turner was Red Three. Billy dropped his bombs on a knot of soldiers pulling an artillery piece up the beach, and then he went in low to strafe something. He got hit, there was a stream of fire coming out of his left wing, but I could see him shooting at the troops on the beach. He went in and exploded."

Wagner nodded and looked at the other two Red Flight survivors. "Hinton? Smith? How about you guys?"

Lt. Hinton shook his head listlessly. "Don't know if I hit shit, Boss."

Smith spoke up. "He got a barge that blew up, damn near tossed me out of control."

"Well, that's good. Then how about you, Smith?"

"Me? Boss, after I got the ship back under control I dropped my bombs on a line of barges at the waterline, sprayed some troops with the guns, stayed with Andy here and got the hell out when he did. We joined up with Ames and were headed home when we got jumped by Zeroes, and you know the rest."

Wagner nodded slowly. Then he looked at Jack. "What happened to Vaughan, Jack?"

"I don't know. I lost him in that first turn. Looked behind me and he wasn't there."

"OK. I know you got at least one Jap. The one you shot off my tail."

"I'm pretty sure I got another one," said Jack. "That last bit, when you pulled that overshoot, I got a piece of two of the bastards, but that's it. And I saw you get three, and someone else got one, but I'm not sure who. And I think that was your wingman we saw get shot down."

Wagner grimaced and looked down. "So, we lost eight out of sixteen, and we can claim what, five Zeroes definitely destroyed, two damaged, one barge and maybe some others, and some Jap infantry shot up on the beach."

Wagner sat down and pulled off his helmet, running his hand through his sweat-soaked hair.

Jack stood for a moment on his wobbly legs and then decided he'd better sit down before he fell down. For a long, uncomfortable moment no one looked at each other.

Then someone stood silhouetted in the tent entrance.

"Jack?"

Jack looked up. Charlie stood there. The right arm of his uniform shirt had been ripped off and his right shoulder and upper arm were bandaged.

"Jesus, Charlie, what happened to you?"

"Nothing much. Just got sprayed with a little shrapnel." Charlie looked around. "Wagner, can I borrow my brother for a minute?"

Wagner nodded. "Sure thing, Davis."

Jack followed Charlie out of the tent. They sat down against the wall of a burned-out building. Charlie handed Jack a canteen. When Jack drank he found it contained whiskey. He choked and for a moment started to refuse. Then he took a deep breath and a long swig of the whiskey, feeling fire flow down his throat to settle into his stomach.

He exhaled and handed the canteen back to Charlie, who took a long swig himself before capping it.

"What the hell is that stuff?" Jack asked.

"I don't know. I had a feeling it didn't pay to ask too many questions. You look like you're OK."

"Yeah. I'm all right."

Charlie nodded. "How did you guys do?"

"We shot down a few Zeroes. Lost half our guys. Scared hell out of some Jap infantry and blew up some barges. You?"

Charlie shrugged. "We dropped our bombs on some kind of ship up around Aparri. Don't know if we hit it, then we ran from Jap fighters halfway down Luzon. Kelly, one of the guys from the 19th, led a mission up to Vigan Bay. He got shot down and the rest of his guys were shot up pretty good. They're making all sorts of claims for ships hit and sunk, but I don't know."

"I thought that was what you guys did best. Bomb from high altitude."

Charlie snorted. "Yeah, well, we're also supposed to put more than six airplanes on the target. For best effect, anyway."

Jack leaned back against the wall and closed his eyes. "So the Japs got ashore."

"Yeah. They're ashore. MacArthur had better get his ass in gear if he's going to whip the little yellow bastards."

Charlie offered the canteen to Jack, who shook his head. "Dad was right," Charlie said as he screwed the cap back on the canteen.

"About what?"

"War. You remember what he told us, that night in the Manila Hotel?"

Jack nodded. "Yeah. I remember."

A jeep pulled up in front of the tent and an officer got out. He glanced at Jack and Charlie and then went in the tent.

"Well," Charlie sighed. "That doesn't look good."

Jack nodded.

A minute later Wagner looked around the corner of the tent. "Jack. Get in here."

Jack sighed and stood up. He reached down and shook Charlie's hand. "Here goes nothin'. Take care of yourself, big brother."

"Yeah, you too, Jack."

Wagner ushered Jack back into the tent where the other pilots were huddled over a map spread out over a small table.

"This is Major Stratner," Wagner told Jack, indicating the officer who'd just arrived. "He's got a little problem he'd like some help with."

The officer indicated was another infantryman, this time with staff tabs on his collar.

"This is an extremely important assignment, Wagner," the major huffed. "And your attitude is insubordinate."

"I don't think there are any unimportant assignments for pursuit pilots in the Philippines today, Major," Wagner replied. "I'm sorry if you find my attitude insubordinate. It's the only attitude I have right now. Do you want this mission to go or not?"

"I'm not sure you've got the guts for this mission," said the Major. "I certainly don't know if you're the man to lead it."

There was dead silence inside the tent.

Jack stood up.

"Jack," said Wagner in a warning tone.

"Wagner's my CO," said Jack. "He saved my life this morning. Where were you when we were getting our asses shot off, Major? Cookie pushing at HQ?"

The other pilots stood up, their faces blank and closed, their hands balled into fists.

The Major looked around and licked his lips.

Before he could speak Wagner said, "Men, sit down. That's an order."

The pilots obeyed. Slowly and reluctantly, but they obeyed. Jack sat last.

"Now, Major, suppose you show me this target again, and then perhaps you'll be needed back at HQ."

The Major looked around the tent. He pointed at the map. "There. Ten miles south of Vigan Bay. Along the coast road to Chamorro."

"OK. I've got it," said Wagner.

The major left.

"What's going on, Boyd?" Jack asked.

Wagner brooded for a moment, looking at the map the major left behind. "Apparently the Japs have made some sort of flanking landing on this beach right here. The major wants us to bomb it."

Jack thought about it. "Any information on how many ships or what kind of troops?"

Wagner looked at Jack and looked back at the map. "A lot of ships and a lot of troops. That's all anyone knows."

After a moment the squadron commander looked up. "Two airplanes. That's all we have in commission right now. I'm going. I want a volunteer to come with me."

Everyone stood up. Not quickly, not eagerly, but they stood.

Wagner nodded. "Yeah. OK, draw straws. I'm going to talk to Chief Willis and see how fast we can get some more P-40s back in commission."

Jack came out of the tent a few minutes later. He looked around but Charlie was gone. He found Wagner talking to Chief Willis next to a P-40 that had the inspection panels off the nose and hole from a Jap 20mm cannon shell behind the cockpit.

Wagner looked up as Jack approached and nodded slowly. He turned back to the Chief. "You got those two P-40s ready for this mission?" he asked.

"Yes, sir. Full ammo, two 100-lb. bombs apiece."

"OK." Wagner turned to Jack. "You ready?"

Jack nodded.

"No call signs. I'm Buzz, you're Jack. We find this beach that's giving Major Whatsisname the trots, we make one pass and come home. Got it?"

"Yes, sir."

"OK. Let's go."

Regroup

Charlie stood under the wing of his Fort, looking at the damage.

"It's not really that bad, Captain," said the 19th's line chief. "You did a good job getting her down. No damage to the spars or the ribs. Just a little sheet metal work, mostly on the wingtip. The biggest problem is going to be raising the wing so we can work on the right main gear."

Charlie nodded. "What about the No. 1 engine?" he asked.

The chief grimaced. "I can find you an engine. I don't like the look of those cannon holes, though. I need to give it a real look-see."

"How long?" Charlie asked.

The chief shrugged. "Major O'Donnell wants every B-17 that can fly. If all we have to do is fix the right main gear and replace the No. 1 engine, this baby won't take more than a couple of hours. I'll move it to the top of the list. The good Lord willing and the Japs don't attack, this evening late or tomorrow morning early."

The snarl of engines running up to full power at the end of the runway reached Charlie. He turned to look in time to see the two P-40s rolling down the runway, throwing up dust, tails coming up. They were off the runway as they came abreast of him, and the trailing pilot waved as he went by.

Charlie raised his arm in reply but the P-40s were already climbing, gear coming up, flaps retracting, turning to the north and what he remembered being described, when he was a cadet at West Point, as "the rattle of musketry from the other side of the hill."

Charlie stood and watched until the two pursuit planes faded into the sky and the blue distance.

Arm 'em Up

Jack's P-40 was damaged during the air raid on the 8th. The damage wasn't bad, mostly to the sheet metal on the skin of the left wing. The fabric on the rudder and elevator had burned off. Sheet aluminum was riveted over the holes in the wing and new fabric stretched over the ribs of the rudder and elevator. It was hasty work that left him a little uncomfortable. There was a vibration in the stick when he followed Wagner into that first tight turn to the north. Jack wasn't sure about the rudder and elevator fabric, either. They hadn't looked really taut on preflight. The controls got mushier and less responsive as they accelerated

309

to 280 mph, all they could manage with the drag of the bombs under the wings. Then the engine started sounding rough. Jack swept the engine gages, which looked fine, and put the roughness out of his mind as imaginary.

"Jack, how you doing?" Wagner radioed.

"This is about what I've got, Boyd," Jack replied.

"I might get a little more but maybe I'll save that for a real emergency."

"Roger that."

They cleared the low mountains and the volcano Mt. Penatubo north of Clark Field. Wagner began to descend. Jack matched him, babying his engine a little by throttling back in the descent. Then they were over dense forest and rice paddies, flying a few feet over the treetops.

Jack kept an eye on the metal patch on the left wing. He told himself it wasn't working loose along the trailing edge. Maybe that would be OK, but if the air flow over the wing got under the metal at the leading edge of the patch, it would blow off in a heartbeat.

Dense heavy smoke rose up in the near distance. Soon he saw another pall, smaller but only because it was farther away.

Wagner altered heading to the west. Five minutes later the shore came into sight and Wagner turned north to stay just over the palm trees at the edge of the beach.

"Arm 'em up, Jack," Wagner radioed.

Jack checked his armaments panel. Guns hot, bombs armed, a nice set of little green lights. The smoke was dead ahead of them now, towering to at least four thousand feet. Jack kept his head on a swivel, looking at the sky above them, from time to time yawing to clear their tails. Each time he worked the rudder to yaw the P-40 he felt the mushy response and grimaced.

If there were any Zeroes they were above the smoke, but once he and Wagner attacked the beachhead any Japs in the vicinity would be down on them. Jack took a deep breath.

The shoreline jogged to the east and directly ahead of them was a mass of ships. The larger ones were at least a mile offshore. As Jack caught sight of them one of the warships fired a broadside, orange flame and smoke obscuring much of the detail of the vessel's upper works. But one thing was clear on all the ships in sight, and that was the fluttering white flag with the red sun-rays radiating from the bold red meatball in the center.

"Dead ahead, that transport," Wagner radioed.

"Roger," Jack responded.

Tracer reached up and past them, dirty black and brown flak burst all around them. The transport was surrounded by barges crammed with men, men who turned their faces to look at the P-40s now just above the waves with all hell breaking loose around them.

Wagner fired at the barges. His .50-cal. bullets walked across the water, throwing tall white splashes into the air, and then bits and pieces flew from the barges as Wagner's bullets struck them and passed on, tearing into the sides of the transport.

Something smashed into the side of his canopy, spraying the side of his head with Plexiglas splinters, and smashed another hole on the other side. Another heavier something exploded under his left wing, lifting it into the air, turning him straight up and down with the water within feet of his right wingtip. Jack reacted automatically, rolling left and hitting left rudder, then straightening and banking a little to the right to begin firing at the barges near the transport. His tracers chewed into a group of barges near the stern of the ship.

Jack saw men thrown clear of the barges by the impact of his bullets, saw bits and pieces of them flying into the air. Then from the corner of his left eye he saw Wagner pulling up, barely high enough to clear the superstructure of the transport, and two dark objects detached themselves from Wagner's P-40. Jack punched his bombs loose and pulled up gently, clearing the stern of the transport but close enough to see sailors screaming at him as he flew past. Then down again, down over the waves with Wagner high on his left side, coming down to avoid the storm of flak breaking around them as they cleared the transport. Jack looked back and saw explosions on the other side of the transport, then looked forward in time to pull back gently, ever so gently on the stick, and follow Wagner in a bank to the right. Dead ahead of them were a knot of troops and some kind of equipment. They fired on it, fired twelve machine guns into the mass. Men dove for the sand, men flew into the air, men came apart like rag dolls as they were struck by machine-gun bullets.

311

Something slammed into the armor plate behind Jack's seat. A line of bullets punched across his right wing and right aileron. Flak blossomed ahead of him and the P-40 shook like it had been seized by the jaws of a hell of a big dog.

The patch on the left wing peeled back. The rear rivets held. It acted as a one-foot square air brake, yawing the P-40 and dropping the left wing from the drag. Jack hit right aileron and right rudder, fed in all the trim he could to counteract the drag and keep the airplane straight and level.

"You OK, Jack?"

"For now. Let's get the hell out of here, Boyd."

The tracers and flak stopped as if by magic. Wagner flew up alongside Jack's airplane, inspecting the damage, and pointed south. Jack nodded and tuned gently to the right.

Once settled on the new heading he looked up and around and saw the six Jap fighters diving on them.

He felt his throat go dry. His heart hammered once, twice and then settled down.

"Bandits, twelve o'clock high," he called.

"Got 'em," Wagner replied, in that impossible calm voice of his. "We'll stay low. They'll have to come up from astern. When they do, leave 'em to me. You run for Clark."

"Boyd..."

"Shut up, Jack."

The Japs began to overhaul them, one element of three aircraft followed by the second element of three. Wagner kept on the south heading. Jack knew in one way that made sense. The closer to Clark they got, the better, the farther away they got from the invading Jap troops if they had to crash land or bail out, the better.

It wasn't as if Jack could do much else with that fluttering piece of scrap metal taking every bit of control authority he had to keep flying straight and level, with the engine at full throttle but making no more than 220 mph. He wished to hell that piece of scrap would come loose, and if he lived through this he was going to find the riveter and strangle the bastard.

"When I tell you, Jack, break left," Wagner radioed.

It was the only direction Jack could break. "Roger," he replied.

He looked over his shoulder and the first element of Jap fighters were close, close! As he watched their noses flared with the flash of machine guns, the cannon in the wings winked fire, tracers licked out and Wagner called, "BREAK BREAK BREAK."

All Jack had to do was relax his hold on the controls and the left wing dipped and yawed, rolled over, impossibly fast, fast enough that Jack let it go through 360 degrees before catching it and continuing his bank to the left. The Zeroes followed him through the turn and the roll, tracers flying all around him, a sudden rapid tatoo of bullet strikes against the armor plate behind his seat. The Zeroes sat on his tail, pulling into a tighter turn than he dared, pulling hard enough that their noses came around again, pulling into the amount of lead required for a deflection shot.

Then behind the Zeroes he saw Wagner's P-40. Wagner fired on the lead Zero and it went off on one wing, crashing into the jungle below. The other two Zeroes broke left and right and Wagner flew up beside Jack.

"Jack, come right to heading 180," Wagner radioed.

"Roger," Jack replied. His right arm and right leg were starting to feel the strain of holding the controls against the drag of the metal plate on the left wing. He looked over his shoulder at the Jap Zeroes. The second element of three was catching up to them; the two from the first element that broke off were forming up behind them.

As Jack steadied up on 180 Wagner slid in close, flying ahead of him on his left.

"Keep it real steady, Jack," Wagner radioed.

Wagner eased his P-40 over. Jack felt the turbulence of Wagner's right wingtip batter at his left wing, causing flutter. Wagner slid his wingtip in front of the fluttering metal plate in Jack's left wing, and the plate, buffeted by the turbulence, fluttered faster and harder and ripped itself clear, flying back in the slipstream.

Jack was abruptly very busy, first keeping the left wing down when the aileron trim wanted to roll it up and into Wagner's wingtip, adjusting the trim until the P-40 was once again flying straight and level – and accelerating with the loss of the parasitic drag of the sheet metal plate.

"How's that?" Wagner radioed.

"Boyd, you're the greatest," Jack replied.

"OK, follow me, I got another idea."

Wagner pulled up. Jack followed him, watching Wagner closely. The squadron leader looked over his shoulder at the Japs, who had immediately pulled up after them. As soon as they committed to the climb, Wagner pushed over into a dive, and the heavier weight of the P-40 let it walk away from the Zero in the dive. The three Zeroes followed them, losing ground in the dive, and at the bottom Wagner pulled up again.

The heavier weight of the P-40 gave it a momentary advantage over the Zero in the climb. Jack saw Wagner's tactic: pull up, walk away, but push over in the dive before the Zeroes could catch up using that impossible climb of theirs.

The Japs bottomed out and chased them on the straight and level for awhile. When they were almost into gun range Wagner pulled up again. The Zeroes followed but as soon as the P-40s pushed over into the dive they turned away to the north.

Jack sighed with relief. He throttled back to take the strain off his overheating engine as they pulled out of the dive.

"Hey, Jack," Wagner radioed. "How does your rudder feel?"

"It's been mushy ever since we left Clark," Jack replied.

"Yeah. Well, there's big strips of fabric coming off your rudder and your elevators."

Jack looked at the jungle below. He was too low to bail out. If he climbed he could stress the remaining fabric on the elevators and expose both of them to Jap fighter patrols.

"I guess we'll find out if it'll last all the way back to Clark," he radioed. He looked across the space between the two airplanes.

Wagner nodded, his face grim.

Coming In

Charlie stood along the side of the runway, watching the progress on his Fort. Chief Dollman had jacks and timbers under the right wing main spar near the fuselage and raised the wing, putting props under it along the line of the main spar to hold it

314

up. Then Dollman's mechanics swarmed over the gear well and found the hydraulic line damaged by Jap fighters, fixed that, tested the hydraulic system, and got the right main gear down and locked. They were just about to pull the Fort back onto the runway when a red flare arced up from the improvised control tower, closing the runway. About the same time the crash truck and an ambulance pulled up on the flight line.

It wasn't an inbound attack, then.

He looked to the north. The only planes out were the P-40s flown by Boyd Wagner and Jack.

In a moment he picked out two specks, one a little higher than the other. Neither were smoking or otherwise obviously damaged.

Then he noticed they were flying in very broad, gentle maneuvers as they lined up on the runway. The first P-40 came in and landed, pretty well shot full of holes, with a long streak of oil down its fuselage. Charlie remembered the markings on the P-40s that took off two hours ago. That one was Boyd Wagner's.

He looked at the airplane on long final.

That had to be Jack, and from the gentle flight maneuvers he had control damage.

Soft Earth

Jack lined up on the battered runway with that "here goes nothin'" feeling. He felt the skid in his turns as the last of the rudder fabric peeled away. He thought of getting the P-40 into a sideslip but rejected the idea since he couldn't kick in rudder to bring the pursuit out of the slip. He had enough elevator left to get a proper descent rate on long approach. He figured on holding power back, maintaining speed with the descent, and rounding out using full flaps just above the runway. When the flaps came down, the change in lift configuration would force the nose up, and he could chop power and bring her in.

Anyway, that was the plan.

He started drifting away from the runway centerline. Jack looked at the trees, whose branches tossed gently, and noticed a jeep kicking up a dust plume. Crosswind, of all the damned times for a wind across the runway! Jack dropped the windward wing a little and the pursuit crabbed into the wind. Now Jack was lined up with the runway again but at an angle. He fed in power to keep his rate of descent constant. He kept his hand on the throttle because judging that last little bit of descent was going to be critical. If he fed in the flaps a hair too late he'd have to give the engine a little power to extend the glide, but it would take a fraction of a second for the engine to respond and give him the power he needed.

The ground got closer, details popping out. He saw the round ragged scars where the craters in the runway had been filled in.

Jack took his hand off the throttle to open the canopy. It slid back smoothly and air blasted into the cockpit. The engine noise increased dramatically. Then he put the wheels down, feeding in a little more throttle as the drag increased again.

He kept the stick centered in the pitch axis and held in a little left aileron to counteract the crosswind. His feet were on the rudder pedals without putting any pressure on them. The ground approached, closer and closer still, and without his willing it his hand on the throttle reached out and pulled down the lever for the flaps. The hydraulics whined, the nose came up; then the mains touched, literally kissed the ground, and the P-40 rolled forward as Jack pulled back firmly on the stick.

The right main dropped into a bomb crater and dug into the softer earth of the crater backfill. The P-40 slewed hard to the right and the wheel and gear strut hit the edge of the crater, levering the nose down hard and crumpling the right wingtip into the ground. The P-40 reared up on its nose, rotating around the gear strut as it broke off, the wicked momentum of its forward speed twisting the fuselage over and slamming it onto its back. Pieces flew everywhere. Something hit Jack hard, stunning, an instant's screaming agony, then darkness.

What a Damned Day

Charlie ran forward as the P-40's right gear slammed into the wall of the bomb crater. The accident was sudden and spectacular, like most airplane crashes, a graceful flying machine turned in the time of a heartbeat into twisted, unrecognizable

316

metal and fabric. Behind him he heard the clang of the ambulance bell and the roar of truck engines.

Chief Dollman ran beside him. They were the first two at the wreck. Dollman ducked down and reached into the cockpit.

"Hold his head and shoulders!" Dollman yelled. "There's gas leaking out of here somewhere, I can smell it!"

Charlie squatted down, got an arm around Jack's shoulders, doing his best to ignore the blood flowing from under his brother's leather flying helmet and the odd angle of his right arm. He gritted his teeth against the pain of his own wounds as he took Jack's weight. Dollman worked for a moment on the harness release and then Jack came free, all 160 pounds of him suddenly on Charlie's arm. All Charlie could do was brace himself and roll back, taking Jack's weight on his body as slowly as he could, gasping in pain. Dollman held Jack's parachute straps and guided Jack's body out of the cockpit, freeing his left foot when it caught on something under the instrument panel.

Then other hands reached forward to help, urgent voices urged hurry, the gas, the gas, this bastard could explode any second! Someone took Jack's body off him, someone else helped Charlie to his feet, and when he looked back to check on Dollman the line chief rolled to his feet running. Charlie ran with him, an airman running by him urging him to hurry, hurry, goddamit!

There was a soft *whoomph* behind him and a rush of heat and the smell of burning aviation fuel and hot metal as the P-40 caught fire.

They ran until they were beside the ambulance. The medics already had Jack on a stretcher, taking his parachute off, running trained hands over his body, gently peeling off the bloody leather helmet.

Then Boyd Wagner stood beside Charlie, looking down at Jack as the medic looked up at them.

"He's alive. Nasty bang on the forehead, probably on the gunsight. Right forearm's broken. We'll take him to the hospital."

The medics lifted Jack on the stretcher and put him in the ambulance, which turned around gently and then accelerated away.

317

Wagner sighed and stripped off his helmet, running his hand through his hair.

"Damn," he said. "I thought he'd got away with it."

"It was a soft spot in the crater," Charlie said. "The right gear dug in."

Wagner nodded wearily, staggering a little.

"Come on," Charlie said. "Let's get you somewhere to sit down. And here, have a swig of this."

Charlie took the canteen from his belt and uncapped it. Wagner took a sip, looked at Charlie, and then took several deep swallows.

"Jesus Lord," said Wagner. He handed the canteen back to Charlie. "What a damned day."

The Hospital

Jack heard a low chorus of moans, punctuated by a scream.

His head hurt like a bastard. So did his right arm. What the hell happened to him? Where was he?

He tried to open his eyes. It took him three tries, and then the light stabbed into his head like steel rods punching into his skull. He gasped and closed his eyes.

"Doctor?" It was a female voice, close by. "Doctor, it's the pilot. He's awake."

A hand touched his forehead. It was a feather-gentle touch, and it still sent a lance of pain through him. He gasped again.

"Easy, son," said a man's voice. "I'm Doctor Thorssen. You've had a nasty bang on the head."

"My arm hurts too," Jack croaked. "And I'm thirsty."

"Nurse, give him some water."

Jack felt a glass straw placed between his lips. He sipped. The water was heavenly, soaking into his dry mouth, evaporating, it seemed, as it touched his tongue. He sipped again, stronger, and got some down his throat.

"Not too much," said the doctor. "Son, your arm hurts because it's broken. It's not a bad break. I'm concerned about this blow to the head, though. Almost certainly you have a concussion. Normally I'd x-ray your skull, but the x-ray machine was destroyed in the bombing."

"OK," said Jack. "When can I go back to my squadron?"

"No time soon. You lie back and rest, now. Nurse, make sure you can rouse him. Check on him every half-hour or so and call me if he won't wake up."

Jack lay back on the pillow in the hot, humid hospital ward, listening to the noises of the other wounded men, and in a few moments he drifted off into blessed unconsciousness. The nurse woke him up every half-hour through the rest of the afternoon and the long, long night.

Fight with What We Have

Charlie stood with Major O'Donnell and Col. Eubanks in the 19th's Operations tent.

"Rosie, I'm recommending to Brereton that we withdraw everything to Darwin," Eubanks said. "There never was any way we could hold Clark, it's too far forward. Del Monte is never going to be much more than a dirt strip in a pineapple field unless we can get a hell of a lot more in the way of reinforcements and supplies from the States than it looks like we will. At least, in the foreseeable future."

O'Donnell nodded. "I understand, Gene. And for what it's worth, I agree."

"Yeah. Then I want you to send Davis here straight to Darwin. We're going to evacuate some of the wounded pilots, aircrew, and tech staff."

"Evacuate?" asked O'Donnell.

"Well, what the hell else would you call it?" Eubanks snapped. "Brereton's got less than twenty pursuits left after three days of fighting. We've got fourteen B-17s and three of those are going to be lucky to get airborne, much less fly as far south as Darwin. If we can get them that far maybe the Aussies can repair them. If not, at least we can keep the Japs from getting them."

"Yes, sir. Sorry, Gene."

Eubanks sighed and put his hand on O'Donnell's shoulder. "No, I'm sorry, Rosie. I shouldn't have snarled at you. But we're airmen, not infantrymen. If we leave a position because it can't be held, that's not a retreat, it's an evacuation, and that's just what we'll have to do. We're going to have to fight with what we have for the next four to six months, and what we have will be whatever we can get out of the Philippines and south to Australia." Eubanks looked at Davis. "Captain, I understand your brother is a P-40 pilot. Got banged up pretty bad in that mission yesterday afternoon."

"Yes, sir."

"Wagner's putting him in for a DFC. He'll get it. You'll get one too for that recon mission."

"Sir..."

Eubanks held up a hand. "We're on the shit end of the stick, Charlie, and so it doesn't look to any one of us like we're doing enough. You let me worry about what the men under my command deserve or don't deserve. And look on the bright side." Eubanks grinned tiredly. "I might recommend you but it doesn't mean you'll get it."

Charlie grimaced, then grinned at the older officer. "I understand, sir."

"Good. How's your airplane? Ready to go?"

"Yes, sir. All we need to do is load up and top off the fuel and oil."

"All right. Off you go then, and God speed."

Charlie saluted O'Donnell and Eubanks, then walked out of the tent into the early morning night.

South to Australia

Jack woke up when he was placed on a litter and strapped down.

"Hey," he protested weakly. "I'm not a loonie. Why are you guys strapping me down?"

The nurse appeared at his shoulder. She looked tired and haggard. There were blood spatters on her uniform blouse.

"You're being evacuated, Lt. Davis," she said. "Our orders are to take you to the airfield."

"Oh. Evacuated where?"

"I don't know. That part we weren't told."

Jack nodded.

They loaded him on an ambulance, which jolted down the uneven road for an interminable time measured only by the interval between the pain each jolt sent slamming into his temple. Then the ambulance braked to a stop and the rear doors opened.

Charlie stood there, in front of the entrance door to his B-17.

"Well, little brother," Charlie said. "You ready to go flying?"

"Always," Jack croaked. "But please tell me someone else is flying this thing."

"Oh, no, I'm the pilot in command, all right. Load him up, fellows, and if he gives you any trouble, gag him."

The medics grinned and carried Jack into the fuselage of the B-17. There were already a half-dozen litters strapped down to the fuselage deck. Elsewhere men were making themselves whatever seats they could. The Flying Fortress was a bomber, not a transport.

A few minutes after the medics left Charlie walked in, closing and locking the door behind him. He knelt beside Jack in the narrow aisle.

"You doing OK?" Charlie asked.

"Yeah, Charlie. I hurt like hell but the doc told me that's normal."

"OK, kiddo. You know the takeoff will be a bitch but after that I'll try to keep things nice and smooth."

"I know you will," Jack said. Charlie gripped his shoulder, smiled, and walked up the fuselage to the flight deck.

A minute later and the engine on the far left started. No. 2 gave some trouble but started eventually. Nos. 3 and 4 behaved, and then the big bomber taxied over the lumpy, uneven surface of the airstrip.

Jack lay back, trying to ignore the jolts, identifying what was happening by the sound. There was the elephant squeal and moan of the brakes, the blattering roar of the propellers, the bump and rattle of the fuselage from the engine vibration. Then they stopped and Charlie ran up the engines, one by one, and taxied forward. There was a long moment while the engines idled. Jack listened, but it was loud inside the uninsulated fuselage. He could see men talking, but they had to put ear to mouth to hear each other.

Then the four engines ran up to full power, smoothly, and the Fort began to move, bumping and jolting. The ride evened out when the tail came off the ground, then the bumping and jolting quit and the Fort was airborne. The wheels whined up into the gear wells.

Climbing, the bomber turned. Jack guessed it was almost 180 degrees. He heard the note of the engines diminish ever so slightly, and realized Charlie had them at climb settings.

The B-17 leveled off ten minutes later. From the shadow of the sun, shining through the left blister, Jack knew they were headed south. For a moment longer he listened to the drone of the four Wright engines. Then he fell asleep as the bomber flew south to Australia through the early morning sunshine.

the end

Look for more from Jack and Charlie in the second volume, A Snowball's Chance, *coming summer 2016.*

Made in the USA
San Bernardino, CA
08 May 2020